Thy Neighbour's Wife

Liam O'Flaherty

Thy Neighbour's Wife

Liam O'Flaherty

WOLFHOUND PRESS
IRISH AMERICAN BOOK COMPANY (IABC)

First paperback edition 1992
WOLFHOUND PRESS
68 Mountjoy Square
Dublin 1

Reprinted 1997

© 1992, 1972, 1924, 1923 Liam O'Flaherty

First edition London 1923

Wolfhound Press receives financial assistance from The Arts
Council / An Chomhairle Ealaíon, Dublin, Ireland.

This book is fiction. All characters, incidents and names have no
connection with any persons living or dead. Any apparent
resemblance is purely coincidental.

British Library Cataloguing in Publication Data
O'Flaherty, Liam
    The Neighbour's Wife. — New ed
    I. Title
    823.912 [F]

    ISBN 0 86327 328 9

Published in the U.S. and Canada by Irish American Book
Company (IABC)
6309 Monarch Park Place, Niwot, Colorado 80503
Phone 303 530 1352 Fax 303 530 4488

TO
MY FATHER

Cover design: Jan de Fouw
Cover illustration: *The Aran Islander* by Sir William Orpen. Private
Collection, courtesy of Pyms Gallery, London.
Typesetting: Wolfhound Press.
Printed by The Guernsey Press Co. Ltd, Guernsey, C.I.

Saturday

ALL'S well that ends well, and Inverara ended in Kilmurrage and Kilmurrage ended in the Pier, which was a fine place — the finest place in Inverara. It stretched out into the waters of the little bay of Kilmurrage, like a spear-head casting defiance at the whole world. It was finely built, all ferro-concrete, with iron ladders down the sides, and iron bitts for mooring purposes, and a promenade and a big warehouse belonging to the steamship company. There was a refreshment room set up in a corner of the warehouse, just as one might see at a big railway station in Dublin, where one could get a cup of coffee, steaming hot, in the cold weather, with four large slices of home-made bread, with a raisin here and there, from Mrs Devaney for the small sum of threepence; and in summer, when the weather was hot, there was a real Italian woman from the Big Town on the Mainland, selling lemonade and ice-cream wafers — not one of these second-hand Italian people, who talk good English and dress just the same as everybody else, but a dark-faced woman with a multi-coloured shawl around her neck, and knowing only enough English to make the proper change for a sixpence, and to make the lemonade, so weak that 'it wouldn't knock down a flea,' as Johnny Grealish said.

It was a fine place, the finest place in Inverara. In winter perhaps it was dreary, when there were no fishing boats, or turf boats from the mainland, or tourists, but in summer during the 'season' in Inverara, it was the gayest place on earth, at least so they said in Inverara.

And Inverara was proud of the Pier. Kilmurrage in particular, being the legitimate proprietor of the Pier, stuck up its head at the rest of the world. Though without the Pier, Kilmurrage was a poor place. It couldn't exactly be called a town and yet it was larger than a village, and it was the capital of Inverara. But a town, in order to be a town, must have streets, and Kilmurrage had no streets, properly speaking. It started off well enough, presumably with the intention of having streets, up at the schoolmaster's house on its western outskirts, but it soon gave up the endeavour. After coming down in a straight line, with six houses on each side, as far as the police barracks, it suddenly ended. Possibly there was some old law against streets in Kilmurrage and that the police deliberately stopped the movement, though the RIC barracks itself did not look very law-abiding. The badge that hung over the door, the harp with a crown over it, had fallen all to one side, as if it were drunk and disorderly. Some said it was that way, as an advertisement for drunkenness, so that the police could get something to do and get a chance of promotion. But the police themselves were a sufficient advertisement for drunkenness without the harp. But that's away from the point.

The street stopped at the police barracks, and beyond the police barracks there was nothing for some dozen yards but a potato garden and the ruins of a large wooden hut that an enterprising gentleman from the Big Town on the Mainland had erected to do duty as a Cinema Theatre. The enterprise was of course a failure, for the theatre was wrecked during the first performance, owing to Pat Farelly coming in drunk, and being under the impression that the murder of the heroine by the villain was real, and being a chivalrous gentleman, brandished his stick and led a mass attack on the screen. So there was the hut, never been used since, rotting in the sun, a monument to the prowess of Farelly.

Then came a row of labourers' cottages, right across the ruins of the cinema, and this row of cottages ended in Mulligan's public-house, a building that would have ruined the most respectable street, for there were empty porter barrels always lying outside in the roadway, in everybody's way, and people sitting on them drinking porter, and stopping everything that passed to have a talk. Then came the court-house and the dispensary, jumbled up in a corner, behind the new house that a shopkeeper had built as a residence for the curate, though the curate had never used it. It was too big, and he could neither afford to pay the rent nor the up-keep on the small sum that the parish priest allowed him. So the big house had the blinds drawn on it all the time, in summer and winter. A miserable-looking place, almost as miserable as the court-house, its neighbour, which was hardly ever used either, because the police were generally too drunk to bring anybody to court, and even if they did bring forward a case of trespass or assault and battery, 'it was thé divil itsel' ov a job to git the magisthrate to come and thry it,' as Sergeant Donagan was fond of saying over his pint in Mulligan's.

This brought Kilmurrage as far as the Hill, and after that it would be impossible to describe it. Taking the court-house as the centre, it branched off in all directions, going a few yards in a straight line, and then ending suddenly in a potato patch, or a cul-de-sac, or a wooden hoarding, or the new store that Jim Shanaghan was building at the back of the Post Office. It ran around corners like a man trying to get away from the police, and it was as crooked as a drunken man in a gale of wind. It had seven different street levels, which was a great achievement for a small town like it. The lowest level was reached by the residence of the Protestant minister, a beautiful place surrounded by trees, in a glen, and the highest level was reached by the parochial house, where Fr O'Reilly the parish priest lived. The natives of Kilmurrage, being ninety-nine and a half per cent Catholic, reasoned from this contrast that the Protestant vicar was down in the hollow because he was well on the road to Hell, and the parish priest was on a height because he was well on the road to Heaven.

However, all's well that ends well, and Kilmurrage ended in the Pier. A wide, level, pretty limestone road stretched from the town to the Pier, along the shore of the harbour, and on a steamer day, when the *Duncairn* came on her thrice-a-week trips, weather and other circumstances permitting, from the Big Town on the Mainland, that road was crowded by an endless stream of people going down to the Pier. The steamer days were the most important days in the life of Kilmurrage, and even in the life of Inverara, and on those days everybody who was not bedridden, or extremely busy, came to the Pier to await the arrival of the steamer, to do their business or just to hear the news and have a look at the new-comers.

In the summer time there was always somebody of importance coming on the *Duncairn*. One day it would be Fr So and So, coming to preach a mission to the young on temperance or some such popular subject. Another day it would be an official from the Congested Districts Board, coming to find out what the islanders could be induced to pay for the land, or whether they could be induced to pay anything at all. Another day it would be a committee from the Geographical Society, coming to examine the ancient ruins. Another day it would be an organizer from the United Irish League, coming to 'rally Inverara to a man behind the Home Rule Programme.' Another day it would be a party of Gaelic League propagandists in kilts and spectacles and long hair, Smiths and Joneses and Hodges and von Strakers, urging the islanders to cultivate 'the language of the ancient Gael, which they had inherited from their proud forefathers.' Another day it would be somebody coming from the United States, or the District Inspector of Police, or the naval officer coming to examine the coastguards. There was always somebody coming.

A stream of people would wander down to the Pier an hour or more before the steamer's arrival. Groups of young girls, without their hats, would skip along arm in arm, laughing and talking. Cissy might expect a new hat from the Big Town on the Mainland, or Mary might expect her sister home from the convent, or Susie might expect her older brother, who was away in a college in Dublin 'going to be a priest for the foreign mission.' The shopkeepers and the publicans had to be down on the Pier, so that they could quarrel with the captain and the steamship company's agent, about paying the freight, and about whether their goods were entered correctly on the ship's manifest, and stand around, making a fuss while their goods were unloaded, so that nobody could steal anything, though nobody ever stole anything in Inverara, except a commercial traveller, who once stole fifty pounds from the till of Mrs Moroney's public-house, while Mrs Moroney was at the door talking to a neighbour.

Then the Protestant minister and his wife came down there. The wife, a pretty up-to-date kind of a woman, with a perky nose and a painted face, looked far more respectable than her husband, the vicar. The vicar was a sleepy individual, always wandering around talking to himself and reading Greek literature. They said that he was a brilliant man at college but that residence in Inverara had turned his intellect into incipient idiocy, and if the stories told about him were even in part true, the idiocy instead of being incipient was highly developed. Before his marriage he had lived alone in the vicarage, without any servants, and the place, under his sole control, had gone to rack and ruin; to such an extent that a carpenter who had gone to mend a staircase found the vicar lying on his back on a couch reading the *Wasps* of Aristophanes, while two hounds and a donkey shared with him the room. Of course, it might be asked how did the carpenter know that he was reading the *Wasps* of Aristophanes? And the fact that Mr Blake told the story, in the first place, and could not remember the name of the carpenter, although there were only two in the whole of Inverara, does not render the story very credible. There was also the story that he, the vicar, told John Sweeney that a mountain in India was three hundred and twenty-seven feet higher than the moon, but he might have said that to make fun of Sweeney, who was a religious maniac. Still the vicar was a silly fellow, a very silly fellow.

The hotel-keepers came to the Pier also, and the agent of the Glasgow merchants who bought the kelp, and everybody, in fact, who on any pretext whatsoever could claim to have business with the steamer *Duncaim*. The schoolmasters and the schoolmistresses were there, in a compact group, away from the rest of the people, as befitted people of their intellectual importance, talking about their schools, and the good looks of the inspectors, and the clergy, and the shameless way the British Government and the National Board of Education paid their school teachers. They were very careful to keep apart from the common or garden islanders from the west of Inverara, 'the natives,' as Mrs Cassidy the doctor's wife called them, who stood around in the background sheepishly, in their rawhide pampootees and thick homespun garments, looking down at the fishing boats, scratching their heads and spitting zealously, while they discussed the weather, fishing, and the price of pigs.

But all these people merged into the background when compared with Fr O'Reilly, the parish priest, and the most important man in Inverara. His was always the position of importance on the Pier, standing out in front, down at the far end, where the *Duncaim* came alongside, with the principal people around him, talking. On steamer days, when he stood down at the end of the Pier, he looked like a well-bred English country gentleman, and many people said he greatly resembled a fox-hunting squire, standing on his hearth-rug before a roaring log fire, with fox-terriers scattered around the room, and the local gentry singing 'Tally ho! Tally ho!' or whatever they do sing. He was a tall man and well built, except for the prominence of his waistcoat at the fifth button, where it bulged into a rotund point, and made him look slightly, very slightly of course, like a cask with head, arms and legs attached to it. Apart from that, he was a fine-looking man. His head was firmly placed on his shoulders and always thrown back at a decorative angle, showing his firm jaw, piercing blue eyes and broad forehead to perfection. His hair had turned grey, but it was a greyness that suited the rest of him, a greyness that could be associated with a well-fed body, and the due respect given to fifty-one years of age, by a parish priest who knew that his reputation for sanctity was secure, as secure as his bank account, which ran well into four figures sterling. His rosy cheeks showed that he had good health. His fleshiness, which was not too apparent, showed that he had a good appetite, and the reddish tinge in his nose, and the pimple on the tip of it, showed according to his enemies that he was a 'little fond of the bottle.'

Whether he was or not, he was a clever man, the cleverest man in Inverara. The people said he was the best man that ever came to the island since Fr McBride, who had built the Pier. They claimed that it was due to his efforts that the Congested Districts Board purchased the land from the landlord, though of course it was the Land League agitation did that. Then they pointed to the fishing industry with tears in their eyes. There it was 'on a sound business footing' (to use Fr O'Reilly's own words) and it was all due to Fr O'Reilly. He got the harbour blessed by the archbishop, and he got a committee of the Board of Fisheries to do something with the fishing grounds, plant seeds there or something (nobody knew definitely what the committee did beyond drinking whisky in Shaughnessy's hotel). Whether as a result of the archbishop's blessing, or the planting of seeds by the Board of Fisheries, there were good catches of fish every year since.

Further, Fr O'Reilly allowed the fishermen to break the Sabbath when there was a glut of fish. So he was popular, extremely popular. He was popular with the fishermen, with the 'natives,' with the business men of Kilmurrage, with the officials of the Congested Districts Board, with the officers of the law — in fact, with everybody.

Of course he had enemies. Everybody has enemies, even in Inverara. And those enemies of Fr O'Reilly claimed that 'he made a good thing out of Inverara.' They pointed to the fact that when he came to Inverara he was as poor as a church mouse, only a few years ordained, with a large circle of poor relations hanging on to his coat tails, so to speak. And he was now a wealthy man, measuring wealth of course by Inverara standards. He had married his sister Ellen to Charles Bodkin the Government contractor, who was a man of good social position, and a man who had a pull with 'the Government.' Of course, the marriage was in a way unfortunate, since Bodkin died within a year after his marriage and his will showed that he left only a mass of debts, and his estate outside Kilmurrage had to be sold by auction, but Fr O'Reilly saved something out of it. Then there was the house that the islanders built for him as a mark of their appreciation. It was the finest house in Inverara, fitted out with all the modern conveniences, even with electric light. However, the electric light was a failure, being a hotch-potch affair, that went out when it was most wanted, just like the night when the archbishop was dining at the parochial house, during confirmation time, and they had to finish the dinner with candlelight.

It was said too that Fr O'Reilly got considerable sums from the Government officials for his services in bringing the islanders to heel in the matter of payment of rents. But the large sums that he received legitimately would make it very improbable that he would descend to low means for the purpose of swelling his bank account. If he accepted money from the publicans in return for keeping the sale of potheen within reasonable limits, it was the reward of just efforts, and why should not a priest be rewarded for so doing as well as a policeman? And who had a better right to reward him than the publicans who profited by these acts? But there it is. Evil-minded people like John Carmody, who came back from the United States a Socialist and an agnostic, were always in search of some scandal to cast a blemish on the fair fame of the parish priest.

Fr O'Reilly was the most important man in Inverara and what was more he was a coming man. His star was in the ascendant. He had just married his niece Lily to Mr McSherry, who had just come back from South America, 'rotten with money.' He had loads of it. He had built a great new house at Coill Namhan on the American plan, with a flat roof, and had brought an architect all the way from England to plan it. Ten thousand pounds it had cost, every penny of it, even though he had most of the materials for building, stone and sand, on the land he had bought, just beside the site of the house. And now he had married Fr O'Reilly's niece.

Of course Mr McSherry was fifty-five if he was a year, and the niece, Lily O'Reilly, was only a young girl of twenty-one, just after leaving the National University in Dublin, but what could the poor girl expect. It was hard enough for the poor girl to get wealth without expecting youth into the bargain they said in Inverara, for Lily had absolutely nothing of her own, not a stitch of clothes to her back they said, and her uncle had paid for her schooling, and maintained her since her mother died when Lily was a little girl of ten.

So here was Fr O'Reilly, fifty-one, the most important man in Inverara and bound to be a bishop one day, as soon as Bishop Donnelly, a doddering old man, died and made room for a successor. Here he was standing on the edge of the Pier at Kilmurrage, on Saturday the 22nd of June, with the *Duncairn* puffing along towards the Pier, waiting for the arrival of his niece and her husband, back from their honeymoon trip on the Continent. Fr O'Reilly spread his legs wider that day. His look was more dominant than usual. He was crustier and more condescending in his answers to the drivel, with which the Protestant vicar was trying to engage his attention, about the decline of classical education in the Irish schools.

The *Duncairn* drew alongside. The captain on the bridge shouted to the mate on the fo'c'sle head. The company's agent on the Pier, a long lanky fellow, with boots three sizes too big for him, and a moustache that got mixed up with his tongue when he tried to talk, bustled around telling everybody to get out of 'the bloomin' way.' A line was cast ashore. The steamer was made fast. There were calls from the Pier to those aboard the ship. Handkerchiefs were waved. The women giggled. The captain, a handsome fellow with a fair moustache, puffed out his chest and smirked at everybody, in an endeavour to make the most of that moment of importance of coming alongside. Then the gangway was fixed into position and the passengers began to come ashore. Young pigs began to shriek in the hold. A swarm of men and boys struggled over the side and began to hustle around the cargo, and finally Mr McSherry and his wife appeared from the cabin and walked on to the deck.

A cheer went up from the Pier, and it was noted that day that the only other time anybody was cheered on his arrival from the *Duncairn* was when Hugh O'Malley had returned to Inverara, after being acquitted of the murder of three landlords during the Land League movement. A cheer went up from the Pier and Mr McSherry gracefully raised his hat in response. Mrs McSherry did not appear to take any notice. She stood looking out to sea, tapping the deck with her umbrella. 'Poor girl,' they said on the Pier, 'perhaps she is sea-sick after the journey.' But few people noticed her. All eyes were concentrated on Mr McSherry, the man who was rotten with money, who had travelled the world, and could talk seven languages, which of course was the sum total of languages in current use, as Pat Coleman the postmaster said, and Pat Coleman was a man who was supposed to know.

McSherry stood with his hat in his hand, smiling. He was a tall man, with a sallow face, clean shaven, square jawed, dark eyed, thin lipped, just as if he had stepped out of the New York Stock Exchange, or had been a hero in a film mystery serial, playing the part of 'the handsome middle-aged villain about town.'

'There he is himself,' shouted the people on the Pier, and McSherry smiled with the air of a man who is making a speech to his constituents after an election. And then Fr O'Reilly stepped forward, crossed the gangway and shook McSherry by the hand warmly.

'Welcome back,' he said, and then turned to Lily, who still dabbed the deck with her umbrella, and looked sad and gloomy, not a bit like a woman coming back from her honeymoon. But women have a peculiar way of behaving at times, or was it that she . . .

'Well, Lily, how are you?'

Lily took the outstretched hand and murmured something about a nice passage, and then Fr O'Reilly turned again to Mr McSherry with as much speed as was consistent with his dignity as the most important man in Inverara, and taking Mr McSherry's arm led him to the gangway. Then having seen McSherry safely on his way ashore, he assisted Lily in like manner and then followed in her rear, having nodded to the captain. Then he paused for a moment, with his right foot on the gangway and his right arm on the support, looking around him proudly like a fashionable Frenchman entering a restaurant with the air of saying to the whole world 'me voyez vous vous autres.'

Ashore there was more hand-shaking and more 'Welcome back, Mr McSherry, welcome back, Mrs McSherry, me dear.' Mrs

McSherry was kissed by Mrs Cassidy, the wife of Dr Cassidy, a portly woman, with a loud and discordant voice, of marked proletarian origin, though imbued with very high social ambitions. She was kissed by Ellen her aunt, and widow of the late Charles Bodkin, the defunct Government contractor. The wife of the vicar shook her hand and murmured in a cultivated and high-pitched voice, after the fashion then current in English society, 'how dye do, my deah.' Mr Blake, the local replica of the British squire, shook her hand and said 'pon me soul, Mrs McSherry, yere looking well, pon me soul you are.'

Then Fr O'Reilly, again pushing himself into prominence, came forward and took Mr McSherry's arm and said, 'Come along to the house. I am sure ye are famished after that trip on the *Duncairn*, terrible tub.'

He invited Mr Blake to dinner. He invited Mrs Cassidy to dinner and Dr Cassidy (Dr Cassidy was too old to make his way to the Pier and was then resting in his trap at the head of the Pier, where he was always deposited by his wife, to keep him out of danger of being walked on, or falling into the harbour, he was so old and doting and absent-minded). He invited Mr Renshaw, the retired RIC inspector. He would have invited Mr Wilbert, the Protestant vicar, and Mrs Wilbert, his wife, but it was not considered good form in Inverara that the Protestant vicar should be on terms of too great intimacy with the parish priest, considering that the parish priest and the vicar were supposed to be deadly enemies, and waging constant war for the possession of the souls of the islanders, Fr O'Reilly, of course, representing God, and the vicar representing the Devil, or the British Crown, or some such equally vicious power.

So off they marched to the head of the Pier, with Fr O'Reilly continually raising his hat to the people, and the pimple on his nose shining like a ruby. And at the head of the Pier they met Dr Cassidy sitting in his trap. He stretched out his lean old shrivelled hand, and grasped Mr McSherry's plump one and said, 'How are you?' in a loud, shrill, birdlike voice.

Mr and Mrs McSherry and Mr Blake got into Fr O'Reilly's landau, a fashionable carriage that was given to him as a present by Judge Bodkin of the Circuit Court and was considered to be the smartest carriage owned by any priest in the diocese, or in Ireland for that matter. Mrs Bodkin got into Dr Cassidy's trap and Mr

Renshaw, valiantly refusing a seat in the Cassidy trap (he was a humane man and the Cassidy mare was old), went afoot by the short cut up the hill, and arrived at the parochial house, just as soon as the others, who took the round road by the post office.

So they all gathered around the big dining-room table in the parochial house, with the parish priest at the head, in the seat of honour. Mr McSherry was on his right and Mrs McSherry was on his left. Mr Blake took a seat at the far end, and Mrs Cassidy sat beside Dr Cassidy, to look after him. Mr Renshaw sat beside Mrs Bodkin, and as Fr O'Reilly saw him sitting beside her, he thought for a moment that worse things might happen than that Mr Renshaw should marry the widow of the late Charles Bodkin. And then looking around the table, Fr O'Reilly suddenly discovered that the curate had not yet arrived, and asked Polly, his servant, whether Fr McMahon had yet come in, and Polly answering in the negative, he gave orders to go on with the dinner. But just then the curate entered the dining-room.

He went up to Fr O'Reilly and explained that he had been detained in Kilmillick visiting a sick old woman, who was dying, and had to give her the last sacraments. 'Poor woman,' said Fr O'Reilly, tucking his napkin under his chin, 'it would be a mercy to her if the Lord took her to Himself.'

The curate shook hands with Mr McSherry and said he was glad to see him back, and hoped that he enjoyed his honeymoon, and in his excitement he was on the point of saying that he hoped that McSherry would see many happy returns of the day, when he overturned a glass on the sideboard to get at Mr McSherry's hand. Then he blushed to the roots of his ears and went over to Mrs McSherry, whether it was on account of Mrs McSherry or spilling the glass of water, or being on the point of making a fool of himself with Mr McSherry, or whether Mrs McSherry was the cause of his spilling the water and being excited and . . . Anyhow Mrs McSherry reddened too and bent down her head as he took her hand, and the curate bending over her, could see her long drooping eyelashes, and that made him still redder in the face. So he just was mumbling something when Mr Blake relieved the situation by calling loudly to Fr O'Reilly, 'have ye got any potheen in the house?' And in the laugh that followed, the curate made his way to his seat unnoticed, and proceeded to busy himself with the soup.

'Potheen, Mr Blake?' said Fr O'Reilly. 'Well, of course you

know my attitude towards it, but I'm not the man to say that it hasn't got its uses, for people, of course, who have sufficient control over themselves to use it in moderation. It has its value as medicine, and Dr Cassidy will agree with me on that point, and for drinking purposes it appeals to some people with a refined palate. I won't deny that I keep a jar of it in my house. Polly, bring the potheen. Mr McSherry, have you ever tasted potheen?'

Mr McSherry said that he hadn't, but that he would be eager to try it after Fr O'Reilly's recommendation, and then the potheen arrived and they all filled their glasses except the women and the curate, who was a total abstainer. Mr McSherry drank his glass at a draught, and said it was great stuff, and laughed down his throat, and Mrs McSherry looked across at him for a moment with a look of fear in her eyes. But they were all laughing good-humouredly and didn't notice that look, except the curate, who had not been able to keep his eyes off Mrs McSherry since he entered the room.

There he was crumbling up his bread with one hand and dabbing his spoon in the soup with the other hand. Now and again he laughed forcibly at some joke of Mr Blake's or at some witty sally from Mrs Cassidy. Sometimes he laughed at the proper time and at other times he laughed in the wrong place, or didn't laugh when he should laugh. And all the time his eyes wandered in the direction of Mrs McSherry. When he saw Mrs McSherry look at her husband, with fear in her eyes, the curate's brow clouded and a strange look of suppressed emotion appeared in his countenance. He looked not like a peaceful country curate, but like a man of strong passions and a highly sensitive nature.

That's just what Fr Hugh McMahon was, a man of strong passions and with a highly sensitive nature. In Inverara they thought he was young and foolish, just that. He wrote poetry. 'The Death of Maeve' had been pronounced the best poem of the year. He wrote articles for the clerical periodicals. Worse still, there were rumours that he contributed to revolutionary papers in Dublin. Not exactly revolutionary papers, like Jim Larkin's Socialist paper *The Worker*, he was too respectable for that, but seditious papers, plotting treason against his Britannic Majesty, and advocating an Irish Republic. But the people paid no heed to these latter rumours, except to say that he was young and would learn as he grew older. Outwardly the curate was amenable to Church discipline during the eight months that he had been in Inverara. He was polite to the gentry and to the business people. He was attentive to his duties, very attentive. He was liked by the 'natives,' because he mixed with them and praised their language and their old customs, and used to tell them that by right they should pay no rent for land that had been stolen from them by the English. But that was in private, and the people with a stake in the island did not hear of it. The only people who did not like him were the potheen vendors and the school children. He nearly thrashed the life out of Patsy Brannigan one evening he caught him bringing home a keg of potheen that had been landed from a smuggler's boat from the mainland. And he thrashed the school children for staying away from school. This he did because he considered that potheen was the curse of the country, that and lack of education, for Fr Hugh McMahon was an extreme and enthusiastic Nationalist. He dreamt of a great Irish Catholic Republic, an Ireland that would again become the torch of learning and sanctity for the whole world. And the people with a stake in the island just smiled at these foolish notions of his and said that he would get sense as he grew older. And Fr Hugh McMahon, looking at Lily McSherry, wondered whether these ideas were going to be robbed of their materialization by . . .

Mr Blake began to tell a story and everybody laughed, because nobody believed Mr Blake.

'There isn't a word of a lie in it,' said Mr Blake. 'I was fishing at high tide, on that cliff on my land, you know the place, Mr Renshaw. A big pollock bit that bait and I was pulled over the cliff with the wrench. One hundred feet I fell into the water, as sure as I am alive. Only for it was high tide I would have been smashed on the rocks. As it was, I had great difficulty in swimming over to the low rock a little to the west, you know the place, Renshaw,' and Renshaw nodded, twisting his moustache and looking out over his eyebrows, same as he used to do when trying to impress people with his intelligence. 'I swam over to the rock and be damned but I dragged the line, with the fish at the end of it, with me. It was only then that I found that my right ankle was sprained. What d'ye think o' that?'

Mr Blake laughed and everybody laughed, even the curate, who never heard the story — thinking of Lily McSherry. Lily O'Reilly he called her in his own mind. He found it hard to think of her as Mrs McSherry, and that he could never call her Lily again. When he had the chance to call her Lily for ever he cast aside the opportunity. His dreams, his vocation forbade it. That evening at Dungarvan, just two years back, last August, just the year before he was ordained, that was the evening when he had come to a decision. And yet it was hardly a decision. She did not seem to him of much importance that evening compared to his vocation, to his ambitions as a priest who was to achieve fame and prominence. He wondered was she thinking of that evening now. If she were she would look at him. And yet why should she look at him after what he had done to her that evening . . . no, not done to her, but what he had said to her, or rather what he didn't say to her. They had been out cycling down by the sea road beyond the village of Ring, just at sunset. He would never forget that sunset. Perhaps if he had been less conscious of the beauty of the sunset and more conscious of Lily's beauty that evening . . . No it was not the sunset. It was his vocation. What would have happened to him if he had forgotten his vocation that evening and listened to the voice of the Devil that was tempting him, tempting him to forget his vocation and marry Lily? 'Eh,' he asked himself, 'what would have become of me?'

Of course it was hard. Christ, how hard it was, and harder still now, when he thought he had forgotten her, to see her another man's wife, looking so sad too. Probably hated her husband . . . They were standing on the brink of a cliff looking down at the sea beneath. Would he ever forget that moment. It was like an opium dream, beautiful and yet with the suggestion of sin and impurity that made it hateful. There were shadows on the water, here the shadow of a rock beneath the water, like a black pool, here a green patch, the shadow of the mossy cliff, while right across was a long shimmering streak of light gold, the shadow of the setting sun. Lily was standing beside him looking down and he said something about the beauty of the scene, and she said nothing in reply and he looked at her, and saw a light in her eyes, more wonderful than the gleams of the setting sun. Her bosom was heaving and the roses in her cheeks were flaming red, coursing through the whiteness of her skin, reaching to her neck. Her body shivered as she leaned closer to him and he caught her in his arms. 'Lord, I should have kept her.' But the next moment he thought of his vocation, of what people would think of him if he didn't become a priest, that he would never come to any good in life, saddled with a wife and poverty, having to fly to some foreign land, just as they all did, when they lost their vocations. He had to persevere and . . . He told her all that.

She said nothing, not a word, all the way back to Dungarvan, and next morning she had left with her aunt. Then he tried to forget her. He prayed and prayed and prayed. He sought the assistance of the Jesuit priest, who preached the retreat in his college that year after the holidays, and the Jesuit told him to make a novena to St. Joseph, that it was a temptation of the flesh and that he must overcome it. He made a pilgrimage to Lough Derg the following summer and then he was ordained and he thought that he had forgotten Lily. In the first joy of his ordination, of saying Mass, of hearing confessions, of having people raise their hats to him, of having his poem 'The Death of Maeve' published and praised, he forgot Lily.

'What a fool I was to think that I had forgotten her,' said the curate to himself as the fish arrived.

There was a rumble of plates, a rubbing of mouths with napkins, a 'ha, ha!' here and there, as the guests settled down to the fish, and the curate leaned back in his chair and sighed.

'I think you will find this turbot to your liking, Mr McSherry,' said Fr O'Reilly. 'It left the salt water this morning, and in Inverara we are proud of our turbot, almost as proud as we are of our reputation for sanctity, ha, ha, ha!'

Everybody laughed and Mr McSherry murmured something about his believing it, but that it would take a lot to beat the River Plate fish in the Argentine.

'I prefer a roast bream myself,' said Blake. 'I think it's the best fish out of water if cooked properly.'

'They catch pretty good fish in Donegal,' said Mr Renshaw, curling his moustache and looking in the direction of the potheen, as if he could do with another glass.

Fr O'Reilly signalled to Polly to help Mr Renshaw with the potheen. 'Always thinking of their appetites,' said the curate to himself as he toyed with his turbot.

Then Dr Cassidy, speaking for the first time and trying to eat his fish without spilling it all over his napkin, which was already covered with crumbs and the drippings of claret, just like the child Achilles at the Homeric banquet, for the doctor was in his second childhood, poor man, and it was rumoured that in the privacy of his own home his wife used to spoon-feed him, Dr Cassidy started off to tell Blake the proper way to cook a bream, when Mrs Cassidy nudged him severely in the ribs with her elbow, upsetting a piece of fish that Dr Cassidy was conveying to his mouth, and preventing Dr Cassidy from pursuing his remarks for a moment. But the impetus that had been given to the doctor's conversational powers by the first attempt soon induced him to turn to the curate, his neighbour on the right, and forcibly point out that a fish diet had a remarkable effect on the average healthy person, namely that it led to longevity and a considerable brain development.

'Do ye see how long they live in Inverara?' said the doctor, warding off the attacks of his wife with his left hand, and leaning over against the curate.

'Yes, quite remarkable,' said the curate, thinking of the day when he saw McSherry and Lily O'Reilly getting married and how he almost fainted when he saw McSherry putting the ring on her finger.

'Yes,' said the doctor, delighted to have somebody to talk to, and being warmed by the few glasses of wine that he had drunk. 'I heard a story, and I have no reason to doubt that it is a true one, about an old woman, who lived in Inverara before my time. Here is how the story was told to me. The old lady said: "Arise, daughter and go visit your daughter, for your daughter's daughter had a daughter last night" Ha, ha! she was old, wasn't she? Very old. I always eat fish. Always. Ha! very old. True story that.'

And then Dr Cassidy, exhausted by the effort that he had made, leaned forward with his head on his breast ruminating, and his lips moved as if he were talking to himself, probably measuring in his own mind the chances he had of living for another century or so, if he increased by so much the quantity of fish he consumed each day. And Mrs Cassidy, having brought her husband to heel and respectability, turned to Mr Blake and asked him when he was thinking of getting a second Mrs Blake for Blake house — this in a low voice, just sufficiently loud for Blake himself to hear, for Mrs Cassidy was a devilishly sly woman, devilishly sly.

So the meal went on, with the curate gloomily dreaming his dreams, answering questions now and again in monosyllables, with Fr O'Reilly even in the process of satisfying his healthy appetite maintaining the prominence and dignity that was his on all occasions, with the witty sayings of Mrs Cassidy and the jovial though sometimes uncouth remarks of Mr Blake, with sudden conversational lapses on the part of Renshaw, when that gentleman made a remark totally out of place and having reference solely to his readiness for another attack on either the wine or the potheen, with Mr McSherry attending to his meal with a bored air, and the mysterious facial expression of a stock-jobber.

The meal rolled on to a conclusion and the women departed to the drawing-room, for in the house of Fr O'Reilly, the most important man in Inverara, these social conventions were respected.

And then when the women had departed there was a pause and a slight yawning and a surreptitious rubbing of waistcoats under the table, and a general leaning far back in chairs, as if the male company had just finished some arduous task, and were taking advantage of the segregation of the sexes to gloat over it. There was a filling of glasses and an emptying of glasses. There was a drowsy hum of conversation, without any other seeming purpose than to prevent the company from going to sleep. Then cigars were smoked, and the men went into the drawing-room.

And then the company having eaten Fr O'Reilly's good food and drunk Fr O'Reilly's good wine, began to find excuses for departure. Dr Cassidy and Mrs Cassidy left on the plea that they had to make a call in the west of the island. Mr Renshaw proclaimed that he had promised to go to John Hanrahan's to shoot a lame bull. And the curate, finding that it was impossible to sit looking at Lily McSherry, left too. He had to go to visit the school at Kilmurrage. Then Mrs McSherry whispered to Mrs Bodkin and they both retired to Mrs Bodkin's room, leaving Fr O'Reilly alone with Mr Blake and Mr McSherry, discussing the possibilities of starting a factory for the treatment of kelp in Inverara.

And after ten minutes or so, the discussion was disturbed by the appearance of Mrs Bodkin, who beckoned to her brother, and Fr O'Reilly excused himself and left. In the hall he asked Ellen what was the matter. Ellen raised her hands to her eyes.

'It's dreadful,' said the widow of Charles Bodkin, and again she repeated 'it's dreadful' in an agonized tone, with, however, a certain feeling of satisfaction pervading her tone, as if she enjoyed the dreadfulness in a certain mysterious way.

'Lily,' she concluded, 'refuses to go home with her husband.'

'What?' ejaculated Fr O'Reilly, and the effort that he made to produce the ejaculation caused the rounded protuberance at the fifth button of his waistcoat to empty itself for a moment as if it were a bladder just punctured, and then the protuberance filled out again to give impetus to the next ejaculation, 'Where is she?'

'She's in my bedroom,' said the widow of Charles Bodkin, drawing her lips tight together and arranging a wisp of her hair at the back of her head.

And then picking up the rim of her skirt to a modest height below the knee, she led the way upstairs.

Mrs McSherry was in the bedroom, lying on the bed face downwards and in tears. The priest went up to her and touched her on the shoulder gently.

'Lily, what is the meaning of this, my child?'

'Leave me alone,' cried Mrs McSherry, suddenly starting up and facing her uncle. The slight, girlish form that had stood on the deck of the *Duncairn* had disappeared. In its place stood a woman, fully matured, fully developed, the lines of girlhood changed in that moment of acute distress into the mature curves of womanhood. Her black eyes were blazing. Her brown hair was tossed in myriads of curls about her head. The heightened colouring of her cheeks emphasized the pure whiteness of the neck and arms. The heaving bosom swelled the veins of the shapely neck.

Lily McSherry had ceased to be a girl. She had become a woman.

'You are the cause of it,' she cried. 'You forced me to marry him. You did it, because I was an orphan in your house and you wanted to get rid of me, to sell me, you, I — I — I hate you.'

And then she lay back again on the bed, checking her sobs.

'What on earth is the matter with the girl?' murmured Fr O'Reilly with astonishment written as plainly on his face, as on the face of a man who had laid a trap for a rabbit and caught a wild cat. 'Tut tut, calm yourself and get rid of these stage utterances. I sell you? I your uncle, that has looked after you all your life . . . that has educated you and cared for you like a father. Look at all the money it cost me to send you to school, clothes and premiums and everything. And then three years in the University and you never had to bother about anything . . . kept you out of every danger that a young girl has to meet with, and then married you to a suitable and God-fearing husband.'

'God-fearing?' cried Lily, springing up again, with her hair streaming. 'God-fearing, did you say? . . . You married me to a vile beast and you knew what he was all the time. I was mad to be persuaded by you. God, if I had only known then what I found out during the last few months . . . no, no, I am not going back with him. Do you know what he did in London, when we were on our way to Paris? Do you know that he . . .'

'Stop stop, woman,' cried the priest, rising from his chair and putting his hands to his ears. 'Stop, I tell ye, you are mad.'

But Lily did not stop and Mrs Bodkin went to her and sat on the bed beside her and calmed her, casting a look at her brother the while with her lips drawn together and her eyebrows contracted, signalling him to keep silent.

'There, there now, child,' she murmured, 'don't get excited, everything will be all right.'

And presently the sobbing stopped and the heaving stopped and the hands that were clutching at the pillow relaxed their hold and Lily was quiet. And then Mrs Bodkin rose, clasped her hands in front of her, nodded her head several times and then looked at her brother.

Fr O'Reilly coughed, pulled a chair near to the bed and sat down. Then he coughed again and sighed.

'Lily,' he said in a meek and humble tone. 'Lily, my child, you are young . . . too young perhaps to bear the cross that the Lord in His divine providence has thought fit to impose upon you. Nevertheless you must struggle to bear it. It sears my heart to think that you are unhappy, but remember, child, that God rewards those who bear His cross with courage and patience. The road to heaven is narrow and strewn with thorns, but the reward, the reward, child, is a glorious compensation for any troubles that we may be called upon to bear in this life. Go to your husband, child. It is your cross. You must not let any — er — momentary revulsion overcome your sense of duty. The Devil is strong in all of us. He moves in mysterious manners. He has many voices, but God will watch over you and protect you. Come now, child. Be brave, be brave.'

The priest stopped and waited, toying with the cross on his watch-chain, and after a few moments Mrs McSherry rose from the bed. The tears were still on her cheeks, but they were drying on her cheeks. Her eyes too were drying, but there was a light in them that was sadder than tears. The words of the priest had indeed succeeded in drying her tears, but they also seemed to have made her grow older. They had cast a shroud over her and she seemed to bury herself beneath it. Perhaps it was that the grace of God, to which the priest had invited her to appeal, had come to her assistance and had bestowed on her the gift of resignation. Or perhaps that she had become callous, finding that even her relatives would offer no assistance, but that they would compel her to bear the chains that were loathsome to her 'because God had ordained it so.' Perhaps.

She rose from the bed, outwardly calm and collected. She smoothed her dress, and wiped the tears from her face with her handkerchief. She arranged her hair, and all the while she wore a fixed expression on her face, like a drowning man, who, finding that he can no longer keep a grip on the plank, folds his arms and resigns himself to the deep.

Then the parish priest, telling the women to hurry to the drawing-room, lest the guests might be uneasy, hurried downstairs in front. But McSherry had not been one whit uneasy, and was still conversing in an animated manner with Mr Blake on the possibility of starting the kelp factory. And as soon as Fr O'Reilly entered, Mr McSherry asked him whether it would be possible to get sufficient labour locally to work the scheme, and whether the natives would be willing to use scientific machinery instead of the primitive methods they were using at present, 'for sometimes, you know, it is difficult to make people change habits that have been current among them for centuries. Look at the cotton operatives in England, for instance, who used to break up the machines when they were first invented.'

McSherry hardly looked at Lily when she entered the room, but kept on talking to Fr O'Reilly about the factory, and even Fr O'Reilly became so interested in the project that he also forgot Lily. And then the McSherrys left, and Fr O'Reilly and his sister accompanied them as far as the outskirts of Kilmurrage, and then returned home.

But when they arrived at the parochial house again, Fr O'Reilly walked up and down the drawing-room with his hands behind his back muttering to himself, paying no heed to his sister, until at last Ellen spoke in a hard, sharp voice.

'Father John,' she said, 'what do you think of this?'

'Of what, Ellen?' said Fr John, pausing in the middle of the room, and looking across at her. 'Were you talking of this scheme of McSherry's about the kelp factory? Yes,' he continued, walking down the room again without waiting for a reply, 'there is a lot to be said for it, and then again there is a lot to be said against it.'

Ellen did not interrupt, but stood looking at her brother, nodding her head slightly and with her hands clasped across her bosom.

'It would do a lot of good, certainly,' continued Fr O'Reilly. 'What with all the money it would bring into the place . . . but then again, on the other hand, wherever these factories come, atheism follows in their trail, and all kinds of new doctrines. You would have Socialists like that devil Jim Larkin, God forgive me, preaching socialism and organizing trade unions and . . .'

'I wasn't referring to a factory or to anything of the kind,' said the widow of the late Charles Bodkin, slowly and with emphasis. 'I was referring to Lily.'

'But goodness me, what of her? Isn't it settled?'

'H'm. Settled indeed! H'm. I think you HAVE settled her.'

'What the devil are you talking about, Ellen?'

'Just this,' said Ellen, stamping her foot, 'that you married Lily to a heathen dissolute wretch for the sake of the thousand pounds he paid you to clear the debt off the new church.'

And the widow of the late Charles Bodkin swept out of the room.

Sunday

1

THERE were two churches in Inverara — that is, there were two Catholic churches, because the little Protestant church in Kilmurrage was not considered to be a church at all. 'How could it be a church,' said the people of Inverara, 'when there is hardly ever a service in it?' And that was true enough, for the vicar had given up the habit of preaching to an empty church. There were only six Protestants in Inverara, and of the six, not one was sufficiently religious to go to hear the vicar preach on Sunday. The clerk of the Petty Sessions was too drunk on Saturday to leave his bed on Sunday. The lightkeeper could not very well leave his post to go hear 'a crazy parson,' as he sacrilegiously termed Mr Wilbert. The two coastguards who were Protestants did not go because there was no officer to parade them, and the other two Protestants were not really Protestants at all, but said they were in order to escape paying dues to Fr O'Reilly and his curate.

Of the two Catholic churches, one was in Kilmurrage and the other was a mile to the east of Coill Namhan. The church in Kilmurrage was new, and a splendid building. The islanders thought that it was a finer church than St Peter's in Rome. And Fr O'Reilly had built it — that is, of course, he had collected the money that built it, because it would be ridiculous to expect a poor priest to build it out of his own pocket. He collected the money in Inverara and throughout the diocese. He preached sermons in the pro-Cathedral in Dublin in aid of the fund. He got a convent of nuns to organise a bazaar in aid of the fund. He even sent a personal letter to every Inverara man and woman in the United States and got money from the majority of them. Even Tom

Manning, the son of old widow Manning, sent him one hundred dollars, and a splendid letter with the money, which the parish priest read from the altar of Coill Namhan church on the following Sunday. Everybody was surprised that Tom Manning had done so well, because there were rumours that he had become a Socialist, and nobody was more surprised than the widow Manning herself. Tom had never sent her a letter when he sent her money at Christmas and Easter and in midsummer to buy the turf, but a little note, 'dear mother, I am well and working, your son tom.' Just like that. But there was the letter in the parish priest's hands on the altar, and he read out every word in it. 'Dear Fr O'Reilly. . . . I cannot tell you how glad I am that the poor people are at last going to get a fitting place to worship their God, and it always hurt, out here under the sweltering sun of irreligious America, to think that my poor old mother had to kneel on the bare, cold stone flags of Coill Namhan church. . . .' And the poor widow wept salt tears of joy as she listened, and did not even once wish that he had sent her the hundred dollars, although she had not had a pound of tea or a pound of sugar in her cottage for the past six weeks, and her joy had turned into pride when the neighbours congratulated her, after Mass, on her splendid son.

But the new church in Kilmurrage was not for the widow. It was for the business people of Kilmurrage and the gentry of Kilmurrage and the tourists. The 'natives,' and among them was the widow, still went to the old church at Coill Namhan. Fr O'Reilly said Mass at nine o'clock in Kilmurrage and the curate said Mass at eleven o'clock in Coill Namhan. Sometimes Fr O'Reilly said Mass at Coill Namhan when he wanted to make a collection for some fund or other.

The church of Coill Namhan was not much of a building. It was very old, and the roof was leaking at the eaves, and the water ran down the whitewashed walls on the inside, in yellow streaks. The flooring was of limestone flags, and there were only a few pews, up in front outside the altar rails, for the gentry when they went to Mass. The poor people had to kneel in the rear on the bare flags. There was a wooden gallery, but that was used by the men, because the conversation that was carried on there during Mass was not fitting for any woman to hear.

But the church had a fine high roof, and the door was never closed during Mass, so that it was very seldom that anybody fainted with the cold in winter, or for want of fresh air in summer, though a stranger who visited the place one summer was heard to say that 'the damn place is insanitary and should be blown up.' If it was insanitary Pat Conneally, the rate collector, was largely responsible, for whenever the schoolmaster opened the stained-glass windows during Mass, Pat Conneally went to shut them again, 'to keep out the draught,' he said to himself, but really to show his spite against the schoolmaster.

It was prettily situated, the old church at Coill Namhan, on the brow of a hill that overlooked the stretch of sea, between Inverara and the mainland. The pale blue mountains of the mainland blended with the dark blue sea, and the sky overhead was nearly always streaked with red and blue and yellow, like a piebald horse, so that it was a beautiful picture. And beneath the hill, Inverara descended in rocky terraces, with grassy plots here and there, to the sea, so that the sea looked like the smooth floor of an amphitheatre, between Inverara and the mountains of the mainland. In the yard in front of the church, there was a sloping green sward, with long silken grasses that were never eaten or mown, and bushes of evergreens and roses growing here and there, and a cross in a corner by the gate, erected to the memory of a temperance missionary, who once upon a time converted the whole population of Inverara to teetotalism, for three days, or the duration of the mission.

Out on that grassy slope the men lay on the grass, smoking their pipes, waiting for Mass to begin. Some of them lay there all during Mass, being satisfied in coming so near to God, without enduring the monotony of kneeling for an hour in the sickly air of the church. They knelt when the people within the church knelt and they beat their breasts at the 'Sanctus, sanctus, sanctus,' and at the 'Domine Non Sum dignus' and they drew near the door at the sermon in the hope that the priest might be saying something interesting.

The Sunday after the arrival of the McSherrys was a beautiful sunny June day. The air was heavy with the ozone that is always in Inverara, bringing sleep and idleness and forgetfulness. But it did not bring forgetfulness and peace to Fr Hugh McMahon, the curate. As he cycled to the church at Coill Namhan to say the eleven o'clock Mass, his mind was busy with the thought of Lily O'Reilly, who was now Lily McSherry. She had occupied his mind since the moment that he saw her in the parochial house the previous day. While he was inspecting the boys' school at Kilmurrage, listening to the pupils reciting their catechism, he had been thinking of her, and forgot to correct the mistakes made by the pupils, and the schoolmaster had looked aghast when he allowed little Michael Devaney to say that idleness was one of the seven works of mercy. He was thinking of her when he retired to his room at Mrs Shaughnessy's hotel at night, and when he tried to write the article he had promised for the *Church Monthly*, on 'Art in Pre-Christian Ireland,' he could not concentrate his mind on the subject. When he tried to think of Pre-Christian Ireland, he thought of Lily. The sad look on her face that day in the parochial house always came between the writing-pad and his eyes.

In the morning, when he was reciting his office, her vision disturbed him several times, and he had caught himself staring at the page, while his mind was far away, busy with memories of the past. And not alone had memories of Lily disturbed him, but other thoughts had come to him in those moments of distraction. He had begun to doubt about the wisdom of the step he had taken, when he renounced Lily for the priesthood. They came to him, those doubts, like the thought of crime comes to a youth for the first time, with fear and abhorrence and yet with a seductive craving, and even though he checked them as soon as he discovered them and murmured a prayer to his favourite saint, they returned and sometimes stayed for whole minutes at a time in spite of all his efforts.

As he cycled along towards the church, he forgot Lily and his doubts. The people saluted him as they passed, and always when people saluted him he felt proud of being a priest. The scenery and the delicious calm of the day appealed to his poetic nature. His body was enjoying the warmth of the sun. When he turned the corner of the road and came in sight of the church, he felt a sudden surging of piety and zeal for his priesthood and pride in himself and his flock. The peasants were coming along the grey limestone road that stretched straight to the west, coming in a long straggling line. They walked in groups, with shoulders thrown back and arms swinging, with the loose rhythm that is peculiar to peasants. The men were dressed in black and grey and white homespuns and the women in red petticoats and heavy cashmere shawls of many colours. The curate, looking at them proudly, felt that they would make a wonderful picture, and then he felt a wave of fervent nationalism sweep over him. Those peasants they were his, to train, to educate, to rouse, to make the vanguard of the great Catholic Republic of Ireland.

He dismounted at the church gate and leaned his bicycle against the whitewashed wall. He paused for a moment to talk to the schoolmistress of Coill Namhan school, who arrived just then. He had news for her. The schoolmaster in Limerick who had been suspended for preaching sedition in his school was going to be reinstated. Mr Murphy, the member for Tipperary, had raised the question in the British House of Commons. The schoolmistress clapped her hands with glee and thought that Fr McMahon looked very handsome when that bright light was in his eyes. Then Fr McMahon advanced up the yard and entered the sacristy.

He put on his soutane and his stole and went through the church to the confessional box at the back, and sat for a few minutes, to see if anybody wanted to go to confession. Nobody came. He left the confessional box, and stood for a minute at the door looking out, and wondering why the grass was never cut. It looked very unkempt running wild that way, and then looking out at the sea and the mountains, he felt that it looked better that way, long and wild, a picture of the past, the unchanging past.

As he walked back up the church, he determined to write a poem about it, and when he was kneeling in front of the altar on his way back to the sacristy, he suddenly wondered whether Lily would come to his Mass, or whether she had gone into Kilmurrage in the morning to the nine o'clock Mass, and as he rose from his knee, he stood looking at the ground for three whole seconds, thinking of Lily, and then shrugging himself, he passed into the sacristy. And a woman seated in the church remarked to her neighbour that Fr McMahon was 'a regular saint, always meditating and praying, did ye see how he stood that time?' And the other woman remarked in a hushed whisper, 'Fr Ignatius, the redemptorist whom I heard preach the last time I was in Dublin in the Jesuit church off Grafton Street, had the same look on him, and sure Fr Ignatius is sure to be canonized as soon as he is long enough dead, though that'll be a long time, since he only died last year, and they say too that when he died strange music was heard in the room, like angels singing, and Glory be to the Blessed Mother, who's going to gainsay it?'

The curate closed the sacristy door behind him, took off his stole, kissed it and laid it on the dressing-table. 'What possessed me to think of her again?' he asked himself, 'just when I am going to say Mass.' And he threw the alb over his head viciously. Then he saw the vestments were green, and they reminded him of the fields in spring, when they were wet with dew in the morning, with the sun sparkling on the dew, and one could almost see the grasses grow, but then again, when he tied the girdle around his waist over the alb, he thought of how beautiful Lily looked in that green dress that she wore the first day he saw her. It was at the feis at Athlone, when she was staying for the holidays at a cousin's house in Ballinasloe and he was visiting in Moate and had come into Athlone to see the feis and hear Fr O'Connor speak on the future of the Gaelic League. What a glorious day that was, and how little he thought then that he would be a priest. He was then in two minds, whether to throw aside his vocation and give his life for the liberation of his country or persevere, perhaps it was all for the better. 'O Jesus, Mary, and Joseph protect me,' he murmured as he discovered himself thinking of Lily and doubting. He began to look for the missal to mark the passages he had to read for the Mass, and cursed softly when he couldn't find it, and became still more vexed because his temper had got the better of him and he had cursed, and then the altar boy — a big rosy-cheeked lout, with hobnailed boots — entered with the book, and the curate snatched it from his hands, and said, 'What do you mean by coming to serve Mass in those boots?' and then he bit his lips as he turned over the missal, for he remembered that the boots the poor boy was wearing were two odd ones, and had been picked up from refuse heaps. And he became so angry with himself that he forgot Lily and his doubts.

He marked the book and put it on the altar. Then he finished dressing, the altar boy tolled the bell a second time, the curate put on his biretta, took the chalice, and marched into the church preceded by the two altar boys. The people rushed to their knees with a terrific noise, that jarred on the curate's nerves and he decided to ask them during the sermon to kneel with less noise in future. He genuflected before the altar, handed his biretta to the altar boy, and marched up the steps to the tabernacle. He placed the chalice before the sanctuary, genuflected again, and then took up a little black book that lay on the altar and prepared to read the prayers before Mass.

He read the prayers in Irish, though he could not speak the language very well, but the people did not mind, for the majority of them were under the impression that priests always talked in Latin. Further, they were too busy with their own thoughts to pay any attention to the prayers, and their thoughts related to no spiritual questions, but to the price of pigs and the price of cattle and fish and whether the following day would be fine for weeding potatoes, how they could meet the demands of the shopkeepers who were pressing them for payment of their debts, when they would hear from their relatives in America, and when they would send home any money, the 'poor devils who were out in the cold great world, where people worked through the year, day in day out without rest, and murdered one another for money, like the heathens and ignorant people they were.'

Fr McMahon droned out the 'prayers before Mass' and the 'Acts of the Apostles,' looking up now and again to watch somebody enter. Lily had not yet come, and he was waiting impatiently for her to come. He knew that it would be a strain on his endurance to have her sitting in front of him, looking up at him perhaps, but it would be a still greater strain not to see her. If he didn't see her today he might not see her again for a week.

The Acts were coming to an end and Lily had not yet arrived, and then he heard a footstep approaching the door and his heart beat wildly. He looked up quickly to see if it were Lily. But it was only John Hanrahan, who kept two bulls for hire, and who always waited in the field with the bulls until everybody was safe at Mass, less some fraudulent neighbour might steal a march on the bulls and thus rob him of his hire, and even when John Hanrahan did leave the bulls and come to the church, he knelt at the door on one knee, with one eye on the altar and the other on the field where the bulls were grazing, so that he could kill two birds with one stone, save his soul and his hires at the same time.

The curate looked at Hanrahan, who was kneeling at the door and gazing at the altar with the devout expression of a monk during Holy Week, and he began to wonder whether, after all, religion had any real hold on the islanders, beyond the reverence they had for it as something they could not understand, and which was supposed to help them without much effort on their part. There were the old pagan customs they still maintained, relics of the pagan religion that St Patrick found in the country, the worship of Crom

Dubh, who still had a special Sunday to himself in early autumn. 'I wonder does it really matter after all what they believe in,' he mused, and considered that it was an injustice to threaten them with eternal damnation, since most of them never committed a crime throughout their lives, but lived more in accordance with the laws of God than most of the bishops whom he knew. The only crime they committed was to yawn during Mass and sometimes not go to Mass, and hardly ever make an attempt to understand the mysteries of religion. 'But could anybody understand a mystery,' asked Fr McMahon of himself as he finished the prayers and closed the little book.

He turned towards the altar. He bowed before the tabernacle. He walked down to the foot of the altar to begin Mass and just as he turned towards the altar, he caught a glimpse of Lily entering the church. She was dipping her finger in the holy-water font at the door and the sunlight from the stained-glass window was shining on her face, yellowishly, making her look like an old woman, and when Fr McMahon saw that drawn yellowish face he felt a biting pain in his breast.

Lily walked up the church to her pew and everybody looked at her, and Pat Conneally, the rate collector, remarked next morning in the forge at Kilmurrage, while he was having a mare shod, that the look on her face as she walked up the church, 'was as like as two pins to the look on the face of Mary Joyce, the day she was condemned at the Assizes in the Big Town on the Mainland for the murder of John Breen, the gamekeeper.'

'Introibo ad altare dei,' murmured the curate with his lips, while his hands behind his vestment trembled and he could hardly enunciate the words, with the hot rush of blood to his head almost choking him. He knew that Lily was behind him and he wondered what was in her thoughts, whether she still felt towards him as she did in the old days, or whether she hated him for the callous way he had treated her. He thought that the whole church saw his excitement, especially when he stumbled going up the steps, having finished the prayers at the foot of the altar. But the people did not notice that there was anything out of the ordinary, except Mrs McSherry and the two old ladies who had before been edified by his piety. These two old ladies did remark the stumbling and the excitement, but they ascribed it, the one to a spiritual ecstasy, 'just the same as Fr Ignatius, who is about to be canonized, used to have on similar occasions,' and the other to overfasting and lack of proper care in that draughty and slatternly hotel of Mrs Shaughnessy's, and she was surprised that the parish priest allowed his curate to stay in such a place, while she herself would be only too delighted to look after him and see that he 'took his nourishment properly,' and have a hot drink of gruel ready for him when he returned 'from a sick call on the cold winter nights, God help us.'

The remainder of the congregation were not paying any attention to the curate just then. They were too deeply engrossed in a scuffle that was in progress at the door. Pat Farelly, the gentleman who had caused the wreck of the cinema, had just entered, making a terrific noise with his hobnailed boots, and hustling the congregation with his huge body in an effort to get at the holy-water font to bless himself. And then, not content with having caused that degree of disturbance, he knelt on Johnny Corrigan's heels, and tumbled Corrigan with the impact, with the result that Corrigan scrambled to his feet and seized his stick with a view to hitting Farelly, when another man, eager to save Corrigan from committing a sacrilege and damning his immortal soul by hitting a fellow-man in the 'House of God,' seized the stick. But Corrigan, not at all appreciating the neighbour's solicitude, turned on the neighbour with the intention of hitting him instead of Farelly; but by that time, everybody was giggling and pushing to get out of the way, and Corrigan was carried away from the neighbour, and out of the door in the rush.

And Lily McSherry sat in her pew, with her rosary beads entwined around her hands, looking up at the statue of the Blessed Virgin, that was placed in the corner to the right of the altar, thinking of her husband, who was sitting beside her, with the smell of whisky from his breath, that she detested so much, since the first day she noticed it in the parochial house last autumn, when he came to the island first from South America, and he had tried to kiss her in the drawing-room, and she put her hands before her eyes and he put his arms around her from behind, and his hot breath, smelling of whisky, was coming over her shoulder, and she turned around suddenly and struck him as hard as she could with her clenched fist in the face, and then crouched in a corner, while he put his handkerchief to his mouth and grinned horribly, like the picture of the Devil that used to hang in the refectory of the convent at Skerries, and he said that he would make her sorry for that yet.

She was looking up at the statue of the Blessed Virgin, trying to pray, for she was a child of Mary, and had always found comfort in praying to the Holy Virgin, and this same statue of the Virgin appeared to her, when she was a little girl, in this church at Mass, to be alive and smiling when the sun shone on it through the stained-glass windows, and she thought in those days that the Holy Virgin would never refuse her anything, but now, even though she tried with all her heart to pray and feel devoted, there was something hard down in her heart that prevented her from praying, something that made her feel bitter and gave her a dead feeling all over her body, as if she had been turned into stone. She thought that perhaps that scientific book, written by an American, was true, that book she had picked up in a book-shop on the quays in Dublin, one day she was going back to the convent after the holidays, and had hidden it in her pillow-case, lest the nuns might see it, because it was forbidden by his Holiness the Pope. It said that people had two brains, and that one brain might be thinking of one thing and the other brain thinking of something else, both at the same time.

And there she was with her rosary beads entwined around her fingers trying to pray, and even though she was already at the second decade, she had not succeeded in concentrating on the Blessed Virgin for one moment, for her mind was wandering from one thing to another like a man who has made himself drunk to forget some great sorrow and finds that his brain, muddled with alcohol, becomes filled with fantastic visions of the very thing he has tried to forget.

On the altar the curate proceeded with the Mass. He raced over the words, reading them from memory, for he could not see the written page of the missal. It was a blur of many colours. Sweat stood out on his forehead in beads. The more he tried to feel devout and attentive to the sacrifice he was performing, the sacrifice of 'the body and blood of the Divine Saviour,' the less attentive he became. The impulse of the flesh was stronger in him than the impulse of the spirit. Within five yards of him, just outside the communion rails, was Lily, and although he had his back to her, her face was on the book before him, and when he turned to the tabernacle and spread out his hands over the chalice and bent his head, her face was still before his eyes. And when he turned to the congregation to give the Blessing, he tried not to look at Lily, but in spite of himself his eyes wandered towards her. As he was turning back towards the altar, he caught a fleeting glimpse of her. She was looking at the statue of the Blessed Virgin. 'She is praying against temptation,' he thought, and he was shocked that he himself was surrendering to that temptation. But again he felt glad that she was tempted. He was sure that it was the sight of himself in front of her that tempted her. She had not forgotten him.

As he crossed the altar, he turned his eyes to have another look at her, but he missed her, and his eyes met the face of old Dennis Lanigan the tailor, who was looking up at the altar praying, with a saintly look on his face, that the men in Jack Yeats's pictures have. The curate saw that look and envied the tailor. He felt that he would willingly at that moment change places with Dennis Lanigan and be a tailor instead of a priest, and he remembered that when he was a little boy, and full of his own intellectual superiority, and confident of a brilliant future, he pitied the calm stupid look on the faces of the peasants and thought that he would rather die than have to lead their lives. But now when his great trouble was upon him, engulfing him in misery, ambition or the glory of his intellect did not weigh anything in the balance of life, compared to the peace and tranquillity of mind, of which old Dennis Lanigan and people like him were possessed.

But all have their troubles, and each thinks his own troubles insurmountable and not to be equalled by the troubles of anybody else. In spite of the meek and peaceful look on Dennis Lanigan's face, there was grief in his heart. For the rosary that he was at that time reciting was the third of ten decades that he was offering to Saint Anthony in an effort to effect a cure for his daughter Ellen, who was suffering from epilepsy, poor girl, and was then in St. Vincent's Hospital in Dublin, undergoing an operation and costing him a 'mint o' money.' And there was the letter that he had received from America, six weeks last Friday, telling him that his only son, Dennis, had been killed in Butte Montana, the sorest blow he ever got, for his heart was centred in the boy, and he had been so proud when he heard that Dennis had joined the police force and was doing well and he had received a newspaper cutting last January with Dennis's photograph in it, when he had been given a medal for saving a man's life in a street-car accident, and now he was dead.

And old Dennis Lanigan was perhaps capable of suffering mental torture as intense as Fr Hugh McMahon, author of the 'Death of Maeve,' which had been pronounced to be as good as anything that Yeats had ever written. For old Dennis Lanigan, the tailor of Coill Namhan, was a poet too, in his own way. He used to sit curled up on his table, with a huge scissors beside him, stitching flannel bainins, and weaving romances about his son Dennis. He used to picture to himself that his son was doing heroic deeds and that he would one day be chief of police of Chicago City. He pictured Dennis, who 'was a good-natured lad, God bless him, before he went away,' kind to the poor and the weak and the humble, and loved by all. And these dreams made it all the harder for him to receive news of his son's death, especially since he got that letter from Fr McCarthy, of the Knights of Columbus in Butte Montana, saying that Dennis had been killed by strikers out in the mining hills of Butte, and that he had been a detective in Pinkerton's Force. So that Dennis had not been a policeman at all, but a detective, and John Carmody, who had come back from the United States a Socialist, said that Pinkerton's detectives in America were 'a gang of thugs, who shoot down workmen when they try to get their rights, same as the RIC shot down the Irish peasants during the Land League days.' Of course, John Carmody didn't tell that to old Dennis, but what was worse, he said it in Mulligan's public-house in Kilmurrage, one night he had been drunk, and was having an argument about religion with Pat Conneally the rate collector.

'Is it old Dennis Lanigan yere calling a religious man?' he said. 'Why, I knew that no-good son o' his in the States, one o' the worst thugs that ever took Pinkerton's rotten money. Sure I knew him. Joined the Knights o' Columbus and called himself Dennis J. Lanigan and threw the bull around that he was the heftiest gunman in Butte, until he got a job with Pinkerton's sluggers. All a damn bunch o' rotten rum swillers and hypocrites. That's what I call 'em, all these craw-thumpers.'

Of course, nobody believed Carmody, and Pat Conneally had almost split open his skull with a blackthorn stick when he said it, for saying such a thing about an honest man's son and casting aspersions on religion, but the words sank into the old tailor's heart and they smashed his dreams to atoms.

'Sanctus, sanctus, sanctus.' The altar boy rang the bell. The congregation sank to their knees. The supreme moment of the Mass approached, when the priest would hold aloft the Sacred Host. The altar boys climbed up the steps and knelt behind the priest, to hold up his vestments, when he raised the Host. All bent their heads and prepared to worship. There was a dull silence in the church, and the twittering of the sparrows in the eaves could be heard distinctly. Even the small boys in the rear of the gallery, who had been chattering in low voices, comparing marbles and talking of the bonfires they were going to have that night, St. John's eve, were silent now, awestricken by the impressiveness of the ceremony.

Dong, dong, dong. The bell tolled sleepily and mysteriously as if it too were conscious of the ceremony, and the sounds lingered in the eaves, dying away slowly and mellowing as they died. Every time the bell tolled, the congregation struck their breasts three times, and murmured prayers and begged forgiveness for their sins, of the great invisible and mysterious Power, who at that moment was being sacrificed to save them. The old woman who had cast herself face downwards in the aisle just outside the communion rails, with her shawl thrown far over her head, rose with each tolling of the bell and casting her hands out wide above her head, cried in a deep and mournful voice, 'O God of Glory, O God of Power!' And then her voice died away like the sounds of the bell, as she threw herself prone once more and rocked herself in an ecstasy of devotion, to the great delight of the small boys, who watched her.

Lily McSherry had bent her head, and had struck her breast with her little smooth hands, and had murmured each time the bell tolled, 'O Lord, have mercy on me.' A well of self-pity gushed from her heart as she meditated on the death of Christ on the cross, which this sacrifice symbolized, and unconsciously she felt a kinship with that suffering, on account of her own sufferings. And this kinship of suffering loosed the hardness that had rested around her heart since the evening before, when her uncle had failed to comfort her, and his words had made her callous. She was almost on the verge of tears, and was feeling a surge of happiness in the superlativeness of her sorrow. She experienced a salt feeling in the throat, and a throbbing of the nerves in the throat, as if she were feeling an excess of joy. But when she was again going to raise her head to look at the altar and give thanks to Christ for having solaced her in her sorrow, her elbow touched her husband's and a tremor of repulsion ran through her body. She shivered and looked at him instead of the altar and the look that she saw in his eyes put a look of terror and hatred into her own. He had that far-away evil look in his eyes, that steely, cold, sensuous look, as if he were dreaming of some evil incident in his past life, dreaming of something afar off that was lurid and sickening.

McSherry was dreaming of something far away, for he was not a Catholic or even a Christian, and was dreadfully bored with what he called 'a superstitious mummery.' And his mind was comparing his present boredom with the jolly Sundays he used to spend in the 'Jockey Club' in Buenos Ayres, sipping champagne with his cronies, and then perhaps in the evening going in search of a . . .

Lily was brought back to reality by seeing that look in her husband's eyes and she became vexed with herself for having thought that anything, even the influence of the Saviour, could help her to endure that terrible punishment to which she was condemned for life, always to feel her husband beside her, and to see the devilish look in his eyes, the same look she had seen on the faces of the men at the platform of the Broadstone station in Dublin, who stared at her girlish beauty, when she was coming from the convent. In those days she would not believe that she would marry a man like them. She expected a man young like herself, some one whose eyes would shine with love for her, pure love, self-sacrificing love, the kind of love that Hugh McMahon had for her, but then, what was the use of thinking of that. He was as bad as the rest and only thought of himself, for if he were not thinking of himself how could he be so cruel to her that night at Dungarvan. And she felt that she hated him as much as she hated her husband, and she felt glad that he was suffering now. She knew that he was, when she saw him at dinner in the parochial house the day before, when he stumbled against the sideboard, while he was shaking hands with her husband, and was so excited that he could hardly speak.

The curate saying Mass on the altar was not thinking at all. A torpor had seized him, dulling his senses, turning his mind into a plasmic mass, that did not reason but accepted the objects around him, the missal, the chalice, the tabernacle, the flowers, as things outside of himself that he could not understand, but was forced to endure through some cause beyond his control; just in the attitude of a bullock being herded to the slaughterhouse, that rushes wildly hither and thither in an effort to escape, and then giving up the effort succumbs wearily, and stands with downcast head and foolish look, waiting for its death-blow.

The Mass rolled on. The people were yawning in the pews and on the gallery. At the door the people were looking out at the sea, watching the little boat that was sailing drowsily along, with a black patch on her white sail, with her crew perhaps sitting lazily on the sun-scorched decks, smoking their pipes and thinking how deliciously cool the porter would taste in Mulligan's when they arrived there in the afternoon. The congregation had by now exhausted their capacity for prayer. Even the most devoted had got tired of constantly repeating the decades of the rosary and they had read their prayer books from cover to cover. They were now scratching their heads and yawning and trying to think of the Mass, but in spite of themselves they were wondering who was going to speak at the United Irish League meeting in Kilmurrage that afternoon, and whether Mr Donovan, the lame organizer from Ballinrobe, was really coming on the *Duncairn* as reported, and whether Fr McMahon was going to preach a sermon, and hoping that he was not, because the day was too fine to be sitting in church, while the sun blazed outside 'glory be to God.' The little boys were bursting with impatience, and some of them had already sneaked out so as to escape being caught by the schoolmaster and forced to stay for catechism, and Pat Conneally's two sons and young Jimmy Grealish had already scampered away to the south of the church, where they had a donkey tied in a boreen, intending to ride him up and down the boreen, until it was time to go home and prepare for the bonfires.

'Domine non sum dignus ut intres sub tectum meum.' The bell tolled and the people struck their breasts again, but this time without any enthusiasm, and with a bored look in their faces. But the curate on the altar was now animated. He would soon have to turn around to the congregation and read the notices for the week, the gospels for the Sunday, and then preach a sermon. He would gladly pass over the sermon, but Fr O'Reilly had strictly enjoined on him to preach a sermon that day, in view of the sports and Pattern coming on the following Saturday, St Peter and St Paul's Day, when the people were in the habit of getting drunk and creating disturbances. But he was vexed that he should have to preach against the evils of intemperance and the evil of potheen that day, because Lily was in the church and she had seen the potheen in the parochial house the day before. Of course, he told himself, he had taken none of it, he had never tasted drink in his life. Though, of course, he was not so much a teetotaller from the religious point of view as because drink had been the curse of his family, and also because he considered that it was the drunken habits of the Irish that kept Ireland in subjection to England. He had read that in some temperance tract written by a Jesuit, and he believed it was true. She could not believe him to be a hypocrite for preaching against drink, simply because she had seen potheen in Fr O'Reilly's house. Of course, he admitted to himself, some of the clergy should set a better example on this matter of drink. It was a well-known scandal that a majority of the shares in Guinness' Brewery in Dublin were held by priests, and some of them stanch temperance advocates. And he remembered how shocked he had been, one time he was at a temperance congress in the Gresham Hotel in Dublin, and he heard Fr Rocke of Knockadoon say that a man with a pledge against drink was like a dog with a muzzle on him, while he himself was touring the country denouncing drink, and paid by the society too. But he himself would never forget the promise that his poor mother exacted from him when he was going to be confirmed, never to touch drink in his life, and she told him how his father, who was an eminent solicitor in Dublin, never really died of fatty degeneration of the heart as was reported, but died in an inebriate's home at Rathgar, and because his mother said that the curse of drink had been the ruin of his father's people for ages, he had always shunned even the sight of drink, as he would shun the plague.

He turned around to face the congregation and began to read the notices. There was to be a holy day of obligation on the following Saturday in honour of the feast of Saints Peter and Paul. The usual monthly confessions would be held on Friday instead of on Saturday. Mass on Saturday would be at nine o'clock, to allow the people time to get into Kilmurrage in time for the commencement of the sports. The usual benediction for the Blessed Sacrament would be given after Mass on Sunday. Finally the parish priest asked everybody to come into Kilmurrage in the afternoon to attend the United Irish League meeting.

Then he read the gospel for the Sunday, both in Irish and in English. When he came to the passage, 'Look at the birds of the air, they sow not neither do they reap, and yet they are clothed,' old John Hourigan, who was trying to raise a family of ten children on five acres of scraggy land, murmured to his neighbour that he wished he were a bird, and then he thought that it was very unjust on the part of God to make it so easy for the birds to earn their living and compel his own children to languish in the direst poverty, and the only people who resembled the birds of the air were the landlords, who never did a stroke of work, but lived by robbing the poor, and how could the landlords be living in accordance with the laws of God since they were nearly all Protestants. And then old John Hourigan, finding the problem insoluble, scratched his head, and fell to thinking of the money he owed Tim Sullivan, the stone cutter, for the headstone that had been erected over the grave of old Mick Hourigan, his father, and the money was owing for nine months or more, and Tim Sullivan himself was badly in need of it, poor man, having been laid up for the last six months with the influenza.

The curate laid down the gospels, put his hands under his vestment and coughed. Then he looked out through the stained-glass windows as if to get inspiration. The people settled themselves in their seats to listen, and those who had been until then lying outside on the grass crowded around the door, in the hope that the priest was going to denounce the potheen vendors by name, for even in Inverara the people liked to hear their neighbours vilified in public, and more especially when the neighbours were people who were making money with greater ease and rapidity than was becoming.

But that Sunday the curate did not mention anybody's name. He was too conscious of the great struggle with temptation that was going on within himself to be in a mood to deal heavily with the sins of others. How could he abuse the potheen vendors, when he himself was in danger of falling a victim to a sin, compared to which the sale of potheen was but a mole-hill. Instead he preached on temptation. He preached better than he had ever preached before, appealing to the congregation to resist temptations. Some of the women were moved to tears when he rose to a pitch of eloquence, and the old lady who had compared him to Fr Ignatius who was about-to-be-canonized, lifted up her eyes and whispered to her friend, that she had never heard such a wonderful sermon since Fr Dominic the Trappist preached his famous sermon against Socialism in the pro-Cathedral in Dublin, and she felt sure that Fr McMahon would be a greater preacher yet, and be sent on a tour of the United States to collect the money for building the new cathedral in Dublin.

But Fr McMahon was not conscious that he was preaching a great sermon. He was preaching to himself. He was trying to empty his soul of the wild torrent of passion that he felt was going to overwhelm him. He was crying aloud, like the prophet in the wilderness, casting his voice to the four winds of heaven, appealing for help against his temptation. His soul was contracted in an agony of pain, fearful of the chasm that stretched before it, magnifying the chasm, so that if it did fall, if it did succumb, if it were defeated in the struggle with sin, its conscience would understand that it did not fall without a superhuman struggle.

'Saints,' cried Fr McMahon, and his body trembled as he spoke, 'when they found themselves assaulted by the temptation of the flesh, cast themselves into bushes of piercing thorns, and then wrapped their bleeding bodies in rough sackcloth.' And his eyes closed and he crossed the altar, holding his hands before his eyes as if to shut out the vision that his words called to his mind. For there in front of him was his temptation of the flesh, looking up at him, and he knew that he could not cast himself into a bush of piercing thorns to escape it. He knew in his heart that his temptation was stronger than he. He knew that his soul was filled with desire, unconquerable desire for Lily McSherry, and he knew that he was a priest and that she was 'His Neighbour's Wife.'

So he turned once more to the congregation and losing himself, he surged into a paroxysm of eloquence. Without thinking of what he was saying, he poured out periods that flowed with the smoothness of a mighty river, but running like the river, with a power that was irresistible. And then he finished in a welter of perspiration, with every nerve on edge with excitement, tired as if he had just climbed a steep cliff. He finished and turned back to the altar and, in spite of the effort he had made, he felt that he had not silenced the voice that cried within him, the voice of his love for Lily.

The people crowded to their knees again, and some thought that the priest had spoken well and others wondered what he had been talking about, because he had spoken in English, a language which they did not understand, and would therefore have to wait until Pat Conneally retailed the sermon to them that night in Patsy O'Brien's, any of them that felt a desire to hear it.

And the only one that understood the message of the sermon was Lily McSherry and she was vexed with the curate for having preached such a sermon. 'It's just like him,' she said to herself, 'in the first place trifling with a girl's love, and then making a martyr of himself, and appealing for aid to the whole world.' And the sermon, instead of softening her in her attitude towards the curate, hardened her against him. She resolved that there was nothing in religion but rank hypocrisy, and laughed down in her heart, in the way that those other women laugh, who are pariahs, at the world, and she determined that she should live like the rest and get the best out of life that there was to be got, without reference to any religious or moral scruples that might restrain her.

The curate finished Mass and retired to the foot of the altar to recite the 'De Profundis.' 'From the depths I cry out to Thee, O Lord, hear my voice.' But he was not crying out to God. He was wearied to exhaustion by the struggle that had been going on in his mind and by the long fast since the night before, so that he just mumbled the prayers, rushing through the words of the psalm without waiting for the altar boys to finish the responses. And with equal celerity he recited the prayers after Mass, reading them in Irish and jumbling the words together so that the people thought he was still reading Latin. Then he rose, genuflected and retired to the sacristy, and before he had left the church, Mr O'Hagan, the schoolmaster from Coill Namhan school, commenced to recite the rosary, a duty which he arrogated to himself at the request of the parish priest, who was too lazy to recite the rosary when he said Mass in Coill Namhan.

Mr O'Hagan recited the rosary in a loud sing-song voice, and McSherry, who had arisen to leave the church, on the disappearance of the priest, looked in the direction of the schoolmaster and scowled and then sat down deliberately in his seat, to the manifest scandal of the remainder of the congregation who were on their knees as was proper. They were surprised to see McSherry, who was one of the 'gentry' and therefore expected to give a good example of piety in public, pay so little respect to the rosary of the Blessed Virgin. And when McSherry, having endured as much as he could of the 'superstitious mummery,' tipped his wife on the elbow and motioned her to follow him, and stalked out of the church, while Lily stayed in her seat, the congregation looked at one another, as much as to say 'what d'ye think o' that for goin's on.'

The schoolmaster reciting the rosary still droned out the Ave

Marias, and paid no heed to this distraction. His eyes were fixed on the altar of the Blessed Virgin, and there was a wild light in those eyes, a light that Mr O'Hagan had often rehearsed before the mirror in his lodgings, for Mr O'Hagan was a holy man, a very holy man, and never so holy as when he got an opportunity of manifesting his holiness in public. A holy man truly was Mr O'Hagan. The good woman in whose house he lodged, said that his favourite recreation after school hours was reading the *Imitation of Christ*, and that he was also learning to read the Roman missal off by heart, so that when he had enough money saved to pay for his college expenses and could 'go on for to be a priest,' he would be already well on the road to sanctity and sacerdotal learning.

Poor Miss Milligan, the schoolmistress of the adjoining girls' school, in spite of the almost transparent pink blouses that she bought especially in Clery's of Dublin to attract his attention, couldn't get Mr O'Hagan to look at her, even though she managed every evening to close her school at the same time that he closed his, and she always smiled and blushed shyly when he talked to her. She was making no headway and Mr O'Hagan seemed to be getting more saintly every day, and people said that he had more the appearance of a priest than Fr O'Reilly himself and that 'you had only to turn his collar backwards and there he was ready to say Mass and hear confessions.' But others who disliked him said that he was more like a Protestant minister than a priest, and John Carmody, who had come back from the United States a Socialist, said that Mr O'Hagan was 'a God damn hypocrite, and I got wise to him as soon as I gave him the once over.'

Mr O'Hagan finished the rosary. The people rushed to their feet in a hurry and pushed and struggled to get out of the church, like boys rushing from school on a summer's day. They never troubled to dip their hands in the holy-water font, and the old lady who had compared Fr McMahon to the Fr Ignatius who was about-to-be-canonized, remarked that day, as she had remarked every Sunday for twenty years, 'it's a disgrace the irreligion that's setting into the island, to see people in such a hurry to get out of the House of God, but there you are.' And the old lady, as was her habit for the past twenty years, stayed behind doing the stations of the cross in company with another old woman who had imposed upon herself three stations of the cross, in the hope that she would get a cure for a cataract on the left eye, by doing bodily penance. And in a few minutes the church was empty and silent, except for the groans and prayers of the old lady with the cataract, while outside the people lying on the grass talked and smoked and laughed, glad to be out in the sun, for after all perhaps the natives of Inverara had never really been converted by St Patrick, but that they retained their old sun worship, and looked upon God only as the God of the conqueror St Patrick, and were glad when they had finished their weekly homage to this God of the conqueror and could return to the worship of their old native God, the sun, and his prophet Crom Dubh.

In the sacristy the curate sat eating his breakfast, which Michael Sweeney, the clerk of the parish, had cooked for him in the neighbouring cottage. But although he had fasted long, he could just barely drink a cup of tea and eat half of a soft boiled egg. The food choked him and he felt a terrific craving, a gnawing desire down in his breast, a gnawing and a craving that he feared more than the first signs of a deadly plague. He felt the craving for drink.

2

A political meeting was a popular event in Inverara, but not because the people understood politics or felt interested in that universal game of chicanery. The people of Inverara, and by the people one must be understood to mean the 'natives,' excepting the inhabitants of Kilmurrage, knew nothing of politics. There were of course exceptional cases like old Dennis Lanigan, the tailor of Coill Namhan, who bought the *Weekly Independent* every week in the year, and read it aloud to the whole village on Saturday evenings in his cottage, and could tell offhand and without a moment's notice, what constituency John Dillon represented in parliament and the meaning of the 'Representation of the People Act,' which even Pat Conneally, the rate collector, didn't understand.

A political meeting was a popular event in Inverara for the reason that Pat Farelly expressed, when he said that 'a meeting is a great thing, upon me sowl it is, for begob ye'd never know when they're goin' to come to blows and kick up a hell ov a row.' What the meeting represented nobody cared. It sufficed that the parish priest should 'be at the back of it,' and that some strangers should come from the mainland, with a priest or two to back them up and give the affair a respectable aspect, by standing on the platform smiling and wiping their faces with red silk handkerchiefs and calling for three cheers for 'the cause' when the meeting was finished. The Kilmurrage people were in the habit of cheering and waving their hats, but the peasants were never guilty of such indecencies, disdaining such civilized expressions of savagery. Having a greater respect for themselves than the average civilized person, they would look on calmly enjoying the show. For, after all, they asked themselves, what was the sense in getting excited over the prerogatives of the British King, since the majority of them did not know who he was or what was his name, and even those who pretended to know were under the impression that Queen Victoria was still on the throne, though it was common knowledge among the people of Kilmurrage that George V had already mounted the throne as the successor of that honourable lady, nobody even in Kilmurrage being aware that a man named Edward had reigned in the interval. But then, of what account was King George V in Inverara, since Fr O'Reilly was the only person approximating to royal power with whom the islanders were acquainted. He had even more power than the average monarch. He collected taxes, all for himself too, having to spend nothing on armies, navies or court favourites of the opposite sex. He arranged lawsuits without having to pay for a police force or the cost of a judiciary. He gave people away in marriage and charged a good round sum for doing so. He baptized people when they were born, at three and eightpence a head if male and three and fourpence a head if female. He allowed corpses to be buried respectably in consecrated ground, and for that service also collected a considerable sum, not only from the owners of the corpse but from the general public, who might be suspected of having even the most distant relationship with the deceased.

There, of course, were the police, who were outside Fr O'Reilly's control, but they were only 'a drunken lot of wasters,' and if they were the best defenders that the King George V could requisition, his power, in the opinion of the islanders, did not amount to very much.

The peasants had got excited over politics but once in the course of several generations. That was the time of the Land League Agitation. But even then their excitement manifested itself in a more sensible manner than the political excitement of civilized people. They fought the landlords and the bailiffs sturdily, but they did it with their old duck guns, going around in the middle of the night to shoot them and disdaining speeches and platforms and silk handkerchiefs to mop clerical faces. And they won too, for not a single landlord remained in the island, and for that reason the peasants were not interested in Home Rule, having nothing to worry them any longer, and because they were too stupid to see the difference between having the police controlled by a king in London or by an archbishop or a president in Dublin.

'Yerrah, is it the King that's bothering them,' said old Nick Carmody, who had shot two bailiffs in one night during the Land League days, 'then why the divil don't they go an' shoot 'im if he's interferin' with them? Musha the divil much good they'll do by shoutin' at him.'

However, that Sunday after Mass the people crowded into Kilmurrage to attend at the meeting. The *Duncairn* had come from the Big Town on the Mainland on an excursion, carrying among her passengers, Donovan, the well-known organizer of the United Irish League, Fr Considine, one of the most noted clerical political speakers in Ireland, and a number of priests and politicians of lesser importance. They had come, to use Donovan's own words, to 'rally Inverara to a man behind the Home Rule Programme.'

The *Duncairn* was met at the Pier as usual by the parish priest and his retinue of important people. Mrs Cassidy was there waving a green flag amid cheers. On board the *Duncairn*, as the ship came alongside, a blind fiddler from the Big Town on the Mainland, sitting on a deck-chair beside the lame organizer Mr Donovan, played the 'Wearing of the Green,' while Mr Donovan held his hat in his hand, with a serious look on his face, in respect for the nationalist sentiment of the song.

'A great sight,' said Pat Conneally the rate collector. 'Nearly as good as the day Michael Davitt came about the "Plan o' Campaign."'

As usual, the important people accompanied Fr O'Reilly to the parochial house for lunch, while the ordinary people, who had come on the *Duncairn*, scattered around the town of Kilmurrage to get refreshments in the hotels and public-houses. The blind fiddler settled himself on an empty barrel outside the door of Mulligan's public-house and played jigs and reels in the intervals of drinking pints of stout, while the boys and girls of the town and the tourists danced on the flags. The Kilmurrage girls made eyes at the young men from the mainland and young Cissy Carmody, who had the blackest eyes and the curliest brown hair ever seen, and was the 'belle of Kilmurrage,' walked around in her new green blouse, with her head in the air, pretending not to notice anybody, driving all the young men mad with jealousy, the Kilmurrage men jealous of the young men from the mainland, and the young men from the mainland jealous of the Kilmurrage men for having in their sole possession such a gem of feminine beauty as Cissy. And Cissy walked around happy in the attention she was attracting, and yet dissatisfied with herself for being compelled to waste her time in bleak and desolate and uncultured Inverara when she might be earning twenty pounds a week in Dublin 'for her figure.'

A wooden platform had been erected in the town square, on the town side of the harbour, opposite the Pier. Towards three o'clock the people began to crowd into the square. The whole town of Kilmurrage came and most of the male population of the west of the island. And then on the stroke of three Fr O'Reilly appeared, accompanied by Fr Considine and the rest of the important people. McSherry was with the priest and mounted the platform, while Mrs McSherry remained with Mrs Bodkin in the parish priest's dogcart beside the platform. Behind them were Mrs Cassidy and Dr Cassidy and young Miss Cassidy home from college, in the Cassidy trap. Mr Blake, the squire, was with Mr Mannion, the solicitor from Athlone. Everybody of importance in Inverara was on the platform or around it except Mr Renshaw, the retired RIC inspector and the vicar and the vicar's wife. Mr Renshaw was not there because he had a pension from the Government and he had to be a Loyalist in order to keep his pension, while the Protestant vicar and his wife stayed away for the same reason, though the vicar himself had absolutely no interest in politics, either seditious or loyalist. He much preferred to stay in his rooms poring over Greek literature and writing his perpetual tracts on the Homeric Metre, reasoning whether accents should be on the peri-spomenon or on the pro-perispomenon and considering this was more important work than endeavouring to give a salary to an Irish Catholic Commoner instead of to an English Protestant Lord-Lieutenant, which was all the Home Rule Movement amounted to.

The important people had mounted the platform amid cheers

and the waving of hats, when young Hugh O'Malley created a disturbance by holding a counter-meeting over at the corner of Jim Shanaghan's new store. Fr O'Reilly and the important people on the platform looked around with surprise and indignation. Sergeant Donagan and his two constables, Moriarty and Snell, elbowed their way through the crowd towards the point where O'Malley was speaking. Their passage was barred however by several young peasants, who held up their blackthorn sticks in a menacing manner, and Pat Farelly's son, Michael, stuck his fist in front of Sergeant Donagan's nose, crying 'If ye lay a hand on Mr O'Malley, I'll bate ye as flat as a pancake.'

Intimidated by this attitude of the peasants, the sergeant halted his men and addressed O'Malley from a convenient distance, asking O'Malley what did he mean by trying to obstruct a legal gathering of law-abiding subjects of his Majesty.

'What the devil has it got to do with you, you pig?' yelled O'Malley, and the peasants yelled and waved their sticks, for even though they did not understand what O'Malley had said, since he spoke in English, they knew that he had said something agreeable, since he had spoken to a policeman.

For Hugh O'Malley was the son of Hugh THE O'MALLEY, who was the son of Hugh THE O'MALLEY, and the descendant of countless generations of O'Malleys, who were chiefs of Inverara for the past two thousand years or more. And the peasants were the descendants of free clansmen of the O'Malleys and had elected O'Malleys for countless generations to protect the clan and defend its territories, and these peasants would still support an O'Malley against the Devil in hell or the Pope of Rome, even though the present O'Malleys were in sadly straitened circumstances and no longer chiefs. They were as poor as the peasants themselves in fact, but that made no difference to the peasants. To the peasants an O'Malley was by nature an aristocrat and did not need to have money in order to command respect. The O'Malleys belonged to an age when 'the possession of a few filthy banknotes of unknown origin,' as old Hugh was fond of saying, did not make a man a gentleman. Valour in the field, intelligence in government, and generosity and honour in private life, had been their claims on the allegiance of their clansmen. So that even though they were no longer chiefs of Inverara, even though old Hugh was living in a cottage by the old fort at Coill Namhan, and young Hugh, after leaving Trinity College, Dublin, had to earn his living by writing for the newspapers and reviews, the peasants of Inverara still thought more of the O'Malleys than they thought of the British King, or of the Pope, or even of Fr O'Reilly, the parish priest. Of course the parish priest did not share this respect for the O'Malleys, and the people of Kilmurrage, who were 'the compact mass of public opinion,' sided with the priest and were more bitter against the O'Malleys than Fr O'Reilly himself.

The cause of Fr O'Reilly's dislike of the O'Malleys was their anti-clericalism. Old Hugh O'Malley had been excommunicated in '67, for taking part in the rebellion against the British Crown and he had remained excommunicated since. His son followed in his footsteps, and was an 'agnostic,' and the people of Kilmurrage said that it was 'small wonder they should lose their religion, seein' the bad blood there was in the family, for look at Hugh's grandfather, Bald Hugh O'Malley, who had been fightin' the priests all his life, and who when he was on his death-bed in the tower room of the old O'Malley Castle, that had been knocked down since by the Hand o' God, Lord preserve us from all harm, had his little finger burned off him by a flash o' lightnin' that came in through the window and he drinkin' a flask o' brandy on his death-bed and playin' chess instead of preparin' his soul to meet his God, and sure everybody knows that that was a sign of God's vengeance, Blessed be His Holy Name.'

If all the rumours were correct, Bald Hugh was a thoroughly bad man, for 'it is a well-known fact, me dear, that he had three illegitimate children, and not all by the same woman either, and they are all alive yet and respected people too.' This rumour was true enough, for one of the children, Martin Dignum, was the wealthiest man in Inverara, and the best Pillar of Society in Kilmurrage, while another of them, Thomas Kiernan, was a wealthy manufacturer in Dublin, a millionaire in fact, since he had a bank account of £50,000, while the third had done remarkably well in the United States in the political trade. And old Mrs Sears, the literary woman who came every year to Inverara for her holidays and in search of 'copy,' said that there was a certain poetic justice in the fact that the bastard children had done so well and the 'legitimate offspring had gone to rack and ruin, my dear.'

But Mrs Sears being of course a foreigner did not understand. Martin Dignum or Thomas Kiernan could amass wealth or gain a position in society, because they had no ancestral traditions to uphold, and could scavenge for scraps in the industrial gutter, but an O'Malley would rather fall on his ancestral sword than demean himself and cast a stain on his escutcheon by taking part in the low vice of commerce or trade. It was quite possible for Martin Dignum to accept a half-penny change when he was buying a hat, but if an O'Malley were offered five shillings change out of a pound, he would throw it into the gutter to some children. Of course Martin Dignum made money, but there was no poetic justice in the fact that he did make it. There was on the contrary a deal of injustice in the making of it. When Martin was rising in the world and had a number of men working for him in the kelp business, and he was boarding them in his own house, in order to be able to give them less wages and feed them on Scotch porridge, he used to come out on the hill beneath his house, and call loudly to the men in the hollow beneath, so that the whole town could hear and admire his generosity, 'Hallo there, men, hey there, men below, come up to yer dinners of praties and mate an' cabbage, with a pot o' tea and a whole gridiron loaf after it.'

So here was Hugh O'Malley holding an opposition meeting to the official meeting of the United Irish League, because Hugh was a Republican like his father, and a member of the Irish Republican Brotherhood, though nobody knew that, of course, since the IRB was a secret society, and only the Government knew about it. The Republicans, later known as the Sinn Feiners, were opposed to the United Irish League, and didn't believe in sending men to the British House of Commons, which was the aim of the United Irish League.

'Ye'll have to stop that meeting,' said the sergeant.

The peasants growled and there would have probably been a few police corpses in the square but for the timely intervention of Fr O'Reilly, who came up at that moment, wearing his best smile, and with the pimple on his nose shining like a star or a piece of lemon in a glass of whisky punch.

'Now, Mr O'Malley,' said Fr O'Reilly, and the very sound of his voice was as captivating as the voice of an American Insurance Agent. 'We are willing to give you a quarter of an hour on the main platform if you have anything to say, but it will do you no good to hold an opposition meeting. Bitterness or disunion will never get our beloved country to the goal we all desire.'

O'Malley considered for some time and looked around at his supporters. Some of them nodded their heads, suggesting that he should proceed to clear the square of his opponents, but others were clearly afraid of the parish priest and seemed to suggest agreement with Fr O'Reilly's proposal. And O'Malley, for a moment dallying with the tempting prospect of clearing the square, yielded to the desire to speak and denounce his own and his country's 'enemies.'

'I agree,' he said, 'if you let me speak at once.'

'All right, Mr O'Malley,' said the parish priest, 'come along and get up on the platform.'

The peasants rent the air with cries of 'Mailleach Abu' (the Irish for 'O'Malley to victory' being the battle cry of the O'Malley clan) and the Kilmurrage people grumbled and made wry faces, and sneered at the peasants, whom they considered to be wild men, and uncivilized people, who couldn't talk English or smoke cigarettes or wear tanned boots. But the important people were interested and Dr Cassidy said to Mrs Cassidy in his bird-like voice, that he was damned, but he thought there were no people like the old people, until Mrs Cassidy threatened to have his life unless he shut his mouth and not make a fool of her in public.

Mrs Bodkin and Mrs McSherry moved up closer to the platform in their dogcart, and the curate, who had been keeping as close as possible to Mrs McSherry since she had arrived, saw her looking intently at O'Malley as Hugh mounted the platform proudly and looked around him with his head high in the air and his chest thrown out. The curate saw that Lily never took her eyes off O'Malley and he felt sure that he saw love or awakening love in her look. His heart sickened within him and he said, sufficiently loud for those around him to hear, 'Christ!' The people around him heard the word and started in surprise at hearing the saintly curate swear, but the curate, immediately realizing what he had said, bent his head and murmured 'Christ have mercy on me,' and then the people understood that he was praying and were highly edified, and Cissy Carmody, the belle of Kilmurrage, who at that moment had been looking at Hugh O'Malley and wishing that she could feel his arms about her and feel the impress of his lips against hers, was shocked at hearing the good priest praying, while she herself had such bad thoughts running through her head. She blushed to the roots of her hair and was thoroughly ashamed of herself, but next moment she looked to her left and saw a young man from the Big Town on the Mainland, in a new tweed suit and a straw hat, ogling her, and she smiled at him, and she moved to a position where he could get a better view of her eyes and her new green blouse, that showed her figure so well.

Hugh O'Malley as he stood on the platform was a fine figure of a man, tall and well built and with the proud look on his face that all the O'Malleys had since the first of them came to Inverara, though if tradition were true, it would be hard to see how the first one of them could have been proud with justice, since he came to Inverara in his bare feet, with a handful of followers, flying from the pursuit of an O'Connor. O'Malley raised his hand for silence and settled his body in position to commence his speech. Another cry came from the peasants — 'O'Mailleach Abu.' Mrs McSherry was still looking at O'Malley with parted lips, and her bosom slightly heaving, and the curate, looking from her face to O'Malley, had a look in his eyes that was not a look of love.

'Friends,' began O'Malley in Irish, addressing his peasant followers. 'I am glad to have an opportunity to speak here today to these gentlemen who have come from the mainland. I am going to address these gentlemen in English since they do not understand their own native language, but I ask you as the descendants of the ancient clansmen of the O'Malleys to see that I get a hearing. If anybody wants to create a disturbance in order to prevent me from saying what I have to say, let us see to it that he will get the worst of the argument. We ruled this island for centuries before the foreigner came with their yardsticks and their beer measures to rob us of our birthright, but we are not conquered yet and we will today make that clear to them.'

There were loud cries of 'O'Mailleach Abu' and waving of blackthorn sticks, and then O'Malley turned to the important people on the platform and, clearing his throat, spoke in English.

'I am speaking now to you priests and politicians, and the deluded people who follow you. You have come here today to hold a meeting, to try and foist your Home Rule programme on the natives of Inverara. As an O'Malley and the descendant of the chiefs who ruled over this island, I came to utter a protest. You priests and you politicians are the curse of this country' (here there were cries of protest, but the cries of protest were drowned in shouts of 'Mailleach Abu,' and Fr O'Reilly raised his hand for silence, although the pimple on his nose was swelling and appeared to be on the point of bursting). 'Ireland needs to be rid of her "Gentry,"to be rid of those descendants of adventurers, who were picked by marauding English generals from the London brothels and foisted on this country as "gentlemen." Ireland needs to be rid of those dissolute, roystering, ignorant scoundrels, who have never done anything for the country but rob it, except when once and again the dung of their stables has been raked by the hand of fate and they have produced a Moore or a Parnell.

'And after them, Ireland wants to be rid of her priests and politicians' (renewed cries of protest, which threatened this time to end in blows, but the parish priest again came to the rescue, even though he himself was trembling with wrath, and Fr Considine's face was hidden behind his red silk handkerchief to hide his anger). 'Ireland needs to be rid of her priests and politicians, for they are the two main forces that are keeping the country in ignorance. When she is free of these three scourges she can advance.

'And I want to point out,' he continued, raising his voice, ' that this objective cannot be gained by begging from British Kings, or by prayer to God, or by speeches. It can only be gained by the same methods by which the Land League men won the land, by reliance on our own brawn and muscle, and by our willingness to die for the mother that gave us all birth' (here there was a cheer even from the natives of Kilmurrage, and the young man in the grey tweed suit and the straw hat, who was now standing beside Cissy Carmody, waved his hat in the air and shouted 'To hell with the King').

Then the parish priest seeing that the meeting was being won over by O'Malley, touched O'Malley on the shoulder and asked him to finish, because it was getting late and they had to allow the speakers from the mainland to get through their speeches before the departure of the *Duncairn*, and O'Malley, with a parting peroration, ended amid terrific applause. The Kilmurrage people cheered louder than the peasants, for who could refuse to cheer such a good-looking young man, who was such a 'powerful orator,' and who showed in his eyes, and voice and gestures, that he was sincere in every word he said, and was as ready to die for Ireland as his ancestor who had fallen in defence of the Bridge of Athlone in the Williamite wars.

O'Malley descended from the platform and as he was making his way through the crowd, he passed close to the dogcart in which

Lily McSherry was sitting. His eyes met hers in passing, and the curate, who was watching, saw the look of joy (that was the only way he could describe it) that was in Lily's eyes as she looked at O'Malley. He saw her smiling into his face as shamelessly as an actress, for Fr McMahon was under the impression that all actresses were by nature shameless, and he clenched his hands and bit his lips with his teeth, for a third torment was now added to the two already in his mind. He had been until now tormented by the conflict of religion and love. Now was added the torment of patriotism. O'Malley represented his own ideas, or nearly his own ideas, on the question of nationalism. He had been in agreement with O'Malley while he was talking. He had felt a corresponding exaltation in his own breast when O'Malley enthused over the present unjust system of government in Ireland. He agreed that the gentry and the politicians and (to a certain extent, of course) the clergy were the curse of Ireland, but when he saw O'Malley being smiled at by Lily his love of Ireland collapsed before his love for Lily. Yet it did not altogether collapse, but now the three objectives of his life, his religion, his love, and his patriotism, surged one into the other in his brain. Neither was powerful enough to assert itself the unquestioned master, but each cried out in turn, begging for support, striving to force itself into the scene of thought, until the curate's brain was like a disorganized and dismembered world with huge mountains toppling over into space, oceans overflowing their banks and flooding continents, amid a thunderous roar that drove out peace. But the impulse of love at last gained the mastery, for its object was there in the flesh, striking his senses by its presence, appealing to him with the force of reality that neither religion nor patriotism could muster in their own defence, and even though his love was clothed in the repulsive garment of sin, clothed in scarlet and labelled in letters of fire, 'Thy Neighbour's Wife,' it was the strongest passion of all. In that smile on Lily's lips, when she looked into the face of Hugh O'Malley, the curate thought he saw the smile of the Devil, mocking his victim.

O'Malley smiled at Mrs McSherry, raised his hat and passed on, thinking no more of her. For at that moment his mind was on fire with the war spirit of the O'Malleys and he saw none of the woman's beauty. Instead he saw serried ranks of soldiers, shouting 'Mailleach Abu,' with himself in front on a black charger, leading them to victory.

Moving out through the crowd, he passed Dr Cassidy's trap, and Dr Cassidy stretched out his shrivelled hand and cried, 'More power to yer elbow, my son. Davitt himself could not have spoken better. That's what they want, men to bare their bosom to the bullets with a song on their lips.' But Mrs Cassidy pinched her husband's arm sharply beneath the rug, and kept her head in the air, with the nose turned up as far as possible, and put her handkerchief to her face, so that the least possible portion of her face would be exposed to the contamination of such close proximity to O'Malley; for O'Malley was not recognized by the best people, and his father kept no servants, except an old woman, and had no bank account, and Hugh was therefore not fit to be recognized in public by Mrs Cassidy, a woman of position in society and of great social ambitions.

O'Malley shook hands with Dr Cassidy and smiled in a distant kind of a way, for at that moment in his mind he was giving the order for the final charge that would annihilate the enemy. He smiled and passed on to the Sea Port Hotel in order to get a drink and treat his supporters.

Then Fr O'Reilly came forward to open the official meeting, and was greeted with prolonged cheers. Those who had cheered for O'Malley a few minutes previously, now cheered for Fr O'Reilly with equal vehemence and in this way they were not consciously inconsistent. For to them Fr O'Reilly was neither a priest nor a politician. He was a kind of reigning monarch, with the combined powers of druid and king, armed with supernatural powers to heal disputes with the same stroke of the magic wand with which he healed diseases of the flesh, able to send souls to heaven with the same ease that he controlled the fishing industry and relegated the relations between the Government officials, the County Council and his parishioners. He was the ultimate expression of the life of the people, social, political, religious and economic. He was, in fact, the brains and thinking power of Inverara, the directing ability, the man who held in his grasp the levers of the mechanism that controlled every pulse and heart-beat, every thought and action of the parishioners, who were the limbs and bowels of the Inverara Social Organism. They cheered him wildly.

He raised his hand for silence, coughed, bowed comprehensively to the important people about him and to the audience in front and began to speak. He did not intend to keep them waiting very long for the eloquent orators who had come from the mainland. He was merely going to say a few words in introduction. In the first place, he would say that he regretted the incident that had just occurred, but he would say nothing beyond regretting it from the bottom of his heart, as he felt sure that nothing could be gained for the national cause by arousing bitterness concerning a matter that concerned the domestic life of Inverara. There was no necessity to introduce Fr Considine, or Mr O'Donovan, the organizer. They were both men who had given their whole time and energies to the cause of Ireland a nation, men who were known throughout the length and breadth of Ireland, wherever a liberty-loving heart beat in an Irish bosom. They were men whose efforts, he felt sure, would be appreciated by every man and woman who loved his or her motherland, and he ventured to predict that one day their efforts would be rewarded by a fitting position in the Government of a liberated Ireland. (Hear, hear, and a voice, 'Long life to them.') There were others on that platform, not so well known perhaps, but they were coming men, and their presence there that day augured well for the reserve of talent that the nation had arrayed behind the front rank of its leaders. He referred to Mr Loughnane, a member of the County Council, and to Mr Geraghty, the solicitor from the Big Town on the Mainland. And now, in order to give the speakers an opportunity to speak at length, he would retire and give way to Fr John Considine. (Loud cheers.)

Fr Considine came forward and received an ovation, but the cheering mingled with the noise of disorderly revelry from the small Pier below the platform, where two boatmen from the mainland had come into conflict with the crew of another boat over the possession of a mooring rope. The attacking party had come down from Mulligan's under the influence of a liberal supply of porter and finding their rope or their alleged rope, as Sergeant Donagan said, being used by the neighbouring boat to moor itself to the Pier, immediately began to untie the rope and cast the neighbouring boat adrift. The other boat's crew protested violently, and one of them ran along his deck swinging a grappling hook and threatening the attackers that he would burst open their skulls unless they stopped interfering with his rope. The fight had reached this stage when the RIC, led by Sergeant Donagan, moved to the scene of conflict accompanied by a large portion of the crowd. But when Sergeant Donagan attempted to arrest the attackers he was pushed from behind by the crowd and his cap fell into the sea and was carried away by the tide. The other two policemen came to the sergeant's assistance and seized the two culprits, but the crowd ordered them menacingly to let the men go, saying they were doing no harm, so the police released their captives and departed. And as soon as the police had departed the dispute was settled amicably, to the satisfaction of both parties, and the people crowded back to the platform to listen to Fr Considine's speech.

'Ladies and gentlemen,' he began, bowing to the important people on the platform, 'and men and women of Inverara,' he continued, looking at the people in front. Then he paused and gave a finishing mop to his face with the red silk handkerchief.

It was with mingled feelings of joy and sorrow that he was there that day. Joy at being once more among the beloved people of Inverara and sorrow at being a witness of the unfortunate incident that they had just experienced. He referred to the speech of Mr O'Malley, a young man of ancient and famous lineage, he might almost say noble, a young man for whom he had the greatest personal respect, but to whose opinions he would humbly place himself in opposition. He held that youth and disordered political and religious thought went hand in hand. He held also that this disordered political thought was again showing its head in the country, in spite of the sad lessons that had been taught in the past, and the perpetual failure of these doctrines of force and anarchy to remedy the evils against which they were all fighting. He had listened that day, he feared, to the same doctrines that had been preached by the Fenians. (A Voice: 'Up the Fenians!') But he was willing to pass over that, since it merely marked the youth and inexperience of the speaker, were it not for the association with these remarks of the gross condemnation of the clergy and the trusted political leaders of the country. (Cries of 'Shame.') Yes, he agreed with that remark. It was a shame, a dire shame, that here in Inverara of the saints, a voice could be raised with impunity against the holy ministers of the National Faith, against our glorious priests, who fought against the pitch cap and the triangle, against abuse and contumely, in sorrow and in pain, and triumphed over the forces of the Devil, who were trying to quench the sacred lamp of Holy Religion on every holy hill of holy Ireland. (Cheers, and 'He never said that,' and 'Yer a liar, he did.')

He would have silence. He would not be put down. He would make his voice heard in spite of all opposition. All his life he had been a fighter in the cause of Ireland, without reward and expecting no reward; he had given his life to the cause of Ireland and the cause of religion, and he would not be put down by interruptions, no matter from what source they came. He saw in these interruptions, and in these cowardly and insidious attacks on their Holy Church, the agency of the Devil, yes, he would say it, the agency of the Devil, and he was going to fight that agency. (Hear, hear.)

Fr Considine paused, wiped his face with the red silk handkerchief, and then he proceeded in a lower and sadder tone than before, appearing to be almost on the verge of tears.

At that moment Ireland was faced with a future in which he saw dangers. The sky was dark. He saw lowering clouds on the horizon. On the one hand, there was the danger from the Orange faction in the North, the danger that force might be used by the enemies of the national religion and of the national traditions to hold the people in bondage. On the other hand, there was the danger of the spread of anarchical teachings among their own people. He referred to the danger of Socialism. There were people among them who were advocating the impossible ideal of human equality, the impossible ideal of the abolition of poverty and suffering, and under the cloak of this idealism were scheming and plotting to destroy all vestiges of private property and disrupt all their social and moral ties. He felt that Ireland had no room for that pernicious imported doctrine, and he would confidently assert that he and his Church, and his comrades in the struggle for Home Rule by constitutional means, would put up a successful fight against it.

Fr Considine also finished amid cheers, but there were also voices raised in protest against his denunciation of O'Malley and extremism, and the young man in the grey tweed suit and the straw hat got excited and shouted out, 'What the hell d'ye mean by denouncing the Fenians?' Everybody looked at the young man. Some cheered him, while others threatened him with assassination, and an old lady with spectacles, a very pointed nose and a green umbrella, who stood near him, waved her umbrella in his face and said that he should be ashamed of himself for talking to a holy priest that way. But Cissy Carmody, who by now had established herself on terms of intimate friendship with the young man, and had her hand on his shoulder, turned on the old lady fiercely and asked her what had it got to do with her anyway, and wanted to know further who was she to come around with green umbrellas, poking them in people's noses, and solicited information from the old lady on the delicate point as to whether her brains were as green as her umbrella, and finally whether anybody saw her, the old lady, coming, for she, Cissy, felt sure that nobody would see the old lady going unless she minded her own business. And the young man in the tweed suit, encouraged by this support from Cissy, waved his hat and shouted, calling for three cheers for the 'Irish Republic,' so that Cissy had to hustle him away to a position of safety, for the people resented this conduct on the part of the young man, not so much on account of his political opinions, as because he had appropriated the belle of Kilmurrage.

Then the chief speaker came forward to address the meeting, Mr Donovan of Ballinrobe, 'a man,' as the parish priest said on introducing him, 'who was known not alone throughout the four corners of Ireland, but whose fame had also spread to the sun-kissed plains of California.' Mr Donovan came forward, leaning on a stick on account of his lameness. His head seemed to be placed directly on his shoulders, so short and so thick was his neck. His jaws were very broad and very heavy and his eyes perpetually winked. His head was turned slightly sideways as if he were always in the attitude of a man who is trying to make headway in a storm of hailstones.

He also ventured to remark that he had spent his life in the service of Ireland. He also saw dangers ahead, but he was not so pessimistic as to the outcome as his eloquent and venerable friend, Fr Considine. He felt sure that the dawn was nigh and that Ireland was at last going to take her place on a fitting pedestal among the free nations of the world. He advocated moderation in political demands, and in the methods used to gain these demands. Nothing could be gained by rashness. They must trust their leaders. They must take their time and go slowly. They must not listen to the voice of the tempters who counselled violence and the taking up of arms. Neither Republicanism nor Socialism had any place, any roots, in the holy soil of Ireland. He had the interests of the working people at heart, and he ventured to say that the only hope of better conditions for the common people was in the establishment of better understanding between the employer and the employed. ('Hear, hear,' from the important people.) He asked them all to stand solidly behind the United Irish League and victory was assured.

The organizer spoke at length and with a great deal of eloquence, and the people listened in silence and with rapt attention, for in Inverara they dearly loved an orator, without any reference to what that orator was saying. But the curate, being an intellectual, was beyond being impressed by the oratorical buffoonery of Mr Donovan, and being a Republican in his soul, though he dared not confess it in public for fear of being suspended, he hated the British Empire and he hated the United Irish League and Mr Donovan, as representing the British Empire. Further, being an intellectual, he understood that all politicians would sell their souls along with their country for private gain, and he knew that they were not out for the love of Ireland, but for the sake of the emolument that might accrue to them by advocating the ideals of Irish liberty. He was not impressed.

Lily McSherry, too, stared at the speakers heedlessly without enthusiasm, but not because she disagreed with their political views, for she herself had no views on politics. The Mother Superior in the convent had instilled into her mind that politics were not at all suitable things for women, and as a result of that inspiration, Lily could never understand how women could get interested in politics and ridiculous subjects like economics. She remembered an evening in Dublin, while she was a student in the University, and she had gone to a 'literary tea' to a friend's house. She had met a woman there, who was then very prominent in the labour and advanced revolutionary movement, and she had thought the woman was disgusting and 'mannish,' and ever since she had looked upon politics with the disgust with which that woman inspired her.

She was uninterested in the meeting especially because she was now thinking of O'Malley, and comparing him in her own mind with her husband, wondering what it would be like to have O'Malley for a husband. She thought he would make a delightful husband, for he reminded her of the knights of old, that she read about in Sir Walter Scott's novels. She knew he was a descendant of people who resembled those knights. She wondered whether she would be able to make any impression on him or whether he was in love with some other woman. And she had no scruples on this question of falling in love with O'Malley, she a married woman, married but six months. Unlike Fr McMahon, the impulse of religion had never been very strong in her, just a superstitious weed that the nuns had cultivated in her mind, instead of the flower of mysticism that Fr McMahon had cultivated by long hours of thought, meditation and penance. And that superstitious weed had been killed in her by her forced marriage, by the callousness of her uncle and her failure to find any solace in prayer to the Blessed Virgin. It had been killed in her by the cruelty of fate that had married her to McSherry.

'The next speaker,' said Fr O'Reilly, 'is Mr Loughnane, the County Councillor.'

Mr Loughnane repeated all that Mr Donovan had said and all that the Rev Fr Considine had said. He passed tributes to various organizations and to the work of several individuals, including Fr O'Reilly, and he would not include himself because he knew his own limitations. In conclusion, he uttered a denunciation of Republicanism and Socialism, and voiced his confidence that nothing could be gained by casting aside the advice of the clergy and of the tried leaders of political opinion.

Mr Loughnane concluded. There were faint cheers, but there were many yawns, for the audience were by now getting tired. A timely liveliness was at that moment given to the meeting by Patsy O'Brien, the shoemaker, asking the speaker what did he mean by saying that nothing could be done by violence. Patsy declared that he himself had an old pike, and that he hoped the day would come when he could get an opportunity to use it, preferably on the person of the King, or the British Prime Minister. Everybody laughed at Patsy, for Patsy was famous for his fanatical views on the national question, for being the most harmless man in Inverara, a man who would shrink from hurting a fly, like all harmless people, he had to be fanatical and warlike on some question, and preferably on a question that would be least likely to call into action his fanaticism or his warlike spirit. And assuredly that occasion would never arise for Patsy, for he was too old and too small and too deformed to be expected to fight by even the most heartless government, and all he knew about the national question was taken from the pages of *Old Moore's Almanack*, which was read to him by the lads of the village, since Patsy himself could not read a word in any language. And because Patsy was credulous the lads were in the habit of reading from the almanack prophecies as wonderful as their imaginations would allow. They imposed on him in other ways. Patsy had an idea that the rocks of Inverara sheltered within their bosom wealth untold, in minerals, which he himself was destined to discover. The lads therefore deposited two sacks of coal beneath a rock in Kilmillick, and came to Patsy with the story that they had found traces of coal under the rock. Patsy sallied forth immediately armed with shovels and crowbars to investigate. He paid two men five shillings apiece to dig up the rock, and lo! there were the two sacks of coal scattered beneath, ready to be taken away and burned. Patsy, wild with excitement at the thought of having discovered a valuable mine, celebrated the event by spending two pounds fifteen shillings and ninepence that night in Mulligan's public-house in Kilmurrage, and the following day he went into the post office with the intention of getting the postmaster to write to Dublin to the Department of Mines for a man to come down and inspect the samples, when Bartly Broderick, who had received none of the porter and was jealous of the other lads, told Patsy the trick that had been played on him, and there was, as Pat Farelly expressed it, 'a hell of a row with skin an' hair flyin'.'

But Patsy O'Brien was happier than Fr McMahon, in spite of the fact that he was only a poor illiterate cobbler, and the laughing stock of the parish. Patsy had only one guiding impulse in life, his fanatical nationalism, and he was as happy as a nigger with a water-melon in his one-roomed cottage in Coill Namhan, and enjoyed fame that Fr McMahon could never hope to enjoy, even though the latter had written the 'Death of Maeve,' and was an intellectual. For Patsy's quaint sayings would be remembered in the homes of Inverara long after the 'Death of Maeve' was forgotten, lying buried in desolate solitude in the vaults of Trinity College Library, and the British Museum, or remembered for a passing moment by sentimental ladies around a suburban tea-table.

Patsy O'Brien, having failed to elicit any reply from the platform, retired amid the cheers of the crowd to a corner, in the shelter of Jim Shanaghan's new store, where a group of admirers gathered around him, while Patsy, with his little sunburned face stuck high in the air, and his little eyes blinking like a bird on a perch, seriously gave his views on the national question and on world affairs, as disclosed to him through the ferocious prophecies of *Old Moore's Almanack*.

Then the lawyer from the Big Town on the Mainland spoke a

few words. He enumerated dangers that hovered on the national horizon. He declared his confidence in the final victory of the cause. He deplored many things, and he ventured to remark several things without fear of contradiction. He disclaimed any association with the ideas of certain individuals, and he went so far as to say that there were no worthier or more patriotic men in Ireland than Fr O'Reilly and Fr Considine, and Mr Donovan and Mr Loughnane, and that he also knew his limitations, but would do his best without hope of reward for the cause. And then he also finished and the meeting came to an end.

The Home Rule Meeting that was to 'rally Inverara to a man behind the Home Rule programme,' came to an end and joined the shades of myriads of meetings that had been held to 'rally Ireland to a man' to the same edifying goal. Soon the square emptied, and it looked dreary and desolate, occupied only by old Tom Milligan, who sat under the monument smoking his pipe, like another Rip Van Winkle, left aged and lonely amid the relics of the forgotten past. And the monument, too, that had been 'erected by the grateful islanders to the memory of their beloved priest, Fr McBride,' looked desolate and forgotten, as if the winds and the rains that had washed its face and furrowed its figure with the lines of time, were mocking it with the truth that it served no other purpose than as a useful place for Tom Milligan to come and smoke his pipe, and meditate on the fickleness of mankind.

The people *en masse* followed the parish priest and the important people to the Pier to witness the departure of the *Duncaim*. The concourse of people advanced to the Pier like an army, with small boys running ahead as scouts, with the important people heading the procession and the common people coming behind as the main body. And last of all came Cissy Carmody in company with the young man with the grey tweed suit and the straw hat, conversing intimately, as if they had known each other from childhood. He was promising to get a perfectly new photograph taken during the week in his perfectly new set of kilts, a photograph that he would bring up to her on the following Saturday at the sports. And he was trying to get Cissy to promise to come to Dublin with him on an excursion in July, and Cissy pretended that she couldn't go, though all the time she was dying with eagerness to go. She loved Dublin and had been there once before in the capacity of a domestic servant, though she had not stayed very long on account of a disagreement with her mistress. She was only seventeen at the time, that was two years ago, and she had gone into service in an advanced family, a family which had advanced views on the question of treating servants. In pursuance of the 'advanced treatment of servants' plan, the mistress had brought Cissy one evening to the theatre to see Oscar Wilde's 'Importance of Being Earnest.' But the mistress's own niece was playing the part of the governess in the play, and when Cissy saw the niece, in the capacity of governess, kiss the parson in the last act, she was highly scandalized, because never having seen a play before, she understood it to be real, and when she left the theatre and the mistress asked her her opinion of the play, she said:

'Oh, ma'am, would ye believe that Miss Alice could behave that way?'

'What way?' cried the indignant mistress.

'Oh,' cried Cissy, 'didn't ye see her kissing that terrible old parson. I wouldn't half mind if he were even a priest.'

And the mistress, being vexed at this suggestion of looseness in the conduct of her niece, and despairing of ever being able to train Cissy on the 'advanced lines' that she had in view, sent her back to Inverara. And as Cissy walked down to the Pier, keeping step with the young man and leaning against him, she felt that she was not a bit sorry that she came back, for if she had not, she would not have met HIM.

The *Duncairn* blew her whistle, the moorings were cast, the fiddler struck up another tune on his fiddle, the people on the Pier waved handkerchiefs, a drunken man began to sing 'When Irish Eyes are Smilin',' and the steamer pulled out into the harbour, while Fr O'Reilly, standing on the edge of the Pier in the attitude of the fox-hunting gentleman, waved his stick at the parting ship and wondered whether Fr Considine would vote for him at the next election for the bishopric. And the curate went up to the church to celebrate Benediction.

3

Having wearied of 'Rallying to Home Rule,' the inhabitants of Inverara rallied to the worship of their pagan god Crom Dubh. Officially, of course, they rallied to the worship of St John, for the 23rd of June, since St Patrick came to Ireland, has been called St John's Eve, and on that night bonfires are lit in the saint's honour, just the same as they were lit before the arrival of St Patrick, on that self-same night in honour of Crom Dubh. St Patrick, one must understand, was the first of the long and successful line of Irish politicians. Together with banishing the snakes, he introduced into the country the gentle art of politics. He never tried to root up a tree when he could walk around it and gain his objective. He never broke a rock when he could get a pole and vault over it. So when he came to Inverara and found that the natives lit bonfires to their god Crom, he meditated a long while and communed with himself as follows: 'Now if I take away their bonfires they will be grieved, and they will very probably stick to their old religion as being the more entertaining, so I will fashion it thus. I will allow them to light their bonfires and do their war-dances around them as of old, but I will persuade them to sing a different war-song the while, and the new war-song will be in honour of St John.'

So the bonfires remained and the night was called after St John, though there was not a soul in Inverara among the natives, even to this day, who knew anything about St John. However, the people no longer sing the war-song taught by St Patrick. Perhaps the song was in Latin, and that owing to the decline of classical learning, bewailed by Mr Wilbert, they have forgotten it. The celebration around the bonfires is still as pagan as it was in the days when the Firbolgs ruled in Inverara, and built their forts on the southern cliffs, and as Pat Farelly expressed it, 'committed many kinds of depredations and divilment that nobody ever heard tell of.'

That Sunday night, when the curate left the church after celebrating Benediction, and the last words of the 'Laudate Dominum' were still ringing in his ears, he thought of the night it was, St John's Eve, and the piety of the islanders who were contributing from their slender stocks of turf and paraffin oil to do honour to the blessed saint, and he was comforted and felt contented. Religion was now the predominant impulse. Somehow or other he always felt comforted after Benediction. There was a mysticism about the chanting of the 'Tantum Ergo' and the 'O Salutaris' that enchanted him even more than the Mass, and then the incense pervading the senses and the brilliant lighting, the raising aloft of the Host, dressed in a scintillating cloak, everything tended to make him comforted at Benediction. But this calmness and comfort that pervaded him now, he attributed to the Grace of God, and the effect of the Blessing of the Blessed Sacrament that he had just received himself and conferred on the congregation.

And then, as he walked up the road, the wondrous stillness of the June night in Inverara, stillness broken only by the chirruping of the birds and the distant lowing of the cows crying out to be milked, solaced him. He felt surprised that he had been so troubled in the morning with his temptation. The temptation seemed to be so distant now and so unreal, like a wicked nightmare appears to a man, who wakes up to find himself snug in bed, instead of being on the cliff, where he had imagined himself to be.

As he walked up to his hotel his face wore a glad smile for everybody that passed, and even when Mrs Connolly's daughter stopped him outside the gate of Shaughnessy's hotel and asked him to come and visit her mother on the following morning and give her Extreme Unction, he was not a bit irritated, although this question of Mrs Connolly was really a very irritating one. For the old lady was continually dying and requiring the administration of the last sacraments, for no other reason than that somebody told her that there was a cure in them for rheumatism. But on this evening Fr Hugh McMahon was not irritated by this manifestation of impiety on the part of Mrs Connolly, for the administration of Extreme Unction to any person who is not on the verge of death is a gross mortal sin, and he remarked kindly to the daughter that he hoped her mother was not very ill. And the daughter, forgetful of the dreadful condition in which her mother was supposed to be, misled perhaps by the kind expression of the curate, remarked that her mother was 'just the same, father, only for a fresh cold she got yesterday washing, and I'm gettin' a Red Ticket from the relievin' officer, so that the doctor will be comin' too, and you can go over in his trap and save yer bicycle.'

Fr McMahon, leaving Mrs Connolly's daughter, was just on the point of entering Mrs Shaughnessy's gate, when he was stopped again by Michael Corbett, the most disreputable man in Inverara. Corbett never did any work, but earned his living begging. And everybody hated to give him charity because he abused those who gave him charity if the amount didn't please him and he abused even the priests, and was fond of saying, when the parish priest refused him money, that there was nothing in Inverara but 'the Grace of God and the British Government.' And now he raised his tattered hat to Fr McMahon and wiped his red beard with the sleeve of his coat and begged the good priest to give him something, for his children were starving with the hunger and he himself wouldn't know the taste of bread from a raw turnip, it was so long since he had eaten any, what with the bad times and the way the people were forgetting their duty to the poor. The priest put his hand in his pocket and gave him a shilling and Corbett went away laughing to himself, saying that money that was that easily got was easily spent, whether he meant for himself or for the priest, it would be hard to say, and Fr McMahon went in through the gate, and entered the hotel.

His dinner awaited him in the dining-room. He had an appetite after the calming effect of the Benediction, and Mrs Shaughnessy's establishment, in spite of the bad character that the old lady in the church had given it, was in the habit of serving an appetizing meal. Mrs Shaughnessy herself, with her slightly greyish hair piled up in a dizzy heap on the top of her long head, hurried around the room, talking in her usual fast and agitated voice about the great meeting, and prodding the mass of hair with a crochet needle, with which she was knitting some altar lace, as a birthday present for her young nephew, God bless the boy, who was a priest in a Redemptorist College. 'Lord protect the boy and he so young to be out alone in the world.'

The curate ate his dinner with an appetite, while he listened amiably to the woman's chatter, and in order to please Mrs Shaughnessy he took a second helping of the rice pudding after dinner, even though he knew it always disagreed with his digestion. And then he retired to his rooms, as was his habit after dinner, to read and write. When he sat in his easy chair, by the window on the east, showing a clear view of the sea, he felt a strange calm steal over him. And then he said, 'I will read some poetry, it's just the evening to read poetry.'

He took a volume of Yeats's poems from a shelf, and for a long time he turned over the pages, without reading, for his own dreams were filling the pages. He felt as if all the world had stopped about him and he was enjoying a blissful rest before it should start again on its rounds. And then suddenly his eyes caught the open page. He sat up in his chair and his brow furrowed and he bit his lips. He bent over the book and read:

'I wander by the edge
Of this desolate lake
Where wind cries in the sedge:
"Until the axle break
That keeps the stars in their round
And hands hurl in the deep
The banners of East and West
And the girdle of light is unbound,
Your breast will not lie by the breast
Of your beloved in sleep." '

God, had Yeats written those lines to him? Never to lie by the breast of his beloved. Never through all the eternities of eternity. Always to wander alone thinking of her, forgetting her for a moment, and then being brought back again to the reality of his desolation, by the written page of a book, by a poet's dream.

The book dropped from his hands and fell to the floor. His head dropped on the arm of the chair. Never, never to touch her. Never to look into her eyes and tell her that he loved her. Never to feel the hot breath from her lips against his, and the light in her eyes shining into his, and the heaving of her bosom, heaving with love for him, pressed against his. Never to take her hand and walk side by side through life, sharing sorrow and joy and gladness and pain. Always when he looked at her, even in thought, he must stare across an impassable abyss, the abyss that he himself fashioned when he forsook her love for the priesthood, the abyss that he fashioned when he allowed another man to take her and brand her as his, with the indelible brand of marriage. Always they would be divided 'until the axle breaks that keeps the stars in their round.' Had sickness or death or war or poverty divided them, did they watch and wait divided by the stretches of ocean, there would be hope. But the abyss that divided him from his beloved was wider than death, wider than the widest ocean, and it was of his own making. He had wrought it of his own free will. He had wrought it, blinded by the pursuit of an impossible ideal. An impossible ideal? Yes, impossible, for were not the grapes of sanctity soured, almost before they had touched his lips. They were mirage fruits that rotted in his system, generating remorse and sorrow and sin. His love was now sinful and scarlet as a flaming devil, corroding his blood like arsenic, stupefying his thoughts like a drug, goading him awake and asleep. And he would be goaded, and stupefied and tempted, through the centuries of centuries for 'never until the axle break . . .'

'G-o-o-d,' cried the curate, and the sound of his voice came from out his throat like the bursting of a blood-vessel, 'God, why hast Thou forsaken me?'

He rose slowly from his chair and threw himself on his knees before the crucifix that stood on the little prayer-stand in the corner and he tried to pray. But prayer did not come. Instead tears filled his eyes and he lay motionless and without thought. He lay there a long time until the sun sank in the west and the twilight grew dim.

Then he arose and left the room, quietly as if afraid to rouse his slumbering thoughts. 'I'll go,' he murmured, 'and look at the bonfires.'

He took his bicycle from the hall and was going out the door, when Mrs Shaughnessy came out of the sitting-room and said that he had better take his overcoat, as the night was going to be chilly, and there was no time of the year as dangerous for colds as June, and she began to tell him about a brother of hers, who had died in June, '88, owing to a cold he caught at a dance on a night just like this, but the curate, murmuring something about the night being fine, wheeled his bicycle through the garden path and out the gate, and Mrs Shaughnessy retired to the sitting-room, prodding her pile of hair with the crochet needle and murmuring to herself that young men, priests or no priests, 'are the divil to manage, God forgive me.'

The curate mounted his bicycle and rode westwards. In the distance he could see the flames rising on many a hill-top. On the distant mainland, among the mountains, there were pale red tongues, more bonfires in honour of St John. On the road, here and there, he passed groups of girls chatting and singing and giggling, followed by groups of young men, who called out to the girls by name, bantering them. All were happy on the wondrous summer night. Here and there he met a stray man, who staggered in his gait, laughing loudly to himself and singing snatches of old ballads, wandering home after having worshipped at the shrine of Bacchus in Kilmurrage.

And as he rode westwards he saw nowhere any sign of veneration for the saint whose festival it was. Everywhere the people were merrymaking, and around the bonfires by the roadside, he could see old people sitting smoking their pipes and telling tales of long ago, and the young people dancing on the open spaces near by to the strains of melodeons and violins. He could hear merry laughter from the girls, and screams at times, when the young men pinched their arms in the rounds of the dance and his face clouded. They were not thinking of St John. They were not thinking of God. They were enjoying themselves as they would at a dance or at a fair. They were having a festival, while he had thought that they had lit their bonfires out of piety and veneration for the saint.

Their merriment mocked his own sadness. He a priest of God, whose communion with God put him on a pedestal above the level of the rest of mankind, was sad and sorrowful, while the peasants were glad, thinking of nothing but the simple pleasures of the flesh, song and dance and laughter. As he rode on he thought that there might after all be some truth in the contention of the atheist sociologist who had written that these bonfires were a relic of the pagan religion of the pre-Christian inhabitants. They were the first bonfires he himself had seen, because in his part of Ireland they never lit bonfires except on election night, but of course he did not believe the sociologist. These people wrote purely for the purpose of undermining the influence of religion among the better educated of the people. Still . . . he had to admit that there was not much religion attached to the bonfires, and he wondered why the parish priest did not visit the fires and get them to sing a hymn or something like that . . . a decade of the rosary for instance around each fire, so as to point out to the ignorant peasants the religious significance of the feast they were celebrating. Otherwise they would believe it to be a pagan festival as soon as some malicious Socialist came along and told them so. And then, perhaps they would be less zealous in their religious duties, since most people preferred a religion that would allow them to sing and dance and light bonfires on a fine night to a religion that was dull and pleasureless.

'But what right have I to accuse them? What have I gained by it, this religion?'

The question seemed to be prompted by some hidden voice within himself and he was shocked by it. It brought him again to . . . But he rode madly to get away from the renascence of these thoughts and kept his head bent down low over the handles of his bicycle, pedalling madly until he arrived at Coill Namhan. There he dismounted at the bonfire. As soon as he dismounted, the music stopped and the dancing stopped and the old people about the fire took their pipes from their mouths and saluted him reverently. While Pat Conneally, being the most important person about the place, arose and came over to him, and said it was a fine evening 'thanks be to God.' The curate nodded assent and stood in silence looking at the fire dully. The people around the fire, ashamed of the priest's presence, stood and sat in silence, for in Inverara it was considered in all ways immodest and indecent and unbecoming to dance, sing, or show any signs of levity in the presence of a priest. Perhaps it was because the peasants were, or considered themselves to be, in the position of members of a secret society, caught in the act of performing their forbidden rites by the policemen of the New Order, for the priests were the policemen of the New Order that had been introduced by St Patrick, and the bonfires were really the forbidden rites of Crom, not really forbidden but allowed solely on the condition that around them were focused the veneer of Christian worship. And the peasants were perhaps conscious that they had disobeyed the ukase of St Patrick and were not singing the Christian war-dance, but were celebrating and enjoying them-selves, just as their ancestors had done under the benevolent rule of Crom, who was a jolly dog of a god in every way.

The curate noticed this restraint and he merely nodded to Pat Conneally's salutation, but Pat did not notice the curate's gloom, for he was always eager to show off his knowledge of English and his sang-froid in the presence of priests to the rest of the islanders. He proceeded in his usual long-winded and round about way to declaim on the happiness it gave him, as representing all good people, to see the young generation enjoying themselves in inno-cent fashion, instead of hiding around shebeens, drinking vile potheen. And the curate agreed with him, without exactly know-ing that he agreed with him, for in his mind he was thinking that

Pat Conneally was really singing the praises of the old pagan order and its superior moral effect, compared with the gloom of Christianity.

He said 'Good night, and God bless you,' and walked away, and Pat Conneally put on his hat and returned to the fire. The music started again, and the dancing and the laughing and the giggling and the pinching, and the old men around the fire returned to their pipes and prepared to listen to the story that old Seameen Gill, the oldest man in Kilmurrage, was telling, about a grey mare of his that had been carried off by the fairies or by Crom Dubh. For when the mare died suddenly in a field, a whirlwind was seen sweeping a string of hay away with it, and that was regarded as a certain sign that Crom had taken the mare, for the theft of the hay was to ensure the mare a good meal when she arrived in the stables of the god. And the peasants around the fire shook their heads and said that there was 'no goin' beyond the power of Crom and it's best to be always on his side,' and one said that the best way to take the spell off the field in which the mare died, was to place a hen there at dawn, decked with red ribbons and with her feet tied together, so that she could not escape, and if she were alive in the evening, it could be regarded as positive proof that the anger of Crom was appeased and the spell broken. And the old men believed this, for old men everywhere are superstitious, but the young people danced and sang, forgetful of Crom and of superstition, forgetful of everything but the strong red blood that flowed in their veins, and the joy that was in their hearts in the fire-bright gloaming of the June night.

The curate took the by-road that led to the beach of the little harbour of Coill Namhan, and leaving his bicycle on a sand-bank at the head of the beach, he wandered down slowly over the white sand to the edge of the water, where the wavelets were breaking querulously on the shore. 'And he walked silently by the loud-sounding sea.'

Up and down the sandy beach he walked, musing, stopping at times to turn his face out to sea, so that the gentle breezes could fan his forehead. He felt that there was a world in Inverara that he did not understand, a world which neither he nor the religion he represented had any control over. He was a stranger among the peasants in some ways. They had shrunk from him when he approached the bonfire. And there were traces of paganism and of the growth of paganism among them in other ways. There was John Carmody, for instance. He had come back from the United States a Socialist, and was now preaching materialism to the natives of Kilmurrage. He had a book entitled '*The Works of Robert Ingersoll*, Memorial Edition, Price Two Dollars, Chicago,' given to Carmody as a farewell gift by the branch of the Socialist Party of America to which he belonged in Syracuse, New York, when Carmody was leaving for Ireland. Carmody himself called it 'The monumental works of Bob Ingersoll, the greatest of America's sons.' And Carmody had already made converts in Kilmurrage, Jim McDermott, the RIC pensioner, who was one of the best-read men in the town, was already nearly as bad as Carmody, and Pat Milligan, who had been drummed out of the Connaught Rangers in India for refusing to fire on Indians or something, was with him too. And the worst of it was that these men were the best-living young men in the place. 'Of course,' said Fr McMahon to himself, 'of course. The Devil is always wise in choosing his instruments.' Of course, these doctrines of Socialism and materialism would never spread among the peasants of the west of the island, but they too had their backsliders. Tom Rafferty, for instance, who had a strange religion of his own and believed that God and the Devil were waging perpetual war, and that neither side had as yet gained the mastery, and that it was foolish to take sides, but wait until one or the other had secured the victory, since men were placed in between the two combatants in a position of danger, between two fires, so to speak. And Tommy, in order to keep friends with both sides, went one Sunday to Mass and the following Sunday stayed away from Mass and trespassed his donkey on his neighbour's land.

And then there was O'Malley, and as the curate thought of O'Malley he dug his heel into the sand and clenched his fists. O'Malley. O'Malley. O'Malley was no doubt an agnostic, but he could forgive him his agnosticism, beyond the official pity he felt for him as a soul lost to salvation. But he could leave him out as an influence that would tend towards the spread of irreligion among the people. The people did not look upon O'Malley as one who should have religion or be obedient to the priests. O'Malley was the descendant of Irish chiefs, and Irish chiefs, like kings in other countries, were more or less beyond the domain of religion, being as it were on terms of intimate relationship with the supernatural by virtue of their divine right. O'Malleys, like kings, could be put in the category of people who could with impunity make alliances with the supernatural and have enmities with the supernatural and with the servants of the supernatural, if the latter irritated them, just like a man might find fault with a friend's footman, if the footman dropped his silk hat while he handed it to him, or with his friend's butler, if the butler spilt the soup over his shirt front. It was not on the question of religion that the curate found fault with O'Malley and dug his heels into the sand and clenched his fists when he thought of him. It was on the question of Lily.

He had never seen him talk to Lily, or look at her with desire in his eyes, but he had seen Lily smile at him. And even though he himself was conscious that he had no right even to think of Lily, since he was a priest and she was his neighbour's wife, still, he was enraged that anybody else could find even passing favour in her eyes. Her husband he did not take into account, of him he was not jealous, but O'Malley. O'Malley was a handsome man, and he was moreover an O'Malley, a man whose lineage and traditions might attract any woman.

And thinking this, he dug his heel deeper into the sand, until the sea-water soaked through the hole he had made, wetting his shoe. He told himself that O'Malley was an agent of the Devil, and was in Inverara for the express purpose of turning people away from their allegiance to God, and inducing virtuous women to be unfaithful to their marriage vows. For a moment he thought of himself as a scrupulous and dutiful priest, who was called upon by his mission to protect Lily and keep her faithful to those marriage vows, to protect her from the insidious allurements of the hand-some O'Malley.

But that thought lasted only a moment, sweet and self-satisfying, like the sound of music that comes through a window to a beggarman, giving him the passing idea that he is within in the mansion amid luxury, and then when the window is closed, waking up to the realization of his misery and destitution.

The curate was swept back to the reality, and the reality told him that he was jealous of O'Malley, jealous because he was afraid that Lily would fall in love with O'Malley, she who had loved himself once. And now, having found himself unashamedly and confessedly jealous of O'Malley, his mind began to try and discover means to belittle O'Malley, to prove him an impostor and a historical buffoon. His mind wandered around searching among the mass of things that he had ever read or heard, abusive of the old Irish aristocracy. Very probably, said his mind, O'Malley is not the descendant of the Milesians, who were the real old Irish aristocracy, but rather a descendant of the Firbolgs, who were a race conquered by the Milesians and reduced to a position of subjection. He recalled the fact that an English professor of history, having been to Inverara on a tour of investigation into 'Ancient Irish Customs,' went back to London and wrote a three-volume book on the subject, which was declared by a London newspaper to be a book 'scintillating with knowledge, and written after the best British historical tradition.' In that book the professor declared that the ancient Irish inhabitants of Inverara were called Firbolgs, meaning 'Stomach men,' since 'Fir' meant men, and 'Bolg' meant stomach. He further declared that they got this name as a result of their prowess at the dinner-table, when they were in the habit of consuming vast quantities of potatoes. In spite of the fact that in ordinary times he would repudiate this statement of the professor's as an insult to the national honour by an ignorant and bigoted Englishman, at that moment the curate accepted this discovery with satisfaction. He passed over the fact that Irish writers had since denounced these historical discoveries as malicious lies, pointing to the fact that potatoes were not introduced into Ireland until the sixteenth century, being along with canned beef and 'pep' the principal benefits accruing to Europe from the discovery of America. These writers had further pointed out that the Firbolgs got their name from their capacity for carrying heavy weights on their stomachs, outside and not inside as claimed by the Oxford professor, but the curate in his jealousy had become anti-national and dwelt more on the discoveries of the Oxford professor than on the diatribes of the irate Irishmen. He had sunk his nationalism for the moment in his love for Lily. He had sunk his religion in his love for Lily. At that moment nothing weighed against his love for Lily in the balance. Perhaps it was the still sea air, the gentle breezes, the crooning of the surf, or perhaps it was that a man's love for a woman, even though that man be a priest, bound by everlasting ties of celibacy, will on occasion burst through the mock-heroics that are labelled nationalism by the ignorant, and the self-hypnotism that passes for religion.

He might have arrived at important and far-reaching decisions had he not been disturbed at that moment from his reverie by the advance of the tide, which compelled him to retreat from his position. He looked at his watch and found that it was already eleven o'clock. He hastened up the beach to where he had left his bicycle, and he looked longingly in the direction of the hamlet of Coill Namhan, where McSherry's new house was built on the western outskirts. It was only then that he admitted to himself that the reason of his coming west to Coill Namhan was the hope of seeing Lily, in the hope that she might come down to the beach in the evening.

'She must have retired for the night,' he said, as he proceeded to pump his bicycle, and just then he heard footsteps approaching from the direction of McSherry's house, and looking up he saw a woman coming in the night, but in the darkness he was unable to recognize her. At first the thought flashed into his mind that the woman was Lily, and when she came nearer, he noticed a shawl around her head and a bundle over her shoulder and he heard her weeping softly. He felt a sudden rush of blood to his head, and a thumping of his heart, hoping and fearing that it was Lily, and that she was coming to him for help in distress, and he murmured a prayer and said 'Jesus, help me.' But when the woman came within a few yards of him and pushed back the shawl from her head, as peasant women do when in a hurry, he saw that she was not Lily, but Kate Mahoney, McSherry's servant. He did not know whether he was glad or sorry, glad to be saved from the embarrassment and temptation of meeting Lily, or sorry for having lost an opportunity of talking to his beloved.

Kate Mahoney started and stood still in the roadway when she saw the curate. She crossed herself and said 'Jesus, Mary and Joseph,' for that corner of the road was noted for ghosts and the night was moonless and ghosts of course had the habit of rising from the ground. But in the next moment she recognized the curate's voice as he said 'Good evening,' and with a sigh and renewed weeping she came forward and tried to pass. But the curate blocked her way.

'My child,' he said, 'what is your trouble?'

'Oh father, I'm in trouble, I'm in trouble.'

'What is your trouble, my good girl?' the priest repeated.

The girl wept again, and her well-developed bosom heaved with sighs, and she pushed back her shawl from her head, showing red cheeks wet with tears, and dark eyes over which the lashes drooped as if in shame, and black straight hair that hung dishevelled over her face.

'Come, let me help you, child,' pursued the priest, hiding from himself that his desire to help the girl was really his desire to find out what was the matter, since Kate Mahoney was a servant in Lily's house, and her trouble must in some way be connected with Lily.

'Oh, I had to leave my place,' cried Kate Mahoney, 'the master . . . he . . . he, oh I had to leave . . . I must go home,' and she swept past the curate into the stillness of the night. For she had been ashamed and afraid to tell the curate what had really happened. She could not tell him that her master had returned that evening from Kilmurrage with his wife and Mr Blake, that Mr Blake had dinner with them, that after Mr Blake's departure, the master retired to his study, and had punch mixed for him by Dennis the farm hand, and had stayed for hours in the study drinking the punch, and once when she passed the door, she heard him swearing out loud, worse than a soldier. And then he rang for her and ordered her to light the lamp in the study, and when she had lit the lamp, he called her over to him, where he was sitting at the table, with an empty glass upset on the table and a punch jug beside it, with one hand resting on the table and the other hanging, lifeless-like, by his side, and a queer look in his eyes, and his lips moving as if he were going to speak but couldn't. He called her to him and afraid of him, she approached and stood by his chair. He put his arm about her waist. She was afraid to go away, she was but a young girl in her first situation, so she stood there trembling, waiting for him to speak. And then he said: 'What's your name . . . yes . . . Kate . . . ha . . . that's a nice name, a very nice name . . . make a very nice girl, Kate, if you were dressed up properly . . . I must see a-a-bout it . . . well developed too.' And then he pulled her towards him and he tried to . . . But then she screamed and struggled and struck him in the face with her fists, and he fell back from the chair to the floor and she fell with him, with his arms still around her, and he laughed as the two of them rolled over on the floor together, and he kissed her on the back of the neck, and dug his teeth into her flesh, and she thought his lips were burning her skin, she was so terror-stricken. She tore herself free and was running from the room, when Mrs McSherry opened the door and came in and 'she was awful to see, standing there with a hard smile on her lips, that Judge Bodkin used to have when he was condemning a prisoner at the assizes.' She had a book in her right hand with her finger between the pages, and Kate Mahoney crouched past her, and ran out of the room and then waited outside the door in the passage, afraid that something was going to happen to her young mistress 'with the master in the state he was.' She waited, looking in through the slit in the hinges, so as to be ready to help.

But Lily McSherry did not need any help. She was perfectly composed. She stood waiting until her husband struggled to his feet and laughed down his throat in the queer way he had.

'What the devil are you looking at?' he said.

'I'm looking at a beast,' said Lily.

McSherry took a step forward as if he were going to hit her, but he fell back again, with fear in his face, and sank into his chair. His mouth opened wide as if he were laughing, but no sound came from him. His lips just trembled flabbily, as if the nerves around his mouth had been cut loose.

'You are the cause of this,' he snarled. 'It's your fault, damn you. You won't touch me and I must have women.'

He leaned forward his head on the table and Mrs McSherry without a word turned and left the room. She looked at Kate Mahoney as she passed her, but she did not speak, so that Kate Mahoney became as much afraid of her as she was of her master. She ran to her room and put her clothes in a bundle and ran out by the back way, afraid every moment that her master would catch her and kiss her again on the back of the neck, or worse still on the lips; she was afraid of her life of that, since John Carmody, who had come back from the United States a Socialist, had told her 'that these rich guys, who been runnin' loose around South America, are chuck full o' disease, and no good woman should let them kiss her on the lips.' All the way down the road she felt the impress of that kiss burning the back of her neck, and several times she put up her hand to see was there a hole burnt into it, and wiped it with her handkerchief and said a prayer to St Theresa.

So afraid to tell the curate what had happened, she hurried past him, home to her old mother in Kilmurrage. The curate stood with his bicycle pump in his hand looking after her, wondering what had really happened, too ignorant of the world to suspect the truth and yet surprised that McSherry should have sent her away at this hour of the night merely because he found fault with her, and then he forgot her and mounted his bicycle. When he passed her again on the road, he merely nodded to her and rode on. In fact, the sight of her going home weeping merely suggested to him that she was an ignorant peasant stupidly magnifying her troubles, weeping for her dismissal from a position for which she received a mere eight pounds a year, while he himself, a priest of God, and the author of the 'Death of Maeve,' was in deadly danger of sacrificing his immortal soul, his mission and his career, on the altar of his illicit love, a man who was pursued by a thousand devils, and was yet battling valiantly, while the ignorant peasant girl was hopelessly overwhelmed by her petty troubles. And his spiritual and intellectual pride was satisfied by this contrast of his own courage and determination and the girl's weakness.

While really the poor peasant girl was superior to him. She had resisted her master's advances without a thought of surrender, even though she knew full well that resistance meant dismissal, and dismissal meant that she and her mother would be plunged again into the depths of poverty, her mother, who was an invalid, without land or any means of support since her husband died, unable even to take in washing. And now, because she had left McSherry's, Kate knew that she would be unable to get another situation, since nobody would believe her if she told them why she left. She would, in fact, get into serious trouble for doing so, for McSherry was a relative by marriage of the parish priest, and she had no witnesses, and people would say that she had encouraged her master in making advances and that she was a loose woman and an idle slut, who ran away from her first job. So she hurried home, wiping her eyes with her handkerchief, and walking on the grass by the roadside lest anybody might see or hear her, with that spot on the back of the neck still smarting, where the drunken man had kissed her, and praying the while to all the saints she knew to get her another situation.

The curate arrived at the gate of Shaughnessy's hotel, comforted now by the cloak of pride that he had cast about himself. He paused for a moment to look at the bonfires that were still burning and reddening the moonless sky, and he thought that the sight might inspire him for another poem, better even than the 'Death of Maeve.' But as he got into bed, he felt sorry that he was not like other poets and could not write of his sorrow, of his grief, of his love for Lily, since he was ashamed to show it to the world, but must carry it always with him locked in his breast, hidden from the world, like a great weight dragging him ever downwards.

And Kate Mahoney entered her mother's cottage, and throwing herself into her mother's lap told her everything. And her mother wept too and said 'Don't cry a leanbh bawn, don't cry, for God's help is nearer than the door. Say nothing of this, for the evil tongue of scandal is the cause of all evil.'

And nothing was ever said of it, and it was well that it was so, for nothing like that ever, ever, ever happens in Inverara.

Monday

PAT COLEMAN, the postmaster of Kilmurrage, took life seriously, very seriously. As an indication of how seriously he took life, it is recorded that once while he was on a two-days' holiday in Athlone, he cut short his holiday by twenty-four hours owing to seeing a gentleman of his acquaintance eat meat on Friday at the hotel table d'hôte. And Pat Coleman made a point of relating this story on all possible occasions, laying particular stress on the table d'hôte, an expression which he did not understand, but which he had heard used by an English tourist in reference to hotels and which he understood to be fashionable. Pat Coleman, though he was generally recognised in Inverara to be 'a man of many parts,' was of limited intelligence, and his only consolation in life was religion. Being a man of importance in Inverara for the reason that he was a kind of connecting link between the power of the British Crown and the power of the parish priest, since he stamped letters with the British King's head, and hung up emigration advertisements and facsimiles of dog licences and notices of elections to the British Parliament outside his post office window, Pat Coleman considered himself in duty bound to show a good example to the rest of the islanders in the matter of moral conduct.

Perhaps also that he was scrupulous in the matter of religion, lest people might think that his professional association with the British Crown, which of course was pagan and in communion with the Devil according to the good people of Inverara, might be thought to have dulled his sensibilities on the matter of the national creed, and cast a stigma on his moral reputation. Be that as it may, he was devoted to his religious duties. He tiraded against every kind of levity on the part of the people of Kilmurrage, and was known to consider the peasants of the west of the island as people who might any day be swallowed up and devoured by the evil one, owing to their laxity in the matter of divine worship, their lack of respect for the clergy and their devotion to the potheen flask. He tiraded against the rise of what he termed 'pernicious influences' in the country and particularly against the evils of Socialism and labour unions. His antagonism to these two national evils originated in the huge cost of building his new post office owing to the exactions of the stonemasons and the carpenters who insisted on working for union wages. These union men and Socialists were, according to Pat Coleman, in 'league with the Devil,' and he kept a copy in his office of the episcopal denunciation issued the year previous against Socialism, as a menace that was going to drown the country in a river of blood. This episcopal tract he read to Pat Conneally, the rate collector, regularly once a week.

Pat Coleman went to Mass on Monday morning. He went to Mass every morning. Very few people in Kilmurrage went to Mass on weekdays, owing to what Pat Coleman described as lack of moral principle and too great a devotion to their worldly affairs, though the real reason was that owing to the ozone in Inverara the people of Kilmurrage were not in the habit of rising earlier than nine o'clock, and Mass, the last one, was at a quarter to eight. Even the two old ladies who were ardent admirers of Fr McMahon went to the parish priest's Mass at seven forty-five instead of to the curate's Mass at seven, but they persuaded themselves that it was not on account of a desire to stay a little longer in bed, but a desire to keep in touch with fashion. For the fashionable hour in Dublin was eight o'clock, and 'even though I am living in the country, my dear, I like to keep in touch.'

But Pat Coleman went to the curate's Mass at seven, because he was under the impression that the earlier the hour the greater the reward. 'The early bird,' reasoned Pat, 'catches the heavenly worm.' So on Monday morning he went into the new church at Kilmurrage at four minutes to seven in the morning, as soon as the clerk of the parish opened the door. He advanced with stately steps up the church, making a terrific noise with his heavy boots. He knelt in the front pew and crossed himself. He meditated as was his wont, pitying the others who had not the religious impulse sufficiently developed to send them to Mass, and considered himself as a fine fellow and one who would one day force himself on the minds of the islanders as a fitting candidate to represent them on the County Council, leading one day perhaps to Parliament, who knows?

He raised his head when the curate entered the church from the sacristy. He was shocked to see a hard and angry look on the curate's face and to see that the vestments hung about him carelessly and slovenly, contrary to his wont. And Pat immediately wondered what was the matter. The curate to him was a holy man, a priest who should approach the altar with love and veneration, feeling joy in his heart and as careful of his dress and appearance as a young man going to meet his sweetheart. In spite of his limited intelligence, for even the most limited intelligences are acute when it is a question of noting faults in their neighbours, he noticed that the curate was in a hurry, rushing through the prayers and through the Mass, and that he had a note of anger in his voice, as a schoolboy who had just been whipped and was saying his lessons unwillingly under his master's eye. And Pat, intent on these thoughts, never said a prayer during the whole of the service. Instead he told himself that he was not sufficiently appreciated by the world, the wicked world, that did not pay him his proper meed of honour and respect for his sterling qualities. If he had been a priest, for instance (as he should have been, were it not for his father lacking sufficient intelligence to appreciate his son's remarkable gifts and sending him to Dublin as an apprentice to a grocer's instead of to a college to be trained for the priesthood), he would never slacken one moment in his duty to God and his devotion to the Mass.

That morning the curate was in a bad temper. A poet may dream wonders as his head drops to the pillow in sleep, but these dreams are in the morning sometimes uncouth and loathsome. And so with the curate. He had retired to sleep with a cloak of pride about him as a covering, and in the morning he awoke utterly disgusted with himself and with the world. Dr Cassidy would have ascribed this disgust to the double helping of rice pudding that he had at dinner on the previous day to please Mrs Shaughnessy, for the good Dr Cassidy, like all medical men, was fond of saying, probably with a view to increasing his fees, that all human ills were due to the liver and not to psychological causes. The curate awoke disgusted with himself. He was disgusted with himself for being in love with Lily. His mission as a priest appeared to him to be as unreal and fantastic as the rôle of a clown in a circus.

His nationalism appeared to him as vague and foolish as his religion. 'What,' he asked himself as he dressed, 'is the use of anything? What use am I in life, or what is the purpose of my life?' He thought of the poem that he had created, 'The Death of Maeve.' But he confessed to himself that that also was idiotic and meaningless in the eyes of the world as it now appeared to him. He wished himself a day-labourer, a farm hand, incapable of thought, capable only of experiencing the natural instincts, to eat, to sleep, to look at the sun and sky and to vegetate. He thought of a story, as he fixed his collar, that a priest at school related, about a young man who had entered the diplomatic service or something and was earning a salary of five thousand a year in Turkey, and was so disgusted with the cholera and the filthy streets and the idiocy of his fellow-diplomats that he confessed to the priest, while on a holiday, that he would much prefer to earn his living breaking stones on the roads in Ireland. 'That man was right,' murmured the curate. 'It would be much better to break stones at sixpence a day than to be a priest and the author of "The Death of Maeve" and be in love with Lily at the same time.'

Then he wondered whether he was in love with Lily at all, or whether he had ever been in love with her, so ridiculous did it appear on that Monday morning to love anybody or anything. Love that morning meant an appreciation of life that he did not want himself to feel.

So he mumbled through the Mass carelessly, so that Pat Coleman left the church convinced that he himself was holier than some people imagined, and he remarked to Mrs Moroney, the publican, when that good woman came into the post office later in the day to send a telegram to Dublin for six extra barrels of stout for the sports on Saturday, that 'Ye wouldn't believe it, I know, ma'am, but I could tell ye some things about some people that would surprise ye, and some people in this island are not as thankful to God as they should be.' And Mrs Moroney, with her hands clasped across her portly bosom, agreed with him, for she always agreed with Pat on everything, since Pat was an important man and unmarried, and she herself was a widow, 'although she was the last person in the world to set her cap at a man, God forgive her.'

As Fr McMahon was going out the church gates he met Fr O'Reilly coming in. The two priests nodded and said 'Good

morning.' Then Fr O'Reilly turned his head to one side and looked
at the curate closely and said, 'Yer looking seedy this morning, Fr
McMahon.' The curate started, vexed that anybody could see that
he was out of sorts, and then wondering what did Fr O'Reilly
suspect, protested that he was feeling quite well. So the parish priest,
who really thought that the curate was privately addicted to drink,
as many priests were, who to his knowledge were teetotallers in
public and tipplers in private, said something about the warmth of
the weather and about June being 'a very heavy month in Inverara.'
He was passing on when he turned again and said that the curate
had better inspect the school at Coill Namhan that morning, in
view of the approaching visit of the ecclesiastical examiner and the
bishop for confirmation within the month, and 'while you are in
Coill Namhan you might drop in to Mr McSherry's and ask him
to come over on Tuesday to see me. I forgot to tell him that there
is an official from the Board coming and we could discuss that
matter of the kelp factory with him,' and he walked away, thinking
what a deteriorating effect Inverara had on all curates, young
curates with imagination, 'they all fall a victim to melancholy and
I suppose the blood is hot in them, ah well, the young generation
of priests is nothing like the old, none of the ambition and talent
of our type. I wonder now, has Fr Considine himself got an eye
on the bishopric?'

The curate had breakfast and then he settled himself down to
write the article for the *Church Monthly* on 'Art in Pre-Christian
Ireland.' He scribbled it right through without pausing, and he
didn't even re-read or correct what he had written, afraid that it
might not please him and that he would have to write it again. He
put it in an envelope and then went to the post office and mailed
it. Then he walked back to the hotel with his eyes on the ground
and his hands behind his back, and a scowl on his face, 'just like a
man who was after gettin' a good lickin',' said Pat Farelly to
himself, as he happened to pass, for Pat couldn't understand a man
being in a bad temper except for being beaten in a fight.

At the pump in front of the hotel the curate saw Kate Mahoney
talking to Cissy Carmody, with their heads close together. Cissy
Carmody was listening attentively to what Kate was saying, while
she had an eye on Mrs Moroney's assistant, who was leaning over
a gate, trying to make eyes at her, and receiving in response only
a disdainful toss of Cissy's curls, whenever Cissy deigned to notice

him. The curate paused at the gate and listened, wondering whether Kate after all had been dismissed for something else than what she had told him. . . .

'Isn't it awful, Kate,' Cissy was saying in an awed tone, 'how they treat poor girls . . . that's just why I had to leave my place in Dublin.'

'Yes,' said Kate, 'the awful temper he had and the hours he made me keep, and as soon as I can get my passage from my uncle in Laurence, Massachusetts, I'm goin' to the United States.'

'I'm thinkin' o' the same thing, mesel',' said Cissy, while in her own mind she was wondering whether the young man in the grey tweed suit and the straw hat was going to propose to her on the following Saturday and determining to accept him if he did. . . .

The curate banged the gate and went up the garden path to the hotel, wondering what was awful in the life of a domestic servant, since domestic servants could not possibly feel the sorrow of soul that alone made sorrow sorrowful. He thought these two girls were flighty, worldly women, who had no powers of resistance. Then he reviewed his own opinions of women, and he decided that they were the cause of all evil . . . for being a man although he was a priest, and having discovered that morning that there was nothing worth while in life, he had to persuade himself, man fashion, that women were the cause of all his unhappiness, through their fickleness and folly.

He found Dr Cassidy's servant waiting for him in the hall. Mrs Cassidy had sent him down to say that the Cassidys were waiting to go to Coill Namhan to visit Mrs Connolly, and would he go up to the house as soon as he was ready. The curate said he would be up immediately, and in his own mind he cursed Mrs Connolly for her belief in the curative properties of Extreme Unction, and then he cursed the Cassidys. It would be a terrible torment to have to travel to Coill Namhan in the Cassidy trap and listen to the chatter of Mrs Cassidy, and gaze at the senile Dr Cassidy. . . . But being a priest he said nothing, but followed the servant to the Cassidy house.

The Cassidy trap was drawn up in front of the Cassidy house, and the Cassidy mare was attached to the trap. The mare, in spite of her thirty years of age, looked remarkably fit and sleek, and a stranger would readily believe that she could trot a steady ten miles an hour instead of the two which was her limit. The trap, too, was deceptive. It did not look at all like a trap that had been in use since traps were invented, for it looked gay and fashionable and flippant in its new coat of green paint. The true facts relating to the Cassidy trap, however, could only be discovered by making a tour of the four towns and villages of Inverara, for the wheels came from the donkey cart, upon which Mulligan the publican carted his porter from the Pier, before he got a new dray-horse and car to match from Dublin, the spokes belonged to Pat Conneally, the rate collector of Coill Namhan, the frame belonged to Mr Bodkin of Kilmillick, and was bought at the auction consequent on that gentleman's decease, while the tacklings were found among wreckage that were cast ashore on the beach of Rooruck, and were sold to the doctor in exchange for three bottles of cough medicine by the finder, Michael Donnelly. And the trap, when in motion, gave evidence of the discordant and warring elements that went to manufacture it. It emitted strange noises and appeared to be in a state of perpetual civil war and on the verge of dismemberment, each member being evidently desirous of declaring local autonomy and intent on setting up an independent republic, to the grave danger of the occupants.

But all things have their uses, and the internal quarrels of the Cassidy trap had their use in this way, they alone were capable of rousing the Cassidy mare from her natural lethargy and persuading her to advance or to retreat, for she sometimes did retreat, on most unseemly occasions, and persistently retreated, like a pig going to a fair.

The curate entered the Cassidy garden and walked up to the house. As he approached the house he heard the voice of Mrs Cassidy, and he paused for a moment, meditating retreat, for it was only when he heard Mrs Cassidy's voice that he fully realized the significance of having to spend the whole day in her company, with his temper in the condition it was. But that moment that he paused, he was lost, for Mrs Cassidy saw him from the window and hailed him in a loud voice. He advanced and entered the house.

Within there was chaos, for chaos always attended the departure of Dr Cassidy on a professional expedition. It was as difficult to get Dr Cassidy ready for the road as it was to get the Cassidy mare to break into a trot on the outward journey. When the curate entered, Mrs Cassidy had finished dressing the doctor, which in itself was a difficult operation, and she had deposited him carefully in an arm-chair in the sitting-room, 'so that he could not lose himself wandering about.' Having said 'Good morning' to the curate, and remarked on the fine weather and the difficulty of getting anything done in a house like hers, with the stupid servant she had, Mrs Cassidy proceeded to collect the doctor's instruments, which she packed in a little carpet-bag that lay on the floor in front of the doctor's arm-chair. The history of this carpet-bag was as interesting as the trap itself, or the history of Dr Cassidy, that is if anybody had been alive to relate it, for the history of the bag was lost in the dim and distant past, when primeval Cassidys first began to pluck herbs and squeeze strawberry juice into pint bottles of spring water and sell them for a financial consideration to cure the sick.

The curate sat in a chair moodily looking over a copy of the *Lancet* and pretending to listen to the snatches of conversation that Dr Cassidy was carrying on, partly apostrophizing himself and partly talking to the curate, while Mrs Cassidy bustled around all the rooms in the house, including the kitchen and the scullery, in search of thermometers, stethoscopes and bottles of medicine, shouting at the doctor and the maidservant and Brian O'Donnell, the general servant, beseeching them to assist her and railing at each in turn for their carelessness and idleness. The curate was becoming momentarily more uncomfortable, and felt that this was a visitation of Divine Providence to test him further, and he was vexed with the Cassidys for having been made the instruments of Divine Providence for that purpose.

But Dr Cassidy, quite unconscious of being the instrument of any power, divine or human, was quite happy setting the contents of the carpet-bag in disorder, while he related a story of a 'case' he attended in the County Limerick forty-two years ago last July, 'a maternity case it was, this is cow medicine, what does she want that for, and I couldn't find my stethoscope, and there it was lying in the bag all the time, just in this corner here where the vaccine is. I wonder is this vaccine all right; don't ye think that's a peculiar story?' Then, without waiting for a reply, he proceeded to explain that Inverara was undergoing a great change of climate and that he could remember the time when in June . . . But just at that moment Mrs Cassidy appeared with a black bottle which she deposited in the bag, closed the bag and ordered the doctor to stand up and attend to his business and not to bother people with his ridiculous stories.

The curate followed the doctor and his wife to the trap and then the transfer of Dr Cassidy to the trap from the road presented difficulties — difficulties that were only finally overcome by the assistance of Brian O'Donnell, the general servant, and severe pushing from behind by the curate, and strenuous hauling by Mrs Cassidy, who had already got into the trap. Finally the transfer was effected and Mrs Cassidy sat in the front seat opposite her husband, while the curate sat in the rear beside Mrs Cassidy. Brian O'Donnell closed the door, and Mrs Cassidy, seizing the whip in one hand and the reins in the other, shouted 'Go on outa that,' and began to belabour the mare on the flanks. But the mare, forgetting perhaps that she was expected to move, or deliberately endeavouring to delay the dreadful moment when the fratricidal strife would commence between the warring members of the trap, pushed sideways towards the wall of the Cassidy garden, instead of pulling forward, as demanded by the Cassidy wife, and after several pushes and snorts, and tosses of her mane and shiverings of her flanks, and tremulous bendings of her knees, finally succeeded in embroiling the left spoke of the trap in deadly conflict with the wall.

Mrs Cassidy moaned, gave the mare a final stroke of her whip and then asked the curate to descend and help Brian O'Donnell to disengage the trap from the wall, which was effected without causing more harm to either than the loss of some paint by the trap and putting the wall in a slightly more precarious condition than it was in previously. The curate mounted again. Mrs Cassidy belaboured the mare's flanks once more, and the mare, finally deciding that the dreadful journey could no longer be postponed, started forward at a brisk trot, a trot that she sustained until she reached the schoolmaster's house on the outskirts of the town, a distance of three hundred and forty yards and two feet, thereby establishing a record in her racing history. Then she spied a seductive tuft of grass on the roadside and paused to pluck it, but Mrs Cassidy caught her in the act and urged her forward again with resounding strokes, and the mare shot forward, with her head to the ground, and the trap creaked and groaned and rattled, with all the warring elements going at it hot and heavy, with artillery, small arms and machine guns in full cry.

The curate sat in silence looking in front of him, rolling and jumping in his seat in obedience to the movements of the trap. Whenever he looked at Dr Cassidy he felt like getting out and walking the journey, for the doctor sat with his hands crossed in front of him, and his head leaning forward on his chest, as if he were meditating on the folly of his past life, and particularly that part of it that referred to his marriage with Mrs Cassidy. His meditations were, however, suddenly interrupted by Mrs Cassidy, who having got the mare in motion could now attend to other business, ordering her husband to hold his head up and not fall asleep. Then Mrs Cassidy coughed and dusted her face with a handkerchief that was totally out of proportion to her face, for her face was large and comfortable and the handkerchief was small and uncomfortable, but the good woman used a small handkerchief because she understood that smallness in a handkerchief was a sign of gentility, and Mrs Cassidy was a woman of very high social ambitions. She then fixed her large and comfortable face into a smile, which she also considered to be a mark of gentility, turned to the curate and asked him whether in his opinion Lily McSherry had made a good match by marrying Mr McSherry.

The curate busied himself with his own handkerchief to hide the embarrassment caused by the question, and replied that he considered that she had. 'No,' said Mrs Cassidy, warming to the subject and without noticing the curate's embarrassment, 'the match was not as good as it might have been. McSherry was too old and the girl was too young, and I think that Mr Blake would have been a better match for her, though of course there are others that might be more suitable a match for Mr Blake.' And there Mrs Cassidy paused and thoughtfully slashed the mare across the flanks, thinking that her daughter Eileen might one day become Mrs Blake. And being carried by this thought from the contemplation of Mrs McSherry's marital success to her own more interesting affairs, she remarked aloud that her daughter had gone to Kilmillick that morning to visit Miss Blake about the dance that was to be held on the night of the sports. Then, having satisfied herself that her own affairs were well on the way to a successful *dénouement*, she returned to the question of marriage in general. She discussed all the matches that had been made in Inverara, good matches and bad matches, matches among the gentry and matches among the 'natives'; she dwelt at length on the man in Kilmillick who ran away with the wife of a man in Coill Namhan, the first of its kind in Inverara, and while she was talking the trap and the mare ambled slowly towards Coill Namhan.

The curate sat grinding his teeth in silence, enraged because he had to confess to himself that the mere mention of Lily's name by Mrs Cassidy had disclosed to him the fact that he had tried to hide in the morning and until now, that he was still in love with Lily. As he listened to Mrs Cassidy talking about marriages he felt every word burning into his marrow and shouting at him: 'This is not for you. You are a priest and cut off for ever from marital happiness or unhappiness. Love or marriage is not for you. You are a pariah if you but think of marriage.' And the thought of Mr McSherry being the sole possessor of Lily, with full and legally defined rights to her, appeared to him now for the first time materially. He began to look upon McSherry as another one who was appointed by Divine Providence to torment him. He wondered that he had never discovered until now what a hateful and base man McSherry was. He loathed Mrs Cassidy also for having been the cause of his discovering this unpleasant fact, and he loathed Dr Cassidy, sitting there with his head fallen forward on his chest, perfectly unconcerned and pretending to be totally unaware of the vile rôle he was playing, since he was Mrs Cassidy's husband and must necessarily be aiding and abetting her in tormenting him.

And then a voice came to him for the first time, crying: 'Why not be a man and go to her and take her with you, since you cannot escape from loving her?' But he recognized this voice as the voice of the Devil and speedily silenced it, and then the trap arrived at Mrs Connolly's cottage in Coill Namhan.

Mrs Cassidy, as she got out of the trap, cast a glance sideways at the curate and smiled to herself and winked one eye at the world in general, for she noticed the vexed look on the curate's face, and perhaps she understood the reason for that look and its connection with her own topic of conversation, for Mrs Cassidy was a sly woman, devilishly sly.

The curate and Mrs Cassidy assisted the doctor from the trap, collected the doctor's stick and his bag of medical instruments and medicines, left the mare in charge of a barefooted boy, who stood grinning and using his sleeve as a handkerchief, and advanced on Mrs Connolly's cottage. Their arrival threw the Connolly family into a state of great trepidation. The young Connollys who were playing about the cottage rushed indoors as soon as they saw the visitors enter the lane that led to the house. Sounds issued from the cottage, indicating that affairs within were in a chaotic condition. And when the Cassidys and the curate entered the cottage the children were sitting silently in a corner by the fire, while the eldest daughter, the one who had been to see the curate the previous evening, was industriously setting the room in order, and gathering up the scraps of wool on the floor, where somebody had evidently been carding. It could not have been the eldest daughter who was carding wool, for her hands were covered with suds and she was evidently engaged in washing clothes, and the other children were too young to card wool. In fact, nobody could have been carding wool except Mrs Connolly herself, and since she was on the verge of death that was ridiculous.

Mrs Connolly's eldest daughter, having wiped her hands in her check apron, curtsied, and led the visitors into the room, where her mother was lying on a bed. She pulled aside the curtain that was drawn on the window, and severe groaning began to come from the bed, indicating the desperate condition in which Mrs Connolly was. But when the visitors approached the bed the occupant did not at all look like one who was on the verge of death. She was very red in the face, and her bosom beneath the bedclothes heaved, not after the manner of a dying woman, but after the manner of an athlete who had just finished running a very tough race. But Mrs Connolly, eager to deny this appearance of health by word of mouth, murmured in a dolorous voice and with a series of heartrending groans, 'Father, father, it's God that sent ye to me in time, I'm nearin' me last.'

But Mrs Cassidy cut short these lamentations by saying in a loud and angry voice: 'The divil a fear of you dying, and it would be a good job if something did happen to you, God forgive me, you heartless woman. Go and examine her, John, to see if there is anything at all the matter with her. The cheek of these people getting red tickets and bringing honest people on a long journey for amusement. Go and get your instruments, John, and see what's the matter with her.'

The doctor began to open the carpet-bag, while the curate looked on, too immersed in his own thoughts to get vexed with Mrs Connolly, and it was only then, when he discovered that Mrs Connolly was not in any danger of death, that he discovered that he had forgotten to bring the Holy Oils. This discovery did not disturb him, even though it showed that he was becoming exceedingly careless in his duties.

The doctor and Mrs Cassidy got into difficulties with the

instruments, for the thermometer could be found nowhere, not even when Mrs Cassidy emptied the bag on a table. She then began to search her husband's person, but with no result, for when his pockets had each in turn been emptied out and even his hat minutely searched, there was still no sign of the thermometer. And at last, when Mrs Cassidy was on the point of going into hysterics with anger, and the doctor was trembling with excitement and fear of his wife, he gave a little cry and said: 'Begob, but I think I've got it.' He unbuttoned his waistcoat, and sure enough, there was the thermometer hanging around his neck on a string. 'I put it there for safety,' said the doctor, taking it from his neck and disrobing the package that covered the valuable instrument. He took off a canvas covering, then a woollen covering, then a silk covering, and at last the thermometer appeared shining.

The thermometer was placed in Mrs Connolly's mouth, with an injunction to Mrs Connolly not to bite it, and then the doctor seized his stethoscope and proceeded to perform the more difficult task of sounding Mrs Connolly's chest. The stethoscope was as old as the trap and far older than either Dr Cassidy or the Cassidy mare. It was of the wooden-handled type, with wide bell-shaped ends, and at intervals it had strings of red silk tied around it, like charms. The doctor, being old and decrepit and very deaf, had to mount into the bed to get within hearing distance of the woman's chest, but Mrs Connolly seeing him about to do so, and being desirous of not being subjected to any further examination, when she saw no hope of getting Extreme Unction, plucked the thermometer from her mouth and sitting up in the bed called out lustily: 'Don't ye come near me, ye old villain ye.'

There she was sitting up in bed, with all her clothes on, and with her hair hanging around her face, and with pieces of the wool she had been carding sticking in her bodice. Mrs Cassidy pounced upon her and seized the thermometer, and then began to tell her what she, Mrs Cassidy, thought of her. Mrs Connolly retaliated by telling Mrs Cassidy what she herself thought of doctors and of Dr Cassidy in particular, and then she jumped out of bed, stamped on the floor, wrung her hands and gathered her children about her, and finally threw her apron over her face, to cry or to curse or something, for it was difficult to say exactly what she was doing, what with the crying of the children and the tongue of Mrs Cassidy, which was still lashing furiously as she hustled the doctor from the room.

The curate followed them out of the house, unmoved by the unseemly spectacle, for he was then busy with what he was to say to Mr McSherry and wondering whether he would see Lily, and whether she would talk to him.

The Cassidys got into their trap. Mrs Cassidy was fuming with rage and threatened her husband with the whip when he ventured to remark that Mrs Connolly had the finest complexion in Inverara. The curate explained that he had to go to McSherry's and thence to the school, and arranged to meet the Cassidys at the school on their return journey from Rooruck, where they had to go to vaccinate a child. Then the Cassidys drove away, leaving the small barefooted boy standing in the road, curling up his toes and looking sadly after them with his finger in his mouth, because they had not given him a penny for sweets for holding the mare. The curate tossed the little boy a penny and went up the road towards McSherry's, and the little boy, grabbing the penny, ran like a deer to the huckster's shop at the end of the lane to exchange his penny for 'bull's-eyes.' But at the door of the shop he met another little boy, who asked him what he had got, and offered to exchange the penny for three horn buttons that he had cut from the coat of Dennis, McSherry's farm hand, while the latter was weeding McSherry's flowers, and the little boy was standing, wondering whether he preferred the 'bull's-eyes' to the horn buttons, and using his sleeve as a handkerchief in order to assist his brain in coming to a decision, when the curate passed him, and the little boy, pausing for a moment in his comparison of the respective values of the 'bull's-eyes' and the horn buttons, thought that it would be a great thing to be a priest, greatness which he associated with an unlimited supply of pennies.

As the curate approached McSherry's house, walking through the long drive that led to the door, he looked around at the beauty of everything, and his pride was injured. Was it this luxury that had attracted Lily? He himself could not give her this luxury. His poverty appeared to him then as disgraceful and humiliating. But then, he was a priest of God, a follower in the footsteps of the lowly Nazarene. He was not affected by this luxury. He could despise it. He had attained a moral superiority over McSherry and the vulgar and worldly rich, who, without intellectual or spiritual attainments, satisfied themselves by making a parade of their wealth. Rather, this beautiful house, with its spacious grounds, more like a fashionable country residence on the outskirts of Dublin than a house in desolate and backward Inverara, was a gilded cage, where Lily was the bird. Because he was a man, eager to belittle his enemy, he did not inquire too closely into the foundations upon which his own virtues were built. He forgot that the archbishop's house was more luxurious even than the house of McSherry, and that the parish priest's residence in Kilmurrage was as luxurious as the generosity of the islanders would allow. He forgot that all the priests of his acquaintance followed in the footsteps of the Nazarene not from choice but from necessity, those of them that did live in poverty. For those of them that did live in poverty and abstemiously, lived so through the parsimony of their parishioners or because they were invested by a number of poor relations who had to be supported and brought to a higher social level.

As he drew near to the house, the prospect of coming face to face with Lily troubled him. He felt ashamed of his love for her now. In fact, he felt that she was a burden on him, a burden that he longed to be rid of. It appeared to him that it was Lily who was pursuing him, doing her best to tempt him, to make him unfaithful to his sacerdotal vows. He determined to do his best to foil her. He wondered what he had ever seen in her. It appeared strange to him that he could have been upset by such a ridiculous thing as a woman, a weak woman, whose own intellect could not possibly be a fraction of his own. He hoped that he would not see her at all, or rather that he would see her and treat her with cool contempt, show her that he was beyond being affected by her. . . . And then he began to think that after all McSherry was a good man and a good citizen. His attitude towards him changed.

And then he turned a corner, within a few yards of the door, and saw Lily approaching him from the orchard, carrying a basket of strawberries. His whole train of thought immediately changed. He felt his blood rushing to his head. He reddened to the roots of his hair. He stopped and raised his hat and looked at her. She stopped too and stared at him with a cold stony stare. He mumbled 'Good morning,' but she did not reply. Instead she turned on her heel and walked back to the orchard, and the stony stare and the contemptuous shrug of her shoulders as she turned back into the orchard cut into the curate's heart and made him as weak as a feather. He wanted to follow her and throw himself on his knees at her feet, but he remembered that he was a priest and instead he advanced to the door and rang. Lily's scorn only fanned the flames of desire in his breast, and he laughed foolishly, for at that moment he was close, very close, to insanity.

The door opened and the figure of Mrs Murphy, the house-keeper and cook, appeared. She curtsied to the curate. Her great fat face and her expansive breasts were trembling with the heat of the kitchen and the excitement and inconvenience of having to attend to the door owing to the sudden departure of Kate Mahoney, for Mrs Murphy was no ordinary domestic, she had been imported especially from Dublin to serve in the McSherry house-hold, and was not at all used to these irregularities and what she described that morning to old Dennis the farm hand as 'strange goin's on that I'm not goin' to put up with, not when I can have special attendance in the best homes in Dublin.'

The curate said, 'Good day, Mrs Murphy, I've called to see Mr McSherry,' and advanced into the hall. Mrs Murphy closed the door, grumbling to herself, and said, 'He's just havin' his breakfast in the dining-room.' She heaved herself along the hall towards the dining-room, opened the door as sharply as her weight would allow, and called out, 'The curate to see you, sir.' A voice from within, a weary and bored voice, said, 'Show him in.' The cook-housekeeper turned to the curate and said, 'This way, father'; and then when the curate had entered the dining-room she slammed the door after him, just to let McSherry see that she did not approve of his 'goin's on,' and hurtled herself along the hall towards the kitchen, apostrophizing the ceiling with uplifted eyes and an excruciating turning of her upturned palms.

The curate entered the dining-room.

'Good day, Mr McSherry.'

The words almost stuck in his throat, but priests received an excellent training in the control of their features, so that outwardly there was no sign of the struggle within him. McSherry did not trouble to rise, for he was in the stage where he was not sober enough to be diplomatic and not drunk enough to forget that he was not a gentleman. He continued sitting in his chair and gave the curate a look, which seemed to say, 'Oh yes, I remember having seen you before somewhere, you have something to do with the church here.'

'Good morning,' he said, and then lapsing into politeness, probably due to his having spent a long time among Spaniards, 'to what do I owe this pleasure, Fr McMahon?'

Then he coughed down his throat and took up his knife and fork, but he did not use them, for his breakfast consisted of whisky-and-soda, and the plate of bacon and eggs that lay on the table in front of him had merely been placed there to satisfy Mr McSherry's self-respect. Heavy drinking was new to him, and he was trying to hide from himself that he was becoming a victim to it, drink that had been to him merely a relaxation in South America. In South America he could on occasion drink to excess and still control himself, but in Inverara, with no engrossing business to demand his attention, with the dull monotony boring him into a state of dreadful ennui, with a wife who refused to cohabit with him and openly expressed her hatred for him, drink was becoming his master. And trying to prove to himself that it was not becoming his master, there was the plate of bacon and eggs on his breakfast-table, as much as to say: 'There are the bacon and eggs and I could eat them if I felt like it, but a man like myself likes a little relaxation now and again, so I will use the whisky-and-soda instead.' McSherry considered heavy drinking a relaxation pure and simple because it had not the consequence of materially lessening his wealth in great proportion in the past; like most men, writing his own dictionary of vice and virtue, and defining as vice that which injured him materially and as virtue that which made him prosperous.

Then McSherry coughed again and said to the curate:

'I usually take a glass of whisky with my breakfast. I find it's good for the liver.'

The curate coughed too, and blew his nose violently and said something which he himself did not recognize as meaning anything, and which McSherry put down to the utter stupidity of priests and thought to be an invocation of some idol or other. Then the curate explained the cause of his visit, and told McSherry that the parish priest wanted to see him in Kilmurrage on Tuesday.

'What about?' said McSherry, pouring himself out a cup of coffee, to delay the dreadful moment when he would have to attack the bacon and eggs to satisfy his self-respect, for he wanted to show this lout of a curate that he could eat bacon and eggs for his breakfast instead of whisky, for in spite of the fact that he was irreligious and looked upon the curate's religion as ridiculous mummery, and on the curate himself as a superstitious hypocrite, like all atheists he had subconsciously a great respect or rather envy of priests, on account of their supposedly high moral character.

'I think he wanted you to meet some Government official about the factory that you had in consideration.'

'Oh yes, quite so, quite so,' said McSherry, and his brow furrowed. He was already getting tired of this idea of a kelp factory, and regretted having brought the matter forward on the day of his arrival in Inverara. For then he had ambitions which now appeared to him to be vain, since his wife persisted in refusing to have anything to do with him, and the monotony of the place was already getting on his nerves. He was, in fact, longing for the bright lights and the bustle of life in South America.

'Yes,' he said to the curate, 'I will certainly come in. The meeting should be interesting.'

Then the curate rose and said he must be going. He was anxious to bring the interview to an end, for the more he looked at the dissolute face of McSherry and noted the hardness in every line and the puffiness under the eyes, the more he hated him. He rose and said he must be going and then McSherry asked him to have a glass of whisky, and the mere mention of whisky raised the violent desire for spirits that he had felt in the sacristy on Sunday after Mass. He felt a longing to say 'yes,' but his lips said 'no,' and then he said 'Good morning,' and left the room. McSherry with a shrug of his shoulders and a pursing up of his lips sat down again, and said 'damned hypocritical lout,' and filled himself another glass of whisky.

The curate went out and down the avenue. He looked several times towards the orchard, but there was no sign of Lily, and before his eyes on the lawn and on the gravel of the drive, he could see the figure of McSherry handing him a glass of whisky. His tongue was dry with desire for it, and he thought that after all, his father who had died in the inebriate's home had perhaps chosen a good way out of torment, if he were tormented as he was. . . . 'No, no, not that,' he said to himself, wiping his brow with his handkerchief. But if he took a drink now and again, just like Fr O'Reilly drank, he would perhaps have a brighter outlook on life, and not be so unnerved by trivial things like his love for Lily . . . but that was not a trivial thing. To an ordinary priest it might be a trivial thing, but he was not an ordinary priest. He was an intellectual, the most brilliant man of his year at college . . . to him it was a big thing, a stupendous thing. It would be a just punishment for Lily if her scorn for him drove him to drink and destruction. He pictured himself, coming mad with drink, laughing in her face diabolically, crying: 'You drove me to this, you wicked woman, you are accursed.' Then she would know that he was no weakling, but a strong man who was not to be trifled with.

As he walked towards the school he wove a romance about himself. He himself was always the central figure in the romance, the hero, the oppressed, the misunderstood, the unappreciated, the tortured.

He detailed every incident in his mind, when he would come face to face with Lily, drunk. He detailed every gesture, every look, every word with a malicious satisfaction. Every gesture and every look would show his own superiority and Lily's weakness. She would say, 'Oh, Hugh, how could you do it?' He would look at her with scorn, and in silence. He would laugh harshly and when she would burst into tears, he would mock her tears with jests. When she would cast herself at his feet, he would spurn her and leave her, and then he arrived at the school and entered.

Miss Milligan was at that moment standing before a map of Europe with a group of girls around her in a circle, teaching them the principal rivers of Europe, and with the tip of her pointer on Berlin, she was telling them that the best way to remember that Berlin was on the Spree was to memorize the rhyme:

'Dublin on the Liffey,
Cork on the Lee,
Paris on the Seine,
Berlin on the Spree.'

Seeing Fr McMahon enter, she dropped her pointer, gave a touch to her blouse, fixing it nicely down her neck, and advanced with a smile to meet him, with the half-shy, half-coquettish look on her face that she always had when talking to the curate, for Miss Milligan, like most schoolmistresses in Ireland, looked on the curates much the same as the women of the East looked on the eunuchs, as people upon whom they could practise the gentle art of coquetry without attracting attention, or endangering their feelings of modesty.

'Good day, Fr McMahon.'

'Good day, Miss Milligan. Could you take the girls that are due for confirmation to the boys' school, so that I can examine both sexes together?'

'Yes, father, to be sure,' said Miss Milligan, with a joyous smile at the thought of meeting Mr O'Hagan at close quarters. She called out rapidly the names of several girls, all of whom answered their names except one, Cissy Connolly, whom Miss Milligan explained was absent that day owing to her mother being dying, poor thing. The curate did not offer any remark on Miss Connolly being absent to attend her dying mother, for in his present mood he was indifferent to all sense of duty, and the fact that the whole Connolly family, young and old, were aiding and abetting in a conspiracy to put priests and doctors to an infinite amount of trouble did not occur to him. He marched out at the head of Miss Milligan and her pupils to the adjoining boys' school, and disturbed Mr O'Hagan at a moment when that gentleman did not at all wish to be disturbed, especially by the priest and Miss Milligan. For Mr O'Hagan, as Pat Farelly would say, was 'layin' about him' with a stout cane, and six small boys were standing in a row getting caned for mitching.

Mr O'Hagan, having a reputation for sanctity, what with the reading of the *Imitation of Christ*, and his devout recital of the rosary in church on Sundays, and his imperviousness to the smiles of his female acquaintances, and particularly Miss Milligan, was worried at being caught in the act of soundly caning small boys in his own school, merely because they preferred to go hunting for birds' nests instead of coming to school. He looked up when he saw the curate enter and dismissed the boys hurriedly to their seats and the small boys returned to their seats, fondling their hands under their armpits and immediately entered into a dark conspiracy to ambush Mr O'Hagan the next time they found him riding from Kilmurrage on his bicycle.

'Good morning, Fr McMahon, good morning, Miss Milligan,' said Mr O'Hagan, endeavouring to hide the cane behind his back and speaking in the mournful and pious voice that he always used, except when he was alone with his pupils and he had a caning operation on hand.

'Get the pupils for the confirmation, Mr O'Hagan,' said the curate.

The schoolmaster called out several names from a roll. Seven small boys answered their names and six small boys did not answer.

Mr O'Hagan explained that three of these were absent owing to sickness (though he knew perfectly well that they were mitching, and determined that he would thrash them within an inch of their lives when he caught them) and the other three were grown-up boys who had long since left school but had not yet been confirmed.

The curate said nothing. He was thinking of how he could get a bottle of whisky without anybody knowing he got it. He had surrendered to the desire for alcohol and now he was devising ways and means of satisfying his desire, with all the cunning of a confirmed drunkard, for had not his father died in an inebriate's home, a slave to the vice . . . and his mother said that the vice was in the family. Even though he had never touched drink in his life, the impulses and the wiles of the drunkard had been lying dormant in him, and his giving way to the desire for drink had stirred them all to life. They were now squirming and turning within him like a million snakes, with burning tongues, craving, craving for the drug.

He turned to the circle of boys and girls and began to question them on their catechism. He began with the girls. They answered the questions in a sing-song voice, without pausing from the start to the finish, beginning on a high note and going through their answers without drawing breath, as if their soul's salvation depended on their speed. Miss Milligan was delighted with the success of her pupils, and made it an occasion for moving up to Mr O'Hagan and whispering in his ear 'what d'ye think of them?' while she smiled seductively and with her right hand adjusted the neck of her blouse, which she had bought specially in Clery's of Dublin to attract him. She arranged the neck of her blouse in such a fashion that it would show as much as possible of her neck, which she considered the whitest neck in Inverara, and the other hand she lay ever so lightly on Mr O'Hagan's sleeve, in the fond hope that she would receive a corresponding pressure and smile. But Mr O'Hagan stood stock-still, and repressed whatever emotion he might feel, were it not for the inspectors and public opinion and the cruelty of the world in general. He stared out through the geranium pots on the window, wondering whether his own boys would be able to answer anything at all.

The curate finished with the girls and turned to the boys. The first boy answered the question, but the second boy being one of those whom Mr O'Hagan had caned, sulked and said nothing, either through ignorance or a desire to have revenge on the master. The master bit his lip and told the boy to speak up, and the curate asked him again in a louder voice and speaking more slowly, 'What is meant by absolution?' Then the little boy, rubbing the shin of his right leg with the toe of his left foot, and curling his hands behind his back, replied, 'God made the world,' wishing to prove that even though he was ignorant of the meaning of absolution, he had at least a firm grasp of fundamentals.

Miss Milligan turned up her eyes and made an effort to hide a giggle. The schoolmaster bit his lips, expecting an outburst on the part of the curate and hoped that he would give the boy a good caning, but the curate simply told Mr O'Hagan that he would have to pay more attention to the boys in order to get them prepared for confirmation. He refrained from examining the rest of them. At that moment he had devised a plan for getting the whisky and was eager to be alone to think it over in solitude. So he looked at the roll, said a few words to the teachers and left the school.

Miss Milligan ordered her pupils to return to their own school and paused to say a few words to Mr O'Hagan at the door, with her back to the boys, so that they could not see her making eyes at the teacher. 'What wonderful patience Fr McMahon has! now if it had been Fr O'Reilly,' she said, waving her hands in front of her, as if words failed to describe the result of such ignorance in a boy in the presence of Fr O'Reilly. Then she toyed with a medal that hung on her breast at the end of a string of corals, or imitation corals, for Cissy Carmody said that they were not real, not a bit like the genuine corals that her mistress in Dublin used to wear, trying to draw Mr O'Hagan's attention to that part of the neck that was exposed by the cutting of the blouse, for Miss Milligan was persistent in the pursuit of her beloved. But the beloved was more worried than usual and merely nodded his head, remarking that he had a lot of work to do, and Miss Milligan with a parting smile and a dab at her hair left the school. Then the schoolmaster closed the door, turned around to his pupils, slowly and with precision, pulled down his waistcoat to its fullest length, and diving for his cane, called out the miscreant who had such a grasp of fundamentals.

The curate, forgetting his appointment with the Cassidys, walked along towards Kilmurrage, with his hands behind his back, meditating on the plan for getting the whisky secretly. . . . He would get it at Brannigan's shebeen in Kilmillick, after dark . . . he would tell him . . . and then the rattling of the Cassidy trap reached his ears and presently came the voice of Mrs Cassidy, 'Sorry to keep you waiting so long, jump in.'

Mrs Cassidy immediately launched forth into a denunciation of Mrs Connolly, lamenting that such people could not be put in jail for fraud, and from that went on to descant on the difficulty of earning a livelihood in Inverara in the medical profession, 'for the people who get sick, get red tickets from the relieving officer, and the richer peasants never get sick, because they know they could get no ticket; and the gentry prefer to get a specialist from the Big Town on the Mainland whenever there is anything the matter with them; and how can they expect a man to live according to his social position on the miserable salary the County Council pays?'

'Ha,' said Dr Cassidy, 'thank God there are no fees, for no fees mean no sickness. I put it down to the fish diet. I eat quite a lot.'

'Oh, will ye shut up, ye divil, ye?'

On the outskirts of Kilmurrage, Mrs McSherry passed them in her new jaunting car going at a smart pace. The curate, listening gloomily to Mrs Cassidy, did not see her until she had passed, but Mrs Cassidy saw her. She did her best to smile in her most genteel manner and nudging her husband, whispered to him to raise his hat, but Mrs McSherry merely nodded without smiling, and Mrs Cassidy hated her from that moment, determining that Mrs McSherry's stony face was on account of 'airs that she was putting on, although I remember the time when she hadn't a stitch to her back, but, poor girl, ye can't blame her, it's in her blood.'

Mrs Cassidy turned to the curate and said:

'I wonder where she's going in that hurry, there must be something the matter.'

'I hope there is nobody sick,' said the doctor in his squeaky voice.

The curate looked after Lily and vowed that he would make her sorry for her scorn and did not reply.

The trap stopped at the Cassidy gate. The discordant elements ceased their war. The mare put her head between her forelegs, shook her mane violently, shuddered all over and snorted, in celebration of the end of the journey.

'I wonder what she's doing in Mrs Mahoney's,' said Mrs Cassidy, seeing the McSherry jaunting car drawn up in front of the Mahoney cottage.

The curate said 'Good day' to the Cassidys and went home to

his lunch and Mrs Cassidy collected the doctor and his carpet-bag and went indoors, wondering what Lily was doing in Mrs Mahoney's cottage, for since nothing of importance ever happens in Inverara, the people were very interested in the movements of their neighbours, so that when Mrs Cassidy, taking a walk that evening on the Pier, met Mr Blake returning from a fishing trip in his yacht, she made it a point to tell him that Mrs McSherry was already 'putting on airs, and I wonder what she was doing in Mrs Mahoney's?'

'Why, didn't ye hear yet?' asked Mr Blake with a sly smile.

'Ye know quite well,' said Mrs Cassidy with a wave of her arms, 'that I never hear anything. People know that I am not a woman to listen to the tongue of scandal. What is it?'

Mr Blake told her in a low voice, and with evident relish, about Kate Mahoney leaving McSherry's house the previous night, adding various little touches on his own account, together with the touches that had already attached themselves to the story before it reached Mr Blake's ears.

'Just what I expected would happen,' said Mrs Cassidy, nodding her head gravely. 'Just what I expected from such a match.'

So spoke Mrs Cassidy, though it would be difficult for anybody else to discover the relationship between Kate's running away and McSherry's marriage, since nobody knew the real reason, but perhaps Mrs Cassidy did, for Mrs Cassidy was devilishly sly, and having developed a dislike to Mrs McSherry, she associated that dislike with everything connected with Mrs McSherry and attributed to all her actions and movements a certain mysterious criminality.

Then Mr Blake, being himself a man who would not listen to scandal, said that he had heard a story about Mr McSherry, but he did not like to tell it.

'Well, ye needn't be afraid to tell it to me, Mr Blake. I know you too well, ye young villain ye, to believe everything ye say.'

Mr Blake, feeling flattered at being called a young villain, he was well over forty, smirked and curled his moustache.

'Well, I don't believe it myself, Mrs Cassidy, for I have it only on the authority of Renshaw, a sly devil that Renshaw, though an uncommon liar. He tells me,' continued Blake, lowering his voice to a whisper and seizing Mrs Cassidy's arm, 'that McSherry comes from a part of the country where he was doing duty as an inspector of police. There were rumours around there, true or false, probably false, that McSherry's mother was a housekeeper in the parochial house in the parish and they say there is a remarkable likeness —'

'Go no further for the love of God,' cried Mrs Cassidy, waving him away from her as she would wave the temptation of the Devil and walked away. . . .

The curate was finishing his lunch, when he heard Mrs Shaughnessy speaking to old Mrs Mahoney in the hall. He started as he heard Mrs Mahoney use Lily's name. He listened.

'Yes, ma'am, there isn't a woman better than her in the whole world. She just come in an' hands me the eight poun', a whole year's money, an' Kate only there three weeks, an' she offered to get her a place too, in Dublin or somewhere, and after all that was sorry she couldn't do more, and may the Blessed Virgin watch over her and give her a long life and happiness, and yerself too, Mrs Shaughnessy; I don't know what I'd do without ye, giving me mate and bread and milk every day, may the seed of yer seed be prosperous through thousands of generations.'

Then he heard the old woman rambling off through the hall praying, for old Mrs Mahoney, having no other pleasure in life, exploited prayer to the utmost limit. She had developed the art of prayer to such an extent, and embellished her prayers with such wonderful snatches of poetic imagery, that priests came from monasteries and colleges on the mainland to her, when they were editing prayer-books, and got five pounds' worth of prayers for a few shillings, or perhaps just for a blessing and a promise of five hundred days' indulgence.

The curate was vexed with Lily for having been charitable to others when she scorned himself. 'But then, her charity to Mrs Mahoney is the salving of a guilty conscience, it has nothing meritorious in it. . . .'

And yet Lily's act was not the salving of a guilty conscience. She had gone to her husband that morning after the curate left the house, and told him that he would have to pay Mrs Mahoney a year's wages as something in recompense for his brutal attack on her daughter. Her husband swore and said that he would be damned if he would.

'Further, I'll have no more of YOUR nonsense,' he said.

'Very well,' said Lily, 'then I'm going this instant to my uncle and tell him exactly what happened,' and her husband gave her the money.

The curate spent the afternoon in the church, directing the clerk of the parish in making arrangements about the altar. Then he spent an hour on his knees in front of the altar, making a last effort to overcome his desire for drink. He was forgetting his desire for Lily now in its result, his desire for drink. But he could not pray. He was afraid to look at God in his mind. And he got up from his knees without having effected anything.

That evening when the sun was again growing dim and its shadow was falling across the headland at Coill Namhan he retired to his room. It was the June sunset in Inverara, more beautiful than the dream of a poet, when young women sit on the threshold of their cottages, looking out at the pale blue mists on the mountains of the mainland, breathing the still air that is fragrant with the sea, and flowers and peace, dreaming of their lovers whom they do not yet know, when the peasants, tired after the fields, sit by their doors and smoke, and the little sons of the fishermen poke their fingers into the sides of the bright-hued fishes and crow. But the curate was neither a fisherman nor a peasant nor a young maiden dreaming of an unknown lover. The peace of nature was to him more dreadful than a nightmare. It thrust him back upon himself, making him afraid like a child who has lost its mother in the wilderness. He had nothing to comfort him, he had done nothing to merit the approbation of those around him, he was alone in Inverara. What was a poet in Inverara? What was an intellectual? A crank, a dull gloomy man, who might be respected but shunned. The peasants had their own poets always with them, poets they understood, that talked to them always, not by written word, but by sound and by colours, the rumbling of the waves over the rocky shores, the sheen of the sun on the dew-covered crags, the songs of the birds, the million noises of the insects in the fields, the music of the breeze blowing through the growing grasses, they did not appreciate the genius of the curate. To them he was less than those others, the winds, the waves, the sun. He was alone among them.

And the gentry of Kilmurrage? The business people of Kilmurrage? He was alone among them, these worms who were fattening on the rotting graveyard of the old Gaelic civilization of the peasants, too intent on their yardsticks and their beer measures, their silly codes of etiquette and their bigotry to understand life as the curate wanted it to be understood. He was alone among them.

And the parish priest, Fr O'Reilly, that greedy, ambitious peasant, turned churchman, did not care for the poetic expression of intellectuality. Intellectuality to him was always cashed into coin of the realm, and if it were not negotiable he despised it.

The curate was alone. He had no one to comfort him but God, and God had forsaken him. He was alone in the stillness of the evening, alone with the devils that were prompting him to drink and to forget. As the darkness fell and the stillness grew more intense, he arose and said: 'I will go now and get it.' But again he hesitated. That first step. He shrank from the first step. He sat down again. His mother's words of warning came to his mind. His mind that had surrendered shrank from the accusations of his body that would be tortured by the demon. Three times he rose to go for the drink and three times he sat down again.

And then trembling he threw himself upon his bed and wept, and weeping fell asleep.

Tuesday

1

IN great cities, and countries which are highly civilized, a man may spring into prominence in one night as a wit and a humorist, by being, as H.G. Wells said, 'a squirrel-house of other people's brains,' or by burning the midnight oil over the résumé of the writings of a long-deceased wit and pouring out the garnered treasure in a speech in Parliament; but in Inverara, before a man could be recognized as a wit, he had to undergo a long and careful scrutiny. His credentials were constantly and carefully examined from the day when he was an unknown and barefooted urchin until the glorious day when he sat in Mulligan's public-house in Kilmurrage, with an admiring circle around him to do him homage, while he quaffed an unlimited number of pints of stout, free of charge.

Johnny Grealish was such a man. He was the wittiest man in Inverara, or as the islanders called it, he was the 'smartest' man, and the latter term would be the more correct applied to Grealish. No other than an exceptionally smart man could raise a family of twelve children on little or no visible means of support, and more especially since the children were all girls; for girls in Inverara were of no productive value whatsoever to a father until they were old enough to go to America, since they could neither fish nor till the land as hired labourers. However, Johnny Grealish supported his large and female family respectably and bore the calamity of twelve daughters philosophically. Every time that his wife had a daughter, he fared forth to the parish priest to get it baptized, saying good-humouredly: 'It's the same three-and-four-pence again, father,' for the good priest charged three-and-eightpence for relieving a male child of original sin, considering very probably that boys were by nature more 'cussed' than girls.

Johnny Grealish having no land, fell back on various trades in order to eke out a livelihood. It was in the capacity of a carpenter that he first earned his spurs as a humorist. While he was working on the Pier, which was then being built, he stayed one morning rather late telling a story to Pat Farelly, whom he happened to meet as Pat was on his way to milk his cow, and being three-quarters of an hour late, he turned the town pump on his face, and came down to the Pier at a brisk trot, with the water streaming from his face. Then telling the foreman that he had run all the way from Coill Namhan in order to be in time, for his cock had crowed half an hour later than usual that morning, he fell down with exhaustion. The foreman, being an Englishman, believed the story, and gave Johnny a draught of brandy to revive him, and bought him a new alarm clock in Kilmurrage so that he need not depend on the unreliable cock any more; and when they heard the story in Inverara, they laughed for a week at the Englishman and universally agreed that Grealish was a wit and could be quoted in public on all occasions.

Johnny Grealish knew everything. He was everywhere and he had everybody's history on his fingers' ends. So when he came into Pat Coleman's post office on Tuesday noon, just before the arrival of the *Duncairn*, Pat Coleman scowled at him; for Pat being a religious man disliked Grealish for his levity, and because he had once made a joke about the size of his, Pat's, feet. Johnny bought a stamp and began to whistle a jig.

'Stop that whistling,' said Pat, considering that Grealish should have more respect for one of His Britannic Majesty's post offices, and for one of His Britannic Majesty's officials, acting in his official capacity, than to whistle a jig on the premises.

Johnny winked both eyes and asked Pat did he hear the news.

'Now look here, Mr Grealish, you know quite well, sir, that I'm not in the habit of listening to what every Tom, Dick, an' Harry has to say about his neighbours, and I won't have it in my office. What news are ye talkin' about?'

'Oh, nothin' at all, I can see yer busy,' said Johnny, as he industriously stamped his letter, and then proceeded to leave the office.

'Look here, Mr Grealish, ye needn't take a man up that way. Is it anybody sick in Coill Namhan? Lord, between us and all harm, is it anybody taken bad suddenly?'

Johnny winked both eyes again. He approached the counter, leaned his arms over it, coughed and rubbed his moustache backwards and forwards.

'No, it isn't anybody sick, but it's somebody gone mad, if I make no mistake; that's what it is.'

'God preserve us, Johnny, who is it?'

'Now don't ye know very well that if there was anybody mad, I'd be the first man to go an' tell the peelers about it, and not be runnin' around talkin' scandal to every Tom, Dick, an' Harry.'

Johnny walked out laughing, for Johnny knew a thing or two, and a thing or two that Johnny knew told him, that if he told Pat Coleman whom he suspected to be mad, he would get into trouble, either get boycotted by the priest, or even a worse fate, for talking scandal of the parish priest's relation by marriage, Mr McSherry.

For the previous evening Grealish had been mending a table in McSherry's kitchen, when McSherry came running out of the dining-room with an empty bottle in his hand, shouting like a madman, asking for his wife. Grealish and Dennis the farm hand came from the kitchen to appease him, and just then Mrs McSherry came down the stairs from her bedroom, and when Mr McSherry saw her, he attempted to throw the bottle at her, but Dennis caught his hand and the bottle broke into fragments on the wall. 'Go away, go away,' he shouted, 'why can't you leave me alone?' and then he foamed at the mouth, and fell down, dead drunk, while Mrs Murphy the housekeeper threw her hands in the air, crying: 'Ochone, ochone, what did I do to have this trouble come on me, a respectable and God-fearing woman. . . .'

Pat Coleman stood looking after Grealish stupidly, with anger in his countenance. Being a man of limited intelligence, he was always stupidly angry when anybody made a joke at his expense. He had to spend a considerable time trying to understand the joke, and another considerable time trying to get an answer. Very often it took him days to get the answer, and when he had found it, there was no point to it. So when somebody came into the post office half an hour later and said, 'Good day, Mr Coleman, I'll have a postal order for five shillings,' Coleman scratched the side of his head with a blue pencil, and said, 'That scamp, John Grealish, 'll come to a bad end yet, unless the good God is merciful to him.'

Then people began to come into the post office to hear the mail called. The post office during three days of the week was the centre of importance in Inverara. Everybody of importance came there to get their mail wholesale, so that they would not have to wait until the postman retailed it later in the day; for the postmen were not reliable persons, and were known to keep wandering around the island for days at a time with the undelivered mails in their possession, if they were fortunate enough to have a letter for one of the shebeens, and received a few glasses of potheen. Pat Coleman was in the habit of calling out the mails, one by one, while the important people stood around the counter. The people of lesser importance stood in the rear, while the poor people, who were expecting letters from their friends in America, or writs from the County Council or the shopkeepers in the big town on the mainland, stood outside to ambush the postmen, when they were starting on their rounds.

First came the Protestant vicar, Mr Wilbert. He stood before the counter, puffing vigorously. He was always in the habit of running to his destination, lest he might forget it on the way very probably, for he was an absent-minded man. He looked around amiably, mopping his brow with his handkerchief, smiling at Pat Coleman as befitted a man of his calling.

'Warm day, Mr Wilbert,' said Pat Coleman with a serious expression on his face, which seemed to say: 'I hope everybody understands that I'm not saluting the vicar because I have a leaning towards Protestantism, but because I have to live up to my official duties.'

'Good morning, good morning,' said the vicar, and he began to hum a tune from the chorus of the 'Iphigeneia in Taurus,' but which Pat Coleman understood to be an incantation to the evil one, whom all vicars worshipped.

Cissy Carmody came in and stood in the rear opposite the door, with her pink knitted shawl thrown at a fitting angle over her shoulders, so that all the young men who came in could admire her figure and all the young women could be jealous. She was waiting to hear the mail called, hoping that she would receive a letter from her young man of the grey tweed suit and the straw hat.

The curate came in, saluted Pat Coleman and stood beside the vicar. Mr Wilbert took him by the arm, and putting his mouth close to his ear, whispered:

'I saw that lyric of yours in the *Erotic Review*, quite good, I congratulate you; though I consider that the expression was not as good as in the . . . What was it called? Yes, yes . . .' and forgetting about the curate he pulled a manuscript from his pocket and pored over it, mumbling to himself.

The curate looked at the floor gloomily, paying no heed to the vicar. Then he started, hearing O'Malley laughing at the door at something Pat Farrelly was saying to him. He looked around and saw O'Malley enter, and he unconsciously moved away towards the wall where he could get a better view of him.

O'Malley stood in the centre of the floor, talking to everybody in a loud voice. He clapped the vicar on the back and said, 'How the devil are you getting on, Mr Wilbert?' and then turned to the curate and said, 'Beautiful weather we're having, Fr McMahon.'

Pat Coleman stared at O'Malley with an injured expression on his face. He regarded O'Malley as an enemy, since O'Malley was an enemy of the King, and on bad terms with the parish priest, the two great powers that Coleman worshipped.

'Beautiful day, thank God,' replied the curate, boiling with jealousy. O'Malley, thought the curate, imagined that the whole place belonged to him. He was vexed because everybody in the post office was looking at O'Malley, smiling at him, listening to every word he said and admiring his audacity for talking so loudly in the post office at mail time, where only the parish priest was allowed to talk loudly, where Mrs Cassidy was afraid to talk loudly, and where Mrs Wilbert was snubbed one day by Pat Coleman for speaking slightly above a whisper. But Coleman would not dream of asking Hugh O'Malley to lower his voice, for he suspected that O'Malley would very probably horsewhip him, for being impertinent to an O'Malley in Inverara, where his ancestors had been chiefs.

Mr Blake came in, followed by Miss Blake. Mrs Cassidy and Miss Cassidy came. Mrs Wilbert came. Mr Renshaw came, looking as he always looked, as if he had just finished a hard day's work tracking criminals or potheen vendors, or grocers who kept their names in Irish over their doors. Miss Cassidy put her arm in the arm of Miss Blake and began to talk in a low and earnest voice in a corner. Mrs Cassidy smiled in a distant manner, as was proper in presence of natives, at everybody of importance whom she could get to look at her. She began by saying something ridiculously

funny to Mr Blake. Then she turned to salute the curate and came
back again to Mr Blake. But Mr Blake had entered into an exciting
discussion with O'Malley and the vicar about the merits of a heifer
he had just bought, and was not to be distracted, and Mrs Cassidy
was highly indignant that Mr Blake, who was a gentleman of good
social standing, should prefer to talk to an outcast like O'Malley
when he had an opportunity of talking to herself.

But Mr Blake, even though he disagreed with O'Malley on
politics, and often abused him roundly in public, was on terms of
close friendship with him in private, for in Inverara they had not
yet reached that state of civilization when people confound individuals with principles. But then, Mrs Cassidy did not belong to
Inverara and was unable to understand that. Since Mrs Cassidy had
very high social ambitions and was of marked proletarian origin,
she had always to be on her guard to preserve her position. She had
to adopt safeguards in order continually to remind people that she
was a lady. Like her bourgeois fellow-beings on the mainland, she
had to construct a bigoted and narrow code of conduct and obey
it diligently. But the Blakes and the O'Malleys and even the
Wilberts were under no such obligations. They had their traditions,
and that sufficed. In public, Blake said O'Malley was 'a madman
and a damned Socialist,' while in private he said he was 'a damn
decent fellow.' O'Malley said in public that Blake was 'one of the
pests of the country, the descendant of degenerates.' In private, he
considered Mr Blake to be 'the best of chaps, always ready with a
joke.' In public, O'Malley looked on Mr Wilbert as the protagonist
of a vile superstition, while in private he admired him ardently as
a scholar; but Fr O'Reilly was disliked privately and publicly by
both Blake and O'Malley, for they agreed that he was not a
gentleman and 'the Devil couldn't make him one.'

The curate, pretending to be watching Pat Coleman sorting out
the letters, saw Miss Blake casting a shy look in the direction of
O'Malley, and he saw Miss Cassidy throwing back her hair from
her forehead and turning her head sideways, so that O'Malley could
admire her eyelashes, of which she was very proud, and the curate
felt that he hated O'Malley more than he hated anybody in his life.
Then Mrs McSherry entered the office with Mrs Bodkin, and he
moved slightly, so that he could see her without moving his head.
Hats were raised, and 'How d'ye does' filled the air. The curate
took out his handkerchief, and holding it to his face, glanced at

Lily. She was standing beside O'Malley. O'Malley had his hat in his hand, looking straight into her eyes, while she looked into his.

'I'm afraid you didn't remember me on Sunday, Mr O'Malley,' she said, with the girlish ring in her voice, the same ring and intonation she had for him in the old days.

'Curse this fellow O'Malley,' he said to himself, 'he is following in his grandfather's footsteps, ruining married women,' and he returned the handkerchief to his pocket, and then he wiped the perspiration from his forehead with his sleeve.

'I'm sorry, but you have grown up so much since I saw you last. Let me see, it's about six years . . .'

And then Fr O'Reilly entered the post office. Being the most important man in Inverara, and availing himself of every opportunity of showing his importance, he entered by the back, behind the counter. He paused for a moment at the door, with his hand on the jamb, while he finished his conversation with McSherry and the official of the Board, who accompanied him, just to show the people that he was perfectly at his ease. Then he came up to Pat Coleman, who awaited his pleasure respectfully, and said:

'Well, Pat, have ye got my letters ready? Good day, Mr Blake, good day, everybody, let me have them, I'm in a hurry.'

He spoke with the air of a man, who a king himself, in his own dominion, holding his own levee, might talk to the ambassador of another king whom he tolerated, and allowed certain concession within his realm, for Pat Coleman might be said to be the ambassador and His Britannic Majesty the concessionaire, in the parish priest's realm of Inverara.

Fr O'Reilly took his letters, said, 'I'll expect to see you later on,' speaking comprehensively to Mr Blake and Mr Wilbert, and walked out. Then Pat Coleman began to read the mail.

The curate still watched O'Malley and listened intently to catch his conversation with Lily. Neither had looked up while the parish priest was in the office. O'Malley was looking into Lily's eyes and Lily was making circles with her parasol on the floor, looking up now and again and smiling.

'Yes, my father is quite well, as well as can be expected,' said O'Malley to Mrs Bodkin, and then he turned once more to Lily: 'Let me see, that's the year you went to the University. Oh, I was away that year in London. . . .'

The curate determined at all costs to warn Lily of the danger she was running into blindly, the danger of being ruined by O'Malley, she a married woman, and O'Malley, a man with such a grandfather. And then the postmaster called out a letter for him. As it was passed along O'Malley took it and handed it to him saying, 'This is yours, I think, Fr McMahon.' As the curate reached out for the letter he touched Lily's sleeve, and said, 'Pardon me, Mrs McSherry,' but she took no notice. His hands trembled as he tore open the letter and commenced to read it, to hide his emotion, so that Mrs Cassidy, who stood beside him, said:

'I hope you didn't get any bad news, Father.'

'Oh, it's nothing,' said the curate; 'the heat, I think.'

He moved towards the door to get the fresh air, and everybody looked up, and Mrs Cassidy bustled the people out of the way, and the postmaster paused calling out the letters, and the curate became still more embarrassed. He stood at the door mopping his brow, and insisted to Mrs Cassidy that he felt quite well. Then the calling of the mail commenced once more and the old woman who stood beside Cissy Carmody said, 'It's fasting too much he is, poor man.'

Cissy nodded her head and blushed, for at that moment Pat Coleman droned out 'Miss Cecilia Carmody, Kilmurrage.' There it was, the letter she had been expecting from the young man in the straw hat. She immediately hurried outside to read it, and pulled her shawl far over her head, lest anybody might see what she was reading. She looked at the address, just as she told him to put it, Miss Cecilia Carmody, and she thought the writing was grand, just the kind of scrawl that was on her father's dog licence in the magistrate's signature. She opened the letter daintily and carefully, smelling the interior to see whether there was any scent in it, and 'Lord bless and save us, it was full of it, just like brilliantine,' she afterwards told Kate Mahoney. Then she settled herself against the sill of the post office window and began to read: 'Dear Cecilia, I'd love to call you Cissy but I'm ashamed, since you — ' and then Cissy hurriedly closed the letter, for Nell Brady came over to talk to her. 'Mean cat, she wants to see what I'm reading,' she thought, as she said to Nell, with a bright smile, 'Hello, Nell, those new shoes fit you lovely.' And she walked back to the post office.

The vicar was talking excitedly to the curate about a letter he had just received; there was to be a presentation of three plays by Euripides, produced by the University Classical Society, in Dublin.

'I'd love to get up to town for it, it will be a historic event,' the minister was saying, when his wife called out to him:

'This is for you, Henry,' handing him another letter.

'What, my dear?' said the vicar out loud, and everybody giggled, except the vicar's wife, since she was the only one in Inverara who did not consider the vicar's eccentricities humorous.

Pat Coleman droned out the mail, almost as dolorously as O'Hagan recited the rosary, possibly in the effort to give the ceremony as religious an aspect as possible. Pat himself considered that he resembled not the voice of Mr O'Hagan but the voice of the parish priest, when Fr O'Reilly was reading the list of contributions to his upkeep at Christmas and Easter, though when collections were bad, Fr O'Reilly's voice was not a droning sound, but it had a harsh and angry tone, interspersing the list here and there with remarks like 'If ye can do no better than five shillings, Pat Farelly, it's a pity ye don't turn pagan and be done with it.'

'Mr Blake, Mr Wilbert, Mr O'Malley, Mr Blake, Miss O'Brien a parcel, marked fragile, look after that, Miss Blake, Pat Farelly registered letter, come and sign for it, RIC Barracks . . .'

The mail finished and the people went outside to talk and exchange news and read their letters. Mr Blake got into an argument with Mr Renshaw about a report in the *Irish Times* relative to the Home Rule question. Hugh O'Malley stood talking to Lily and Mrs Bodkin. The curate stood at the door, pretending to read his letters, watching Lily furtively. It seemed to him that she looked wondrous beautiful in her dark navy blue costume with white frilled blouse, showing her well-moulded lines remarkably well. He felt that she was twice as beautiful as she was before she got married, and then wondered whether it was her scorn for him that enhanced her beauty in his eyes.

He glanced over the letter in his hand. It was from his mother. She was going to come for a visit to Inverara in July. He flushed. It seemed to him that he was ashamed to read his mother's letter while he thought of Lily. His mother to him was pure and his thoughts of Lily were . . . He watched Lily walk away with Mrs Bodkin. He followed, still holding the open letter in his hand, so that Pat Farelly, who had come out of the post office, counting the money he had received in the registered letter, the price of fish he had sold, raised his hat to the curate and said to himself, 'I'm damned but that b — y curate is nearly as bad as the minister,' as he went up to Mulligan's to pay his bill.

The curate left his letters in Shaughnessy's hotel, told Mrs Shaughnessy that he would lunch at the Oceanic Hotel, he had to attend the parish priest's meeting there with the Board official.

'There now,' said Mrs Shaughnessy, 'and I had such a nice bit o' lunch ready for ye, but some poor mouth'll be glad of it.'

Outside the Oceanic Hotel the curate found the parish priest and Mr McSherry talking to Mr Blake. Blake was arguing with Fr O'Reilly heatedly and rapping the ground with his stick.

'There is no use going behind people's backs,' he was saying (while Fr O'Reilly rubbed the pimple on his nose and smiled amiably, trying to pacify him); 'if there is going to be a meeting O'Malley must be at it.'

'Have ye seen Mr O'Malley?' said the parish priest to the curate.

'I saw him go to the forge to get a shoe on his mare tightened.'

'All right,' said Fr O'Reilly, 'I'll send a boy to look for him. Go on in, you three.'

The Oceanic Hotel was a poor place for a meeting of the important people of Inverara. It had been chosen by Fr O'Reilly for the reason that Fr O'Reilly had been designed by nature to be a diplomat, had not fate intervened and sent him into the still more lucrative calling of the priesthood. The Oceanic Hotel had once been a prosperous place before its owner, John Tierney, took to politics, and then it went to ruin because the owner, being so interested in getting elected to the County Council, had little interest in his business, and as each vote in the election cost him a number of free pints of stout and a number of free dinners, the cost of getting elected one year reduced him to the verge of bankruptcy for several years. But because John Tierney was on the verge of bankruptcy permanently and always, and because he was 'in politics,' the parish priest cultivated him. He gave him small sums now and again to stave off bankruptcy for a few months, and in return John Tierney was able to carry with him the vast number of people who owed him money, to the support of the parish priest in local politics, such, of course, as getting a relative elected into a salaried position, or a sum of money voted for a church or a purse or a bazaar or anything like that. The number of people who owed Tierney money was the chief characteristic about Tierney. It was, in fact, what made him important in political life to the parish priest, for Tierney's debtors, having no intention of paying their debts, said Tierney was 'a damn dacent man, who don't give a damn what anybody owes him,' and they voted whatever way he told them.

Tierney leaned up against his bar counter, smoking his pipe, watching the important people passing along the corridor to the room where the meeting was to be held. He nodded intimately to the parish priest, shook his head importantly at the vicar, winked one eye at Mr Blake, with the familiarity that was born of the appreciation of a good glass of whisky, and then he turned once more to his cronies, spat thoughtfully into the fireplace behind him, and with a slight shiver of his fat body, hit the counter with his fist, and said, 'I always said that the secretary of the County Council had no right accordin' to th' Act to — '

And then the important people having all gathered around the luncheon table 'in the second room along the passage,' ate the meal in silence, broken only by a casual remark about the weather, Mr Blake's prize heifer, and the judgment passed at the last assizes by Judge Bodkin on the case of Murphy McIntyre, the famous right-of-way lawsuit. The curate listened to Mr Wilbert, who sat next to him debating heatedly on the controversy which was at that time raging among scholastic circles in Ireland, as to whether there were any grounds for believing that the pre-Christian civilization in Ireland had any relation to the Greek civilization of that period, or whether it dated farther back, and the curate was on the point of taking up the controversy with the vicar when he suddenly remembered Lily and decided that it was not worth while discussing anything.

The meal finished, Fr O'Reilly coughed, wiped his mouth with his napkin, and said that they might as well get on with the business that brought them there together that day. All coughed and wiped their mouths. Silence fell, waiting for the parish priest to open the discussion. The official of the Congested Districts Board, a lean-faced sour-looking individual, who seemed to be suffering equally as bad as Mr Renshaw from chronic boredom and lassitude, sat trying to balance his cigarette holder on the tip of his right forefinger.

Fr O'Reilly coughed again and commenced to speak.

'I called this meeting here today, gentlemen, so that we might be able to form a judgment on the advisability of going ahead with a project that Mr McSherry had in his mind, namely, the starting of a kelp factory in Inverara. Now I feel sure you will all agree that there are many advantages in the proposition, but still we have to take into consideration the elements of danger, I mean danger to the financial success of the undertaking, and for that reason I availed myself of Mr Crotchett's visit, to ask him to tender his advice on the matter, for everything depends in a case like this on the good-will of the Government. If the Government is against the undertaking it is bound to end in failure. I am sure everybody will agree to that. The extracts of kelp as you all know are carbonate of soda and from the alkali of kelp the very important substance iodine is manufactured. For that reason I may say that kelp is a substance that is very important to the British Government, and over which it must exercise a certain control, since iodine is used in large quantities by the army for medical purposes. Picture to yerself the advantage that an iodine-producing factory in Inverara would give to a native army in rebellion against the Government.

'For that reason I say, and I think you will all agree with me on the point, perhaps the Government might be desirous of getting the crude kelp sent to Scotland as it is at present, to be treated there under their own eyes and control. But Mr Crotchett will be better able to tell us what attitude the Government will be likely to adopt. Then there is the question of labour for us to consider. There is the possibility that local labour would not be available in sufficient numbers, since the majority of the islanders are small peasant proprietors and averse to working for wages. And the importation of labour from the mainland would have a questionable effect on the moral character of the parish. But these are only minor drawbacks and I am sure we will be able to circumvent them and start the scheme, which I feel sure will start Inverara on the road to wealth and a part at least of the greatness that was hers in the distant past.'

Fr O'Reilly sat down. There was a murmur of 'Hear, hear,' and low coughing and clearing of throats as if each expected to speak next, and only through humility, or pretended humility, wished his neighbour to precede him. Finally Mr Blake stood up.

'In my view, gentlemen,' he said, 'we might as well let the matter drop for the present. For even though the scheme might bring money to the place, and we can all do with a little money now and again (laughter), still the island to my mind is very well as it is at present. My people have lived for a very long time in Inverara, even though Mr O'Malley here would say I am a damn foreigner (renewed laughter), and I'm rather proud of Inverara and fond of keeping it as it is. I don't want to see smoking chimneys and lots of ignorant people running about disturbing the peace and quiet of the place. A man couldn't get a duck to shoot within six months or take a walk in the evening without being run over by a tram-car or some damn thing or other. Inverara is well enough as it is and I don't see the use of changing it. The trouble nowadays is that there is too much rush and bustle and too little enjoyment of life. Factories are all right for Dublin or New York, but in Inverara we can get along all right without them.'

Then the parish priest asked the Government official's view, as to the Government's possible attitude. The official ceased balancing his cigarette holder on the tip of his finger and sighed. In his opinion there might be a difficulty, in fact there might be a marked difficulty, in getting the Government to take a friendly view of the matter. He felt that there would be a great difficulty, but he would not commit himself to a definite opinion one way or the other. The matter, of course, would have to be gone into in detail in the proper official department. And then with another sigh he returned to the balancing of his cigarette holder.

The parish priest asked Mr Wilbert's view. Mr Wilbert scratched his chin and said that he really had not got an idea on the whole thing. Mr Renshaw was in the same position, but he inclined to agree with Mr Blake. Mr Dignum, the agent of the Scotch company who bought the kelp, considered that the present arrangements were the most profitable for the islanders, namely, selling the raw product to the Glasgow people. The parish priest was going to turn to Mr McSherry when Mr Blake demanded that O'Malley's views should be heard.

'Quite so,' said Fr O'Reilly, 'what are your views, Mr O'Malley?'

'Well, my views are in a measure the same as Mr Blake's, but with this difference. He is opposed to the starting of a factory for sentimental reasons. I am opposed to it on principle. I am in favour of industrializing the country, of putting it in line with the rest of the world, for it is only by industrializing it that we can get rid of superstition, in which it is merged at present. But I am not in favour of industrializing Inverara, at least not just yet. Inverara, and places like it, is the breeding ground of the nation. It must be preserved as such until machine industry has ceased to have the effect of demoralizing the races that come under its sway. Peasants are the backbone of a nation, and if we stop breeding peasants in the pure air of our Inveraras, free from drudgery, the race will degenerate. I look forward to the day when the introduction of factories and machinery into Inverara will have the effect of adding wealth and culture to the islanders as a whole and not the effect it would have at present of making fortunes for a few and making stunted and degenerate serfs of the remainder. Let it go on as it is. Let Mr Dignum buy the kelp from the islander at five pounds a ton and sell it to the Scotch firm at ten pounds a ton. He may rob the islanders —'

Here Mr Dignum rose angrily to protest, and Fr O'Reilly asked Hugh O'Malley to apologize. But O'Malley smiled in scorn and Blake put his handkerchief to his mouth and his shoulders shook with laughter.

'I never apologized to anybody in my life,' continued O'Malley, 'and I am not going to begin now. If John Dignum thinks that he has been insulted at being told the truth, he knows the remedy among gentlemen. I said gentlemen.

'Further, even if we were all in favour of starting a factory, there is Mr Crotchett's Government to contend with. Mr Crotchett's Government will see to it that no factory is started in Inverara. It is their policy to keep Inverara as a recruiting ground for their Army, and in order to keep it as a recruiting ground they must have it poor, with a surplus population that must either emigrate or become cannon fodder. That is all I have to say, gentlemen.'

'I want to protest against the remarks made by Misther O'Malley,' cried Mr Dignum in a rage. 'I won't stan' for it, him callin' me a robber in my own native town, a man like meself that has done more for it than any other man, barrin' Fr O'Reilly —'

'There is no use in getting excited about nothing, Mr Dignum,' said Fr O'Reilly; 'forget the remark. Well,' he continued with a sigh, 'I am sorry to see that our project is meeting with so little support, Mr McSherry.'

And he leaned back in his chair, apparently in dejection. He was a clever diplomat. Having decided finally that the kelp factory would not be to his interest, as the most important man in Inverara, he had taken careful precautions that the project would not materialize. While the peasants were poor, he held undisputed sway over them, but he foresaw that if the peasants became comfortably rich and had money to spend, his power would not be so great. He had read history, and history told him that in countries where modern industry had firmly established itself the power of the clergy had become a minor quantity, and in some instances Catholicism had disappeared altogether, and because he preferred to be a dictator in a poor kingdom, to being a satrap in a wealthy empire, he had schemed before the meeting to antagonize everybody to the scheme. He had told the official of the Congested Districts Board to throw cold water on the proposition and that gentleman readily complied, because he needed very little encouragement to throw cold water on anything that demanded energy on his part. Fr O'Reilly had pointed out to Mr Blake that a factory would be bad for Mr Blake's interests, since Mr Blake received rents for the seaweed that was collected on the foreshore (rents which Fr O'Reilly told him he would lose if a factory were established, since he had no right to them by law). He had pointed out to Mr Dignum that his profits as a middleman would be endangered, and then having successfully antagonized everybody of importance he expressed sorrow to Mr McSherry that there was no support to the proposal, lest McSherry might be offended with him.

McSherry rose and coughed down his throat.

'I have listened,' he said, 'to the various opinions expressed on this matter of a kelp factory, and for the life of me I cannot understand how the scheme could meet with such universal disfavour. I took this project on hand for the simple purpose of bringing some money into the island, and to give the people employment. I need not mention that I had no ulterior motive in doing so. I see that there is greater opposition than I expected. For that reason I am willing to let the matter drop, and I hope that some other scheme will be taken in hand, involving less difficulties. In which case I am still ready to lend financial assistance.'

And he sat down without saying one word of what was in his mind, for he also had come to the meeting with the intention of backing out of the scheme, since the refusal of Lily to live with him as his wife had altogether changed his outlook towards Inverara. He had come to Inverara with the intention that most returned Irish emigrants had, of founding a family, becoming a pillar of society and going into Parliament. He had dreamt of that goal while he was struggling with life in South America, piling dollar upon dollar, sacrificing himself, his honour, his principles and his soul, just to make money, so that he could come back to Ireland and found a family, he whose father was a . . . He had told himself many a time, while he was sweating under the burning sun of the tropics: 'I will one day go back and grind them, and plant my heel on their chests, because they despised me and called me a bastard, when I was poor and helpless. They drove my mother to her grave in shame and they drove me a wanderer out of the country. I will have my revenge.'

But while he was planning revenge for his wrongs he lost the power of revenge. He had lost his soul and his honour, to get wealth that would help him to get his revenge. But when he got his wealth and returned with it to secure his revenge, he found that his revenge recoiled on his own head. He came to Inverara. He bought Fr O'Reilly's niece with his money. He had laughed to himself at the ease with which he was succeeding in his plans. He was hailed with cheers by the islanders. He was greeted by the smiles of the Cassidys, and the Blakes and the Wilberts and the Renshaws. He had visions of Parliament and of a power that would be greater than the power of the priests whom he hated, because they had made his youth sorrowful. But then . . .

Although his gold bought Lily's body it could not buy her soul. Her body that he had bought faded from his grasp every time that he tried to seize it. With it faded his dreams of power and greatness, of fame and influence, for fame and influence was monotony and boredom to a man who had no soul to enjoy it in Inverara. He had lost his soul in South America, lost it in the bodies that he had robbed in order to get his wealth, in the souls that he had raped to get his pleasures; and the pure air of Inverara, and the peasants living careless of life on the bleak crags, looking out wistfully at the sea and dreaming, hurt him and made him ashamed, as a dissolute man would feel ashamed coming from a brothel into a sanctuary.

Poor McSherry. He sat in his seat with the hard firm look on his face that had earned for him the reputation of being the 'tightest business man in Buenos Ayres.' He sat in his seat and thought that he had made a hopeless mess of life. He thought that he had better get back to the bright lights of the great world that he knew and that knew him, away from the dreaming world of Inverara that he could never know and that could never know him. Poor, weak, broken reed. He was a victim of the demon that was now too strong for him to conquer, the demon of greed and lust and avarice.

Then Mr Blake suggested that it would be a good thing if a first-class hotel were built to attract tourists to the island, and Mr

Dignum suggested that the fisheries should be developed by the purchase of steam trawlers, and then Mr Renshaw, suddenly taking an interest in the conversation, asked Mr Blake whether he was willing to sell that grey mare of his, and then the meeting forgot all about kelp and fisheries and hotels and the development of Inverara, and for the first time during the meeting everybody became enthusiastic and prolific of opinions and advice, discussing the merits of Mr Blake's mare. Another bottle of John Tierney's whisky was ordered. The time was passed in cheerful banter until the *Duncairn* blew her whistle and all accompanied Mr Crotchett to the Pier, and the scheme for the introduction of a kelp factory to the desolate island of Inverara was buried and forgotten.

2

Everybody in Inverara denounced potheen as a curse and nearly everybody drank it, whether because it was a curse, or because it was illicit and forbidden by British law or because they liked it, would be difficult to discover. Certain it is, however, that in Inverara potheen was used to a great extent, to a greater extent even than Holy Water. There were boats continually chartered, in a small way, carrying the stuff from the mainland, stealing in under cover of darkness and landing their forbidden casks in a small cove, to elude the watchfulness of the police. Really this secrecy was unneeded, except perhaps to feed the romanticism of the islanders and the smugglers from the mainland, who had a fancy for playing at being pirates and buccaneers, for the police were never watchful, unless the potheen vendors refused to pay them their commission. In fact, the police themselves preferred potheen to the tax-paying whisky, and it was told in Inverara that Big Dan Mulcahy, the biggest sergeant in the force, burst himself drinking it. Or at least so it is told.

Everybody drank it. Pat Farelly was always in the habit of catching cold whenever the weather gave him an excuse for so doing by changing even in the slightest, so that he could go to bed and wrap the blankets around his head and order his wife to bring him a quart of potheen 'to drive the could outa me bones, or I'll be a corpse before morning.' For potheen in Inverara was considered the only cure for a cold, since in Inverara, as everywhere else, people discovered remarkable cures in liquids whose consumption was at the same time a pleasure and a vice.

There were more shebeens in Inverara than churches, which of course was natural enough, for alcohol cannot be put into a condensed state like the Grace of God, to be consumed on or off the premises. It takes up more space and has to be consumed in greater bulk and oftener in order to produce the desired effect. The most important and 'notorious' shebeen, according to the publicans who sold tax-paying liquor, was Brannigan's shebeen in Kilmillick. Brannigan's cottage was admirably situated. Kilmillick was two miles from Kilmurrage to the south up on the top of the hill. Brannigan's cottage was on the slope of the hill to the Kilmurrage side. It commanded an excellent view of the surrounding country so that nobody could approach by day without being seen and by night . . .

Well, by night the approach to Brannigan's cottage was in itself the best defence against sudden intrusion by unappreciated individuals like policemen or priests. The road to Brannigan's cottage, after it passed Blake Lodge, was the most desolate road in the world. It was sunk between two cliffs that hung dark and menacing over it. And that piece of road was reputed in Inverara to hold a ghost to the square inch. Countless stories were told around the firesides of the islanders about ghosts that were seen there, bad-minded ghosts who cast an evil spell on those who saw them, with now and again a good ghost thrown in, to give the bad ones colour. It is even told that during the term in which Fr McBride was parish priest (for in Inverara, as in ancient Rome, the dates are remembered by referring to the ruling priests as the Romans referred to the consuls), a curate approaching Brannigan's shebeen by night was attacked by the Devil himself, and the curate had to read three and a half pages of his breviary before he could banish him. Perhaps the ghosts, good and evil, were attracted by the potheen, being good when the potheen was pure and evil when it was mixed with paraffin and methylated spirits, or perhaps the ghosts were invented by the wives of the island in an effort to terrify their husbands and keep them away from Brannigan's shebeen.

But it's easy to scoff at ghosts when one is far away from that road leading to Brannigan's. It's another matter scoffing at ghosts when one is walking along that dark and dreary road at dead of night, listening for every sound, seeing shadows at every corner, hearing the weird noise the wind makes through the crevices of the cliffs, and the mournful roar of the sea waves rolling over the sandy beach at Coill Namhan. Even the bravest will tremble and their hair stand on end, when a donkey stands silhouetted against a break in the cliff or a bird flashes past in the night, or a bat strikes one in the face with the noise and impact of a cannon-ball, and all the while one remembers in spite of oneself the weird stories that have been told about that road and the terrible visions and apparitions that have appeared on that quarter of a mile of craggy approach to Brannigan's. And strangely enough more ghosts have been seen going to Brannigan's than coming from Brannigan's, which went to prove in Inverara that the Devil does not worry those who are in his power.

The curate, as he walked towards Brannigan's late that Tuesday night, was afraid. He would never confess to himself that he was afraid of ghosts. How could he be, an intellectual, who had written the 'Death of Maeve,' the most brilliant man of his year, and beyond all that kind of mediæval superstition? Still, there are ghosts and ghosts, and the ghosts that the curate feared were real ghosts, ghosts that were within himself, that were always with him, day and night, persecuting him, but who were now more active than ever here on Brannigan's road in the darkness, as if they were nourished and made bolder by the congenial surroundings. They were ghosts of conscience, accusing ghosts, and he was so much in their power that he thought he saw their replicas in the rocks by the roadside and in the sounds that reached his ears.

It was not the first time he had come up that road by night to Brannigan's. He had come several times before to try and catch Brannigan selling potheen. During the six months that he had been in Inverara he had been an inveterate enemy of potheen and potheen vendors. He had particular enmity against Brannigan, because his place was the most popular and the most secluded. And Brannigan had two daughters, two marriageable daughters, whom he was not in a hurry to marry because they attracted custom. And the curate considered that Brannigan's was a haunt of immorality because of these daughters and had denounced Brannigan publicly from the altar at Coill Namhan for allowing his daughters to endanger their virtue by keeping them in a den where men made beasts of themselves with drink.

For, of course, the curate knew nothing of Inverara. The virtue of Brannigan's daughters was safe in the hands of Brannigan, for he would knife any man that would insult them and had, in fact, slashed Mick Kiernan from one end of the jaw to the other for having used a licentious word in their presence. But, of course, the curate took his ideas of moral conduct from the mainland and could not know that because in Inverara the people were ignorant of the whole ten commandments they were not tempted to break the sixth.

And now here were his morals all blown away on the weird winds of the June night. He was going to Brannigan's to get potheen. The ghosts within him were mocking him. Going to Brannigan's, Brannigan whom he had beaten with a stick but a month ago, when he had caught him bringing a cask of potheen from a boat, Brannigan against whom he had preached a special sermon, Brannigan whom he had denounced from the altar as a public menace.

Thus shouted the demons of conscience as he hurried along, but there were other demons within him who scoffed at the demons of conscience, the demons who were craving for the drug to satiate them. They were urging him on faster, faster, faster towards the shebeen. Even his love for Lily was now swallowed by a demon, a demon that sang in his ears, singing hate and murder and revenge, and the angels that had hovered around him that day when he had been ordained and was saying his first Mass had all vanished or were hiding in shame. He was in the hands of the demons.

Then coming around a corner of the road he halted and his hair stood on end. An apparition darted from the roadside and fled in the direction of Brannigan's with noiseless steps. The curate took off his hat and said a prayer, for in spite of himself he thought that it was a ghost. But the apparition was only Patsy Brannigan's young son who was out scouting, and then the curate remembered that he had seen the same apparition before and walked on to the cottage.

He knocked at the door. The cottage was in darkness. For several moments there was silence save for the barking of a dog in a barn to the rear. Then Brannigan himself began to move within the cottage, groaning after the manner of a man who is forced to leave a comfortable bed to open to an unexpected visitor. Then the door opened and Brannigan's grizzled head appeared looking out into

the darkness. Seeing the curate he affected great surprise and said:
  'Lord, save us from all harm, is that yersel', father?'

The curate, without replying, walked past him into the kitchen.
Brannigan closed the door, and a look of hatred came into his eyes,
hatred for the curate. He was a vicious man and there still rankled
in his breast the memory of the beating he had received. He was
waiting for an opportunity to get his revenge. For Brannigan,
whether by nature or on account of his profession, had murder in
his heart against mankind in general, just like a cur who is
perpetually whipped, may lick the hand that whips him, but will
fly at the throat at the first opportunity.

The priest stood in the centre of the kitchen and looked around.
The fire was still burning on the open hearth, casting a glow about
the room, showing the shining brown delftware on the dresser and
the rafters in the roof overhead, and the strips of sod that covered
the roof beneath the thatch, hanging down in patches between the
beams dried by the heat of the fire, and the wooden benches along
the walls and the earthen floor smoothened level by the tramping
of many feet. Then he turned to Brannigan.

  'You have no company tonight, Brannigan.'

  'What company, yer reverence? We're in bed this ages.'

  'You went to bed in a hurry then and forgot to put out the fire.'
Brannigan scowled and said nothing.

  'Brannigan,' continued the curate, 'you have been going on in
your evil ways a long time, but the Devil will one day get you
unless you mend your ways. I have done my best to stop you selling
your vile potheen and yet you take no notice of my warnings. You
will have to put a stop to it or I will curse your house with bell,
book and candle-light. I will put a curse on it that will wither
everything you possess and poison the very air you breathe. I will —'

The curate paused and shuddered. A sudden shame seized him
for the hypocrisy that he was uttering, terrifying Brannigan with
threats so that he could get whisky to satisfy the demons within
him, prostituting the reverence that his priesthood inspired in the
breast of the ignorant and superstitious peasant in order to terrify
him into obedience to his demands. And Brannigan stood by the
door trembling, afraid of the priest, afraid of the curses, yet hating
the priest with his real pagan self and determined to fight him to
the last, like a wild beast driven to his last fastness and facing the
pursuing enemy. For several moments he stood watching the priest

with trembling lips. And in the centre of the room the curate stood also trembling, undecided, fearful, waiting for Brannigan to speak. And then Brannigan, overcoming his superstitious fears with his hate, snarled:

'To hell with your curses, ye can do yer best.'

Immediately a scream came from the room to the left. Brannigan's wife, a middle-aged, pale-faced woman, who spent most of her time on a sick bed, rushed out and threw herself at the priest's feet.

'Oh, don't listen to him, father, don't listen to him, he's mad. Oh, father, don't put a curse on us, don't put a curse on us; what have I done to, oh, father, oh, mother o' mercy, don't put a curse on us. Oh, Patsy, do what he tells ye, do what he tells ye.'

Brannigan stood at the door scowling. He looked at his wife and his lips formed a curse, cursing her for her interference when he had resolved to revenge himself, and then in a moment glad that he had found an excuse for submitting to the priest, he said:

'What d'ye want me to do, father?'

'Hand me over all the whisky you have in the house.'

'Oh, hand it to him,' moaned Mrs Brannigan, still rolling herself from side to side on the floor. 'Oh, hand it to him, Patsy, for God's sake, before he puts a curse on us.'

'It's there in the cupboard behind the dresser,' said Brannigan, without moving.

'Then get it for me, or I'll thrash you within an inch of your life!' cried the curate, forcing himself into a rage, to drown the voice that was crying within him, 'Shame on you, Fr McMahon; shame on you, you hypocrite!'

Brannigan, muttering curses under his breath, pulled the dresser aside, disclosing a cupboard in the wall at the back. He opened the cupboard and took out three quart bottles of potheen. He placed them on the floor beside the priest and then went to the hearth and sat on a stool.

The priest stooped, took up the three bottles and then, without a word, left the cottage. As soon as he had gone out the door Brannigan jumped up from his seat and, running to the door, he shut and bolted it. He ran to the paraffin lamp that hung on the wall and lit it. Then he turned to his wife, who was still lying moaning on the floor.

'I'll make you pay for this!' he hissed in Irish.

Then he went out to the back door and opened it, and called out: 'Come on now, boys, he's gone.'

The woman rose from the floor and hobbled to her room, and three young men entered the shebeen from the rear. They laughingly took seats by the fire and told Brannigan to get out the bottle. Brannigan, grumbling and cursing, moved towards the cupboard once more and took out another bottle. . . .

The curate hurried down the dark road between the towering cliffs, hugging the three black bottles. He paused when he reached a distance from the cottage and put two of the bottles in his overcoat pockets. The third he threw away because he could not carry it hidden on his person. Then he laughed. He laughed because he had lost control of himself. His brain was swimming around and around. There were a million noises in his ears, just as if they had been smitten and were smarting after the blow. He did not know whether he was sorry that he had succumbed to his temptation or glad that he had got the drink. He was hurrying; hurrying to get to his rooms with the whisky. He whispered to himself as he walked, 'Hurry, hurry; I must hurry.' His hands touched the smooth sides of the bottles in his pockets and he chuckled to himself, just as the father who had died in the inebriate home might have chuckled; he was now in complete control of the hereditary craving of which his mother had warned him.

But he laughed because the craving drove out all memory. For one moment, indeed, the memory of Lily arose in his mind, but in that moment he cursed her. He cursed her with a curse that he had never used before, and when the words of the curse had passed his lips he shuddered at the nameless horror that the words inspired. But then he cursed again, the same curse, in mockery of the horror, and he hurried on stumbling and cursing, mumbling and laughing down the road, looking neither to the right nor to the left. He feared nothing now. The demons had all left him but one. There was only one demon within him, in sole possession of him, the demon of his craving for drink. He had the bottles in his pockets and the demon was satisfied. And as he hurried down the road he saw no ghosts, for no one coming from Brannigan's shebeen ever saw ghosts.

He left the cliff road below Blake Lodge and took his bicycle from the field in which he had left it, and mounting the bicycle he rode as fast as he could into Kilmurrage. Passing the schoolmaster's house on the outskirts of the town he almost rode over Seameen O'Toole, the fisherman recluse, who was returning from a visit to Mulligan in Kilmurrage. Seameen, having taken more porter than was good for him, made the sign of the Serpent on his forehead, for Seameen was admittedly a pagan, but when he arrived half an hour later in Pat Conneally's in Coill Namhan, with the perspiration pouring from his face, and trembling with fright, he said he had seen Crom Dubh riding past him on a winged horse, and that he would have been burned alive with the fiery wind that flew about the horse had he not crossed himself in time, and he was in such a fright that Mrs Conneally had to sprinkle him with holy water, and send one of the boys home with him to keep him company until morning.

The curate arrived at the hotel just on the stroke of midnight. He stealthily opened the front door and placed his bicycle in the hall. Silently he crept up the stairs to his rooms and silently he turned the key in the lock. Then he listened at the keyhole like a thief to see whether anybody was awake. Not a sound but the noise of the breakers on the beach afar off and the boom of the buoy in the harbour to warn the ships off the rocks beyond the bar. He sighed and sat down. He took the bottles from his pockets and placed them carefully side by side on the table. Then he lit the student lamp.

For several minutes he sat looking at the bottles without moving. The muscles about his mouth twitched and twitched as he looked at the bottles. His eyes gleamed as he looked at the bottles. He kept looking at them without moving. Then he rose, took off his overcoat and threw it on the floor beside him. He stood for several minutes looking straight in front of him into space, like a man in a dream. Then he said aloud:

'I have done it; I have done it. God forgive me, I have done it.'

He sat down in the chair. He stretched out his right hand and touched the nearest bottle. He withdrew his hand immediately and shook it as if he had thrust it into a flaming fire and the touch had burned it. He rested his head in his hands and stared at the bottles as if they were horoscopes in which he was trying to read his fate. There was now a look of terror in his eyes. His breath hardly came from his lungs, so intent did he watch the bottles. Then he rose again and walked around the room. He paused near the door, stretched his arms out full length in front of him, held them rigid, clenched his fingers gradually, and then drew his arms downwards and inwards, holding his breath, like a man doing exercises in a gymnasium. Then he let his arms drop limply by his side. His body relaxed. His head sank forward on his chest. He stood bowed and defeated. He had finally succumbed.

For several minutes he stood thus, with his head bowed, and then he took a glass from a cupboard and placed it slowly on the table beside the bottles. He went to the window, pulled aside the blind and looked out. He could see nothing in the darkness, strange shapes in a dark sky without a moon or stars to brighten it, everything dark, pitch dark like his soul. He let the blind fall back into its place. He went to his chair and sat down.

'I wonder was drink really the cause of his death?' he said aloud, thinking of his father, and then horrified at hearing the sound of his own voice, he shuddered and said to himself, moving his lips silently:

'I must be going mad.

'But then if I were going mad I would not be conscious of it.'

He became busy now with the idea of proving his own sanity. He recalled a lecture that he had heard a priest deliver in Maynooth, a priest who was chaplain of the asylum at Ballinasloe, in which the priest had declared that the lunatics were all perfectly convinced that they themselves were sane and that the rest of humanity were insane, and the priest went on to prove from that, that the lunatics who were trying to prove that science refuted the Biblical theory of creation were all insane in the same manner as the inmates of a lunatic asylum. Thinking of insanity, the curate forgot his troubles and the whisky and Lily. He contemplated the serious menace of insanity in Inverara. He wondered whether it was owing to the intermarriage of blood relations or to heavy consumption of strong tea, as the doctors claimed, or owing to the climate and the surroundings, the monotony of the life and the weird noises of the sea at night. Then he wondered whether insanity was really insanity, or whether it was as yet an unknown form of genius, the abnormal development of particular nerves and . . .

He found comfort for some time in these calculations. He was completely absorbed in himself. He had woven a shroud around his mind that hid the present from him, just as a soldier on a battlefield, waiting for the signal to advance into an engagement that may probably mean death for him, is carried away to a few moments' happiness and forgetfulness reading a letter he has just received from the post-corporal, from his wife at home, telling that the baby has successfully recovered from an attack of measles, and dreams of the baby's future and happiness and his wife's embraces, until the officer's whistle and the sudden thunderclap of the artillery barrage suddenly bursts in upon his happy dreams and plunges him into the jaws of death. . . .

So the curate, wrapt in his thoughts, was suddenly brought back to reality by the mewing of a cat outside his window, a weird and pathetic mewing that sounded like the funeral pæn of a dead race. He shuddered again and stretched himself. He reached out his right hand and toyed with the nearest bottle. Presently he drew it towards him slowly, as if he were playing with it. He stretched forward his left hand and seized the cork in the bottle's neck. Then he paused again. His eye had caught the figure of the silver crucifix on the prayer-stand, dazzling in the lamplight. He looked at it, fearfully as if it were an apparition. But he suddenly became too tired to be afraid or to think. He stared at the crucifix unashamed, unremorsefully.

'What about it?' he said aloud, without knowing what he meant, just casually, as a man would speak, waking from his sleep and murmuring something irrelevant, just to prove to himself that he was awake and could hear himself speak.

'What about it?' he repeated, becoming enamoured of this phrase, since he could not understand it to mean anything. With a sudden jerk he pulled the cork from the neck of the bottle. The fumes of the whisky, strong and bitter, yet sweet, with an overpowering, captivating and repulsive sweetness, filled the room. They surged up his nostrils and took his breath away, and then once he had smelt the fumes, he seized the bottle hurriedly in his hand that was trembling, and poured out the whitish grey liquid into a glass, until the glass was full and overflowed on to the table with the trembling of his hand. He put down the bottle carefully. He carefully wiped the stains with his handkerchief slowly, eager, in spite of his craving, to delay the moment when he would put the liquid to his lips and burn his boats, and share the fate of his father . . . the thought of his father was still surging through his brain subconsciously, the thought of his father dying in the delirium tremens in the inebriate's home in Dublin.

Then, having put the handkerchief into his pocket, he seized the glass suddenly and emptied it at a draught, with a fury of movement that tried to hide from his conscience that act that his hand was doing. He held his free hand before his eyes while he gulped the spirits, and threw the empty glass on the table and then grabbed it again as it rolled off, for excited as he was, he was watchful that no noise should disturb the house and bring Mrs Shaughnessy up to see what was the matter. He felt the whisky burning his throat, coursing through his veins and rushing to his head. His body surrendered to the strange invasion. Every nerve throbbed and every muscle twitched. He waited excitedly without thought, waiting to see what would happen, expecting something terrible to happen and yet not knowing what would happen. And then, when after several moments nothing happened, he seized the glass again and filled it. This time his hand did not tremble as he poured out the whisky. He raised the glass steadily to his lips, looked into it and licked his lips and then he swallowed it, again at one draught. He laid down the glass and stared viciously at it. Gritting his teeth as if he were about to strike the glass and the glass were his deadliest enemy, he said:

'Now I have done it, damn it!'

'Ha!' he said again with a smile, 'it was ridiculous to think that there was any danger in it. See. It has no effect on me, absolutely no effect. I might have known that. An intellectual cannot become the victim of drink. We are above that. Drugs are our servant. Our intellect soars beyond them, on another plane where ideas conquer matter. Drink can only cheer us, act as a stimulant . . . of course, my father might have died of it . . . but then he was a solicitor, a being that was on another plane from me . . . by Jove! I'm beginning to feel better. It was the tonic I needed. Ha, ha! a tonic, that's just it, a tonic. Just what Mrs Cassidy told me, too . . . an intelligent woman, Mrs Cassidy . . . though, of course, this is much better than the vile things they give you in the chemists . . . all right for the common class of person, but for us who are . . . .'

Then weariness seized him and he lost the thread of his thoughts. He leaned back in his chair. The strong spirit roamed through his blood, heating it, stirring it up, roaming around and about through every crevice and inlet, down to the marrow and around the heart and back again to the brain, and then straight down at one mighty rush to the feet and up again along the shins, until gradually a mist began to form before his eyes and gradually, very gradually, he began to feel a looseness about the limbs and a willingness in his hands and feet that was beyond the control of the nerve centre. His hands began to move without the direction of his brain. He was surprised when he discovered his right hand stretching out and seizing the leg of the table. He checked it. It dropped back to his side. But presently his right foot shot out and hit the table sharply and the glass rattled. The bottles shook and a little spout of whisky shot up from the neck of the open one. The curate swore at his leg, but he swore humorously as if he were amused at the childish pranks his leg was playing. Then he became afraid that the noise would wake Mrs Shaughnessy.

'Faugh!' he said, laughing at this idea. 'Hang Mrs Shaughnessy, what has she got to do with it? What has anything or anybody got to do with it, to do with me, eh?'

He spoke in an irritated tone as if somebody were trying to contradict him, and he was determined not to be put down; and then, as nobody answered his voice, that resounded slightly in the weird stillness of the night, he laughed through his nose without making any articulate sound, as if he were scoffing at the idea of anything being the matter, or anything or anybody mattering in the least.

For perhaps half an hour he sat without moving, while a delicious peace pervaded his mind and his body, thinking of nothing actively, absolutely passive, allowing ideas to float about him and above him and below him, without making an effort to grasp them or to reason with them or to refute them, making no effort to control his limbs or anything belonging to himself, within him or without him, feeling a delightful warmth in his blood, with everything painted in a rosy hue, while before his half-closed eyes there wafted a pale blue mist, like a veil that shut out from his contemplation all the wickedness and pain of the world. Then the pleasant sensation gradually lessened, and then it died and left him. A slight tremor of pain shot through his frame. It shot through his body, but it was not physical. It was his mind awaking from the stupor and beginning to think, and, thinking, it thought of his father who had died in the inebriate's home. Then a host of thoughts, terrible thoughts, rushed at him pell-mell, overwhelming him, screaming at him and gesticulating, as if in revenge for having been suppressed for so long. There came the thought of Lily, the thought of his career destroyed, the thought of his soul damned, the thought of devils devouring him in everlasting torments. Chasms opened up before him. His head seemed to be rising, rising from his shoulders, going to float off into space and desert his body to the devils. He grasped the table with his hands in an effort to steady himself, to keep himself from vanishing then and there into the open gaping chasm that would engulf him in the eternal fires. He almost screamed with fright. He tried to scream, but no sound came from his lips. His parched tongue clung to his palate. His throat emitted no sound, but a low gurgling noise like the last drop of water being sucked down a drain-pipe. Then the visions charged at him with redoubled fury, until they became so numerous that they devoured one another. The vision of Lily was devoured by the vision of the Devil. The vision of the Devil was in its turn devoured by the vision of his father being strangled by snakes. The vision of his father was again devoured by the vision of himself writhing and squirming in the roaring flames of Hell, and then the whole galaxy of visions came to life again and whirling around joined together into a ball, and the ball faded away from his eyes until it was lost in infinity.

He stretched out his hand and grasped the bottle. Strangely enough, his hand did not tremble and he wondered at it. He poured out the whitish grey liquid and emptied the glass eagerly. The spirit coursed once more through his veins. His limbs loosened once more and he sighed with satisfaction. He filled the glass again and again he swallowed it. Then his head fell forward with the empty glass clutched in his hand and he shivered.

'I will write a poem now,' he said in a thick voice, raising his head, 'I am inspired.'

He recalled the stories he had heard of men who could only dream of beauty, dreams of genius, when they were drugged with alcohol or opium. He remembered a famous actor who always went on the stage stupefied with drink, and how they locked him in his room once in order to get him to the stage sober, thinking that he would act still more wonderfully, and how he got a bottle of whisky secretly and acted that night as he had never acted before, and the management thought he was sober until he fell on the stage in the last act blind drunk. He thought that he himself was just like those men. He thought it in that moment when his vision was clear. He tried to rise to get a pen and paper, but he staggered. His head swam and he sat down again.

'Why should I write?' he muttered querulously.

'Why should I do anything but dream?'

He sat dreaming. For some time his dreams were pleasant. He was dreaming now about Lily. At first his dreams pitied himself and Lily. Tears came to his eyes and he wept. Then the weeping passed, and he had other visions, visions that made his blood rush madly through his body; desires for Lily awoke in him. She appeared before him in all the seductive poses in which he had ever seen her, that evening in Dungarvan, the moment when she sank into his arms and his lips touched hers . . . then back again . . . farther back to the first day he saw her with the eyes of love . . . then the evenings at college after the summer in which he had fallen in love with her. He used to sit at his desk in the study with his head resting on his hand, and her face would come before his eyes on the page of Virgil that he was translating . . . the dreams he had of her . . . he recalled the day he told his confessor that thoughts of her were troubling him, and the confessor told him that he must put her out of his head, and told him to pray to St Joseph when these thoughts came. . . .

'Why the hell should I put her out of my head. . . . Maybe he had thought himself about somebody. Eh? I'm sure he had. Eh?'

He thought of her in Inverara, McSherry's wife, and then he saw her smiling at Hugh O'Malley and he became furious. He clutched at the table and his face darkened. His eyes blazed. The hot sensuous look left them and they opened wide like the eyes of a startled mare. He struggled to his feet, and then his head swam again, round and round . . . everything blurred . . . and then everything appeared ridiculous, and he said to himself:

'What am I talking about?'

He sat down heavily in his chair, and laying his head on his hands he fell asleep.

Wednesday

IT WAS broad daylight when the curate awoke. When he opened his eyes, the sun was streaming in through the window into the room. He could hardly believe his senses at finding himself leaning on the table, with his head between his hands and his clothes on, as if he had been there all night. He thought that he had a nightmare and had dressed himself while asleep, but then his head brought him back to the realization of what had happened to him. It smarted when he moved. He put up his hands and pressed it tightly to keep it from bursting. He felt sure that it was going to burst. The events of the night flashed across his memory. He felt a terrific shame and remorse within him. He wished that the ground would open up and swallow him. He wished that he could die that instant to forget the shame of what he had done. His crime appeared greater to him than the murder of a nation would appear to a statesman, if a statesman existed who had a conscience. He, a priest of God, ordained to the service of the Divinity, to be shepherd of the weak, to be the guide of the doubtful, the comforter and saviour of sinners, fallen a victim to temptation. He was on the point of throwing himself on the prayer-stool, to kneel before the silver crucifix and beg for mercy; but when he raised his eyes, he caught sight of the black bottle. There it stood on the table, jauntily, unashamed and unmoving, beckoning to him. His whole body stretched out to it. His parched tongue craved for it. His head that was throbbing cried out: 'Give me to drink.' He seized the bottle with a hand that was trembling as with the ague, and was on the point of filling a glass when a knock came to the door, a heavy knock. He started and called out:

'Who is there?'

'It's me, father,' came the voice of Mrs Shaughnessy, 'it's eleven o'clock. Is there anything the matter? I called three times before, but I couldn't make ye hear and yer door was locked. Is there anything the matter, father?'

'I had a headache and didn't sleep until morning,' said the curate. He spoke glibly with a curious cunning that he found new to himself. It seemed to him that somebody within had spoken, somebody whom he himself did not know, some one who was born within him during the night and had come to live within him and was now taking control of the old being who had lived there until now, the ghost of his father, perhaps.

'I will be down presently,' he added.

'Thank God,' murmured Mrs Shaughnessy, moving away from the door, 'I was afraid of me life, rememberin' that Fr Fullerton of Rossmare was found in his bed just that way one morning, but Glory be to God it's only a headache.'

The curate licked the sides of his mouth with his tongue and then he bit his tongue. His eyes, opened wide, stared in front of him. He had lied. He was going down, down . . . sinking farther at each step into the moral degradation that his surrender to drink had started. He swallowed two glasses of the whisky, one after the other without pausing. The first glass burned his throat and almost made him vomit, but the second glass relieved the unpleasant sensation. It warmed him and eased the pain in his head. It made him feel strong and courageous and careless and defiant. He pulled off his coat and his clerical waistcoat and his collar. He rolled up his sleeves and immersed his head in the wash-basin. Then he combed his hair, brushed his clothes and dressed himself again, doing everything in a hurry. Then with a cunning smile and a chuckle he hid the glass and the bottles in the cupboard. He was going to lock the cupboard when he paused and took a silver flask, that he used to carry altar wine, a present from his cousin who was a nun in a Dominican convent, and he filled it with whisky. He put it in his pocket with a smile, thinking that he was a very clever fellow and that he had at last learned how to live his life, that he had been a fool for a long time, allowing himself to be buffeted by fate, but that he was now the master of his fate and could laugh at the world. His love for Lily, or anything else so trivial, would no longer cause him any worry. He would play with Lily and with the world with a devilish cunning and find pleasure in doing so. He would scheme and plot and . . . He wiped up the stains on the table carefully, and set the books and manuscripts in order. Then he gave a final brush to his clothes and looked at himself in the glass . . . He paused in wonder, looking at his own reflection in the mirror. Funny that he had never before thought how good-looking he was. He decided that he would get his hair trimmed in the new fashion the next time he was in the Big Town on the Mainland and could visit a decent barber.

Then he went downstairs into the dining-room. Mrs Shaughnessy asked him was he going to have breakfast or was he going to say Mass, with a plaintive ring in her voice, as if she felt sorry for him to have missed Mass, and thought it a bad sign. . . . Perhaps not being so sure about the headache and thinking that he had stayed up too long, writing those terrible things for the papers. 'And it isn't at all a good thing for a priest to pay so much attention to the things of this world, poetry and that kind o'rubbish, and forget about his Mass, God forgive me,' she afterwards told Mrs Mahoney, when that lady came for her daily supply of food.

The curate detected that ring in her voice and suspected that she had discovered the real cause of his getting up late. For the first time, too, he discovered that Mrs Shaughnessy was a very curious, skittish and flighty woman, who would be far better employed minding her own business, instead of busying herself with his affairs. He determined to be on his guard in future against her and to keep her at a proper distance, for the less ignorant and scandal-mongering people like Mrs Shaughnessy knew the better. Then he remembered the new cunning that he had discovered within himself and availed himself of it for the discomfiture of Mrs Shaughnessy. He looked down at the ground with a sad and disconsolate look and said mournfully, with intense pathos in his voice:

'He who goes late to the banquet of the Lord should be whipped with scorpions,' saying it as if it were a quotation from the Bible. And as Mrs Shaughnessy had never read the Bible, but heard it second-hand, and had a great respect for that literary masterpiece of Semitic tradition, she believed the quotation to be genuine and very suited to the occasion. She lost her suspicions of the curate's delinquency in her edification at seeing the saintly look that came into his eyes as he said those words. She took care to add this episode in her conversation with Mrs Mahoney, and Mrs Mahoney, whether inspired by these words or eager to show her own superior knowledge of prayer, recited one of her most imaginative chants when she heard it.

The curate had breakfast. He ate a hearty breakfast, better than he had eaten for a long time. This morning his mind was at ease. He felt elated. There was a comfortable springy feeling in his body, just the feeling one gets walking through a clover field on an April morn when the larks are singing overhead. He wanted to sing a song. He wanted to laugh at everything. In the middle of his breakfast he took a crumb of bread and threw it at a statue of some saint or other, that stood on a wooden pedestal in the corner. He laughed like a child and when his conscience pricked him for being disrespectful to the saint, he murmured 'Silly rot,' and went on with his breakfast. When he finished breakfast he went upstairs, humming a tune, and Mrs Shaughnessy, who was listening to him, said to herself: 'He's always that way when he has written a poem or something, God forgive him.' He took a towel and a bathing-suit from his room, and told Mrs Shaughnessy that he wouldn't be back until four o'clock and not to bother preparing any lunch for him. He was going to Coill Namhan for a swim. Then he took his bicycle from the hall and rode off.

As he passed Dr Cassidy's on his way westward, Pat Coleman was coming out from Cassidy's after delivering a telegram. He looked after the curate, who was cycling away as if he had not a care in the world, and Pat was worried. He had waited for half an hour that morning in the church, waiting for the curate to say Mass and felt sure that the curate was ill since he had not come. He was surprised to see him cycling towards Kilmurrage, looking perfectly fit. He made it a point to call into Mrs Shaughnessy's on his way home.

'Good day, Mrs Shaughnessy,' he said. 'Is the curate in bed ill? I was sure that there was something serious the matter with him when he didn't say Mass at the usual hour this morning.'

'That so,' said Mrs Shaughnessy; 'well then, Pat Coleman, yer losin' yer time as a postmaster, and it's up in Dublin Castle ye should be, for ye were born to be a policeman, an' inquisitive people don't always hear what's good for them.'

Mrs Shaughnessy was eager to preserve the honour of her charge, and she was not over-fond of the postmaster, whom she considered a hypocrite and 'a nosey person,' for in Inverara and in Kilmurrage in particular the people were imbued with some of the vices of the mainland, in so far as each thought his neighbour a hypocrite.

'Well now, ma'am,' began Coleman, but Mrs Shaughnessy cut him short, saying that she could not afford to loaf around all the morning, talking to people that had nothing to do and were getting their money too easily from the Government 'that no honest person would work for' to be able to mind their own business.

So Coleman went away in a temper and went into Mrs Moroney's for consolation, and found it. For Mrs Moroney always listened to him attentively and agreed with him on everything. She raised her eyes and hands to heaven respectfully when Pat told her that there were things going on in Kilmurrage, to his private knowledge, that would bring no good to the island, or luck to Kilmurrage.

The curate went westwards until he reached the beach at Coill Namhan, but when he reached the beach, he changed his mind about having a swim. Instead, he left his bicycle and his towel and swimming kit in a cottage to the west of the beach and trudged on westward by the seashore. The land rose before him as he walked, until gradually the seashore became a rising cliff, soaring sheer above the sea beneath. In the distance in front of him stood the old fort of Coill Namhan, standing on the highest cliff in Inverara, four hundred feet above the sea-level. It was thousands of years old, and its weather-beaten walls, that had withstood many a siege, were still standing intact, evidence to prove that the natives of Inverara had degenerated like the Egyptian, for the descendants of those who had built that monstrous fort, without technical appliances, had, like the descendants of those who had built the Pyramids, reached a stage of ignorance when they had not sufficient social energy or skill to build a first-class pig-sty.

A long grassy slope led up to the fort, almost perpendicularly, and the curate had to pause now and again in his climb to take breath. Once he sat down on the ledge of a rock, panting and with parched throat. He looked around him cautiously, took the flask from his pocket and took a draught. Then he went on upwards, looking to his left now and again towards the hamlet of Coill Namhan. The hamlet lay sheltered among the low hills that stretched inland, falling terrace upon terrace. Slim columns of blue smoke rose from the cottages, rising straight upwards on the still air. He could see the long low building of O'Malley's house beyond the village, beside the ruins of the old O'Malley castle, while the grey square concrete house of McSherry stood near it, like the castle of a foreign conqueror, standing amid the ruins of the conquered.

'I wish I could see her now,' murmured the curate as he looked at McSherry's house. 'I wish I could see her now and laugh at her.'

He climbed upwards until he reached the Hill of Slaughter, and there found Seameen O'Toole, perched on the summit of the cliff, with his legs dangling over the edge, smoking his clay pipe moodily and fishing in the waters, that were two hundred feet beneath him. The curate looked at him as if he were an apparition. It had been so hard to see him in his grey homespuns, the colour of the rocks around.

'Why, it's Seameen O'Toole,' he said with a smile.

He remembered that he had often scolded Seameen for not going to Mass on Sunday and he said to himself: 'Poor devil, I should not be so hard on him. He has a hard time of it.' For today he felt lenient towards everybody.

Seameen looked down the slope of the hill and saw the curate. He scowled and then put his hand to his hat to salute the priest. Seameen was a recluse who lived alone in his one-roomed cottage in Coill Namhan and he had a dislike for everybody, and particularly for priests, for they worried the life in him, trying to convert him from getting drunk on Saturdays in Mulligan's and then staying from Mass on Sundays. He never worked as other men work, with an objective, to raise a family or perpetuate themselves. Seameen just worked to exist. He had five acres of barren crags and on these he raised a few sheep and sowed a few potatoes every year, potatoes which he never dug or weeded or sprayed, but scratched a few from the ground when he needed them. He fished most of the time, when the weather was fine, and when the weather was not fine he slept. He fished to get food or to buy himself whisky or tobacco. He never sold the fish for money. When he wanted whisky he brought a few fish to Mulligan and exchanged them over the counter for spirits. So he had not a hard time of it and was happy, if it were possible for him to be happy, for nobody could tell whether Seameen was happy or not, since he never disclosed his thoughts to anybody, not even to remark on the weather. And it would be impossible to judge his happiness or unhappiness from his looks, for a red beard hid the lower part of his face, and the upper part of his face was always hidden under an old tattered hat, that hung down around his ears, with a piece of string tied around the crown and under the chin. Nobody ever knew whether he was laughing or crying or smiling or scowling when they looked at him. In fact, people went out of their way to avoid him. They considered that he was under a spell and brought bad luck to those that met him, but people always say that of a man they don't understand, and who does not give them an opportunity to pity his faults and exalt their own virtues. The people did not like Seameen's independence, for Seameen was independent, as independent as Diogenes in his barrel, when he asked Alexander to get out of his sun as the greatest favour the conqueror could do him.

'How are you, Seameen?' said the curate in Irish, coming up to him on the cliff-top.

'I'm all right,' replied Seameen in a surly tone, as if to say, 'Get out of my way, I'm fishing.' And he looked out over the sea, scratching his red beard and dangling his line.

The curate stood watching him, like a superior being watching an insect in a field trying to get from one blade of grass to another. He wondered why he had never noticed before that Seameen would make a wonderful setting for a poem, sitting here on the Hill of Slaughter where the Firbolgs and Tuatha De Dananns had fought thousands of years ago, when the Firbolgs threw the vanquished Tuatha De Dananns down the steep cliff into the sea. He thought that Seameen was the spirit of the Tuatha De Dananns, brooding over the scene of their defeat. He laughed out loud at this idea and slammed his thigh and Seameen looked up, muttering something to himself. The curate thought it to be a curse and got vexed.

'What's that you said, Seameen?' he said sharply.

Seameen dangled his line thoughtfully for a time and then he looked up at the curate over his beard.

'There are more madmen in this world than sane men,' he said, and then he looked out at the sea again and spat, as if he had swallowed something bitter, and then wiped his mouth with his beard.

The curate laughed, thinking that Seameen himself was mad, and wishing to humour him in his lunacy. He walked up towards the fort and sat down in the shade of the ramparts, looking down towards Seameen. Seameen was now pulling furiously at his line and presently he landed a big glittering fish on the cliff-top. He cut the fish's mouth from the hook with his knife and then he rose, knocked out his pipe on the rock, stretched himself and, shading his eyes with his hands, looked at the sun to see what time it was. The curate, feeling the dryness in his throat again, took another draught from his flask. The blood began to flow warmly in his body again. He felt a tingling in his head and the rosy tinted mist came before his eyes. He began again to think of Lily. He strained his eyes down towards McSherry's house and thought he saw the figure of a woman coming along through the fields towards the sea path by which he had himself come to the fort. He trembled with excitement. He felt sure it was Lily. 'She is coming to me,' he cried aloud. His breath caught in his throat. He felt a wild desire for her seizing him. He looked down towards Seameen. He wished Seameen would go away and not interrupt his meeting with Lily, but Seameen was quite unconcernedly collecting brambles on the cliff-top to light a fire. Presently he put the brambles in a pile between two stones and taking a little can from his basket he placed it on the fire. There he lit the brambles and sat down.

The curate, straining his eyes towards Coill Namhan, could now see distinctly that it was Lily who was coming towards him. She was dressed in a grey tweed skirt and a green sports coat and she was wearing no hat. His heart began to throb more violently. He kept ripping up the grasses with his hands. He kept trying to plan out in his mind what to say to her. How would he begin the conversation? It would be now or never. This was his last chance. If he failed now to bring her back to where they left off at Dungarvan. Oh, what mattered his vocation or his priesthood, silly lout; that was when he was mad, a child, he was sane now. He completely forgot that he had determined to scorn her, to humiliate her. The moment that he saw her he forgot his strong determination to flout her. He only remembered that he loved her.

'Great God, I wish that fellow would go away. He will spoil everything, the fool.'

But Seameen had now taken a frying-pan from his basket and, placing a small fish in it, he held it over the blaze to broil. He poured some tea from a paper bag into the boiling water, then some milk from an old tin can, then sugar from a paper which he took from inside his blue woollen shirt. Then he twisted and turned the fish on the pan with the edge of his knife.

The curate looked at him vexedly but dreamily. He was too

engrossed in his passion to be angry actively.

'If he weren't there, I could throw myself at her feet and overpower her with my begging. Only poets can make love.'

He began again to rehearse what to say to her, but he couldn't frame the phrases that he desired. She was now beginning to mount the slope. God, how beautiful she looked, with her hair waving in the breeze, just like the evening at Dungarvan. Was she coming to him? Had she seen him coming up the hill and followed him? She must have. Otherwise, why would she have come just then? He would ask her to come with him away somewhere, to America. He remembered he had an uncle in St Louis, editing a daily paper. He would be able to get something to do, a man of his literary talents. His uncle wouldn't mind his leaving the Church. His fare could be arranged somehow. Some of the Republicans in Dublin who were anti-clerical would see to that. Of course, everybody was anti-clerical who was worth anything. What was a priest anyway? All silly rot. As for Fr O'Reilly and priests like him, they were only in the Church for a living. He should have known that long ago. They almost spoiled his life with their clericalism. A critic in Dublin had said that a priest could not write poetry, since his imagination was carped by reverence for dogmas. What were dogmas? Folly and superstition. Everything was folly but Lily. God! what poetry he would be able to write about her. . . .

Lily had now reached old Seameen, who was munching a hard oaten loaf and picking pieces of the broiled fish from the pan with the tip of his knife and his forefinger, sitting on a ledge of rock, with his can of tea beside him, just as Diogenes might have sat. Seameen touched his hat to Lily and she nodded to him and paused for a moment to talk to him. Then she continued up the slope with her eyes on the ground.

The curate clawed the grasses viciously. His brain was in a whirl. What could he say? Could he say anything? His blood was rushing so madly that it clogged his brain and made thought impossible. For a moment he felt like running away, and as if he were afraid that he was going to run, he said in a low voice, as if talking to some one beside him: 'Don't run.' He began to swallow his breath and put his hand to his throat to ease his breathing. He gloated over every line and contour of Lily's body as she approached him. She was only twenty yards away now and he could hardly restrain himself from rushing out to her, but he looked at Seameen and he swore.

There was Seameen sitting unconcernedly drinking his tea and looking out over the sea, pulling his hat down farther over his eyes, with his knees curled up under him, sitting like a rabbit.

The curate almost stopped breathing, waiting like a panther for its prey. He was hidden beneath the shade of the ramparts, so that Lily did not notice him until she was within a few yards. Then she put her hands to her hips and paused to take breath. She sighed with weariness after the stiff climb. He could see the roses in her cheeks heightened and glowing after the exertion. Her eyes were soft as she looked out over the sea, holding her chin up so that she could drink in the salt breeze that came from the waves beneath. Her eyes had a shining light in them and he thought they were like pearls dipped in water in a moment of poetic abstraction. And then his eyes wandered to her lips. Her lips were . . . But he looked around at Seameen. A furtive look came into his eyes as he looked at Seameen and his mouth opened into a gape like a dog going to snarl. He hugged himself close and shivered, watching Seameen as if Seameen were some wicked demon who might turn any minute and devour him and throw Lily down the cliff like the Firbolgs had thrown his ancestors, perhaps. . . . But Seameen at that moment had seized his line and pulled it in with long sweeping hauls a few fathoms and then let it fall again. A fish had bitten the hook and missed. . . . And the curate, looking back again at Lily, met her eyes. She saw him and stiffened like a statue.

Volumes could be written of that thirty seconds that Lily and the curate looked at one another without speaking. Centuries upon centuries of the development of human thought were exploited by those two in that thirty seconds. Waves upon waves of thought, countless millions to the second, passed from one mind to the other, jostling one another on the way, counteracting one another, fighting, defeating, conquering, smothering one another, advancing, retreating, surging, flowing, ebbing, while Lily and the curate looked into one another's faces and said nothing. The thirty seconds seemed an age, so much happened, and yet not a word was said. Not one articulate sound passed their lips. The duel of the minds was won and lost in silence.

Lily stood staring at the curate. Her face was frozen into a hard substance like ice. Her eyes glittered in the sunlight and stared without a twinkle, without a movement of the lashes, into the curate's face. Her mouth was firmly shut, the lips forming a shapely curve, one against the other. Her brain was sending out waves of thought against the curate, waves of accusing thought, waves of scornful thought, turbulent eddies of mockery, and deep rolling breakers of revenge that smashed into his consciousness with overwhelming force. Her eyes were piercing the curate's mind, with millions of penetrating rays that read his thoughts, reading them in his eyes that quivered and blinked as if they were looking at the sun at noon in summer, reading them from his mouth that twitched with a thousand tremors as if his body were on the rack. Her ears listened for his breathing that was troubled, listening for the sound of his heart-beats, his breathing and his heart-beats that came troubled and irregular. And then her brain sent out fresh waves of thought, that rushed against the curate's waves of thought, defeating and routing them.

And then the thirty seconds passed and the curate's mouth ceased its twitching. His eyes ceased blinking. They settled into a steady stare. He was defeated. His face settled into a flabby replica of the firm set face before him. Slowly he stretched out his hands, like a drowning man appealing vaguely as the waves close about him to a God in whom he no longer trusts for succour. He mumbled the one word 'Lily,' and his voice came up from his throat, harsh and coarse and cracked, as a sound from a broken violin.

With his hands stretched out towards her he waited, waiting for her to speak. His mouth fell open with the lower lip sagging. Lily remained motionless, looking at him for two seconds and then she shrugged her shoulders and her bosom heaved upwards, in a long swelling heave. It sank again suddenly, she shrugged her shoulders a second time, and taking the tip of her skirt in her right hand, she walked past him into the fort, looking away from him out to sea. She entered the fort through a gap in the ramparts, while the curate without moving his body or turning to follow her with his eyes, stared into the spot where she had stood. His hands gradually lowered and fell to his sides with a low thud, and then he became conscious of Seameen O'Toole sitting on the cliff in front of him. Seameen was now tying his line to a ledge. Then he took his pipe from his pocket, put his finger into the bowl, shook out the ashes, struck a match and puffed at the pipe, threw the match out to sea and the breeze caught up the match and whirled it back over the edge of the cliff on to the land. The curate watched it eddy around on the breeze and then light on a tuft of grass. Then he shivered and bent his head down to his knees. He put his hands about his knees and bit into his right knee with his teeth. Then grinding his teeth, he stood up, and began to walk slowly down the slope.

Lily stood behind the rampart, looking at him walk down the slope. Her face was now relaxed and her lips were twitching. There was a look of pity in her eyes and she seemed to be on the point of weeping.

The curate walked down past Seameen, and Seameen looked up at him over his beard and pulled at the rim of his tattered hat with his hand, while he held his pipe in his mouth with the other hand. He noticed the sad forlorn look on the priest's face, like a murderer being taken into the condemned cell after hearing sentence pronounced by the judge 'to be hanged by the neck till dead.' Seameen looked after him and spat into the sea and rummaged in his beard with his hand. That night when he was cooking his supper of porridge in his cabin and talking to his cat Phoebus, who was his only companion, he said: 'Phoebus, that priest is mad; he is, Phoebus; Phoebus, they are all mad but you and I, aren't they, Phoebus?'

The curate stood on the cliff-top farther down. The breeze flung his coat-tails away behind him, like a flag of distress. He stood with his feet together and his arms folded, looking down into the sea. Lily, seeing him, thought that he was going to throw himself down. She started and put her clenched hands to her mouth and watched him with wide-open eyes, murmuring, 'God have mercy on me.' He stood for several seconds stiffly silhouetted against the sky, thinking of . . . thinking of nothing, just letting the breeze flow through his hair and cool him. Then he turned and walked downwards and Lily heaved a sigh and rose from the wall. She turned around . . . and there was Hugh O'Malley coming towards her from the other side of the fort, raising his hat and smiling at her as her eyes met his.

'God, what did I do it for?' cried the curate aloud, going down the slope. He was seized with a sudden access of fervour and devotion. His refusal, his failure to make an impression on Lily threw him back upon his religion. He was seized with remorse. And he cried out to God. And then as his words died away on the breeze and there was no response, no word of courage came back, no inward bracing of his soul by an invisible hand, no rush of Divine help and Divine grace to cheer him, the fervour waned and vanished. It gave place to rage and hatred against, he knew not what, against the world, against everything. And he found a certain pleasure in his sorrow as a man does when he is thoroughly miserable and has given up all hope of positive happiness. Sitting down suddenly on the brink of the cliff, he took the flask from his pocket and drained it. Then he waited with the empty flask in his hands, waited for the rushing of his blood, for the warmth that he expected to steal through his body, following the entry of the alcohol into his veins, waited for the rosy mist to come before his eyes, dulling his strained nerves into an artificial calm. He waited and waited but nothing came, no rosy cloud came before his eyes, no delicious warmth pervaded his body. Instead, it seemed as if a whole horde of melancholy demons seized him and bound him with bolts of steel and daubed his soul through and through with black, and threw a whole avalanche of blackness over his brain and his heart and his lungs, and over the air and atmosphere about him, until the whole world was black. In a fury, he hurled the silver flask far out over the cliff into the sea. He watched it as it curved in the air and fell with a thud into the waves. Then he rose and walked downward to the beach.

Lily smiled at O'Malley, shyly digging into the grass with her foot. O'Malley approached also smiling, holding his hat in his hand.

'Admiring the scene from the old fort, Mrs McSherry; I think it's the most beautiful sight in Inverara.'

Lily said she thought so too, and wondered whether O'Malley had come there expecting to see her, just as she had come expecting to see him, for she had questioned old Dennis the farm hand that morning about the O'Malleys and old Dennis had told her that Hugh never did a 'damn thing while he's at home but traipse around visitin' all the old ruins and forts and lioses, an' he spends hours, ma'am, sitting up there on the walls of Coill Namhan fort, lookin' out at sea, tryin' to see Hy Brassil or somethin'; a quare man, ma'am, there's no doubt about it.' And she had come along, hoping to see him sitting on the ramparts.

They stood in silence for some moments looking out at the sea, like a pair of lovers gazing into a fire. Then O'Malley looked at her and she blushed and O'Malley's face flushed too.

'How do you like living in Inverara?' he asked.

'I think it's splendid,' she said readily.

She thought it splendid since she had seen Hugh O'Malley, but before that she would have given the world to be out of it. She was looking at Inverara now in a new light; because Hugh O'Malley was there it was the most wonderful place in the world.

Then O'Malley began to talk about the history of the fort, and while he talked, she heard not a word of what he was saying. She was looking at him from the feet to the hair. How lovely she thought his hair, long, sleek, thick hair. She longed to smooth it with her hands. She stood listening to him for a long time and then became afraid of herself standing there in the loneliness of the fort with him, with the thoughts of him that were running through her head, and the knowledge that she would be powerless to refuse him if he tried to kiss her, and she did not want to kiss him yet, not yet, he was too sacred as yet to be touched. She interrupted him talking and said it was time she were going home. He made a movement to accompany her.

'You mustn't, we should be seen.'

Then she blushed to the roots of her hair, conscious that she had unintentionally spoken her thoughts aloud. She had not meant to say that. It showed that there was something between them which they did not want other people to know. O'Malley saw that too and his eyes brightened. He made a gesture of a movement forward and then stopped. Then he flushed too, and in that instant each knew that the other cared, and that henceforth they were not acquaintances or friends, pretending to be interested in one another's society, and hiding from themselves the real cause of the interest, but that they were lovers.

Lily turned around and walked back through the gap, while O'Malley stood looking after her with his hat in his hand. When she was going through the gap, he called softly:

'Lily, when shall I see you again?'

She paused with her foot in the gap and smiled. But she did not turn back or reply and passed on hurriedly down the slope, and as she went, she kept smiling to herself and presently she commenced to sing, for her heart was singing within her. When she reached the beach and was about to turn up the road towards home, she saw a crowd on the eastern edge of the beach beneath the road. They were carrying something between them up from the beach to the road. She saw a man pick up from the sand what she saw was the broken frame of a bicycle. She stood staring until a little boy came running along towards her from the direction of the crowd. She stopped him to ask what had happened and the little boy, pausing a moment, shouted out:

'It's the curate, he's killed.'

But the little boy, like everybody in Inverara, was fond of exaggeration. The curate was not killed. He had mounted his bicycle at the door of the cottage, where he had left it on his way to the fort, and started on his way to Kilmurrage. But when he got on his bicycle, the whisky that had lain dormant in him until then, began to work with the exertion. His head swam and he felt reckless. Although the road was narrow and covered with a deep layer of sand, blown up from the beach by the wind, and the road was unprotected on the left, and eaten away by the sand in places, the curate rode as hard as he could, driven forward by a strange youthfulness and exuberance of spirits. When the bicycle gripped in the sand and began to wobble he drove it harder, and then it skidded over the edge of the road and fell twenty feet on to the beach beneath. He and the bicycle rolled over and over down the slope of sand and rested on the level beach at the bottom, and Pat Conneally said afterwards that the reason the curate was not killed was because he was a saint, for any ordinary man would have been killed by the fall, and that the only other man besides a saint that could have escaped alive was a drunken man, for it was well known that drunken men always escaped uninjured from falls and Sergeant Mullery of the RIC, who fell down fifty feet of cliff three years before, had escaped with a broken ankle, although he had just drunk a quart of potheen for a bet, and, of course, since the curate, 'God between us and all harm, never tasted a drop in his life, it must be that he is a saint.'

The curate, stunned by the fall, lay unconscious on the beach, with the broken bicycle entwined between his legs, and a few fishermen who were drying their nets on the rocks and some women who were picking sea-moss came over to him. A fisherman brought a bottle of holy water from a curragh near by and sprinkled it over him, murmuring a prayer to the Blessed Virgin; but he never opened his eyes or moved. Then an old woman, who was noted for her spells and was on that account feared and suspected of witchcraft, got on her two knees and said she was going to put 'the spell of Crom on him.' Pat Conneally asked her was she mad, or did she want the earth to open up and swallow her and them, by putting a heathen spell on a holy priest. But the others said that there might be some good in it and told the woman to go ahead. 'It's better not to interfere with her, Pat, and anyway the curate'll never know.' The old woman began to chant and throw sand over her head. She took a package from the breast of her bodice and untied the strings that bound it, disclosing a huge periwinkle. She blew into it three times, mumbling, and then filling it with sand she poured the sand over the curate's forehead, and surely enough the curate stirred at that moment and opened his eyes.

Whether he had been brought back to consciousness by the spell or not, is still a subject of controversy in Inverara. Most people think that he was, but Pat Conneally still swears that he was brought back to consciousness by the holy water, but that his recovery was delayed by the presence of the old woman who was suspected of witchcraft. . . .

And Lily was terrified when the little boy told her that the curate was killed. The thought struck her that if he were dead, she herself was the cause, for she was certain in her mind that he had killed himself. She began to walk fearfully towards the cottage to which she had seen the men bringing the body, and with every step she became more nervous and excited. Although she had hardened her heart against the curate, because he had wronged her so much, by sacrificing her love and her happiness for the sake of his own personal ideals, yet now when she had found real love for O'Malley, a woman's love and not the girlish infatuation she had experienced for Fr McMahon, she was sorry for having caused the curate suffering. She was, too, a woman, and as a woman she pitied him, so that the happiness she had felt a few minutes before now left her, like an opiate, worse than she was before she had met Hugh at the fort. . . . But then she arrived at the cottage, and they told her that the priest had been merely stunned by the fall. The peasant woman, who owned the cottage, came running out to meet her, wiping her hands in her check apron.

'I'm afraid to ask ye to come in, ma'am, the place is in such an awful state with dirt,' although her cabin was as clean as a new pin.

'That's all right, I won't disturb you,' said Lily with a smile, 'I will send down the side-car to take him into Kilmurrage, and if there's anything else he needs, send up to the house for it.'

She walked away and a load of care was lifted from her bosom, happy that nothing serious had after all happened to him, but then in another moment she became vexed with him for having caused her such anxiety, forgetting that it was the little boy who had caused it.

'It's just like him,' she said; 'he's always trying to be theatrical.'

When she arrived home, she ordered old Dennis to harness the bay stallion and take the curate into Kilmurrage on the side-car.

'Lord save us from harm, ma'am, what happened?'

She told him and Dennis went off hurriedly to the stables. On the lawn, as he was driving away, he met Mr McSherry coming up.

'Where the devil are you off with my horse?' he said surlily.

'It's the curate, sir. He had an accident and I'm takin' him home. The missus told me.' And Dennis told him about the fall from the bicycle.

McSherry laughed and turned on his heel.

'Go ahead,' he said. 'He was drunk, I suppose. We're all drunk in this damn place.'

And walking towards the house, with his hands behind his back, he said to himself, 'Wish I could fall that way and not wake up, only I haven't got the courage.'

Dennis crossed himself to protect his soul from being affected by such blasphemy, hearing a blessed priest accused of being drunk, and drove down to the cottage. Inside they were all standing around the room with their heads bared, for the curate was lying on the couch where they had laid him, reciting his rosary, with the beads entwined in his fingers. He had been shocked by his fall and grateful for his recovery. The shock had unnerved him and made him weak and fearful, and in his weakness and his fear he turned back to religion for consolation, the religion that he had scoffed at in the morning. He turned back with fervour, praying to the Blessed Mother, and comforted by his prayers. It seemed to him that his soul was again pure, purified by his fall, that he was now free from temptations, the temptations that had oppressed him for the past days.

And the people about him were edified by this manifestation of sanctity, so that Pat Conneally was convinced that he had been miraculously saved from death owing to his sanctity. Even Dennis was impressed by the sight and took off his hat reverently when he entered the room, and murmured a prayer.

'It would do ye good,' he said that evening to Mrs Murphy, the cook, 'to see him lyin' there on the couch with his rosary in his hands, prayin', an' it's a pity, ma'am, that some people only had the faith that he has. It ud make them happier and more content than they are.'

'Oh, don't talk to me, man,' said Mrs Murphy; 'can't I see who yer referrin' to, and it's meself that knows that to me sorrow, God forgive me.'

But when they were putting the curate on the car, Johnny Grealish, who was supporting his arms, got the smell of whisky from his breath. But Johnny was a wise man and said nothing, until the car drove away.

'He'll be a canonized saint yet,' said Pat Conneally, looking after the car.

Johnny Grealish laughed.

'What the divil are ye laughing at?' said Conneally, turning on him angrily.

'Nothin' at all, Pat. Woe to him that giveth scandal,' said Grealish, walking away.

'That scamp Grealish 'll come to a bad end yet,' said Conneally, quoting a phrase which his friend Pat Coleman always used when referring to Grealish.

Conneally looked at the crowd around him and added, 'That's what he gets by talkin' to ministers,' for Grealish had been working in the vicar's house, and presumably he had learned the Bible there, and in Inverara it was considered the height of indecency to quote the Bible in public or outside a church, either because the islanders considered the Bible indecent, or because they regarded such action as an encroachment on the prerogatives of the parish priest.

They had to carry the curate into Shaughnessy's hotel, and Mrs Shaughnessy became so excited when she saw him, that she dropped her crochet needle and fainted then and there. She was carried into the sitting-room and attended by several women who came running from all quarters into Shaughnessy's as if mobilized urgently by the accident. The whole town bestirred itself into activity and advanced on Shaughnessy's to hear the news. So that within half an hour there were seventeen different versions of the story spread around the town. A crowd collected in Mulligan's to discuss it, where Pat Farelly held the floor, since he had spoken to old Dennis and received firsthand information.

'This is how it was,' said Pat, 'will ye listen to me, Mickey Corrigan, an' not be tellin' yer lies. The curate went up the Hill o' Slaughter to try and persuade ould Seameen O'Toole to go to Mass, and begob, ould Seameen, the bould lad that he is, struck him across the head with a welt of a stick and cast a spell on him and the divil a bit of the curate but fell over the edge o' the broken road when he was comin' down on his bicycle to call for help. It's the spell that done it; fill 'em again, Mary.'

A crowd collected in the post office to listen to Pat Coleman philosophize on the lessons taught by the accident.

'It's these new-fangled notions,' said Pat, 'that's the cause of everything that's harmful, these bicycles that no Christian should get up on. What in the name o' God do ye think legs were given people for if not to use them? I'm surprised that the archbishop doesn't issue a warning against this kind o' thing, tryin' to go faster than God decided we should go; it's all this hurry that's goin' to be the ruination o' the place.'

Dr Cassidy and Mrs Cassidy arrived the same time as the parish priest to visit the curate. They went upstairs to the curate's rooms. Fr O'Reilly stood for a few minutes by the bedside while the curate described what had happened.

'It's a pity about the bike,' said Fr O'Reilly, 'it was a Pierce, was it not? D'ye think is it damaged beyond repair?'

The curate said that he had not thought of looking, the bicycle was still in the cottage at Coill Namhan.

'Well, ye better take a rest. I must be going. I have work to do.'

'I'll see about getting the bicycle fixed,' he said as he went out the door. And going down the stairs he said to himself, that it was just like the curate getting himself hurt and losing his bicycle just when a busy time was coming; he supposed he himself would have to buy him a new one if the old one was damaged beyond repair, and then he wondered if, after all, it would not be better for him to stay in Inverara than to go forward for the Bishopric, for he told himself that even though the position of a bishop might be higher, still the expenses were greater and he had wide powers in Inverara.

'Better the reality than the tissue, or what was it — ah, yes — better have substance than the shadow, as the poet said, nice phrase that begob; I must think over it, but I hate to let that devil Considine get away with it and I'm sure he's planning behind me back, although he told me himself . . . Well, how are ye now, Mrs

Shaughnessy? . . .'

Dr Cassidy took the curate's temperature, and inquired whether there were any bones broken. The curate said that he did not feel anything the matter with him except that he felt shaky and had a violent headache. Then Dr Cassidy went over to the window to look at the thermometer, almost a minute after he had taken it from the curate's mouth.

'H'm,' he said and rubbed his chin. Again he said 'H'm' and came back to the bed.

'Put out yer tongue,' he said.

The curate put out his tongue and again the doctor rubbed his chin and said 'H'm.'

'Did ye have drink taken?' he asked suddenly.

'Mother o' Mercy, is it mad ye are?' cried Mrs Cassidy, almost on the point of swooning. She seized her husband roughly by the shoulder and pulled him over to the window and said in a low angry voice:

'Is it losing yer sense ye are to think that he'd have drink taken.'

The curate on the bed started at the question and went hot and cold for a moment, but then remembering the cunning that he had discovered in himself that morning, he put on a mask of injured sanctity and kept silent, considering that his silence was the best rebuttal of the monstrous suggestion of the doctor's. And when Mrs Cassidy bent over him on the bed and murmured, 'Don't mind what he says, father, he's getting old and at times he forgets himself,' the curate held his breath, so that Mrs Cassidy, in spite of all her efforts, had to rise to a standing position again, without being able to smell his breath.

'I'll make up a bottle for ye and send it along,' said the doctor, 'and ye had better eat a lot of fish, it's good for the health, I eat it myself. I remember —'

But Mrs Cassidy cut short his reminiscences by bustling him out of the room, being eager to hear from him in private whether he had any definite proof that the curate had 'drink taken' when he fell.

But the doctor had no proof, and the following day when Mrs Cassidy met Mr Blake at the post office, she could only throw out hints that he had been intoxicated, and she was forced to add that even these hints were based on the slender proof of her husband's professional investigations.

And the curate, left alone in the room, prayed and prayed, until the constant repetition of the prayers wafted him into sleep.

Thursday

THE arrival of the *Duncairn* on Thursday caused great excitement in Kilmurrage. The steamer carried the tents and equipment for the sports field on Saturday. In her cabin she carried 'notables' connected with the Gaelic Athletic Movement, who were coming to Inverara to arrange about the sports. On her decks, fore and aft, she carried a motley assembly of people, people who made the rounds of every fair and race meeting in Ireland from one end of the year to the other for the purpose of earning an honest or dishonest livelihood as opportunity might offer. They were twentieth-century nomad tribes, moving from place to place with all their goods and chattels. They were Irish, English, Jews and legitimate gipsies. Along with their wives and families they carried their means of livelihood, an assortment of goods that would put an Eastern bazaar to shame. There were boxes upon boxes of sweets and biscuits; baskets of oranges and apples, that had been collected on all the fruit markets of Europe in the distant past, picked up casual-like, as O. Henry would say; there were parcels of 'lucky bags, a penny each, and you are sure to get a surprise'; there were tin cans packed full of succulent sticks of 'peggy's leg'; there were whole army corps of miniature saints in plaster and in mufti, mostly in the possession of Jews, who, however they might differ in principle with the religious beliefs of the islanders on the matter of the coming of the Messiah, were quite willing to pander to their opinions in practice for a financial consideration; there were strings upon strings of rosary beads; there were medals inscribed with portraits of theologians, saints, and scholars; there were Agnus Deis and Gospels in quires, all ready to be blessed by the parish priest in order to administer the usual indulgences to the wearer; there was a gipsy woman, with large and massive features, with her ears bedecked with ear-rings, like an old-time pirate, dressed in all the accoutrements of a fully fledged and practising fortune-teller, with a basket containing paper packets that would tell anybody his or her future or past life for a penny; and a hut to accommodate inquirers into the unknown who wished to hear the good news by word of mouth; there were three sharp-eyed gentlemen, with very pointed noses, carrying a three-legged stool, 'three-card-trick men' according to their official designation given by Sergeant Donagan, coming on the offchance that there were innocent people in Inverara with spare half-crowns to lose in the hope of finding the lady; there were fiddlers with black beards and red beards and grey beards and alcoholic noses; and, finally, there was the old chap from the Big Town on the Mainland, with a wooden leg, who played the concertina.

They all trooped ashore on to the Pier and quarrelled with the steamship authorities about paying freightage on their goods, and one of the fiddlers commenced to fight with one of the gipsies and the Pier was in a turmoil, until Sergeant Donagan and his two constables commenced to break heads and restored order.

Then the secretary of the County Board of the Gaelic Athletic Association came ashore and was heartily welcomed in Irish by Hugh O'Malley. The secretary of the GAA had come to officiate at the sports of Inverara, which was under the auspices of the GAA He was a short, stocky, bull-necked man, with rosy cheeks and whimsical blue eyes, a large stock of curly brown hair, large ears and a nose that bulged at the extremity, a large man in every way except in height. He was dressed in a grey tweed coat and waistcoat, the waistcoat being embroidered with green, grey tweed knicker-bockers, homespun grey stockings and brown brogue shoes, made in Cork. He was an advertisement, from his grey tweed cap made in Dublin to his brown brogue shoes made in Cork, of Irish manufacture. He was an active man, an energetic man, a well-read man. He knew Keating and the Annals of the Four Masters and the Tain Bo Cualgne off by heart. In all respects he lived up to the best traditions of the Gaelic Athletic Movement, which represented the best traditions of the Young Ireland Movement, that was out to 'capture Ireland for the old Gaelic civilization.' Like Hugh O'Malley, he was a member of the Irish Republican Brotherhood.

He hated England as the Devil is supposed to hate holy water, and he adopted the slogan of the GAA, namely, to burn everything English but English coal. He talked English only when he met somebody whom he knew could talk Irish, and he was privately anti-clerical. He had broad-minded views on the social question, and considered that the peasants were the backbone of the country and were bound to be cultivated like the land. He was a teetotaller. He eschewed everything English in literature, art, poetry, and the theatre. He hated Bernard Shaw, whom he considered to be an anti-Irish bigot. He considered that the poetry of Yeats and the novels of George Moore were deteriorating from a national point of view and therefore to be discouraged. In short, the secretary of the County Board of the Gaelic Athletic Association was a man after O'Malley's own heart, a man to be cherished as a bosom friend and a soul mate.

O'Malley and the secretary of the County Board walked up the Pier arm-in-arm. They barely nodded to the parish priest, who was 'an enemy of the country' in the eyes of the County Board and of the Young Ireland Movement. They talked vigorously on the latest developments on the national question, and about the new Circle of the IRB that had been formed in the Big Town on the Mainland, about the prospects of a war in which England would be defeated, and about all the things dear to their hearts. And then they began to make arrangements for the meeting of the Sports Committee, to be held that afternoon in order to complete the preparations for the sports on Saturday.

The Inverara Sports Committee was a representative one. Fr O'Reilly had expressly stipulated that unless the control committee was representative he would veto the sports. So the committee was representative. Everything in Inverara under Fr O'Reilly's control was representative. He was always desirous, as he said himself, to give every shade of public opinion and every branch of the community a voice in public affairs, always provided, of course, that the voice was not contrary to his own interests. In important affairs, Fr O'Reilly himself was chairman, general director, manager, secretary, treasurer, and official recorder. But on less important affairs, like a sports committee, he was content to allow the curate to represent that branch of the community known as the Church, since the curate was a young man and it might be considered lack of dignity in the most important man in Inverara to interest himself officially in sports, just as undignified as it would be for the President of the United States to act as manager of a baseball team. The curate, therefore, represented the Church. Pat Coleman represented the professional classes, for lack of a better representative, and on account of his marked religious tendencies. Pat Conneally represented the peasants, because he was a man who had a great respect for the authority of the Church, and a penchant for having no independent views of his own on any question, outside the atmosphere of the village forge at Coill Namhan. Mr Mulligan, of Kilmurrage, represented the shopkeeping class, because he was a man who was indebted to the parish priest for protection against the abuses of the police, who threatened him several times with prosecution for being open on Sunday, and demanded blackmail for not prosecuting him as they were by law allowed to do. And Mulligan, being a publican, was more fitted to represent shopkeepers on a sports committee than a grocer, for naturally the sale of intoxicants had more to do with a public festival in Inverara, than the sale of candles, tea or oatmeal. Mr Blake represented the gentry, and Mr O'Malley was chairman, for although O'Malley was anti-clerical and an enemy of law and order, he was the only man in Inverara who had either the ability or the knowledge of athletics, or the enthusiasm to put the affair through successfully.

At four o'clock the committee met in Shaughnessy's hotel, in order to save the curate, who was still slightly indisposed as the result of his accident, the trouble of going elsewhere to attend. Mrs Shaughnessy had arranged the sitting-room for the guests and dodged around dusting here and there, trying to talk to the whole committee individually and together in one breath. Then the curate arrived, with his unopened mail in his hand and the committee condoled with him on his accident. The secretary of the County Board, whom the curate had met in Dublin at a Republican gathering, exchanged news with him, and then the meeting was called to order, with O'Malley in the chair. The rest of the committee took seats around the table except Pat Conneally, who persisted in sitting away from the table, with his hat held in his hands between his knees and a doleful look on his face, which he probably considered to be suitable to the occasion, but which gave one the impression that he was assisting at the inquest on a murdered man, or had come to pay his rent.

O'Malley opened the proceedings by reading a list of the subscriptions that had been subscribed to the Sports Fund up to date. While he was reading the list, he was interrupted several times by Pat Conneally, who assaulted the veracity of the list at all conceivable points, saying: 'I thought Patsy O'Brien gave ten shillings, but you must be right'; and again, 'As far as I remember, Mr Dignum promised to give ten poun' an' you have only seven, but you must be right.' At last O'Malley got into a temper and asked Conneally whether he suspected that the funds had been tampered with, and Pat relapsed into a gloomy silence that seemed to suggest that all was not well somewhere, but where, was beyond his comprehension.

The list of subscriptions was read and then passed around for inspection of the committee. The list was passed. O'Malley then proceeded to the next business, which was the election of judges. Here a divergency of opinion showed itself. The parish priest was selected unanimously, but when Pat Conneally proposed Mr Blake as the second judge, Mr Blake refused and suggested Pat Coleman. Pat Coleman refused on the plea that he was a servant of the Crown, and therefore that it was not fitting that he should preside at an event that was in a certain sense associated with sedition. Mr O'Malley angrily asked Coleman what the devil did he mean, and the secretary of the County Board looked at Coleman as if he were about to swallow him. Coleman then rose from his seat and said that it was quite clear that he was not wanted there by some people, and it required the united efforts of Mr Mulligan, Mr Blake and Pat Conneally to prevail on him to sit down again. And then Mr Blake, to ease matters, consented to act as judge, and in order to prove themselves equally accommodating, Conneally and Coleman followed suit.

Then Mr O'Malley was selected as a judge and Pat Coleman objected on the plea that since O'Malley was a competitor in one event he could not act as judge.

But Mr Blake asked how could a man be prejudiced in events in which he himself was not competing, since he could not judge and compete at one and the same time, and Coleman withdrew his objection.

At that moment Mr Mulligan proposed that they should leave the business of the election of judges aside and get on with the business that really mattered, which was, whether there was to be permission given for the sale of drink on the sports premises or whether there was not.

'For if there isn't,' said Mulligan, 'I'll have nothing to do with it, and there's me word for ye.'

At that moment the curate, who had been until then reading his letters, started to attention at the mention of drink. He turned angrily on Mulligan.

'Do you want to disgrace the island,' he said, 'by turning the sports meeting into a common debauch? Don't you know that drink is not allowed at a sports meeting under the auspices of the GAA?'

Then he sat back in his chair reading a letter he had received by that mail from a bishop in Dublin, who was organizing a Mission to China, and was calling for young priests to volunteer to preach the gospel to the heathens of that country. China! He shuddered at the thought of it. Why should he go there? It would be running away from temptation.

'I propose Fr McMahon as judge for the boat race,' said Mr Blake.

The curate started again.

'Not on any account,' he said; and then added after a pause, 'I am not sufficiently recovered from my accident.'

He looked at O'Malley as he spoke, for he remembered that O'Malley was competing in the boat race, and he knew that it would be a torture for him to preside as judge, for he knew that Lily would be watching the race with a flush and smile on her face waiting for O'Malley to win.

O'Malley frowned slightly, and thought 'What's coming over that sour-faced priest?' and then he smiled at the curate and said:

'All right, we'll excuse you, Fr McMahon.'

Fr McMahon sat back in his chair again and took up the letter. But he read nothing now. It suddenly struck him that he was years older and more experienced than before he had taken the whisky. He was now a man of the world, he thought, a man who was repenting for his sins, just like St Augustine and St Paul had done, for they, too, had been men of the world and great sinners; it was only a man who had been a great sinner that could become a great saint, and he had been a great sinner; he had been; for that morning when he awoke, he had felt drawn once more towards God and religion and had determined to shun drink in future and lead a life of the greatest sanctity; he had felt all desire for drink and for Lily vanished. And then he bit his lip in anger when he reflected that he had been forgetful of his new position as a man of the world, as a man who was on the road to sanctity, by showing his irritation against the thought of acting as judge for O'Malley. Such a trivial matter. He must show these people around him that he was a man of the world, a man who had known the world and had forsaken it for a life of sanctity, a man who was now immune from temptations.

'Now, we had better arrange about the prizes,' said O'Malley.

Then a heated discussion began. O'Malley and the secretary of the County Board did not wish that any money prizes should be given for the winner in any event. But Mulligan and Conneally and Coleman stoutly opposed this, saying that they didn't know for what purpose anybody should compete unless it were for money. And while the argument proceeded, the curate, leaning back in his chair, began again to read the letter from the bishop in Dublin, who was asking for volunteers for the Mission to China. He began to wonder whether after all China would not be a suitable place to become a great saint. What were the ties that had bound him to Ireland in the past? His nationalism? What was that now? Nothing. Good enough for people like O'Malley, who were too immersed in the material things of this world to have a conception of the greater things that were beyond this world. All men were brothers; the world was his country; souls to be saved everywhere; China with its teeming millions; a man with ability, with poetic imagination would be sure to have a wonderful influence on that poetic people; he would sweep the country with his eloquence, with the power of his personality; he would learn the language in a few months; a land of teeming rivers, sun and flowers and wonderful colourings; he would preach to them in poems in the native language; he would surpass everything that had been ever achieved by missionaries; his name and fame would be world-wide; it was an opportunity not to be missed; head of a great Church in the East; cardinal one day; the modern Augustine; greater than Paul. . . .

'What is your opinion on the matter, Fr McMahon?'

It was Pat Coleman who was talking, what was he talking about? Oh yes, the prizes.

'I think there should be money prizes,' said the curate. 'After all, what use is a silver cup or a silver medal to a poor peasant; he would appreciate the money more.'

He leaned back again and asked himself why had he said that? Why had he gone against his own personal view that money prizes should on no account be given? Yes, because it was against O'Malley's wishes that money prizes should be given; phew! these materialists like O'Malley must be defeated; they must be put down. Why go to China after all? Here was Ireland that could be made a glorious field for the restoration of the Church, a restoration of the Church Militant, it could sweep Europe again, he would be the evangelist of the restorations, a new idea, save Europe from the materialism that was engulfing it. . . .

'That's exactly what I think mesel',' said Pat Conneally with a serious air, as if the matter had given him serious trouble. Conneally was feeling delighted with himself and proposed to make a great speech that night in the forge at Coill Namhan, telling how he fought the whole committee on this matter of prize money and how he won with the assistance of the curate, and how Mr Blake had said: 'Come now, MISTER Conneally, what is your opinion on this?' And what he said in reply to Mr Blake; and how Hugh O'Malley said: 'Well now, MISTER Conneally, do you agree with that?' and how he persuaded O'Malley that his point of view was correct.

Hugh O'Malley, surprised that the curate had adopted that attitude on the matter of prize money, curled up his lips and thought: 'There are those damn priests, always siding with the mob for the sake of policy,' and then he smiled and shrugged his shoulders and said:

'Well, as you all want to have the prize money, let it go at that.'

And then the secretary of the County Board rose and made a speech, slamming the table with his fist. He talked about the games that were held in the time of Fionn McCumhaill and of King Conor McNessa, and he talked about the Olympian games and the Isthmian games, and said that a great and civilized people like the Irish should be content with a laurel wreath of victory instead of paltry money, and that they were lowering themselves to the level of the commercialized English by striving after money and then he sat down sweating and satisfied.

'Well,' said Pat Coleman, 'people who are supposed to know don't despise money so much after all, no matter how much they pretend to despise it.'

But O'Malley and the secretary of the County Board looked at one another and shrugged their shoulders, as much as to say: 'What can one do with these yokels, they know no better?' For O'Malley was a descendant of kings, and the secretary, since his name was O'Rourke, must, of course, have also descended from kings; and since, of course, the descendants of kings could not be expected to take an interest in such base things as money and personal gain, they both shrugged their shoulders in a superior manner. But both O'Malley and the secretary, in spite of their bloodthirsty opinions on the national question and their total lack of appreciation of the value of money, were quite content to write to the reviews and the newspapers for their living, reviews and papers that were not at all to their own way of thinking; in fact, they might with justice be said to prostitute their brains in a literary sense in order to earn a means of livelihood. And although O'Malley would rather die than work for his living in Inverara he was quite content to do so as a journalist in Dublin, and yet was as proud of his ancestry as a peacock of his feathers, but he questioned the right of Pat Coleman to be proud of the fact that he was a postmaster and of value to the community, or of the right of Mr Mulligan to be proud of the fact that he was a publican and sold bad porter instead of unadulterated porter and made money by his cunning. Nor is this strange. For all people are proud of their ancestry and think it is a wonderful thing to have ancestry, though how anybody could live without having ancestry in the first place it would be hard to discover. But there you are. There are people who boast of their ancestor forty times removed being a clown, because he happened to be a clown in a royal court. There are people who boast of their ancestress forty times removed being a courtesan, because she found favour in the eyes of a king and was given a title. This desire for pre-eminence in ancestry is not peculiar to O'Malley or to the secretary of the County Board. The O'Malleys and the O'Rourkes everywhere all over the world despise the Colemans and the Mulligans. Five-sixths of the population of the United States, whose income is over forty thousand dollars, pretend to be descended from the Pilgrim Fathers and boast of it, while they try to forget that they were useful citizens in their youth and worked for a living.

Then arrangements were made after discussion for the time of starting of the various events, and then the committee came to the question of erecting the marquees and the tents, and the platforms for the dancing and singing competitions. Here further dissension arose. Mulligan wanted the contract for his cousin, while Pat Coleman wanted the contract for a relative of his own. The argument became so heated, and both parties became so intractable, that the matter was finally left in the hands of O'Malley and the secretary of the County Board to dispose of in whatever way they pleased. Then the committee broke up, and Pat Coleman and Mulligan stared daggers at one another going out of the door and Mulligan paused on his way to say to Mrs Shaughnessy, so that Coleman could hear him: 'There are upstarts in this town, Mrs Shaughnessy, that are too big for themselves.'

When they had all gone, the curate went to his room, still dreaming of the future, wondering whether his future rôle in life were in Ireland or in China. He felt it was inconceivable for him to live his life in the old way, without thinking of the future. He was a new man, an older man, a more important man. He closed the door of the room behind him, and then he suddenly hit his forehead with his open palm and paled. He would have to go to confession to the parish priest before he could celebrate Mass; he would have to disclose his sin to the parish priest; he would have to reveal to the parish priest that he was a drunkard. Horrors! he could not do it. If he could only get to the Big Town on the Mainland, or if there had only been a strange priest in the island, but to Fr O'Reilly, it was unthinkable.

As he sat down the thoughts that came into his head terrified him. He was doubting the privacy of a confession made to Fr O'Reilly. And to say Mass without having confessed his sin when he had an opportunity of confessing it, still greater horror. What could he do? What could he do? He stretched out his hands, raging impotently against something which he was trying to prove was beyond himself, some outside force which he could not control. But he failed to satisfy his conscience. He knew subconsciously that it was his own weakness, his own cowardice that was at fault. And then he cried:

'God, have I not suffered enough; have I not been tortured enough, without this fresh torment?'

'Courage,' he cried again after a pause, 'they all had to endure this. Greatness in sanctity cannot be bought cheaply. Paul, Augustine, they all went through these torments.'

He sat in silence without moving, thinking now that this fresh difficulty was assuredly a sign that he was chosen to be a great saint. He held his breath, thinking that the temptation to conceal his sin would roam about him as it were, and finding no movement of mind to encourage it, no support, no acknowledgement, would leave him again; just as a man lies still when he sees a snake hissing in the grass, lest a movement would betray life and bring destruction.

Then as he sat still and passive a strange lassitude overcame him, a thoughtless lassitude. He seemed to be sinking down and down within himself, down through the chair upon which he was sitting, down through the ground beneath the chair, down, down through never-ending chasms beneath the ground. A singing came into his ears and his head began to swim. He seized his head between both hands and jumped to his feet, and without thinking he rushed to the cupboard and opened it. He had taken out the bottle of whisky and pulled the cork, when he suddenly remembered. He put the cork back again into the bottle. He put the bottle back into the cupboard and locked the cupboard.

'No, never again,' he said fiercely. 'I shall NOT be defeated.'

He stood to his full height and crossed his arms, and then he took his breviary and sat in his chair to read. He read through page after page, reading aloud so as not to allow his thoughts to wander. Gradually he found himself becoming interested in what he was reading, but not in relation to the spiritual aspect of the written words. Instead, he began to find fault with the construction of the Latin sentences, wondering what period of the decline of Roman literature the prayers in the book represented, and from that he went on to the thought of Roman literature in general, until he was recalled to his senses by Mrs Shaughnessy's maid knocking at his door to say that dinner was served, and he woke up to find himself meditating on the siege of Troy.

'I will go to Fr O'Reilly immediately after dinner,' he said as he walked downstairs to the dining-room. But he thought no more of his sin during dinner. He felt comfortable in the thought that he had made up his mind to confess his sin, and that he still had a respite before the time would come for putting his decision to the test. He laughed and joked with Mrs Shaughnessy during dinner about the Sports Committee, and about the secretary of the County Board, who was staying in the hotel. He told Mrs Shaughnessy that the secretary was an awfully decent man, a well-known man in

Dublin, and while he was saying this he suddenly thought of the criticism that had been passed on the 'Death of Maeve' by the solitary critic who had denounced it, namely, that it would have passed very well as the production of a convent girl. 'There is no force in it, no virility,' the critic had said. And now the curate thought that that had been correct; he had been too ignorant of life, but in future his poetry would show the wider knowledge. . . .

'Yes,' he said to Mrs Shaughnessy, 'I think Fr Considine is expected to open the sports.'

Declining another cup of tea, he went out to go to the parochial house and confess his sin, but as he was going out the door something prompted him that it would be just as well to wait until the following day; he could feign illness in the morning and not say Mass; but he sternly walked down the drive to put out that temptation. Going down the road he smiled at everybody that passed. He told Mr Dignum, who stopped him to inquire after his accident, that he never felt as well in his life, and he felt that, too. He whistled a tune and swung his arms as he passed Mulligan's, where the gipsies and the fiddlers were sitting on the empty barrels outside the door, dancing and singing and quarrelling, while a crowd of the townspeople stood around them enjoying the entertainment. He turned down towards the parochial house, but when he was about to open the gate leading up to the house his courage failed him, and he walked past it, on to the road leading to the Pier.

'It's too soon yet,' he said to himself as an excuse for his lack of courage. 'He hasn't finished dinner. I will wait for another half an hour.' And he walked on down to the Pier.

Night was falling. The last fishing boat, going out for the night, to trawl, was fading away on the horizon. The curraghs were coming in after casting their nets. The curate listened to the dull rumbling rhythm of the oars as the curraghs approached the shore, while the crew of one boat was singing an old folk-song, about brimming goblets of wine or of beer and eulogizing old Ireland. Groups of boys and girls were walking along the edge of the beach on the sand, laughing and talking. All around were happy, and the curate determined to be happy, too, to enjoy the peaceful moments before he would have to go finally to the parish priest and confess. He sat down in the shade of a rock, listening to the chatter of the groups of young people as they passed him. The young men were all talking about the sports: So-and-so would win this race; no he wouldn't. The brass band of the Temperance Society was coming; no it wasn't, but the Brian Boru Piper Band was coming. 'How d'ye know?' 'Oh, I heard Pat Farelly sayin' it, an' he knows everything.' 'The divil he does!' 'O'Malley is sure to win the boat race; he has the best crew in Inverara.'

Then the girls came along giggling and laughing in low voices, pausing now and again to peep beneath their shawls at something they had bought from the gipsies. Cissy Carmody came with a girl friend.

'Look what I got from the fortune-teller, Mary. Would ye believe it, "Married to a fair man and you will have a large family, of whom six will be boys,"and she doesn't say how many girls.'

The two girls giggled, while Cissy wondered whether the fair man would be her own young man in the grey tweed suit and the straw hat, and thought that she would not like to have so many children, just two boys and two girls, and decided that she would call the boys Cyril and Joseph, the names her mistress's boys in Dublin had, and then she said to her friend Mary:

'I wonder will the parish priest give us the schoolhouse for the dance. Oh, mother o'mercy!' she cried, seeing the curate behind the rock, and the two girls hurried on, panting with supposed fright, crying to one another, 'Oh, Mary!' 'Oh, Cissy, he heard us talking about boys, what will he say?' and they beat their breasts in mock anxiety.

The curate got up and stretched himself. He decided to go now to the parochial house. 'He will have finished dinner by now,' he said aloud, as he were satisfied that that was the reason for his having hesitated before about going in. He walked very fast, as if afraid of not being in time for an appointment. He entered by the gate in the rear and walked around to the front door on the grass, instead of on the gravel path, for he was afraid of the sound of his own footsteps, as if the sound would say to the world: 'Here is this supposedly holy curate coming to confess a serious sin, a heinous sin, the sin of drunkenness.' And just as he was passing the drawing-room window he halted suddenly, unable to advance or retreat, for he heard Lily's voice coming through the window from within.

He heard Lily's voice, then Fr O'Reilly's voice, then Mrs Bodkin's voice, then the three voices jumbled together, so that he could not distinguish the words, but he knew they were quarrelling. Next came Fr O'Reilly's voice, and he heard a tone in the parish priest's voice that he had never heard before, the tone of a dog snarling, then silence for a moment, then a low murmur as of a woman going into hysterics and mumbling something.

'What?' Fr O'Reilly's voice came loud and distinct.

'Oh, Lily, Lily, what are you saying, child?' cried Mrs Bodkin.

He could hear Lily laughing, loudly and shrilly, like an actress in a tragedy; and then she spoke, pronouncing every word clearly and distinctly:

'You damned hypocrite!'

The curate tried to visualize her, bending slightly forward from the hips upward as she said it, with her chin thrust out and her eyes narrowed and her nostrils distended. For the life of him he could not move now. He wanted to hear what was being said; what it was all about. He was not conscious of being eavesdropping because Lily was there. He wondered what they were doing to her. He must wait and hear, but Great God! if anybody saw him there; he must go away. Whist! what was that?

'You abandoned woman, do you mean to say — ' It was Fr O'Reilly who spoke; what did he mean by saying she was an abandoned woman? Great God! had she told him about that night in Dungarvan, the vicious wretch! Had her jealousy of his success as a priest and a poet brought her to that? Surely . . .

'Oh, John, John, don't make it worse!' came the voice of Mrs Bodkin. 'It will help nothing abusing her.'

'What does it matter, aunty? His abuse doesn't matter. I tell you once more that I will not live with him, no matter what you say or do; and you can't hide the fact that you are to blame, you HYPOCRITE!'

Ha! after all it was not about that night at Dungarvan. Ha! Great Scot! what was that? Fr O'Reilly swearing; he must stay there no longer, he must go away; or should he go in; there was Mrs Bodkin moaning and Lily laughing; he had better go away.

As he turned towards the back gate to go, the back gate swung open and somebody entered. The curate walked back a few paces and then walked heavily up the gravel drive to the front door, humming a tune, while his heart beat loudly. The voices stopped as he passed the window, and when he knocked at the hall door Fr O'Reilly himself came to open it, and the curate was surprised to see the nonchalant smile on his face as he stood before him in the hall.

The curate stammered for a moment, trying to say that he wanted to go to confession, but what he did say was:

'When are the confessions in Coill Namhan tomorrow?'

'We had better go over there at noon,' said Fr O'Reilly. 'I will call for you.'

'All right. Good night, Fr O'Reilly.'

'Good night.'

The curate hurried down the gravel path and out the gate, as if a thousand devils were crawling at his heels, trying to catch up with him. As he closed the gate behind him he said to himself:

'How does she mean, refuse to live with him; she is living with him.'

He blushed with shame as it struck him what she really did mean, living with him as his wife. He was overwhelmed with shame as this was made clear to him. He shuddered to think that he had been looking in, as it were, on some immodest scene that it was unfitting for a priest to see, but then. He shrugged his shoulders slightly and thought that he was now a man of the world, a man who knew what sin was and could overcome temptation, and — Well, there was Fr O'Reilly. He was as capable as Fr O'Reilly to look at these things in his mind and not be scandalized; but then he stood in the road and asked himself, 'what things?'

He became ashamed once more. It seemed that this part of him had been asleep until now, that part of him which craved for the reproduction of his kind, to see little children grow up about him, little children in his own image, that would carry on his blood into the future when he himself was dead and forgotten. That part of him had been crushed. It had been lectured against. It had been tiraded against, prayed against, in college during religious retreats, in sermons, in advice from reverend fathers in the confessional box. It had been denounced as an abnormity that must be fought by him and overcome, until he could stand before the world as a sexless being without any desires of the flesh, desiring nothing but the spiritual love of God. And now this desire awoke in his blood, strong and furious, and instead of being natural or good, it was to him horrible and indecent, for everything that is forbidden, no matter by what law, is indecent, and for that reason alone.

He murmured a prayer against these desires and said to himself as he walked, 'O God, O God, it is because I failed to confess my sin that I am troubled with this new temptation.' Then he lost all the spiritual ecstasy of the morning, when he had determined to give his future life to the service of religion. He felt sure now that he was irreparably lost, and he took two decisions: he would drink again when he went indoors, and he would wait on the road until he could see Lily passing on her way home, for if she refused to live with her husband . . .

Outside Mulligan's public-house he met Hugh O'Malley and the secretary of the County Board, and he hailed them joyfully, for he was now by his own volition banned from the contemplation of his own sanctity, of his own mission to convert Europe to Catholicity, and for that reason he felt drawn towards O'Malley and the secretary of the County Board, who were similarly banned through their agnosticism. He fell in beside them as they proceeded up the road towards the hotel, and he began to chatter cheerfully on the national question, about the development of native art, about the rise of native industry, about the prospects of a new war in which England would be involved and defeated, evincing enthusiasm on all the questions that were dear to the heart of the Republicans.

O'Malley and the secretary of the County Board were at first surprised at this enthusiasm on account of his gross betrayal of the national principles on the question of prize money at the Sports Committee. O'Malley suspected that he was drunk, but the secretary, who was too enthusiastic a Republican to be suspicious of even a lunatic's sincerity, not to mention a mere drunken man, was soon chattering as excitedly as the curate, and the curate adopted the rôle of listener, interrupting now and again, when the secretary of the County Board appeared to be on the point of collapse, exhausted by his flow of language. Instead, the curate now became conscious of O'Malley, who was moodily silent. He became conscious of O'Malley's presence in an uncomfortable way. The presence of O'Malley dampened his high spirits and made himself gloomy again. O'Malley seemed to press in on his consciousness like a great weight, and the weight was all the greater because he was unwilling to admit that O'Malley's presence or O'Malley himself was irksome to him in his present state of mind.

And as if there were a strange telepathy between himself and O'Malley, the latter felt the presence of the curate irksome. Now and again, when the curate glanced sideways at O'Malley, he found

O'Malley looking at him, and when O'Malley glanced at the curate, he found the curate looking at him. Neither was able to meet the other's eyes and yet they could not say that they were enemies. They could not for the world abuse one another roundly or come to blows, and then shake hands good-humouredly. It seemed, as it were, that their enmity was something indecent that had to be hidden, something for which there was no excuse, an enmity that was born of folly. And the curate, thinking of O'Malley, said to himself, 'Stupid fellow, that O'Malley,' meaning, of course, 'There is that handsome fellow with royal ancestry at whom Lily smiles, while she scorns me.' And O'Malley, thinking of the curate, said to himself, 'Stupid beast, that curate,' meaning, of course, 'There is that curate who is trying to discover that I love Lily McSherry, another man's wife.'

They arrived at the hotel. The secretary, who was staying in the hotel, invited O'Malley to come in and have supper with him, but O'Malley declined, saying it was getting late, and that he would have to be getting home. As he spoke he cast a look down the road towards the parochial house. Then he looked at the curate and saw that the curate was watching him.

'He knows I am waiting for Lily,' he said to himself.

'He is waiting for Lily,' thought the curate.

And the two men in that moment that their eyes met fleetingly knew that they hated one another because of their common love for their neighbour's wife. They both turned to the secretary of the County Board and began together to talk excitedly of the Republican movement, and the value of games to cherish and cultivate the national sentiment, eager to prove by the vivacity of their conversation and their interest in public affairs that they had no private troubles and no enmities. But they both took care to talk to the secretary, each avoiding to refer directly to the other; and whenever they were forced to refer directly the one to the other, they did so hurriedly, as if it were a scandalous matter that had to be passed over lightly.

And then the noise of a car reached them, and presently Lily McSherry appeared coming up the road alone in her jaunting car.

'Who is that lady?' said the secretary of the County Board.

Neither O'Malley nor the curate replied for a moment, each expecting the other to reply, each thinking that his own personal relations with Lily prevented his talking about her in public, just as if Lily were his wife and her identity were being questioned in public by a third person and waiting out of modesty for his friend to reply. The secretary looked from one to the other and then repeated his question.

'Oh that's Mrs McSherry,' said the two together.

'Parish priest's niece,' added the curate.

'She has progressive views,' added O'Malley. 'She was in the National University, might be of use in the movement.'

The secretary looked towards Lily again and said that she should be cultivated, there was nothing like a young woman of influence in a parish if she were interested in the movement. It would have a great effect. Then he went on to talk of the women of Limerick who had fought William of Orange, and the women of the Paris Commune, and gave a lengthy treatise on the value of women in revolutionary movements, but neither O'Malley nor the curate listened to him. Each was watching the other and watching Lily as she came up the road.

The secretary was dealing with the women of Sparta at the time of the Theban invasion under Epaminondas when Lily reached them. They all took off their hats.

'Good evening, Mrs McSherry,' said O'Malley.

'Good evening,' said Lily to the whole three, looking at no one in particular, but the curate felt that she was looking at O'Malley.

'Allow me to introduce Mr O'Rourke,' said O'Malley.

The curate bit his lip. He thought that he himself was being put into the background, he a priest and the author of the 'Death of Maeve,' while O'Malley, a man of absolutely no intellect or importance, was doing the honours, he himself, who had been Lily's ideal in the past, cast aside for a worthless fellow whom she knew only for a few days.

The secretary, eager to capture Lily for 'the movement,' began to talk about people that Lily knew in the university in Dublin, pointing out that they were all 'heart and soul with the Republican movement, great fighters.'

'What an abandoned woman she is,' thought the curate, abusing her in his mind for looking so happy talking to the secretary, while he had heard her but a couple of minutes before say that she refused to live with her husband; what a deceiving wretch, refusing to live with her lawful husband that had given her a beautiful home and everything she needed, making her poor uncle's heart sorrowful, too, he who had done so much for her, standing there laughing and talking to men who had no thought of God in their souls. He felt that he himself, a priest of God, was disgracing himself by keeping such company, instead of being busy with the affairs of his Church.

But when Lily laughed a moment later, and he heard that thrill in her voice, soft and musical and sweet, like the voice of a lark soaring, he shivered all over him, and that thought came back to him again, the thought of children, the thought of the peasants he had seen sitting amidst their children by the fireside, with the glow of the turf fire on their faces. Then he looked at O'Malley. He was laughing, laughing in response to Lily's laugh. He knew it was mate calling to mate, rejoicing at the urge of summer in their young blood. His heart hardened hearing that laugh. He realized more than ever that his boats were burned. He could not bring himself to feel on a level with these people. There was a barrier that prevented him ever calling to a mate, a barrier between him and the father sitting by the fire-glow amid his children.

He was thrown back again on religion, ever backwards and forwards, rolling like a ship without a rudder in a storm. He went back to religion, conjuring up once more the wild enthusiasm and burning zeal of the evangelist of militant Catholicity that would sweep over Europe like a tidal wave, carrying himself on the summit, as the strong fierce genius of the resurrection, he who had killed man within himself, he who was purified by the force of his intellectual abandonment, purified of all the dross of nature and of natural desires, he who had scourged himself with fiery rods of repression until he was a crystallized flame of spiritual passion, beyond human emotion.

'It's late, I must be going,' said Lily, seizing her reins. 'I will see you at the sports, I suppose, Mr O'Rourke. Good night, everybody.'

She drove away without looking once at the curate, but she cast a glance at O'Malley which the curate saw and understood to mean:

'I will see you on my way home, you are my mate.'

O'Malley almost immediately bid them good night and went to the cottage where he had left his horse. The curate and the secretary went indoors. The curate listened for a few minutes to the secretary who was still talking on the value of women in a revolutionary movement, and then he refused supper and retired to his room. As he was going to mount the stairs he stopped to complain to Mrs Shaughnessy that he had a headache and would not be able to get up for Mass in the morning; he was feeling too seedy. He refused the gruel that the good woman offered him and went up to his room. He was satisfied now that he could stay in bed in the morning and not have to say Mass, but on his way upstairs he wondered whether after all he might not be able to say Mass. Perhaps he had not committed a mortal sin at all. When could a man be said to be drunk? He remembered that even the police could not tell when a man was drunk, and that they had to make suspected persons say 'The British Constitution' rapidly, and if they stammered they were drunk and if they did not stammer they were sober in the eyes of the law. Then he remembered a meeting of theologians who had debated the question and had failed to come to a decision, but gave their general view that a man was drunk when he lost his senses. But when could a man be said to have lost his senses? Supposing a man fell asleep in the ordinary way after a good dinner and a glass of port, that would be losing his senses and yet it would not be a case of drunkenness; or again, a man with weak nerves and a cut on his skull might take a glass of weak claret and reel around the streets with a dagger to assassinate all within reach, just as badly as a man who had drunk a dozen bottles of Guinness's stout and eaten two dozen oysters to solidify the liquid.

'Certainly, it is impossible to decide,' said the curate to himself, sitting down in his chair, heartened by this impossibility to discover whether he had been drunk or whether he had not been drunk. 'Especially in my case,' he continued, without exactly knowing why his case was special, but he had vague ideas that his case was less blameworthy than Pat Farelly's case for instance, for Pat Farelly was only a peasant and could have no other reason for getting drunk than his own natural wickedness.

Finally he convinced himself that he had not been drunk, that he was not in a state of mortal sin, that he was under no obligation to go to confession before he could celebrate Mass and then . . .

He suddenly jumped to his feet, clasped his two hands together and said, 'Great Holy Jerusalem.' Just then he remembered that all his reasoning, all his apologizing, all his clever advocacy of his own innocence were in vain. There was his crime staring him in the face all the time and he had passed over it. There it was written in letters of black on his conscience. He had broken his pledge by touching drink. He had committed a mortal sin by breaking the pledge for life that he had taken at his confirmation, the pledge that he must never touch alcoholic liquor except on the order of a doctor or in a case of great physical necessity.

He was so overwhelmed by this irrefutable proof of his guilt that he covered his face with his hands. All was now lost for ever. As soon as he admitted one sin others came up before his mind and after a few moments he had convicted himself, with a certain malicious pleasure, of having sinned against the whole ten commandments and finally of having also sinned against all the commandments of the Church. With his head between his hands he gazed dully at his own sins. They appeared like a mountain before him, ever swelling to greater heights. He began to compare himself with other great sinners. Particularly he compared himself to a nun about whom he had read during a retreat at school when he was a boy. She had lived a life of outward sanctity and had died in sanctity, and when they were going to canonize her many years afterwards, a messenger came from heaven to the cardinal who was arranging her papers of canonization to say that the nun was damned in hell for having concealed a mortal sin in her third confession and concealed it ever afterwards through pride or shame of whatever it was she concealed. And through concealing this sin all her confessions were in themselves sins, and all her good deeds were sins, and she had accumulated such a multitude of sins through her life of apparent sanctity that she was loaded with sin at death and was condemned to the lowest place in hell. The curate thought over this case, it so resembled his own, for he was in his mind concealing his sin. Then for a moment he wondered what was the sin the nun had concealed. It could not have been very important since it was in her third confession and she must have been only eight years of age at the time. 'Oh yes,' he murmured, 'I remember, she was an Italian; they develop quickly.'

Then he visualized himself concealing his own sin throughout his life. He would have resurrected Europe from its spiritual apathy. He would have enthroned Catholicism as the dominant power in the world. He would stand out as the greatest of God's children, greater than Charlemagne. He would stand out as a burning pillar of sanctity. He would die and be buried with all the panoply of the Church triumphant, with cardinals marching in state behind his bier, and archbishops with their mitres and hosts of parish priests and heads of monasteries and thousands of nuns, and chanters and incense burners, and a choir of ten thousand virgins, followed by another choir of ten thousand youths, chanting the 'Dies Iræ, dies Illa,' and then he would go down to hell and be damned.

He pictured to himself the expression on the face of the cardinal who would be disturbed in the preparation of his canonization papers by the appearance of a stern-faced angel to say that he, Fr Hugh McMahon, was damned and one of the most sinful of the damned, seventeen chasms below Nero, and enduring twenty degrees more heat than either Henry VIII or Martin Luther.

Horrified at this spectacle that he had conjured up in his mind, a spectacle that he had conjured up so realistically that he saw it plainly before him, he rushed to the cupboard and took out the whisky and filled his glass with the spirits. He was already drunk before the spirit touched his lips, drunk with fright. He sobered as he swallowed the whisky, for the alcohol instead of arousing fantasies scattered those that had already gathered. He felt the calm pervading him that he had felt the first night that he drank. He felt brave.

'Bah!' he said as he sat down, 'what silly rot. Perhaps there is nothing in the whole thing but the dream of a lunatic. I wonder what my father thought of it. Probably never thought of it. That Socialist, John Carmody, says that a man never has any peace of mind until he becomes an agnostic. Fine fellow, that Carmody. Must have a talk to him tomorrow. Wonder what he thinks of hell.'

Friday

FRIDAY in Inverara was indistinguishable from any other day in the week, excepting in Kilmurrage, where the important people lived. In Kilmurrage Friday stood out from the jumble of the other weekdays (jumbled together in Inverara owing to the ozone that made the people too sleepy to even keep count of the days like the people of Tennyson's 'Lotus Eaters') because on that day Fr O'Reilly, by virtue of the power of his Church, ordered that all the faithful should abstain from the use of flesh meat. But outside Kilmurrage, where the use of flesh meat was unknown, except at certain clearly defined periods of the year, at Christmas and Easter and in mid-autumn during the feast of some pagan god or other, this landmark was not sufficient to make Friday different from any other day, because on Friday the peasants ate fish just as they ate fish on Thursday or Monday or Saturday.

The people of Kilmurrage, being more civilized than the rest of the islanders, ate meat occasionally. But, of course, the eating of meat is not fundamentally a mark of superior civilization. In fact, Dr Cassidy maintained that it was not, and that a diet of fish, as the rest of the islanders followed, was far more conducive to high cerebral development; but, of course, Dr Cassidy was old and liable to make mistakes, at least so they said in Kilmurrage.

When Friday came the people of Kilmurrage knew that the day had arrived for fasting and abstaining by getting a strong smell of bacon from John Carmody's house. John Carmody, being a good Socialist and an agnostic, never ate meat for breakfast on any other day of the week but Friday. On Friday he opened wide his kitchen door and the kitchen door opened on the main street, or the nearest approach to a main street that the town provided. He brought his frying-pan as near as possible to the door while he was frying his bacon, and several times, while the bacon was being fried, he was in the habit of taking the pan off the fire and out into the open air, pretending to be out for a look at the sun or at somebody passing, but really so that the smell of the bacon could be more widespread, and to show as many as possible that he cracked his fingers at the vile superstitions which ordained fasting on Friday. Then when he had cooked the bacon, if the day were fine he ate his breakfast outside his house door, sitting on the stone wall with his hat on, because he had heard that Jews always wore their hats while eating, as a sign that they did not believe in the Pope.

So on Friday morning John Carmody was sitting on the stone wall in front of his cottage with his hat on jauntily. Beside him on the wall was a plate of bacon, sizzling fresh from the frying-pan. Pat Coleman, passing up the road, halted in front of Carmody deliberately and aggressively. He took off his hat and crossed himself just as deliberately.

'John Carmody, sir,' he said, 'I'm surprised that a man of your education and travel wouldn't mend your ways, sir.'

'You go clean to hell, you God damn hypocrite,' said John Carmody.

Then he said several other things, for he hated Coleman more than any man in Inverara, and Coleman went up the road and met Mrs Mahoney coming out from Shaughnessy's hotel. He told her about Carmody and said that it was a disgrace to the island of Inverara that he should be allowed to live in it.

'Believe me, ma'am,' he said, 'or don't believe me, what I'm goin' to say, but as sure as I'm alive and an honest man some evil is goin' to befall the place on account of him.'

And Cissy Carmody, John's sister, coming up at that moment with a pail of water from the pump, heard what Pat had said about her brother. She dropped the pail of water on the ground, folded her arms and 'gave Coleman a bit of her mind,' saying that if he were as good a man as her brother he could be proud of himself, and that all his brains were wasted in the size of his feet, which were too big, according to Cissy, even for a policeman. Then she picked up her pail of water, shook herself and hurried home, and when she got home she scolded her brother for disgracing herself in the eyes of the whole world, by being such an idiot and letting people like Pat Coleman laugh at him. Then she went indoors and wondered what the young man in the grey tweed suit and the straw hat would think of her for having such a brother, her brother an atheist and a Socialist and she herself so respectable, and he might think that there was bad blood in her family and have nothing to do with her on that account. She was so disturbed all the forenoon that she put three wrong stitches in a bow she was sewing on her new hat, 'same as Miss Blake has on hers,' she told her friend Mary, later in the day, 'and he belongs to the confraternity of the Sacred Heart and is very religious and what will he ever think o' me when he hears that our John is goin' on like that, an' sure nobody ever came to any good that's been in America losin' their religion among all them sky-scrapers.'

Pat Coleman looked long and anxiously after Cissy Carmody as she retreated down the road with her pail of water, trying to think of a fitting retort, but he failed to think of any as usual. Then he turned to Mrs Mahoney.

'Ma'am, I know ye won't believe me,' he said solemnly, 'but there is some misfortune going to happen to that family. They are under a curse, I tell ye. Look at Cissy and then look at John.'

Mrs Mahoney did look at John. She saw him sitting on his stone wall, nonchalantly and with evident relish eating his rashers of bacon that seemed to be more succulent than usual because it was Friday, and she thought that, God help her, it was seldom she got a rasher to eat Monday or Friday, and that perhaps if she did get a rasher and it happened to be Friday that she would not wait for Saturday to eat it. But she threw her hands, sideways and palms upwards, in the direction of Pat Coleman's chest and said in tones of great anguish:

'Musha! I wonder how he can bring himself to do it and break his poor mother's heart an' she that's dead this three years and sufferin' in purgatory on account of him, God be merciful to her soul.'

'Amen,' said Pat Coleman reverently, looking towards Carmody as if Carmody were an evil demon who was deliberately keeping his poor mother burning in the flames of purgatory.

But Carmody was evidently acting on the principle that a man who has a bad reputation might as well live up to it. He could have no qualms of conscience on the question of his dead mother, for he must have slept well since his appetite was excellent, and when Pat Farelly paused, scratching his beard in front of him, and looked at the bacon greedily, Carmody said to him with a smile:

'Have a bit, Pat? it's best Limerick.'

Pat shook his head mournfully, for he had a good reputation on this matter of observing the Friday fast and he had to live up to it, but having a bad reputation on the matter of drink, he thankfully hurried into Mulligan's to drown the irritating smell of bacon in the smell of porter.

Then Pat Coleman suddenly remembered the cause of his walk towards Shaughnessy's hotel, for he had only digressed from his main purpose in discussing the sins of the Carmodys. He asked Mrs Mahoney did she hear was there anything serious the matter with the curate.

'Why so? said Mrs Mahoney, settling herself into a position of attention.

'Well, to tell ye the honest truth, I was afraid there was somethin' serious the matter, an' I'll tell ye the reason why. He hasn't said Mass for three days runnin', an' I waited meself this mornin' for three-quarters of a solid hour an' he never came, so that I'm afraid that there's somethin' serious the matter with him, an' I only after seein' him last night talkin' and laughin' to O'Malley and that stranger from the mainland; bad company, ma'am, for any respectable man to keep, not to mind a priest.'

But Mrs Mahoney had no news. She had heard nothing, but if there had been anything serious the matter, like pneumonia or rapid consumption, she felt sure that she would have heard it.

'That's enough, ma'am,' said Coleman; 'that's enough, ma'am, and I know ye won't believe me, but there are things goin' on in this island, there are things goin' on in this island that shouldn't.'

He walked away as if the load of responsibility of looking after the morals of the whole island were too great for his shoulders to bear. He moved uneasily around Kilmurrage the whole forenoon. He went down by the sports field where they were setting up the tents and marking out the grounds for the sports. He went around by Mulligan's to see who was spending his time and money on 'poisen,' as he called Mulligan's porter, not because it was bad porter, but because it was porter. He went down again to Carmody's to see whether John Carmody was up to any more 'divilment.' And it was not until he saw the parish priest and the curate cycling into Coill Namhan shortly after twelve o'clock to hear confession that he was finally satisfied. Then he went into Mrs Moroney's, and leaning over the counter pulled at his moustache and said:

'Mrs Moroney, ma'am, I know ye won't believe me, but we'll soon have a new curate in Inverara.'

'Why so, Mr Coleman?' asked Mrs Moroney, intensely and respectfully interested.

'Oh, well, ma'am,' he said with a sigh, 'I'm not in the habit of givin' scandal.'

And then satisfied that he had given scandal he walked to his post office.

The curate rode west to Coill Namhan church with Fr O'Reilly. They rode in silence most of the way, for Fr O'Reilly that morning seemed to be brooding over his own thoughts too much to be able to give any time to the curate. In fact, he had hardly ever any time to talk to his curate. He treated his curate much the same as any army officer would treat his batman. Now and again he uttered disjointed remarks, such as: 'You tell me that the girls in Coill Namhan school are ready for the bishop, eh?' or, 'You knew Canon Farelly in Maynooth; what are his views on politics?' or, 'What d'ye think O'Rourke is up to around here?'

The curate answered these questions as curtly as possible without giving offence, for since the previous night he looked upon Fr O'Reilly as a man to be avoided, as a man from whom he was keeping a secret, a man who at any moment might pounce upon him and annihilate him. Because he felt that he was lacking in his duty towards Fr O'Reilly he began to dislike him intensely as an excuse for his own conduct. He thought Fr O'Reilly a worldly man, and not one whit what a priest should be. As he cycled closely behind him, he examined Fr O'Reilly's body. He noted the fleshy lines of the back pressing against the coat. He noted the fleshiness of the red neck pressing against and above the collar. He thought he resembled a shopkeeper more than a priest, a mass of flesh without any spirituality. He reflected that he himself could not possibly be understood by Fr O'Reilly. He felt sure that if he told Fr O'Reilly his sin the parish priest would not understand it, since he was not a priest at all but a business man in clerical robes. Then he thought that he himself had made a vast mistake by becoming a secular priest. He should have become a Jesuit, cut away from the world, so that he could give all his time to the development of the spiritual in him, and have the association of men who were intellectuals like himself, and not vulgar priests like Fr O'Reilly.

He felt that association with Fr O'Reilly was the cause of his temptation, Fr O'Reilly with that fleshy red neck of his and the portly back. 'Enter not into temptation.' Of course that was it. He had entered into temptation by putting himself on a level with priests like Fr O'Reilly, a priest who was not a priest at all; almost the father of a family, as it were, giving Lily away in marriage and having Mrs Bodkin to look after, merged in all the cares of the world, with kelp factories and politics and everything of that kind. Now, for instance, if he went to China . . . ah yes, but China . . . that would be running away from temptation. He should stay in Europe. There was where the great fight was to be fought. He must not run away and allow priests like Fr O'Reilly abolish all vestiges of spirituality in religion . . . reduce religion to a business matter . . . have the people guided by money-changers in cassocks. . . .

'Be as quick as you can; I want to get back by four o'clock; I am expecting a telegram from the Big Town on the Mainland,' said the parish priest as they dismounted at the church gates.

There was a large crowd already in the church when they entered. It was a sunny June day, an ideal day and time of the year for the peasants of Inverara. But in spite of the contention of priests that the Devil reaps a harvest on idleness, idleness among the peasants of Inverara bred sanctity. Having nothing else to do, they went to confession in large numbers. Since they had not got refined consciences like the curate, going to confession for them was just 'passing the time.' They never had anything serious to tell, so much so that a missionary who once preached in the Coill Namhan church threatened fire and brimstone to all the natives of Inverara indiscriminately, saying that they would all assuredly be damned unless they attained a high degree of sanctity, since temptations in Inverara were scarce and Heaven could only be obtained by successfully resisting temptation. And on that account the inhabitants of Inverara had a very difficult acrobatic feat to perform in order to reach the heavenly reward. They would have, as it were, to go around at night with a torch in one hand to discover temptation lurking among the rocks, and with a spiritual sword in the other hand to annihilate temptation when it were discovered. So great, in fact, was the fear inspired by the missionary that Bartly Sweeney, brother of the religious maniac, if he failed to remember anything worth telling when he was going to confess, cursed vigorously for a half-hour in order to load his conscience with sin.

Having confessed this load of sin he could afterwards persuade himself that he had overcome the temptation to swear.

The curate finished his prayers at the foot of the altar and walked to the confessional box to the right of the baptismal font, while Fr O'Reilly went to the box on the left. The curate closed the little door, sat down, and put his stole about his neck, after kissing it. Immediately there was a rush of feet. The penitents shuffled and pushed and squeezed, trying to get to the confessional box first. Heated arguments developed as to the right of way and priority of arrival. Each strove to get to confession first, either afraid of forgetting their sins, or because they had more important business awaiting them, or perhaps just from pure 'cussedness.' Finally Fr O'Reilly had to come out of his confessional box and order them all back to the pews in front, so that they could come to confession in their turn 'and not hang around the boxes listening.' Then there was a scramble for seats in the pews. Each wanted to get to the very edge of the seats near the aisles, while nobody wished to take a seat on the inside near the walls, so that Fr O'Reilly had to arrange every seat individually, and then he marched back to his box and called out 'First two now.'

The curate slid the grating aside on the left of his box. Presently some one knelt on the ledge outside and began immediately to make an act of contrition with great rapidity. Then somebody knelt on the opposite side of the box, groaning and sighing so loudly that the curate lost his temper.

'I confess to almighty God, to Blessed Mary ever Virgin . . .' The first penitent rushed through the confiteor in a hesitating, hurried, girlish voice, hardly able to enunciate the words with haste and excitement. The curate waited irritably until she had finished.

'How long is it since your last confession, my child?'

'One month, father.'

'What sins have you committed since your last confession?'

As he asked the question he became suddenly ashamed of himself, he who was afraid and ashamed to tell his own sin to Fr O'Reilly asking this girl beyond the grating to tell him her sins. 'Ah, yes,' said a voice within him, in response to the first voice from across the corridor in his brain, as if the Devil prompted from one side and his guardian angel from the other, 'you are the deputy of God; she is not confessing to you but to God through you.' 'Then why not confess to God directly,' came the other voice, the Devil's voice; 'God is omniscient, He does not want an interpreter. . . .'

'I had bad thoughts three times, father: I didn't say my prayers one morning; I told a lie once, father . . .'

'Did you give way to these bad thoughts, my child?'

He was wondering what these bad thoughts were. . . . How silly of a mere child to have bad thoughts; how could anybody have bad thoughts but a grown-up person of intellect and comprehension?

'No, father.'

Ha, even this little girl could overcome her bad thoughts, whereas he himself could not . . . but then, perhaps her thoughts were of no consequence. . . .

'I was rude to my sister; I was distracted during Mass once, father; I was, I was . . . was . . . was, that's all, father.'

'All right, my child, you must try and be more careful in future and say your prayers every morning and be dutiful to your parents, and, and, and say for your penance a decade of the rosary. Make an act of contrition: O my God, I am heartily sorry that I have offended Thee.'

He held his hand over the girl's head, giving absolution for her sins. . . . 'Absolvo te' . . . he wondered whether there was any sense in the whole thing. . . . The Devil across the corridor of his brain had the mastery now, and the guardian angel was silent. . . . What had John Carmody said? . . . Oh yes, nobody had any peace of mind until he became an agnostic. . . . Wonder was there anything in the agnostic's point of view? . . . 'God bless you, my child, go in peace.' . . . Certainly many brilliant men had taken up that point of view. . . . 'But they all came back to the faith before their death,' came the voice of the angel. . . . 'Not at all,' said the devil hurriedly, 'that's a canard spread by the clergy; there's no truth in it.' . . . There was Darwin and Huxley and Haeckel . . . they had a good case if one looked at it from their point of view. . . . Without a doubt there was a conflict between the discoveries of science and what had been hitherto accepted as the origin of the world and of God according to the Biblical version. . . .

'Say the confiteor.'

A fresh penitent came. A heavy lumbering voice recited the confiteor with a foreign accent and slowly, as if it were not a habit. The curate listened for a moment, and then, irritated by the slowness of the peasant, wandered off again. . . .

From certain points of view the existence of Hell was ridiculous. It was a crude theory to an educated mind, this mundane idea of fire and brimstone and eternal punishment . . . probably originated in the pagan worship of fire. . . . The Finns had a conception of Hell as a cold place on account of the perpetual cold in that country. . . . Even so, Hell would not be so bad. . . . Look at the company one would have there, all the greatest minds of the world, Plato, Darwin, all the classic poets, the élite of all the civilizations before Christ, the flower of modern knowledge . . . it was difficult to believe that . . .

'How long is it since your last confession? What? You don't know? Nonsense, you must know. Try and remember. Is it six months? Yes. All right. What do you remember since your last confession?'

'You can't escape from the existence of God,' cried the voice of the angel. 'Who created the stars, the universe? The scientists cannot tell you. Why is anything, unless there is some ulterior motive?' . . .

'Try and remember something. Run over the commandments in your mind, that will help you. Don't be afraid, God will assist you.'

The peasant began to tell about the difficulty he had, but instead of accusing himself of being the culprit, he accused his neighbour. It seemed that the neighbour, whom he did not name, had three sheep, and the sheep were continually trespassing on the penitent's grass. The penitent warned the neighbour several times to look after his sheep, but the neighbour took no notice, and finally the penitent, in order not to be out of pocket, sent his horse to graze on the neighbour's land. He didn't know whether it was a sin or not, but he thought that it would be very unfair to allow the neighbour to trespass with impunity, but the priest would be able to judge for himself which of them was to blame; and then there was another man. . . .

The penitent went on accusing his neighbours of trespass and malicious injury and calumny until the sources of his imagination were exhausted. But the curate had long ago forgotten him. He was lost in his own fancies, and kept on murmuring, 'Yes . . . yes . . . is there anything else?' . . . while he wondered if there was any proof that there was really anything beyond this world. He was trying to probe into infinity, and his mind wandered on and on through space until he was totally lost in the hopelessness of conceiving anything capable of filling the void that his imagination had created, the limitless vacuity that rose up before him. He fell back on the contemplation of a prosaic Heaven, with a personal God seated on a throne, with angels and saints about Him, having earthly bodies and musical instruments . . . but then it struck him that it would be very dull to contemplate this scene for all eternity. . . . He tried to imagine an eternity, an endless succession of millions and billions of years, with no other occupation, no end in view, but to sit and contemplate the Deity on the throne. He shuddered, and turned once more to the penitent.

The penitent had now finished accusing his neighbours, and was waiting sheepishly for his penance.

'Say for your penance ten decades of the rosary and . . . make an act of contrition: O my God — '

He raised his hand again and began the absolution, but when he had finished the peasant was still only halfway through the act of contrition, either because he had forgotten it in his excitement, or because he had never known it. The curate had to help him through word by word to the end, and then he said, 'Go in peace, God bless you'; and he heard at that moment Fr O'Reilly's voice from the opposite box, droning out the 'Absolvo te,' his voice falling away slowly to a low and indistinct mumble. He wondered what Fr O'Reilly was thinking of, or whether he had similar thoughts to his own. How awful it would be for him to tell his sin to Fr O'Reilly if Fr O'Reilly were really an agnostic. He knew that many priests were agnostics. . . . There was Fr McManus, of S — , who was well known to be an atheist in the college, but was not suspended owing to his brilliant genius. . . . If he did tell Fr O'Reilly, and Fr O'Reilly ever had anything against him afterwards, he could make use of what he had heard from him if he were an agnostic.

'Say the confiteor: O my God, I am heartily sorry — '

Goodness gracious, what a fool he had been to make his life miserable for the past few days if all this religion were only a sham and hypocrisy. . . . Instead he should have shown a false front to the world and carried on his life as he wished. . . . Certainly there were many things cut off from him by being a priest. . . . There was Lily, for instance; when he had her in his arms at Dungarvan, the evening she told him that she loved him, he could have married her and lived happily . . . but then, what was happiness? . . . perhaps that, after all, a priest could enjoy all these things if he only . . . He remembered the stories he had heard of the priests in the Middle Ages, how a certain priest was in the habit of saying Mass with a hunting hawk sitting on the corner of the altar, and how two priests laid a wager of a cask of wine to whichever of them would get through the Mass first. . . . Then look at Fr O'Reilly . . . what difference did it make to him whether he was a priest or not. . . . Of course, there was the vow of celibacy, but after all, celibacy. . . . oh well, celibacy . . . of course, his mentality was different from Fr O'Reilly's . . . Fr O'Reilly was not an intellectual; look at that red neck of his, sticking out in layers of fat over his collar . . . it was disgusting to look at . . . and the priest at school told him that he had a very refined conscience and would either make a great saint or a great sinner. . . . Well, it was a consolation to know that if he did not become a great saint he would at least become a great sinner. . . .

'That's all, father,' said the penitent.

'All right, say a decade of the rosary for your penance: O my God . . .'

What was sin, anyway? . . . It was impossible to differentiate between good and bad . . . he had read somewhere that it all depended on the conception of the individual . . . where had he read that? . . . Yes, of course it was forbidden to read those books, but why was it forbidden? . . . He remembered that he had been caught reading Mark Twain's *Innocents Abroad* at college, and had almost been expelled for doing so . . . and yet Mark Twain was considered to be one of the best American writers, and he knew that the priests read the books themselves, and worse books than that, for he had seen the Dean of studies in the same college reading *Bel Ami*, by Guy De Maupassant. . . . It was all very well for them to define as good what suited their own interests as priests or what praised their religion, and as bad whatever was contrary to their own interests. . . . 'Bad is a diminution of reality.' . . . Oh yes, that's what that theologian had said, McDonald or somebody, but he didn't say what was reality. . . . 'Good and bad are relative terms; they are relative to the psychology of the individual, and the psychology of the individual is always governed by his surroundings.' . . . Somebody had told him that, a fellow he had an argument with in the 'Hibernian Hotel' in Dublin . . . taken, of course, from the works of some agnostic philosopher or other. Still, there was a lot to be said in favour of it . . . and at that rate how was it possible to denounce drunkenness as bad: . . .

'Go in peace, my son, God bless you.'

He pushed aside the grating on the opposite side to hear the next confession.

While it might have been bad for him to get drunk on certain occasions, very possibly it was good for him to get drunk when he did. It might have saved him from losing his mind. 'You were losing your mind because you allowed temptation to enter,' cried the angel in his brain. But the Devil cried again scoffingly and angrily across the corridor, 'Why should it be labelled temptation? Why should a desire to marry Lily be called a temptation; tell me?' Yes, of course, there was a point of view . . . why should it be a temptation? . . . it was natural in every one to marry a mate; even the animals took a mate and were fond of them; somebody had said that the first instinct in man was the instinct of self-preservation, to reproduce the race, increase and multiply . . . surely it could not be a temptation to conform to the dictates of Nature . . . could it? Of course, it was said that . . .

'Go in peace. What's that? You have forgotten your penance — oh yes, say five Hail Marys for a week every night before you go to bed.'

Of course, they said a priest was celibate so that he could give his whole time to God, but what did they really know of God? . . . and wouldn't it be better if priests raised families, just to show the lay person how to raise their children properly. . . . They would do more good by setting a good example. . . . It was cowardice and shirking their social duties more than anything else, to escape the necessity of rearing children, escaping the responsibility of propagating the race. Certainly the whole thing was ridiculous . . . from a reasonable point of view it had nothing to support it. . . . Wonder why he had never thought of that before?. . . . Why should he confess his sin? . . . what should he fear? He had robbed no man, murdered no man, done no man any harm . . . he was simply tempted to obey the laws of Nature, and now this desire to obey the law of Nature had been turned into a crime by some inexorable deity . . . it was monstrous. . . .

Then he became interested in the penitent who was kneeling at the grating of the confessional box. For a moment he thought that it was Lily, the gentle cultured voice, so unlike the rough voices of the peasants . . . but no, she was a stranger, some tourist or other, and she leaned so closely against the grating and spoke in such a low voice that he had to put his ear close to the grating in order to hear. He asked her to speak more loudly but, afraid of being heard by the others in the church, she still continued in a whisper. His cheek was moistened by her hot breath, and he could smell the scent from her clothes. She reminded him so much of Lily that he trembled and cursed his folly that night in Dungarvan.

The woman began to tell her sins, trivial matters like the sins of the others. She had bad thoughts, but she had not given way to them; she had told lies, but she had not been conscious of them; she had been careless in her prayers, but . . . and so she continued accusing herself and defending herself until the curate grew tired of her and lost interest. He rehearsed again all the arguments that he had used in proof of the futility of the function he was now fulfilling, absolving these people from sin. In short, he proved to himself that the Catholic religion was ridiculous. He paused for a moment and considered the Protestant religion, and he found that still more ridiculous, trying to make infinity and mystery conform to reason, trying to democratize something that owed its existence to a blind belief in the dictatorship of a supreme Being. Then he allowed the existence of a supreme Being and questioned the deity of Christ. He shuddered at this thought, but the accusing voice of the angel was drowned by the cries of the demon from across the corridor, hurling an avalanche of jeers and proofs and reasonings and scientific discoveries against the plaintive voice of the angel that cried: 'You must believe, you have no escape; down in your heart you know.' Then, having drowned the voice of the angel, he reasoned that Christ was a great genius, a great reformer, the greatest of men. And then, having established that point to his satisfaction, he went back again to the question of the supreme Being. He began to wonder whether there was really a hereafter, and wondered how he was going to accept the idea of a hereafter if he refused to accept the religious conception of a hereafter. He wondered what course of action would be guided by what object in view. Then the thought of there being no hereafter and no purpose to his actions in life, no cause for anything but fantastic theories that were incapable of comprehension or of being examined even by reason, disturbed him so much, and it brought such formidable fears to his mind, that he paled in the gloom of the confessional box. He paled so that he could almost see himself turn pale. He was on the point of calling out for help to the woman penitent, so desirous was he of feeling the companionship of a fellow-being to assure himself that he was not wandering alone in a limitless infinity with no bourne to guide him, wandering in an emptiness. But he restrained himself and listened to the woman reciting her act of contrition as slowly and devoutedly as she had defended her innocence and virtue.

Then he fell back on his thoughts again. The voice of the angel was now drowning the voice of the demon, crying: 'Believe, believe, and you are saved; there is no hope but in religion, there is no consolation but in the unquestioning acceptance of the Divine Saviour.' And in order that the voice of the demon might not again assail him he said hurriedly to the woman, 'Go in peace, my child, God bless you,' and rising from his seat he left the confessional box.

He stood outside the church door for a minute, while the breeze played on his brow, thinking of nothing. His brain seemed to be an amorphous mass from which no thought ensued, as if the whole category of ideas and thoughts had been jumbled together in a heap by the mental hurricane which he had just endured and had congealed into a solid mass by the sudden freezing cold of his fear. He amused himself by watching a little sparrow jumping along the branches of the rose bush that grew by the church wall. Then his mind wandered from the sparrow and he looked within the church. The young women were kneeling in the pews nearest to him saying their prayers before confession and whispering to one another: 'Who are you going to, Julia?' — 'The curate, he is the nicest, he never says anything'; 'The parish priest gave me ten decades o' the rosary last time and said awful things to me; I'm not goin' near him.' 'Are ye goin' to the dance tomorrow night, Bridgie?' — 'I am, are you? — but o' course I needn't ask ye; Dan Finnigan'll be there.' 'Go on with ye, yer afther him yersel'.' And then the old man with the parchment face and the bleary bloodshot eyes and the big red muffler coiled around his neck, like the figure of a mummy, mummified from the shoulder upwards, suddenly broke the silence. With a loud wailing cry he asked God and all the saints to have mercy on him a sinner, and then his voice died away slowly and he made a sibilant sound with his lips, as if he were sucking a sweet. The girls all giggled and the parish priest called out in a loud voice from his confessional box 'Silence there.' Then the curate walked back to his box.

The fresh air and the exercise had brought him back to the reality of his surroundings. It had, as it were, shown to him the ugly nature of the world around him — the voice of the old man with the mummified face, the giggling of the girls, the drone of Fr O'Reilly's voice, all showed him the chasm that divided him, a priest and an intellectual, from the vulgar world about him. He felt that if he burst through the dream, even though it were but a dream, that bound him to the worship of God, with all its attendant splendour and intellectual ecstasy, he would become deprived of all that he found beautiful in life. He would deprive himself of the right to clothe anything he did or felt or said in the robes of virtue. It was the power to do so alone that made them beautiful. Without that power he would have nothing. He would have no measure to weigh anything if he broke the one standard he possessed, the standard of religion. It was too late now to establish another.

Then when he looked at the controversy from this point of view, from the point of view of his own personal pleasure, he found it easy to silence the voice of the demon who counselled unbelief. He felt as if his own property had been attacked, and that the demon in his brain who was denouncing religion and scoffing at the existence of God was a burglar, who was clothing his house-breaking implements in the mask of reason. So he said firmly and calmly and proudly, 'I believe, my God, I believe.' But as soon as he had admitted to himself that he believed, the angel within him, eager to take advantage of this first victory, suggested confession of the sin that was still on his soul, and the momentary peace that he had felt by acknowledging his belief changed again into the same torrential flow of recriminations and fears and shames that he had experienced, before reason, eager to save itself from the darts of conscience, had challenged the existence of the whole structure and basis of the supernatural. He felt suddenly and actively angry, like a wild beast who is hunted and turns to an avenue of escape only to find that it ends in a trap. He turned in his rage on the young woman who was now confessing her sins with her shawl thrown far out over her head, so that the edge of it touched the grating and the damp smell pervaded his nostrils. He turned on her and scolded her for her sinfulness, and prophesied that if she did not mend her ways and lead a better life an evil end would befall her. Then he gave her as penance the Stations of the Cross seven times, and the young woman returned to her seat, picked up her prayer book and left the church immediately and told her friends on the way to Kilmurrage that the curate shouldn't be a priest at all. 'Lord save us, he flew at me, just before I had begun telling him anything, and gave me an awful penance without hearin' a word of what I had to say, an' 'twill be a long time 'fore I go near him again.'

The curate's passion spent itself, having nothing upon which it could feed. He sat in silence without thought during the following two confessions and gradually he felt comforted, as if he had rid his soul of sorrow by his outburst. Tears welled into his eyes and a softness came into his heart. He began to pity himself and turned to Christ for succour in his weakness. During the next two confessions, while he murmured 'Say ten decades of the rosary,' or 'Make an act of contrition,' or 'Go in peace,' he was making his own confession to Christ, accusing himself with nihilistic vehemence of enormous sins, magnifying his sins, with a wish to prove his repentance and his humility. But again this ecstasy of devotion gave way to its counterpart of weariness, and the demon in his brain, eager to take advantage of this weariness, cried: 'You have deluded yourself; Christ did not hear you, nobody heard you, for Christ is a myth; He died on Calvary, He has been dead since.'

The curate turned around with a scowl so certain was he that the voice was not within but without him, but even as he turned, looking for something to attack, he knew there was nothing, and feeling his impotency to revenge himself on these malicious attacks on his peace of mind, he became thoroughly miserable.

'I have to be going now,' said Fr O'Reilly, knocking outside his confessional box, 'you must try and get through with the rest.'

The parish priest stalked away, yawning in a loud voice, and the curate swore softly. He felt so tired sitting in that cramped little box, with all the insanitary smells that were thrust at him through the gratings, listening to the dreary and monotonous repetitions of lies told and bad thoughts resisted or not resisted, and trespassing of sheep and donkeys, and scandal listened to and repeated, and immoral desires and all the rest of the sins that were hurled at him pell-mell in endless succession. He felt sure that it was the monotony that was troubling him and not the struggle that was going on within him.

But just then the demon cried aloud in his brain, with a victorious strain in his voice as if he were mocking and jeering the angel: 'If you believed in your priesthood and in the reality of God and in the efficacy of the function you are performing, you would not find it monotonous and uncomfortable.' And in reply the angel cried solemnly and fearfully: 'Believe, believe,' as if it had failed in argument and now wished to save the curate by being dogmatic and imperious. And the curate struggled hard to believe, but nothing came of the struggle, for the demon and the angel now seemed to have rushed at one another from the opposite sides of his brain and were engaged in mortal conflict for the mastery. There was a perfect chaos of impressions flashing across his mind, fleeting impressions that were strangled almost before they reached his consciousness, as if the demon were smiting the angelic impressions and the angel were smiting the demoniacal impressions. A perfect whirlwind of thought floated around his brain in confusion, as if the store-room of his brain had been burst open and looted.

To escape from the turmoil of his thoughts he turned to the old lady who was now confessing. Gradually he became interested. She was telling a story of a neighbour who had put 'the evil eye' on her son. She went to the neighbour and asked her to remove it, but the neighbour denied absolutely that she had imposed the 'evil eye,' 'although the whole village knew she had done it, an' I had to go an' lay me hands on her, father, the good God be merciful to me.' The priest forgot that he should warn her about the gross danger of believing in such superstitions as 'the evil eye,' and began to question her on how she discovered that her son was under the influence of the spell, but the old woman had no further particulars than that 'he wasn't takin' his food proper, an' it's well known that she has got the "evil eye," an' she has a grudge against me since I won the lawsuit against her for pullin' down the fence on me backyard.' The curate was vexed with the old woman for having no more definite information, for he had imagined subconsciously that he himself might be suffering from the 'evil eye' as a reason for his temptations, so he turned on the old lady and abused her for believing in superstitions, and assured her that the ground would open up and swallow her if she persisted in paying attention to such things in future. 'And for your penance make three journeys to St Hoolan's well,' a popular penance for sins of that sort. For St

Hoolan's well was supposed to rid people of evil spells, and every Sunday throughout the year pilgrims went there to drink three seashellfuls of the spring water, and walk around it three times in their bare feet, saying three *Ave Marias* every time they circled it. Then they knelt in front of it after the third round and recited five *Pater Nosters*, and finally left at the well whatever article of property in their possession they valued least, so that the well was always surrounded, like a scarecrow, with pieces of red petticoats and cotton handkerchiefs and rosary beads, and the fact that the pilgrims left their rosary beads there did not speak well for the value they imposed on these means of prayer.

For another half-hour the penitents came and went, stammering and mumbling, remembering sins and failing to remember the time of their last confession, recriminating themselves, their neighbours, and the weather, confessing to Almighty God, and expressing heartfelt sorrow for their sins, while the curate listened carelessly and wearily, delivering penances with the nonchalance of a judge at the County Assizes, and at the same time debating in his own mind whether he believed or whether he did not believe. Sometimes he was perfectly convinced that he did believe, and at other times he was equally convinced that he did not believe; at one time assured of the existence of a hereafter; at another fearful lest it should exist and merit him eternal damnation; at another moment laughing at the idea of a life after death and of a Hell of roaring flames; and then, finally, conjuring up before his mind a vision of Hell, with souls roasting and flaming and burning among the giant furnaces, while myriads of Devils stood around them grinning and taunting them. And then he saw his own soul among the damned, naked and weird, with flames starting from the fleshless skull, and across the fleshless breast a scroll, upon which was written in letters of red 'drunkenness,' and then beneath another scroll inscribed . . . but he was afraid to read that scroll, until the Devil who was raging victoriously in his brain shrieked at him, 'Thou shalt not covet thy neighbour's wife.' And then the last penitent left the grating and the curate rose and sighed.

As he walked up the church towards the sacristy he saw the schoolmistress of Coill Namhan school on the altar decorating it for the festival on the following day. She was rushing from one end of the altar to the other with flowers and vases, pouring water from one vase into another, pouring water from another vase into a pail, with no other purpose than to make the work as hard as possible and thus gain a greater indulgence for personal services rendered to the Almighty, just like women get the Order of the British Empire in England during a war for upsetting hospitals and driving ambulances into ditches. Or perhaps, and this was probably the real reason, that the schoolmistress wished to stay as long as possible on the altar in full view of the people who were still praying in the church after confession, for on the altar she attained a certain prominence that was pleasing to her vanity, since the altar had a distinct and easily recognizable association with the most important man in Inverara, Fr O'Reilly, whose proper place was at the altar, though he was oftener off the altar than on it, metaphorically speaking. And the schoolmistress had still a further interest in decorating the altar, for she thought that if she did it artistically the schoolmaster, Mr O'Hagan, would admire her for having done it so well, and it might arouse in him an interest in herself and her new pink blouse that she had bought specially in Clery's of Dublin to attract him, but there at least her labours were wasted. For the schoolmaster was not artistically inclined, and took no interest in the decoration of altars, or in altars themselves, except in their association with getting rid of inspectors and bishops and the poverty of his profession.

The curate knelt at the foot of the altar to pray, and the schoolmistress, coming down from the altar, bowed reverently to him, just to show the peasants and the lady tourist that she was on terms of almost familiarity with the priest even within the sacred precincts of the church, where even angels whispered, afraid to make a noise. And the curate answered the bow and knelt down, thinking how everybody respected him as a holy man, and how terrible it would be for them to discover the temptations from which he was suffering. He did not pray while he knelt, for he feared that if he prayed to God, God might get vexed and denounce him then and there to the people.

He went into the sacristy. The schoolmistress was arranging more flowers in a vase, flowers for the altar of the Blessed Virgin, and waiting to catch a glimpse of Mr O'Hagan. For Mr O'Hagan always walked into Kilmurrage on Friday evenings, as a set duty, to have supper with the schoolmaster of Kilmurrage boys' school, who was looked upon as the most respectable man in Inverara, and therefore deserving to be cultivated by the respectable O'Hagan.

The schoolmaster of Kilmurrage was respectable as distinct from important, and he owed his intense respectability to the fact that he always wore a very stiff and very high collar (even in bed, according to Johnny Grealish), and this collar caused him to hold his head very erect, giving him the appearance of a man who was standing upright proudly, to be examined in every detail by the scrutiny of a critical world, and concealing nothing that might wound the susceptibilities of the most diligent inquirers into the existence of skeletons in closets.

The curate was talking to the schoolmistress about the benediction for the following Sunday, when a horse approached from the west, coming at a mad gallop. The schoolmistress rushed to the door and immediately uttered a little scream.

'Oh, it's Mr McSherry's servant,' she said. 'I wonder what's the matter.'

The curate ran out to see old Dennis dismounting at the church gate and McSherry's new stallion lathered in sweat, with its sides heaving. Old Dennis ran up the steps with his cap in his hand.

'Oh, father, hurry on over, it's the master, he's dyin', he's been took sudden.'

Then he doubled back to his horse, mounted again, and galloped away towards Kilmurrage.

The curate cycled westwards hurriedly.

'Am I sorry or glad that he's dying?'

He felt that McSherry's death would somehow bring Lily nearer to him, but how, since he was a priest, could that be so? And, again, even if he were not a priest, the fact still remained that she scorned him, and that he was almost certain that she was in love with O'Malley.

'It can only be an infatuation; she loved me first.'

Yes, quite; it was only an infatuation for O'Malley. She could not possibly prefer O'Malley to himself and, further, he himself now had a different way of looking at things that would make much difference in her attitude. The curate of yesterday was dead, the shy awkward priest was dead. The curate of today would be cunning, diplomatic, attractive. He had a different standard of life, he was like other priests, who had not a too-refined conscience, just like the priest who said Mass with the hawk on his altar. This new curate would make a different impression on women. He would attract a woman whom the old curate had repelled. He would be able, without blushing to the roots of his hair and stumbling like a fool, to say the things that the other curate could never say, seductive things. McSherry's death, what of it? What use was he in life? He had lived his life, and by all accounts his living of it was not all to his credit: look at the way he carried on the day he had gone to visit him. Why should he not die? This sentimentality about death was all very well for the old curate with his childish respect for the conventions of religion. These things were all right for the common people, respecting things like that, living up to the very letter of religious beliefs. . . . There was that priest who told him that he needn't trouble about doubts that he had about Jonah being able to live three days in a whale's belly, saying that things of that sort were of no account and only useful to impress the masses, just as they were impressed by sleight-of-hand tricks on the stage. For intellectuals these things were mere trifles to be accepted or rejected according to the taste of the individual; . . . of course, that priest was afterwards unfrocked for writing a treatise in defence of the Materialist Conception of History, but still . . . one had to admit that there were things that the masses could accept but could not be accepted by the better-informed among the clergy . . . though some of the clergy were just as ignorant as the peasants. . . .

He was met at the door of McSherry's house by Mrs Murphy. Mrs Murphy was in a state of great excitement, for this last blow was another insult to her dignity. In the other houses in which she served nobody ever had the indecency to be 'taken sudden like that.' And the new girl who had taken the place of Kate Mahoney was stupid and unsatisfactory, and had taken fright when Mr McSherry collapsed in the dining-room after dinner, rolling on to the floor and gasping for breath. She was now sitting in her room with her apron thrown over her head in a state of horror. So Mrs Murphy, mastering her grief and indignation, said to the curate, 'He is better now, father, thanks be to God for His mercies'; and, groaning under the load of her surplus flesh and her surplus sorrow, she led him to McSherry's room. She stopped the curate outside the bedroom door to whisper, 'Be as quiet as possible with him, for he's in an awful state, God forgive me, swearin' at "herself,"an' she's never gone near him, but sat in the library there as unconcerned as ye like, readin' a book as if he were a heathen Turk.'

The curate entered the room and found McSherry lying on the

bed with his clothes on. He had refused to be undressed, saying that it looked too much like death, and that he might be murdered in his sleep. He just turned his head when the curate entered and said in a low, harsh voice:

'What the hell are you doing here?'

He was trying even in his pain to be the cool, hard, calculating McSherry, who had made a fortune in South America by his hardness.

'Your servant asked me to come.'

'Huh, I will dismiss him when he comes back. Is he back yet?'

'No; he is gone to Kilmurrage for the doctor and the parish priest, I think.'

'Send them away again when they come, what do I want with them? There is nothing the matter with me, I am merely having a rest. Can't I rest in my own house without having the whole island rushing in to disturb me, curse the place?'

And he determined as soon as he got fit again he would leave and go down to South America, where he would have something to occupy his mind other than worrying about a slut of a wife. There was the real life for him down there, making a name for himself and amassing wealth . . . there was that proposition in Antofagasta, for instance, that water-supply scheme they were talking about; it was a half-million-dollar job, and he was the only man fit to take it in hand . . . he was only fifty, not an hour too old, and there wasn't another man in the whole of South America could touch him yet in engineering . . . he was wasting his time in Inverara. What the devil good was there in founding a family? The only thing worth while was the struggle with life, and he could have all the pleasure he wanted besides down there, women by the dozens . . . there was nothing the matter with him, all he needed was a pick-me-up and the voyage out would just set him right; he would be quite fit when he landed there, ready to take up the old fight again. Ha! there was nothing like it, the struggle for the mastery of men. Still, he would be the better for this experience. They would say of him: 'There's that old dog McSherry, the hard-bitten devil went over to Europe, got a beautiful wife and left her without a murmur; wanted to come back to the old grind again. By God, he's got the grit!' Just what they would say. Left her without a murmur. Of course he would leave her, the whore!

The curate had stood standing in silence looking at the floor.

He had been angered by the insulting tone of McSherry, and his anger at being insulted by this infidel layman made him forget the theories of the afternoon, made him forget everything but the fact that he was a priest in the presence of an unbeliever.

'You have a soul to save,' he said in response to his own thoughts.

McSherry started suddenly, being brought back from his reverie of South America and his plans for the future. He stared at the curate. The curate flushed angrily.

'Do you want to confess?' he asked.

'What the devil do you take me for?' cried McSherry, purple in the face. 'Do you think I am a superstitious peasant? What do I want to confess? I have not robbed a bank or murdered anybody, and you're not a policeman, the damn cheek of you!'

The curate was forced farther back into the psychology of the old curate by this outburst, this attack on his prerogatives as a priest and as a shepherd of souls. While it was he himself who accused religion, his opposition had lain dormant. But now, when religion was accused by an outsider, a layman, he rushed to arms immediately to defend it. His whole being responded to the call to arms. The theories of the afternoon fell to pieces. The old loyalty returned. Reason, with her grumblings and her doubts, vanished and pride held sway, pride in his calling and a grim determination to defend his calling against all comers.

'You have a soul,' he said proudly, 'and it is my mission to care for souls. You cannot forget that you have a soul.'

'I have a soul. I cannot forget that I have a soul.'

McSherry repeated the phrases almost to himself. He had forgotten that he had a soul, any kind of a soul — a religious soul, or a moral soul, or a soul capable of appreciating goodness or beauty, or nature or art. He had forgotten it. He had lost it, and he began to wonder whether he had ever had one; or, if he had one, where had he lost it? Was it when he had the fever in Rosario after his first heavy debauch at the carnival, when he had lain seven weeks on his bed, in the burning hot sun, on the verge of death, and he had come back to health so different to the innocent youth he was before; or was it when he had a certain disease in Buenos Ayres, which the doctors told him they had completely cured, but which left a certain dizziness in his head ever afterwards, and caused him violent pains and mental aberrations whenever he took drink in excess; or was it when he was building a railroad in South Africa and paid his native workers with pepper-and-salt waistcoats at half-a-crown apiece instead of their monthly wage of thirty shillings; or was it when he was up in Central Equador, when he was in charge of his first big construction contract and a woman, who had lost her husband in the employ of the company, came to him for assistance, and he offered her help provided she gave him her young daughter for his amusement? Where had he lost his soul, or did he ever have one? It appeared to him that he had never had one, and it vexed him to think that he should be reminded of it, just when he was satisfied with going back again to South America to take up the threads of his life where he had left off. It seemed to him that there was something of which he was deficient, of which no great man should be deficient, and this lout of a priest had reminded him of it.

'What do you know about a soul?' he said to the curate, with as much fury as he could muster.

The curate was knocked completely out of his confident attitude towards religion by this question. It sounded so much like the question the demon in his brain had been hurling at him all the afternoon. It vividly reminded him of his own failure, his own uncertainty, his own doubts. He reddened in the face slightly and kept silent. Twice he tried to speak and to explain, but something held him back, telling him not to be a hypocrite, since he himself knew no more about the soul than McSherry did. But finally he made an effort to save his self-respect, and mumbled:

'You will learn yet, when it is too late,' and he walked out of the room.

And McSherry lay back on his bed and laughed, satisfied now that he was deficient of nothing because of the conduct of the curate. He felt sure now that there was no such thing as a soul, and that all was well with him.

The curate left the room dissatisfied with himself. He felt that he had not done his duty as he should have done it. He had not made a sufficiently hard fight for McSherry's soul. He decided to wait until the doctor came. He would talk to McSherry again after the doctor had left. He would be more amenable then to discussion and reason. He had heard that people on their death-bed were more resigned and religiously inclined after the visit of the doctor than before, probably because they looked on the doctor as the precursor of the undertaker, and take the point of view of the criminal who makes a confession on the scaffold of the murder which he had hitherto consistently denied.

Mrs Murphy showed him into the library to wait for the doctor. He had taken a seat before he noticed the presence of Lily, and when he did see her he did not know whether to advance or retreat. For the life of him he could not come to a decision, but stayed in his seat without speaking.

Lily did not notice him. She was reading by the French window. She had gone to that window when her husband fell in the dining-room, after insulting her vilely and accusing her of having sexual relations with O'Malley, because he had caught her that morning talking to O'Malley at the gate. She had come to the library to read, and in spite of the woman in her that was suggesting that she should go to her husband and nurse him because he was ill, even though he was cruel to her, something held her back and laughed to scorn this sentimentality.

The curate tried to remember what he had decided on the road from the church, about becoming a callous priest and being gallant to women, and making himself attractive by being daring in his conversation. He tried to say something fitting to the occasion, but, try as he would, he could not frame the words. Where was he to begin? Was he to apologize, and, if so, for what? Was he to commiserate with her on the illness of her husband, and if he were to do so, how would she receive it? He drew up a speech in his mind, adding the appropriate gestures, picturing the attitudes he would adopt and the variations of his voice as he delivered it. But when he was near the end of his rehearsal, Lily moved at the window and disturbed him. He lost the thread of his speech and began all over again with a different one. This time he thought it better to lay stress on his own sufferings. He thought that would appeal to her as a woman. He felt he knew what would appeal to women. He had an idea that all women were overcome if anybody wept at their feet and sobbed out their sorrows.

However, when he had his speech completed he still kept silent. He found fault with one sentence. He felt ashamed to deliver another sentence. He failed to find a good rhetorical construction for a third. And in the end he became so absorbed in the making of the speech that he lost the thought of delivering it. He kept repeating it in his own mind for his private satisfaction. He determined to use some of the points that came to his mind in the sermon on the following day. Then he thought it would be a pity to waste it on the Coill Namhan congregation, and decided to write it out and deliver it at some church meeting in Dublin, when important people were present. He would become an eminent preacher one day, the greatest in Ireland . . . and then he suddenly started and sprang to his feet.

Lily had turned her chair abruptly towards the window, so as to get her back to the curate. She had been thinking of him, while he had sat there in silence. She had noticed that he was trying to bring himself to talk to her, to ask her forgiveness, and she was hoping that he would do so. She felt weak and in need of assistance and sympathy, and she had determined to forgive him everything, even the slighting of her love, if he came to her as a friend in that hour of need, when she was alone without a friend. In spite of the firm front she was presenting to the world, she felt weak, and there were tears behind her tearless eyes ready to gush out. Her silence was a bulwark against an outburst of sorrow that the least friendly word might evoke. But as the curate kept silent, this weakness left her. She became hard once more. She thought that the curate looked upon her as a heartless woman, sitting reading while her husband was in danger of death. She said to herself, 'How ridiculous to think that he could be anything else but a hypocrite,' and she moved her chair farther into the recess of the window.

The curate jumped to his feet. His lips moved, trying to speak, but he was saved the embarrassment by the opportune arrival of the Cassidys. The Cassidys were coming up the drive in their trap at a gallop, but the gallop was in no wise due to the efforts of the Cassidy mare. It was due to McSherry's stallion, for the Cassidy mare had at the last moment refused to be harnessed to the trap, and the stallion had to take her place. And the stallion, being full-blooded and in good condition, was so infuriated when the discordant noises started within the trap that he set off at a break-neck gallop, and stayed at his gallop, in spite of the combined efforts of Mrs Cassidy and old Dennis, until he arrived panting and snorting at McSherry's door.

The curate rushed out and Mrs Murphy rushed out to help the Cassidys to alight. Mrs Cassidy gave old Dennis 'a bit of her mind,' and threatened to take an action against him for not having been able to get the stallion under control. Dr Cassidy alighted, groaning and murmuring that he was not as young as he used to be, signifying that, if he were, he himself would have kept the stallion under control.

'Where is the parish priest?' asked the curate.

Old Dennis said that he had been suddenly called by telegram to the Big Town on the Mainland, and had left in Mr Blake's yacht, to escort a bishop to the sports or something. Old Dennis did not know what in his excitement.

Mrs McSherry met Mrs Cassidy in the hall.

'Good afternoon,' she said coldly.

Mrs Cassidy went up to her and said in a low voice, as if it were something that concerned her and Mrs McSherry privately:

'I'm sorry for yer trouble, Mrs McSherry.'

Mrs McSherry said nothing. She could say nothing. She was ready to fall on Mrs Cassidy's chest if that good woman gave her an opportunity, while Mrs Cassidy was waiting for Mrs McSherry to suggest that they should retire into a room and be alone for a few minutes, and Lily was waiting for Mrs Cassidy to suggest the same thing, and Mrs Cassidy thought that Mrs McSherry was too proud because she did not want to suggest it, and Mrs McSherry thought that Mrs Cassidy was unsympathetic and coarse because she did not suggest it, and the two women became cold and frigid the one to the other.

'Show them upstairs,' said Lily to Mrs Murphy, and then she herself retired to the library once more. The curate waited outside, not wishing to trouble Mr McSherry with another visit, or sit with Lily after the ordeal he had undergone.

Upstairs the Cassidys entered the sick-room. McSherry rose on his elbow to look at them.

'Are you the doctor? — yes, good evening. Allow me, Mrs Cassidy, to ask you to withdraw. I hope you will not take offence, but it is not usual; you understand what I mean.'

Mrs Cassidy, who had grown used to attending sick calls with her husband, in order to look after him and 'keep him from making a fool of himself,' suddenly remembered that she was in the presence of a 'gentleman.' She apologized and retired, but outside the door she vowed that she was disgracing herself by associating herself with such low people as the McSherrys, man and wife, 'upstarts of the worst kind they are,' she told Mr Blake the following day at the sports, though she herself was the daughter of a man who kept a little grocer's shop in a town in the Midlands.

'Do you know anything about medicine, Dr Cassidy?' asked McSherry.

The doctor was still standing in the centre of the room, with his carpet bag still in his hand, as if he had been rendered totally incapable by the loss of his wife. He was so surprised by the question that he let the bag drop to the floor.

'Eh, eh, what's that?' he said, with a horizontal forward jerk of his head. 'Ha, ha! Do I know anything about medicine? It's my business.'

'Damn your business; that's the reason I ask you, because it is your business. If it weren't your business, you might know something about it.'

Mrs Cassidy, listening outside the door as carefully as she could without injuring her self-respect, said to herself, 'The low cur, to talk to John like that.'

'I was supposed,' began Dr Cassidy meditatively, rising to a high note, as he always did when he wanted to be impressive, 'I was supposed to be the best theoretician in the country in my time. If I had had the means, I might have —'

But what the doctor might have done if he had had the means was never discovered, for at that moment a discreet cough was heard on the landing, and the doctor remembered that his wife was out there; and since the subject of what the doctor might have done if he had had the means was distasteful to the doctor's wife, and in a way connected with the brilliant theoretician marrying the daughter of the country grocer, who was a nurse in a Dublin hospital where the brilliant theoretician was practising, and because the brilliant theoretician had been indiscreet like many brilliant men in his relations with nurses . . . the doctor veered off from the subject of what might have been.

'I remember —' he began, going to dwell on the safer subject of his reminiscences.

'Do you know anything about the heart?' said McSherry impatiently.

'Do I know anything about the heart, is it?'

The doctor suddenly became all interest. Years seemed to fall from his shoulders. There was a youthful note in his voice. His eyes gleamed.

'It was my special subject,' he cried eagerly and joyfully. 'I never got an interesting case in Inverara, never anything like that.'

He furiously emptied his carpet bag on the table. He hunted for his instruments hurriedly.

'The heart, the most interesting organ, so susceptible to every disease, so responsive to every fault in the human organism, the sounding-board. Where the devil is my stethoscope? Ha, here it is — the heart, the heart. Well now, let me see.'

He assembled his instruments and approached the bed. In a few minutes the shy and retiring and apparently senile Dr Cassidy had become an eager, bustling, energetic, overbearing, dominant man. He began to make a minute and careful examination of McSherry. He questioned him. He browbeat him. He handled him as roughly as an army doctor would handle a malingering soldier at an army clearing-station. He suspected the veracity of his statements. He told him point-blank that he was concealing something. He threatened him. He apostrophized the air, appealing to dead authorities on the heart and living authorities on the heart, as if McSherry were a subject in a dissecting-room and served no other useful purpose than to offer an opportunity to Dr Cassidy of showing his professional knowledge.

Finally, when he had finished, he gazed long and wistfully at McSherry, rubbing his chin through his grey beard, with violent satisfaction showing in every feature.

'The most interesting case I have ever seen,' he said slowly.

McSherry lay on his bed with his firm jaw relaxed and fear in his features. The vision of returning to South America had vanished, before the vision of approaching death that had been conjured up by Dr Cassidy examining him as if he had been a pauper corpse, sold to a hospital for five shillings to teach young medical students their trade. The sight of the senile and browbeaten doctor becoming suddenly young and active, and browbeating instead of been browbeaten, appeared to McSherry as a sign that his end was at hand, and that this was the dissolution of all things that he held important.

But just then Mrs Cassidy's voice was heard in the corridor talking to Mrs Murphy, and the doctor, hearing the voice of his wife, underwent a transformation. Like Oisin returning from the Land of Youth, a strong and comely warrior, became wizened and aged when his saddle-girth broke and he touched the ground, fallen from his fairy charger, so the doctor, hearing the voice of his wife, lost his youth and energy, and McSherry, seeing the metamorphosis in the doctor, shook himself and understood that he had been dreaming.

'If you take any more drink, intoxicating drink,' said the doctor in his old shrill and weak voice, 'you are lost. You might die any minute.'

McSherry smiled in derision.

'Good day, doctor,' he said. 'Send on the bill.'

And the doctor left the room.

Outside on the drive the curate stood waiting, leaning on his bicycle, wondering whether he was really an actor, or a priest with decisions of life or death before him. He was disturbed by the Cassidys coming out, talking excitedly among themselves.

'How is the patient, doctor?' he asked.

'He might live for years,' said Mrs Cassidy, having again assumed control and answering for her husband, 'and he might live five minutes.'

The curate was gravely affected, and as he got on his bicycle and cycled homewards, he wondered whether he himself would live five minutes or five years or fifty years, and whether he was not already dead, the soul in him, or that part of him that believed in a soul.

But as he was passing along the sandy beach of Coill Namhan he gave a low gurgling cry of joy.

'Fr O'Reilly is gone to the mainland. There is not another priest in the island.'

He was overjoyed at this knowledge. He whistled. He could now say Mass without having to go to confession; an act of contrition would be sufficient, since there was no priest to whom he could confess. He had another day's respite, another day to decide whether he would become a great saint or a great sinner, whether he would renounce God or return to untrammelled worship, and as he rode into Kilmurrage the weight of sorrow in his breast almost disappeared, leaving only a tiny sentinel of conscience as guardian of the fort.

Saturday

I

IN Inverara they called an athletic sports a race meeting, probably out of respect for the first recorded race that was ever contested in the island in the year A.D. 457, on the 17th of April (which fell on a Monday that year, according to the testimony of old Mary O'Reilly of Kilmillick, the oldest woman in Inverara, and who was suspected of relationship with the occult on account of her age). It is recorded that in that year, St Patrick, representing Christianity, contested the possession of the island with a Druid, representing the reigning deity, Crom Dubh. They chose a peaceful way (and therefore novel way in those days, as in these) of contesting the supremacy and 'to find a basis of agreement,' as Mr De Valera would say. They decided to race from opposite ends of the island, and whoever was the first to arrive at the centre was the victor. The Druid, a gentleman called Brian of the Silver Tongue, a name which proved that soothsayers and politicians had attained their present-day characteristics even in the distant past, mounted a fleet charger at the west end of the island and galloped eastwards half an hour before the appointed time. St Patrick, being at that period a poor man, mounted a donkey, and, being also honest, he did not start until the proper time. But honesty was the best policy, and St Patrick won. The charger of the Druid was struck dead by a stroke of fire from heaven half a mile to the west of the central point, and the Druid himself went up in a blue flame, so that St Patrick on his donkey won at a slow walk.

Since the 17th of April, A.D. 457, until the 29th of June of the year with which this story is concerned, many races had been contested in Inverara and various feasts had been celebrated, but none to equal the sports that were now about to take place. The Inverara sports was the official designation given to the event by the Gaelic Athletic Association, but besides being a sports, the event was also a regatta, a bazaar, a tournament, and a religious feast combined. For the 29th of June had been celebrated in Inverara as the annual festival since the Fir Bolgs built the first fortress, and since the knowledge of Crom Dubh first reached the prehistoric inhabitants. But in later years the annual festival had degenerated into an annual debauch for the men and an annual source of revenue for the doctor, owing to the numbers of people who became ill, following that day, as a result of eating too many sweet things and drinking too much whisky. But this year the event had again attained importance, for the Gaelic Athletic Association had stretched forth its regenerating hand to 'win Inverara for the Gaelic Revival,' as the secretary of the County Board would say.

The secretary of the County Board had done his best to make the sports a success from the Gaelic point of view. By sunset on Friday the Sports field, Mr Dignum's largest meadow to the west of the Pier, was arranged for the foot-races, the long jump, the high jump, casting the hammer, etc. A platform had been erected in the centre of the field for the dancing. An old hulk had been stationed in the harbour as a turning-point in the boat-race. Everything was shipshape by nightfall. Then the alien element who had arrived from the mainland contributed their share to make the event look like an Eastern bazaar. Being debarred from the sports field by the rules of the GAA, they pitched their tents along the road leading from the town to the Pier during Friday night, and the publicans, who were also banned from the field, followed suit with their drinking-booths, so that when the first rays of the morning sun poured across the bay on Kilmurrage, a long line of white canvas stretched from the town to the Pier, glistening in the sun. The booths of the publicans gazed shamelessly at the sun, with two empty porter barrels as supports at their doors, ready to smile at their clients with their seductive roundness, ready to lure the thirsty islanders into the gloomy recesses beneath the canvas, where Mulligan's assistant or Mrs Moroney's assistant would hand out frothy pints of porter and glistening tumblers of whisky to slake the thirst and set the blood tingling. The booths of the foreign elements stared shamelessly at the sun, with the flaps of their tents thrown back to show that they had nothing to hide from the gaze of even the most innocent, disclosing strings of rosary beads in black and red and grey and green and amber, in glass and wood and ivory, exposed to the admiration and cupidity of the religious and devout, with heart-shaped Agnus Deis in blocks of six on worsted cushions, with crucifixes of wood and crucifixes of iron and crucifixes of tin, gilt with gold, statues of saints canonized last year and canonized a thousand years ago, while the vendors stood within, with their semitic faces smiling blandly, to show the universality of religion and the all-conquering influence of coin of the realm. There were the fruit-stalls staring at the morning sun and the confectioner's stalls and the lucky-bag stalls, and right opposite the end of the Pier stood the most ornate booth of all, where the gipsy fortune-teller had installed herself, ready to peer into the future or the past at a moment's notice.

The grey of the dawn had not mellowed into the morning light when the first visitors began to arrive from the one hundred towns and villages scattered along the shores of the mainland. They came in everything seaworthy, from a full-sized hooker to a little coracle that a man of medium strength could carry with ease on his shoulders. They came singing and playing melodeons and violins to the music of their oars splashing in the water and the swish of the wind through their sails. They landed on the beach with shouts and eager cries, as if they were old-time Fir Bolgs and had come to participate in an inspiring battle instead of a common or garden festival. They gathered around the tents and the booths, to warm themselves with food and drink, after their scurrying race across the stretch of sea in the cold morning. And when Mr Dignum's servant arrived at six o'clock to take his master's cows home to get milked, the road to the Pier was in the full swing of merry-making, so that the servant, being a young man and full-blooded, had two tumblers of Mr Mulligan's whisky and forgetting his duties to his employer, allowed his cows to be milked by the visitors and driven back again to their pasture, while he himself danced a jig outside Mulligan's booth, to the tune of 'Giolla na Mine,' played on a rusty old violin by a black-bearded fiddler from the mainland.

Both churches in Inverara were crowded that day, for all the people went to Mass, even those who had not gone for years, in order to begin the celebration of the festival respectably. People came from Rooruck in the west, who had never left the village before in their lives, and had heard of Kilmurrage only by hearsay, for even though Kilmurrage was only eight miles from Rooruck, the inhabitants of Inverara travelled solely by sea, and feared land travel as much as Columbus's sailors feared the western stretches of the Atlantic. And then, when the curate had finished the last Mass in Coill Namhan, the people all crowded into Kilmurrage, and from Kilmurrage to the Pier, to witness the arrival of the *Duncairn*, that was due at eleven o'clock sharp, weather and other circumstances permitting, according to the prospectus. And at eleven o'clock, as sharp as the prospectus, the *Duncairn* snorted her way alongside the Pier, blowing her whistle more shrilly than usual in honour of the occasion, and loaded from stem to stern and from the keel to the bridge with passengers.

There were passengers stowed in the hold like cargo. They were on the hurricane deck, packed close together like immigrants coming into Ellis Island, New York. There were some even stowed away among the boilers in the stokehold, having been refused a passage by the steamship company, lest they might be prosecuted for exceeding the ship's capacity. There was the Brian Boru Pipers' Band in a position of honour on the saloon deck, with the Temperance Band close behind them. There were scores of young ladies in grey tweed skirts and grey coats and without any hats, and scores of young men in grey tweed suits and without any hats, advertisements, like the secretary of the County Board of home industry and the Gaelic Revival, in clothes. There were men in kilts, with rimless glasses and morose expressions, advertisements of the Gaelic Revival in art and literature. There were young men in military-looking suits and with military demeanour, advertisements of the Gaelic Revival in the ancient military prowess of the Gael. And mingled with them and about them were scores and scores of ordinary people, male and female, who had not reached the high state of culture of the Revived Gael, but who had their Post Office savings in their pockets, and showed in their happy faces that they had come determined to enjoy themselves, if not like Revived Gaels, at least like ordinary people of universal nationality, who feel that life is short and the world made to be laughed at and enjoyed, even though it be to the detriment of the dead soul of a nation.

But even at this moment of historic importance, this landmark in the history of Inverara, Fr O'Reilly stood out as the most important man in Inverara. He stood on the bridge beside the captain, and around him were assembled three canons, a county court judge, and two members of Parliament. It was to Fr O'Reilly that hats were raised; it was Fr O'Reilly who received a cheer when he stepped ashore on to the Pier, accompanied by his important people. It was then that the Pipers' Band struck up 'O'Donnell Abu,' and followed by the Temperance Band and by the concourse of people, and preceded by Fr O'Reilly, the important people, and the small boys, led the way to the sports field to open the sports.

The Pipers' Band halted with a final shrieking blast from the pipes in front of the platform in the centre of the sports field. Fr O'Reilly, accompanied by the three canons, the county court judge, and the two members of Parliament, proceeded to open the sports with a speech suitable to the occasion, laying stress on the glories of the past of Inverara, and the still greater glories of the future, expressing his confidence that the natives of Inverara would that day live up to the greatness of their past, and show the rest of Ireland that Inverara's manhood was as stalwart as it was supposed to be. And then, since he had a habit of turning everything to political account, he proceeded to introduce the three canons and the members of Parliament, as men who were of widespread fame in the struggle for national liberty (taking care to omit the judge, who was a virulent Unionist). Then the three canons and the two members of Parliament began to talk volubly on their own achievements and on their own and their country's prospects, until O'Malley and the secretary of the County Board, vexed at being thus pushed into the background, and disgusted with this performance, which they understood to be a vile clerical intrigue for the purpose of deflecting the forward march of the nation, peremptorily told Fr O'Reilly that it was time to begin, and Fr O'Reilly interrupted the last canon in his remarks and declared the sports open.

Every inch of the sports field was crowded, except the space that was held open for the foot-races. The crowd stretched out beyond the sports field into the neighbouring fields and along the beach, and along the road right up to Kilmurrage. Boats were still arriving from the mainland at all points, and the immense throng of people gave the impression that the ghosts of all who had ever died in Inverara had come to life for a day and were making the most of it. The homespuns and the rawhide shoes of the islanders mingled with the machine-made clothes of the visitors, like two people drawn from opposite poles fraternizing, and laughing, talking, drinking, dancing, fiddling, and cheering, without any other purpose than to show that they were alive and happy.

Even Dr Cassidy was smiling when he arrived with his wife and daughter in the Cassidy trap. Mrs Cassidy, also eager to show that she was enjoying herself, waved her green parasol at everybody she knew, even her social inferiors. Then she spied out Mr Blake in the crowd, and leaving the doctor in the trap at the entrance to the field, she went over with her daughter to talk to Blake, and one of the canons, on his way to the parochial house to get a glass of whisky in private, spied the doctor in the trap and stopped to talk to him. He had known the doctor in his young days, when the doctor was trying to entice a practice in Limerick, and the canon, then a curate, was angling for a parish.

'Ah yes, glad to meet ye, Canon Kelly,' said Dr Cassidy. 'And how is Mr Bailey, the solicitor? Well, ye say. I'm glad to hear it. An interestin' man is Bailey. I remember, he, he, I remember the last time I met him. It was in August, '97, the seventeenth, I think, but I'm not sure, I haven't as good a memory as I used to have. We were talkin' about solicitors and doctors, an' I was saying that solicitors were the greatest rogues in the world; so they are, he, he, and Mr Bailey said: "D'ye know, Dr Cassidy, that there are only two letters of the alphabet separatin' a doctor from a worm?" "How's that, Bailey?" says I, an' he said, ha, ha, he said: "Worms fatten on deceased bodies and the doctors fatten on diseased bodies." Ha, ha, I never fatten meself, though I eat fish, fresh fish, it's good for a long life. I remember a story —'

But the canon suddenly remembered that the doctor was a garrulous person, who might keep him from his whisky for hours, and availed himself of the approach of the curate to murmur: 'Sorry, Dr Cassidy, but you must excuse me; see you again, I hope.'

He turned to the curate and said:

'How d'ye do, Fr McMahon. I read that article o' yours in the *Church Monthly*. I heard the bishop commenting favourably on it,' he continued, lowering his voice; 'keep at it, 'twill mean a parish for ye in no time.'

He hurried off to get his drink and the curate looked after him scowling. It vexed him that all the priests seemed to treat him as a brilliant kind of an automaton, and seemed to think that the only reason why anybody did anything was to gain personal advancement.

No thought of altruistic devotion to their mission. He seemed to be useful solely as a Church propagandist, a useful appendage to the propaganda department of the Vatican in Rome. Now if he had commended him on his poetry, of which he was proud, it would be different, but he remembered that article. It was mere trash that he had written out of pique, praising the Church, because he had been irritated by the truthful remarks of a writer in Dublin who had denounced the clergy as keeping back educational facilities that would benefit the country. He nodded to Dr Cassidy and passed into the field. He walked through the crowd to the open space where the 'two hundred yards open' was about to be contested. At the far end of the course six men were waiting in a line, crouched with the tips of their fingers touching the ground, waiting for the starter to fire his revolver. Two of them being natives of Kilmurrage, and doing their best to imitate the customs of the mainland, were dressed in tights, green tights, significant of their nationalist fervour. The remaining four were peasants from the west of the island. Being prevented by poverty from being able to purchase a suit of tights, or possibly being too modest to appear in public wearing such scanty clothing, they had merely discarded their heavy over-garments and stood in their grey flannel trousers, rolled up above their knees, with their grey flannel shirts opened at the neck and their feet clothed in socks without any shoes. The dress of the islanders caused a certain amount of merriment among the visitors from the mainland, and even among the natives of Kilmurrage, who did not consider themselves peasants, and were eager to associate themselves with the people from the mainland, and the islanders who looked on were irritated and threatened the visitors with their blackthorn sticks, while the visitors jeered them.

Then the revolver shot rang out and the race started. The six men shot forward with heads bent low. The two men from Kilmurrage ran according to the rules of running, as prescribed by the GAA, with their arms doubled, their heads low, with their fists clenched tightly together, moving only from the shoulders downwards, swinging their arms from front to rear, like soldiers on a parade-ground. The peasants ran according to no studied rules. They swung their arms in all conceivable directions. They changed the positions of their heads, so often that it appeared that their heads were a heavy burden of which they were eager to dispose in their flight. They spat out now and again, as if to relieve their insides of extra ballast. One of them wore a cap, and several times he put up his hand to change the angle at which it rested on his forehead. Another tightened his belt several times with a fleeting movement, and all the while the spectators kept up a perfect din of entreaty and encouragement, waving their sticks and their hats in the air and urging on their favourites, as eagerly as punters at a race meeting. At half-way three of the runners were left far in the rear, two of the peasants and one of the men from Kilmurrage. Far in front, running as fleet as a deer, with his arms swinging like windmills in wild circular strokes, bounding off the ground like a ball at each stride, with the end of the red scarf that he wore around his waist floating in the breeze, ran Paud O'Donnell from Rooruck. Close behind him panted the Kilmurrage man, running straight as an arrow, making up by training what O'Donnell gained by pure natural speed. While out on the very edge of the course ran John Walsh, of Coill Namhan, as big and bulky as a bull, with teeth gritted, swaying his head from side to side between his massive shoulders, as if he were gnawing a way through the atmosphere.

The excitement rose to a violent pitch. They had only fifty yards to go. 'Rooruck! Rooruck Abu!' cried the backers of O'Donnell, waving their sticks. 'Coill Namhan! Coill Namhan!' roared the backers of Walsh, while the natives of Kilmurrage, disdaining such barbaric localism, shouted 'Give it 'em, Matt!' Thirty yards to go, and Rooruck seemed to have victory in its grasp. O'Donnell was as fresh as ever. His chest was rising and falling distinctly and evenly. Nothing moved about him but his long arms and his subtle legs. The Kilmurrage man and Walsh were now running neck to neck, showing in their disordered breathing and the violent efforts they made that their powers of endurance were diminishing.

And just then, when O'Donnell was about to let loose his reserve of strength, in order to fly past the winning-post like an arrow, O'Donnell's mother, forgetting herself in her excitement and becoming hysterical with fear, called out in a shrill voice of terror, 'Paud, Paud, ye divil ye, look behind ye, they're comin' up on ye.' And Paud looked for an instant, tripped, tried to keep his feet, stumbled again, and fell head over heels within ten yards of the tape and victory.

A roar of anguish went up from the people of Rooruck. Curses were hurled at the unfortunate woman who had robbed them of their victory, but only for an instant. The next instant they had united with Coill Namhan in order to present a united front to the common enemy, Kilmurrage. The volume of support for Walsh doubled, and Walsh, roused by the danger to the prestige of the peasantry of Inverara, seemed to swell to twice his size. In spite of the heavy garments that he wore and that clogged his progress, he hurled himself forward and shot past his opponent. Five yards from the tape. 'Coill Namhan Abu!' 'Walsh has won!' 'No, he hasn't. Go it, Matt!' The Kilmurrage man was almost level; he was level, he was in front; and then Walsh, exerting himself again, spread out his hands and took a headlong plunge, carrying the tape before his breast and rolling on to the ground with the impetus of a bull being floored in a slaughter-house, and the judge cried, 'Walsh has won!'

The people crowded around Walsh to congratulate him and to beg of him to come to Mulligan's to have a drink, but Paud O'Donnell, smarting under the misfortune that had befallen him owing to his mother's untimely warning, declared in a loud voice that the race was not valid, and that he was prepared to run any man in Inverara, or in Ireland for that matter, any distance from five yards to a mile, or to fight them if they so preferred; and Walsh, being eager to prove himself a man equal to the occasion, refused the offers of drinks, and, going over to O'Donnell, offered to take up the challenge of personal combat. He was, however, restrained by his supporters, who clung to his body, declaring that it was ridiculous for him to want to fight such a skimpy fellow as O'Donnell, who might be able to run, but could not surely be expected to fight such a powerful man as Walsh. Then O'Donnell's supporters took umbrage at this suggestion of lack of prowess in their hero, and declared truculently that there was never a man bred in Coill Namhan who could equal a Rooruck man at any pastime, so that a free-fight seemed imminent between the rival villages, when the secretary of the County Board pacified them by promising that both parties would have an opportunity of settling their differences and of testing their merits in the 'one hundred yards open' half an hour later; and O'Donnell and Walsh, gladly accepting this solution of the question, shook hands and retired together to get a drink in Mulligan's and forget their enmity.

The curate had become interested in the race. He had, in fact, become excited watching the finish. But when the race was over and the Pipers' Band struck up a tune during the interval before the commencement of the next race, his interest waned. He became conscious of his own position amid all this merry-making, as forlorn as a starving man in a gay city. He moved about among the crowd, taking care to avoid meeting Fr O'Reilly and the other priests. He felt that if he went near them they would be able to read his thoughts and the hidden sin in his soul. He felt towards them like a criminal, and yet towards himself he did not feel like a criminal. He told himself several times that he had committed no wrong, at least, no wrong measured in the light of reason. But still, there was the priest's point of view. He was a criminal according to the laws of the Church. And as he was walking around, the secretary of the County Board hailed him to ask him to preside at the singing competition that was being held in the tent in a corner of the field, but he excused himself on the plea that he was not feeling very well, and the secretary walked away murmuring, 'That curate is impossible, like all priests.'

He wandered back to the Pipers' Band. The pipes were droning like a million bees, screaming now and again as a bag emptied or a player missed a note, while the peasants crowded round, wondering at the strange instruments, for even though war-pipes were supposed to be the musical instrument *par excellence* of the ancient Gael, in Inverara, where the people most closely resembled the ancient Gael in customs and language, the popular musical instruments were the melodeon and the jew's-harp and the violin. The curate found distraction listening to the music and mingling with the crowd. He halted close to Cissy Carmody. Cissy was arm-in-arm with her young man from the Mainland. Instead of the grey tweed suit and the straw hat he was now wearing a set of saffron-coloured kilts and a large, heavy saffron-coloured shawl that hung in many folds over his shoulders and down behind, giving him the appearance of a super in a film play, earning his five dollars a day for walking in an ancient Roman procession or something of the kind. But Cissy was delighted with the kilts. She thought that the kilts made him look like an ancient Irish king, and they were so 'different.' She had paraded him around the field so that all her friends could see her and be jealous, and had taken out the new photograph that he had given her several times when the other girls were looking and said, 'It's just like you, isn't it?' She was now talking to him, without listening to the band or hearing the music, telling him of her uncle in America, who wanted her to go out to that country, saying that she was in doubt whether to go out there or not, and watching the apple in the young man's throat going up and down whenever she mentioned America, afraid or ashamed to say what he wanted to say, namely, that she would do quite well as the wife of the young man in the grey tweed suit, etc., instead of going to America. And Cissy, having noticed the apple making constantly more hurried trips up and down the throat, suggested that they should take a walk around and get somewhere to sit down, for she felt that the young man only needed seclusion and the pressure of her body against his to enable him to overcome the resistance of the blockading apple and make the proposal. As they moved away the curate looked at them and said to himself, 'That Cissy Carmody is becoming quite loose in her conduct lately'; and he also walked away.

The sports were now in full swing, several competitions proceeding simultaneously in order to allow the programme to be completed before the departure of the *Duncairn* at six o'clock. The 'hundred yards open' attracted all the young men and old, who were interested in the rivals of the 'two hundred yards open,' eager possibly to assist in the settlement of any difficulties that might arise after the decision of the judge. But the greater part of the people crowded around the raised platform in the centre of the field, where the dancing competition was about to commence, while the competitors in the singing tournament shrieked forth their doleful melodies to an empty tent in the far corner.

The dancing competition, next to the boat-race, was the most important event of the day, for the islanders looked upon dancing as a great art, an art which they cultivated on all possible occasions, and particularly when they had a liberal supply of potheen consumed. There were three events — the jig, the reel, and the hornpipe — and the number of competitors was so great that they had to perform in threes. There were three judges, and of the three Pat Conneally and Pat Coleman were the more important, for the reason that they knew nothing about dancing and might therefore be expected to give an unprejudiced judgement. The third judge was from the mainland and a professor of Irish Dancing. He was a man who was interested in the Gaelic Revival, and had therefore consented to give his services as judge at half the usual rates. Three fiddlers sat on the rear of the platform, tuning up their instruments, each casting a doleful look at the audience, in silent protest at the stupidity of the other two.

At last the musicians started in harmony and the first three dancers took up their position on the platform, facing the judges, ready to commence the jig, and just then the curate noticed a movement among the crowd. McSherry and his wife were coming along the field in their car. 'Is it possible that he can be here today after the condition he was in yesterday?' he thought. He moved away from the platform to get near the car. McSherry was smiling his cold cynical smile in reply to the inquiries after his health made by the parish priest.

'I was unfortunately absent on the mainland,' he said; and then immediately introduced the three canons and the two Members of Parliament and the county court judge.

'Just a slight indisposition; I am quite all right now,' said McSherry.

In spite of the dizziness that was still in his head and the difficulty he experienced in breathing, he had come to the sports to persuade himself that he just wanted a change of air and a pick-me-up in order to make him as well as he felt before his seizure of the previous day. He laughed and joked with Fr O'Reilly and with the other important people, saying in his own mind, 'You yokel of a priest, you nearly killed me, but I'll put you in a peculiar position in a few days.' And the thought of the ridiculous position in which he would place Fr O'Reilly by his sudden departure and his desertion of Lily, made him all the more genial in his conversation. Presently he responded to an invitation to go to the parochial house with the parish priest and the important people, while Lily expressed her desire to see the dancing, and passed over to the dogcart to sit with Mrs Bodkin.

The curate also moved towards the dogcart in spite of himself. He felt some magnetic force drawing him to Lily the moment he saw her. The sight of her drove out every other thought in his head. He said to himself: 'Today I must come to a decision. Today I must put an end to this torture one way or another.' As he passed through the crowd, he suddenly thought of death and he laughed to himself, for he was a poet, and as a poet death appeared to him ugly and not to be thought of, self-inflicted death. 'Ridiculous,' he murmured, 'melodramatic, vulgar.' He felt pleased to find that he considered suicide vulgar and melodramatic. That put it definitely out of consideration and it proved to him that he was normal and had perfect control over himself.

The dancers were now patting the platform with nimble feet, turning around and around in the treble, jumping half their own height, clapping their hands together between their thighs in mid-air, crossing their feet in a series of interminable twists and turns, and then miraculously disentangling them and coming deftly to a normal position at the end of the bar, holding their hands on their hips with their heads erect, looking straight in front of them, moving from the hips downwards without a muscle moving above the hips, moving continually and rhythmically without losing a stroke, up and down the platform, across the platform, circling on the platform and then facing the judges at the end of the bar, changing places, back again, forming figures of eight, triangles and parallelograms, advancing forward, rippling with their feet like the patter of a machine-gun, retiring again on their heels with their toes in the air, and with their toes touching and touching like drum-sticks, and then suddenly raising both feet in the air, they clicked their heels and stamped on the platform, all three together, just as the bar finished. They bowed to the judges and a roar of applause greeted their finish.

The musicians wiped their brows and took a drink from the can of porter that stood beside each. The judge from the mainland ran his pencil over the notes he had taken, sucked his pencil, scratched his head with it, and then turned to his two fellow judges. The two fellow judges were sitting, quite calmly smoking their pipes, having decided beforehand who was the winner, since they knew each of the three competitors, and it was common knowledge in Inverara that Dan Brosnan was the best dancer of that three. But the judge from the mainland had different views and maintained that another of the competitors had won that heat, since he had danced more in accordance with the dancing rules prescribed by the legitimate Gaelic Revival. Pat Coleman and Pat Conneally smiled scornfully at him.

'Excuse me, sir,' said Coleman, 'but people who are supposed to know say that Dan Brosnan is the best, so that's enough.'

The judge from the mainland shrugged his shoulders and had to agree, for the affair was not of sufficient importance to warrant him giving a minority report, in keeping with the rules of the Gaelic Revival in matters of that sort, when there was an anglicized element present, and the next three dancers mounted the platform.

The curate looked at Lily clapping her hands. He felt how

hypocritical she was, pretending to be merry when he himself knew that it was impossible for her to be merry on account of her estrangement with her husband. Then he himself clapped his hands. He felt that it was his duty to do so, so as to give a good example to his parishioners, and encourage them in innocent amusements. Then he looked towards the platform. The next three dancers were waiting to commence. They were three girls. They bowed to the judges. They bowed to the fiddlers. They bowed to the audience. They bowed to one another, eager to make up by their grace and elegance for their lack of dancing ability. Then they commenced to dance. They danced lightly and with less skill than the men and with less speed and agility. Pat Conneally and Pat Coleman talked and smoked, because they had decided that a girl could not possibly be able to gain a prize where men were competing. But the audience cheered continually, encouraging the girls because they were girls and therefore needing encouragement, shouting: 'May God never weaken ye, Ellen,' 'Good girl, Mary,' 'Long life to ye, Bridget.' And Mary and Ellen and Bridget pirouetted and curtsied, with their skirts in their hands, and with their curls dancing on their forehead far more prettily than their feet tripped on the platform, and with the roses in their cheeks glowing with a ruddy glow of youth and health and exertion. The audience never looked at their feet. They watched the curls and the roses and the shapely bosoms heaving beneath the tight bodices. In fact, the only one who watched the dancing was the professor of Irish Dancing. He took notes and sucked his pencil and scratched his head, for to him, being a Revived Gael, the attraction of sex was as nothing compared to the attraction of the cold scientific judgement that was necessary in order to come to a just decision and pick out what was best in the dancing art of the Ancient Gael.

And then in the middle of the dance a commotion arose in the direction of the foot-race, where the 'two hundred yards open' was being contested. The majority of the audience rushed thither, for O'Donnell of Rooruck and Walsh of Coill Namhan and Matt of Kilmurrage were again flying along the course, with the honour of the three rival towns and villages on their shoulders and in danger. And the commotion reached a frenzy when O'Donnell passed the tape when the others had barely covered seventy-five yards, so that a stranger from the mainland took his name and said that he would break the world's record with a little training.

O'Donnell was so proud of his feat that he began to boast, and Walsh then said that he himself would beat him in a half-mile race. O'Donnell swore that he wouldn't, and the two of them retired to a neighbouring field with their supporters to run the half-mile for a quart of whisky.

The three girls finished dancing and three men took their places. The curate, tired of watching the dancing, moved down towards the beach. It was a torture for him to stand watching Lily, just ten yards away from her; he had measured the distance carefully in his mind, wondering how long it would take him to reach her, if nobody were looking. He wondered too what it would feel like to put his arms about her and crush her to his bosom. And because these thoughts had come rushing into his head, he walked away down to the beach and sat on the pebbles. But sitting on the pebbles he kept wondering what was she doing now. 'This is my last day,' he said to himself, 'this is the last day I will see her.' He persuaded himself that it would be the last day. He was decided to put an end to his doubts and his temptations and his uncertainties without exactly knowing how he was going to put an end to them. And then, having decided that this was to be his last day, he asked himself: 'Why not make the most of this day? Why not drink her in, enjoy her every moment of the day? Abandon myself to enjoying her?' He felt tender towards her now. All his bitterness had vanished. He looked upon himself as a man who was voluntarily sacrificing what he held dearest in the world for the sake of principle. Then he had a vision of himself bidding good-bye to Lily, tearing himself away from her, while she clung to him and begged him to stay. And then he, with a tremor in his voice, would say: 'I must go, dearest, but remember you are my first and my last.' He would feel the clinging of her hands about his neck, and then around his waist and then about his knees as she fell to the ground in despair. He would stand over looking down in pity, and then shrugging his shoulders, he would stretch out his hands and say: 'My mission calls me. I am an evangelist. For me there is no escape from the path that has been carved out for me by Fate.'

But that vision faded into the vision, the real vision of Lily of Dungarvan, lying in his arms, passively, looking up into his eyes, with her lips lightly parted, eager for his kiss.

He rose from the pebbles vexedly and uncomfortably and said: 'God! what a fool I am. I should have been an actor.'

'How am I going to finish?' he asked himself, as he walked back to the platform; 'my father finished in a —'

He shuddered at the thought of his father and then suddenly an idea struck him. His eyes sank far, far into their sockets as he thought of this idea. He tried to banish it as he had banished the thought of suicide as being ridiculous, and continued walking. But the idea still remained. He paused in his walk and his lips twitched . . . and then Mrs Cassidy tapped him on the shoulder with her parasol.

'Day-dreaming, Fr McMahon,' she said. 'What d'ye think of the Sports?'

'I think they are splendid,' said the curate hurriedly. 'Beautiful day for them, thank God,' and he walked on towards the platform.

Mrs Cassidy saw Mrs McSherry in front and the curate walking towards her. She said 'Hm' and then again she said 'Hm, hm.' She said the second 'Hm' louder than the first, and on a different note, and then she went off in search of Mr Blake, whom she found talking to Mr Renshaw and a landlord from the mainland, who had an estate somewhere in the mountains, an estate upon which the tenants never paid any rent and which supported him by the sale of the shooting rights to London shopkeepers in the season.

'Good day, Mrs Cassidy,' said Mr Blake. 'Let me introduce you to Mr Lynch, a friend of mine. You knew old Sam Bodkin Lynch — yes, dear me, I remember when old Sam was dying of the cholic and the doctors had given him up as lost and I cured him in half an hour, special drug I discovered in South America, up among the natives in Chili in my young days, wouldn't give it away for the world, although Sir Mark Kelly came down specially from Dublin to try and buy it off me, just a teaspoonful in a half-pint of brandy, and he was shooting ducks the next day as fit as a fiddle, wonderful man, Sam.'

And Mr Blake was so interested in his story that Mrs Cassidy had to leave him without being able to tell him her suspicions.

When the curate reached the platform, the final heat in the dancing competition was about to commence. The struggle for mastery was between Dan Brosnan and Michael Corbett, Michael Corbett the wastrel and beggar. The people, showing that their love of art placed them above such paltry considerations as dress or character, were cheering lustily for Corbett, in this way showing themselves superior to more civilized people, who cheer a prima donna merely because of the jewels she wears and her reputation among the nobility. And the appearance of Corbett would prejudice his chances in any other audience assuredly, unless he were acting the rôle of a clown. Never clean, he surpassed himself that day in the general decay of his clothes, the unkemptness of his beard and the debauched look in his features, for he had spent the previous night in Brannigan's shebeen in Kilmillick, drinking potheen at the expense of visitors from the mainland. He was wearing shoes of raw cow-hide, and the cow-hair on the shoes was very long and of several colours, so that Corbett had the appearance of a satyr, dressed in the skins of wild beasts, with his tangled beard and his eyes grinning devilishly beneath his bushy eyebrows.

But when the fiddlers struck up a tune and the dancers got in motion, everybody forgot Corbett's appearance or the incongruity of his dress. Corbett disappeared as Michael Corbett the drunken beggar. In his place, a lithe figure skipped around the platform, tapping the platform with his feet as an angel might tap it and with the sharp biting sound of hailstones pattering on flat rocks. His arms were swinging and gesticulating in the air, outwards, upwards, circling around his body, one moment on the hips, another moment clasped behind his head. And then his feet and hands would get intermingled and Corbett would present the appearance of an acrobat turning somersaults on a stage, and then again he would stand erect, with his beard standing out straight in front of his mouth as if it had suddenly been transformed into stiff bristles. And then he would utter a wild yell and treble until his feet were lost from sight in a crazy whirlwind of cow-hair, going round and round with dazzling rapidity.

The crowd forgot to cheer, watching Corbett. Even Pat Coleman and Pat Conneally, the judges, took their pipes from their mouths and watched Corbett, while Dan Brosnan hammered away with determination, doing the steps with a manly precision, and watched only by the judge from the mainland, who even in that moment of excitement was not forgetful of his duties as a judge and the responsibility he owed to the rules of dancing as prescribed by the Revived Gaelic Movement.

The fiddlers fiddled until their fiddles vibrated with the power of a brass band, and when one of them paused to wet his lips at the can of porter beside him, the crowd yelled at him to get on with his work, 'and be damned to him,' or they would have his life. And thus for half an hour Michael Corbett held the vast concourse of people enthralled with his exhibition, until at last Dan Brosnan, his rival, dropped with exhaustion to the platform, and then Corbett with a yell gave a few more flourishes, a few more trebles, then a wild whoop and a whirl in the air. He brought his two feet together in the air, touching the soles together so that the dried raw leather resounded like the crack of a whip, and finally he hit the platform, with one foot stretched forward in front of the other and his body bent forward in a graceful bow.

'Is le Corbett a buadh,' yelled the peasants furiously. 'Corbett wins,' cried the natives of Kilmurrage. Even the visitors from the mainland, who were not concerned with 'the soul of the nation,' applauded vigorously, crying, 'Well done, Corbett.' But the supporters of the Gaelic revival in art, literature, manufactures, and military prowess dissented. They favoured Brosnan, because they regarded Corbett as the stage Irishman, a man who should be put down and banished with a strong hand, a drunken waster whose kind had disgraced the country since the English invasion, an insult to the morality and sobriety and steady robust self-respect of the Revived Gael. In agreement with their prejudices they opposed Corbett and shouted for Brosnan, claiming that he had won, since he had danced more in accordance with the rules of dancing prescribed by the Gaelic Revival. So that the professor of dancing from the mainland, being himself a Revived Gael, and eager to curry favour with the Revived Gaels in the audience, suggested to Coleman and Conneally that Brosnan had won.

Coleman and Conneally immediately rose to their feet and looked to the supporters of Corbett in the audience, at the same time casting a deprecatory look in the direction of the dancing master. And then Coleman, taking upon himself the rôle of presiding judge, announced in his most professional voice that Corbett had won. There was a roar of applause that drowned the voices of protest from the Revived Gaels, and Corbett was carried off to Mulligan's, while the secretary of the County Board announced through a megaphone that there would be an hour's recess for lunch and that the boat-race would commence sharply at two o'clock.

Immediately the people forgot Corbett. They forgot everything but the boat-race, the greatest event of the day, the event that had been talked about, wagered on, quarrelled about, and discussed acrimoniously for months past. Everybody hurried to the beach to get a position from which they could see the start. Voices rent the air. 'There are a hundred curraghs competing'; 'O'Malley's boat'll win, Peter'; 'I bet ye anything ye like that Pat Farelly is goin' to win.' 'Go away; he has a fat chance, Walsh of Coill Namhan has the best crew o' that lot.' Everybody had his own favourite. Even the visitors from the mainland, carried away by the popular enthusiasm, pretended to have inside information as to the outcome of the race. They now brought themselves on a level with the islanders, whom they had hitherto despised, and asked them questions about the competitors and listened to their opinions with respect. And the islanders, who had until now been more or less tolerated spectators, suddenly assumed a position of great importance. They swaggered around arrogantly, talking loudly in Irish, and calling to one another from great distances, feeling that this race, which called forth the greatest amount of skill and endurance, they appeared as superior people, compared to the degenerate people from the mainland who could not drive one of the curraghs half a dozen yards without upsetting the boat or smashing their knuckles.

Down on the beach was Patsy O'Brien with a large audience around him, giving his opinions on the race, and claiming that the outcome of the contest would in some mysterious way affect the future history of Ireland, for *Old Moore's Almanack* had prophesied that . . . But his prophecies were lost in roars of laughter. Farther along the beach rested an old man, who had been brought from his home in Rooruck on a donkey to witness the race. He was looked upon as the greatest authority on rowing in all Inverara. A great crowd gathered around him, listening to his account of how he had won the race from the Big Town on the Mainland to Kilmurrage on the occasion of the Cardinal's visit in 1898. He sat on the beach with his aged legs spread out in front of him, in the attitude of a man sitting in a curragh at sea, moving his hands to show all the strokes of which he was a master, while the audience hung on every word, with greater attention than they listened to Fr O'Reilly reading the Gospel. Everywhere along the beach the islanders crowded down to the edge of the sea, while the small boys pulled their trousers up about their knees and waded into the surf, where the curraghs were being drawn up in line, hopping on the gentle swell, with their tar-covered sides glistening in the sun.

The curate took his bicycle and rode up to Shaughnessy's Hotel for his lunch. As he was passing Moroney's public-house, he saw O'Malley, O'Rourke and Mr Blake talking to Mrs McSherry. Blake was inviting the party to have lunch with him on board his yacht, which was drawn alongside the little Pier on the town side of the harbour, by the square.

'I brought some food along and one of the men is cooking it on board, 'twill be rough and ready, but it's just the thing for a day like this. They'll be crowded up at the parochial house, anyhow. I'll send a boy along to say you're not coming, Mrs McSherry. There'll be plenty of room on deck for the whole of us. Hey there, Fr McMahon, you had better join us.'

But the curate declined. He felt that he had no use for company that day and he rode up towards the hotel. When he was farther up the road, he thought of turning back. It was his last day, and he had better spend it as near Lily as possible, but he rode on and entered the hotel.

'I'm sending yer lunch to yer room, father,' said Mrs Shaughnessy; 'the place is so crowded.'

'All right,' said the curate.

There were visitors in the dining-room, in the sitting-room, and in the back parlour that was used as a smoke-room and a library. They were standing in the hall waiting for their turn at table. Mrs Shaughnessy and her maid were reinforced by three other girls hired for the day. They bustled around serving mutton chops and potatoes, huge pots of tea, and baskets of bread and butter, and charging seven times the normal price for each meal, for even though Kilmurrage was in uncivilized Inverara, it had nevertheless become civilized through contact with priests, bishops, county court judges, Government officials and shop-keepers, and had become as corrupt as the most favourably situated portion of the civilized world, to the extent that it had already mastered what is known and appreciated in the civilized world as the 'business instinct.'

The curate had his lunch in his room and he ate it. He ate it because he was in the habit of eating it, and because his appetite was so good in normal times that it was not disturbed during moments of intense emotion. But although he ate his food it took no effect on him. He felt neither satisfied nor dissatisfied, neither hungry nor sated. But he was thinking deeply while he ate. He was thinking that this was his last day, and it was only towards the end of the meal that he asked himself why it was his last day. And just as if a stranger had asked him the question, he shook his head gloomily and murmured, 'Of course it's my last day, it must be.'

And then the 'idea' sprang to his memory, the 'idea' that he had coming up from the beach in the Sports Field. 'Phew!' he said aloud, 'only a madman, a superstitious maniac, would dream of finding that way out, it's too ridiculous.' He became so furious with himself for entertaining that 'idea' that he hit the table with his hand and upset the teapot. It fell to the floor with a clatter and the servant girl came running up the stairs to see what was the matter.

'Nothing,' he said, 'I only upset the teapot. Clear those things away. No, leave that glass; I need it. I broke the one I had.'

When the servant left the room he rose to his feet and stretched himself.

'Well, if this is my last day, I might as well enjoy myself like the rest.'

He laughed mirthlessly, as he placed the second bottle of whisky on the table and pulled the cork.

As he finished the second glass he sighed deeply and smacked his lips.

'Ha,' he said, 'it gives me courage. I will be able now to —'

The 'idea' again came back to him. Now that the whisky was in his blood, warming him, giving him courage, he no longer feared that 'idea.' He took a book from the shelf and laid it on the table, *Early Saints of Inverara*, by Fr Coutts Moore, S.J. He turned over the pages and at page twenty-five he said, 'Here it is.' He sat down and read.

'A peculiar tradition which is told to this day around the firesides of Inverara, tends to show that the early saints of Inverara had attained a wonderful degree of sanctity. It is told that in the monastery of Cregeen, standing on the site of what is now called the village of Rooruck, the holy monks had a singularly severe manner for doing penance for their sins. Each evening they set out to sea in an oarless coracle, and allowed themselves to be carried away by the tide. If any of them were in sin he was drowned, and if they were in the state of grace, Divine Providence brought them back safely to land. I relate this story as a tradition, but it is firmly believed to this day in Inverara, and my personal opinion is that it is deserving of credence.'

The curate closed the book, and putting his head between his hands, he mused. It was surely a way of testing whether he was an enemy of God or still in friendship with God. It was a way of relieving himself of this torture, of ending it once and for all. The book said it was the way the ancient saints had for doing penance and he was in a way akin to those saints. Perhaps the hand of Providence had sent him to Inverara to cleanse him completely of the stains of the world in order that he might be more fitted to take up his great mission, just like Paul and Augustine.

It did not appear to him as a contradiction of this resolve, when he took another glass of whisky and swallowed it eagerly. He was but loading himself with sin in order that his penance might be the more cleansing. And when he poured the remainder of the whisky into a large flask and put the flask in his pocket, he was still satisfied. His conscience did not prick him. The stupefying effect of the alcohol had now mastered him. In fact, he began to wonder whether after all he should test the power of the 'idea,' or whether he should instead become a great sinner.

But as he went downstairs he felt certain that this day was going to be his last and that he must enjoy himself while it lasted. He whistled. He struck the wall with his fist as he descended, as if he wanted to allow the surging joyfulness within him to express itself. As he went to the Pier he thought of Lily. He felt at the moment that he would seize her in front of all the people and carry her away with him, what did it matter what he did? It was his last day. And then as he passed Blake's yacht and saw O'Malley helping Lily ashore, a homicidal impulse seized him. 'How I hate him,' he hissed. 'Before I go I will kill him and her,' and he shuddered.

He took up a position on the wall to the rear of the Pier, facing the sea and the beach where the boats were arranged, ready to start. He must watch and see O'Malley being defeated. He would see the look on Lily's face as she saw him being defeated. His hatred for O'Malley was now the clearest impulse in his mind. As O'Malley came down the beach to his curragh, he tried to find fault with his physique. He told himself that O'Malley's shoulders were too broad, totally out of proportion to his body, and that his knees showing bare beneath the tights as he took off his raincoat, were slanting inwards. 'A sign of loose living,' said the curate with satisfaction. Then he saw Lily. She was only thirty yards or so away from him, with Mrs Bodkin and a lady from Dublin beside her.

He moved along the wall to the end to get closer. The peasants on the wall made way for him now. He took out a pair of field-glasses and looked towards her. She was smiling and waving her handkerchief. Yes, there was O'Malley looking up at her and smiling also, as he took his seat in his boat. 'Shameless woman, letting everybody know.'

The starters were running hither and thither, putting the curraghs in their proper positions in the line. There were thirty-five curraghs competing, all lined along the beach, manoeuvring in and out, to their places in the line. O'Malley was allotted the centre of the line. 'Favour,' murmured the curate, but he smiled immediately. Walsh and Farelly were beside O'Malley in equally good positions. He felt glad and gave a penny to a little boy beside him who was cheering for Walsh.

The boats were ready. It was a wonderful sight. The curraghs were round-bottomed coracles with sharp, high prows, just light shells of wooden laths, covered by tarred canvas. There were four men in each curragh and each man had two oars, long heavy rough oars, but oars that were as light as a feather in the sturdy hands that wielded them. O'Malley's crew were dressed in green tights. O'Malley had bought the tights himself. But the other crews were dressed in grey flannel shirts and loose woollen trousers, with woollen stockings pulled up over the legs of the trousers. Each man had a multi-coloured knitted scarf around his waist.

The boats were in position, the oars stretched out, the crews lay forward on their oars, with muscles taut. Not a move along the whole line. The starter stood with his revolver cocked in the air, ready to give the signal. Perfect silence, and then . . .

Crack. The whole line of waiting boats suddenly moved as if the impetus of the shot had hurled them forward. The oars dipped into calm surf — creak-splash-creak. Every boat of the thirty-five glided away from the beach, like a torpedo from the side of a battleship, leaving a white trail of widening foam in their tracks. The people, silent until now, gave a mighty shout, and waved their hats. Cheers arose from the various groups of partisans. 'O'Mailleach Abu' came loudest of all, and the curate, forgetting his dignity as a priest, and vexed at this demonstration in favour of O'Malley, cheered for Walsh. Then he settled himself down to watch the race. Putting his glasses to his eyes, he looked out to sea.

The boats were now jumbled up together, each trying to get

into the centre of the line towards the hulk, which they must pass before they could double back on the homeward stretch. For a moment he could not distinguish the foremost boat. Then he smiled. It was Pat Farelly's crew, rowing madly, a hundred yards or more in front of O'Malley and Walsh, who were rowing steadily prow to prow, with long slow strokes. He could see Pat Farelly's long brown beard in the prow of his boat, bending forward until his forehead touched the back of the man in front of him, then stretching back until the boat seemed to be empty, the crew lying level with the gunwale. Farelly and his crew, four boon companions, were rowing furiously and the curate was delighted. He began to consider Farelly an interesting fellow, a good-natured man, a worthy man. He wondered could he keep up his speed. And then lowering his glasses he looked at Lily.

She was standing on a rock with her glasses to her eyes, looking out to sea. He thought he could see the veins in her neck running up and down as if she were in a state of great excitement. And then he chuckled and put his glasses to his eyes again. He felt sure that she would be disappointed, that O'Malley was going to lose. The three boats were now nearing the turning-point. Pat Farelly's boat, a dark speck, with eight glittering white oars, rising and falling like flashes of lightning, was still racing in front. O'Malley and Walsh were still prow to prow, while the remainder of the boats came behind in the ruck. Nearer and nearer they came to the hulk. Pat Farelly reached the hulk. His crew paused for a moment, raised their oars in triumph, and then with another mighty stroke they disappeared behind. A cheer went up from the shore and from the hundreds of boats that were scattered around on the outskirts of the course watching the race. All eyes then concentrated on the struggle between O'Malley and Walsh. They were about two hundred yards from the hulk when O'Malley's crew lay on their oars and plunged forwards to get past the turning-point in front of their rival. A great cheer went up from the shore in response to the effort, for in spite of Farelly being far in front, the islanders knew that O'Malley and Walsh were still in the running. The curate, looking through his glasses, trembled with excitement. The little boy beside him was yelling 'Walsh, Walsh, go on, Walsh,' at the top of his voice, but the curate, looking through his glasses, saw O'Malley in front. His green-clad crew had shot out beyond their rival. They had reached the hulk, with Walsh just to stern, and then . . .

A cry of rage went up from O'Malley's supporters on the beach. O'Malley's starboard oars had fouled in the anchor chain of the hulk. He had hugged the hulk too closely in his eagerness. For a moment his boat swerved round helplessly, and in that moment Walsh swung past, with his starboard oars shipped to avoid collision. And at the same moment Farelly's boat appeared from the opposite side of the hulk, coming in on the homeward stretch.

For a moment there was dead silence along the shore. Pat Conneally said afterwards that he could hear Patsy O'Brien breathing beside him. For a moment there was silence with all eyes fixed on O'Malley's boat. Were the oars broken? Was the boat damaged? Was he out of the race? The curate wished that he was and glanced hurriedly towards Lily to see how she was taking it, but before his eyes could reach her, a mighty shout brought his gaze back hurriedly to sea, and he saw O'Malley disappearing behind the hulk again in the race.

The finish of that boat-race will be remembered in Inverara until the end of time. Inverara men will discuss it in the valley of judgment, when the hosts of the dead are assembled to be judged. Inverara men will on that day of judgment grow heated in argument as to whether O'Malley or Walsh would have won if . . . But to return to the race.

The three boats were now on the homeward stretch. They came in a line, Farelly in front, Walsh behind Farelly, and O'Malley last. The spectators crowded down to the shore, some wading knee-deep into the surf to get a closer view. There was silence now, but for a dull rumble of sound. The excitement was intense. The superstitious were murmuring prayers to Crom Dubh. On and on came the boats, with a long wake of foam behind each, with the sun gleaming on the oars, and rippling on the canvas-covered sides, with the boat's sides sparkling as if strewn with emeralds, with the crews rising and falling on their oars backwards and forwards, rhythmically, moving with the precision of machines, with the rattle of the oars in the rowlocks sounding and resounding like the wash of breakers on a rocky shore.

On and on they came, without change in their position until Farelly was within half a mile of the winning post. And within half a mile of the winning post, Walsh began to draw nearer to Farelly. Farelly's crew, exhausted by the superhuman efforts they had made, and weakened by the whisky they had drunk to give them excessive energy, began to flag. The silence broke. Cries became loud and shrill. The backers of each crew began to utter their war cries, exhorting, threatening, entreating, cursing, praising, goading. Farelly's crew became weaker in their strokes, slower to dip their oars, slower to bend their backs, slower to rise, while Walsh's crew, with long steady strokes crept nearer inch by inch, and O'Malley's crew, rowing now as rowing had never before been seen in Inverara, gained on Walsh.

The curate looked at Lily. She was standing on tiptoe on the rock, madly waving her handkerchief. The curate noticed that it was a green handkerchief, the same colour that O'Malley's crew were wearing. He thought that it was disgraceful for a woman of her class to become so excited over an affair in which ordinary peasants were competing. And seeing O'Malley drawing nearer to Walsh, he became vexed with himself for getting excited himself, he an intellectual and a priest. But at the same time he put his hand in his pocket and gave all his pennies to the small boys around him to cheer for Walsh. And then he looked to sea again.

Walsh was now abreast of Farelly. He was passing him, and then a cry of rage came from the shore. Farelly was giving up the race. Raising their oars, his crew cheered and lay back in their boat exhausted, within a quarter of a mile of the winning-post. The spectators yelled in derision. Farelly's supporters, maddened by the surrender of their hero, screamed curses, 'Cowards, drunkards.' But Farelly and his crew rattled their oars in the rowlocks, like the devil-may-care fellows they were, and as O'Malley's boat passed them, they cheered.

O'Malley and Walsh now had the race between them. Their boats seemed to fly over the water without touching it. The clash of the oars in the rowlocks came like the crash of musketry. The plunge of the oars in the water resounded now dull and distinct along the shore. 'Mailleach Abu, Mailleach Abu.' The cries for O'Malley became louder as O'Malley gained inch by inch. They were only two hundred yards from the winning-post. The curate stood up on the wall and dropped his glasses from his eyes. The boats were close to him now, passing beneath him. He could see the play of the muscles on the bare arms. He could hear the sharp groans as the men tugged at the end of the strokes, with their legs planted firmly against the boats' sides. He could see the massive frame of Walsh, with the sweat trickling down through the dark hair on his bare chest, with his eyes distended, his teeth bared, and his lips moving spasmodically as he hurled commands at his crew. He could see O'Malley, with his face lathered in sweat, with the proud look in his eyes that the O'Malleys always had, with his jaws set square, and his lithe body moving gracefully, as he dipped and rose and stretched on his oars, as agile as a leopard.

Within a hundred yards of the winning-post, the prow of O'Malley's boat was level with Walsh's stern. Another stroke and he was on Walsh's quarter. Another stroke and he had slipped slightly to the rear, as Walsh's crew exerted their last reserve of strength to make a spurt to the winning-post. And then, with the next two strokes in quick succession, the second stroke catching the boat before it had time to pause, O'Malley shot out half a boat's length in front of Walsh, amid a roar that almost shook the concrete Pier. Everybody went mad with excitement. Some ran into the sea. Others threw their hats in the air. Some, sitting on the beach, rowed stroke for stroke in company with the boats. Some kept their mouths open, blue in the throat and unable to utter a sound. The curate went black with rage. He almost hurled himself from the wall on his enemy beneath.

And then when the two boats were within six strokes of the winning-post, with O'Malley clear in front of Walsh, there was a tearing of canvas, a sharp crunching sound, and O'Malley's boat began to fill with water. It had grounded on a rock, hidden beneath the water, as it passed close to the shore. The stern of the boat sagged. The prow swerved outwards across Walsh's course. O'-Malley and his crew, careless of the water, pulled madly at their oars. They dragged to the post. They were sinking, and then Walsh's crew, with an enraged yell, charged into the sinking wreck, and carried it on their prow past the winning-post. Another moment O'Malley and his crew were swimming in the sea, with their boat sinking beneath the water, but the judge cried out through his megaphone, 'O'Malley has won.'

Then there was chaos. Amid deafening roars of 'Mailleach Abut' came counter cries from Walsh's supporters. Forgetful that O'Malley was in front before the accident, they claimed that he had won by a fluke. And then O'Malley landed on the Pier, dripping with brine. He immediately shook hands with Walsh and congratulated him on the fight he had put up and then the whole people joined in the cheers for 'Mailleach Abut.' He was hoisted on the shoulders of the peasants and carried in triumph up the Pier, while everybody followed shouting.

And the curate, casting a look at Lily, who was still standing on the rock with a flushed face, cursed and went into the lavatory to get a drink from the flask he carried in his pocket. He took a deep draught, smacked his lips and took another draught. 'If I were a man I would kill him,' he said, as he put the flask back into his pocket, 'and her, too. But the devil take them both. This is my last day, and I'll enjoy myself.'

As he came out of the lavatory, going towards the sports field he met Cissy Carmody with her young man from the mainland. They were walking arm in arm, looking into one another's eyes, careless of the boat-race, for the young man had spoken in the secluded spot in the sports field, and he was now telling Cissy about a nice comfortable three-roomed cottage on the outskirts of the Big Town on the Mainland, that they could have for three shillings a week rent, from a man he knew. And Cissy, feeling that she was already a housewife, was asking him was he sure that it was not draughty.

The curate went into the sports field. There he met Mr Blake. 'Wonderful race, that, Fr McMahon,' said Blake, twisting his moustache. 'Damned if I thought that a lot of peasants could be so interesting. And O'Malley, too,' he added, in a lower voice, 'don't ye think, though, that it was a bit out o' place rowing with those fellows?'

As the curate walked away from Blake, lest he should smell the whisky from his breath, he felt that it was really a ridiculous thing for O'Malley to do, a gentleman to row with peasants. He forgot that he himself was a Republican and an opponent of class distinctions. He forgot that his grandfather had been a labourer on the Dublin docks, before he was able to study law by means of the three hundred pounds legacy that had been left to him by an uncle in Australia. He felt that O'Malley's victory was of no account. He had proved that he was a mere peasant by competing in such a race.

'Quite right. It is funny,' he said to himself, as if in reply to Blake. And then, as if imitating Mr Blake, whom he now considered a thorough gentleman and a man whose opinion was to be highly valued, he said 'Damn peculiar, damn peculiar, and in damn bad taste.'

When he had reached the middle of the sports field he paused, and wondered where he was going. He had merely followed the flow of people without sense of direction. He now realized that he had no interest in the sports. He turned back to the road leading to Kilmurrage. It was now densely packed with people. The peasants had lost interest in the sports after the boat-race. They were gathered around the drinking-booths, drinking the bets they had wagered. Walsh was there in front of Mulligan's with a crowd around him, swearing that if he had not been tired after running three foot races and drinking his share of two quarts of whisky, he would have won easily. Others were around the confectioners' stalls and the fruit stalls and the lucky-bag stalls, while some of the more devout were purchasing rosary beads and Agnus Deis from the Jews. A group of young women lingered around the fortune-teller's booth, ashamed to go in and yet unable to tear themselves away from the hidden secrets of the future and the roseate pictures of the past — the past which perhaps held a kiss or an embrace, or a desire, half-formed, fleeting and sweet, like sin which is not ravished but desired.

The curate passed up along the line of booths, saluted here and there, curtsied to by the women, addressed reverently by the old men, stared at stupidly by the men who were already drunk with whisky. He passed up the line to the base of the hill leading to Kilmurrage, and there he halted and asked himself again where he was going. He turned to go back, but again he asked himself what did he want to go back for. And then he suddenly realized that he wanted to see Lily and O'Malley. He felt his hands clenching and opening without being conscious of the purpose. And then when he found himself staring at Jim Shanaghan's store and laughing silently, he knew he was drunk. He was not ashamed or worried by the discovery that he, Fr Hugh McMahon, priest and author of the 'Death of Maeve,' should be wandering around at a public festival, drunk with whisky. On the contrary, he felt that it was his duty to get drunk that day. It was his last day. When the sun was setting he would . . . Yes, it was at sunset they did it according to the tradition . . . He would set out from the shore of Rooruck and do penance. But why should he? As a man who had a brilliant future, why should he do it? Now, was it ridiculous or was it not? That was the question.

He sat on the low stone fence that protected the road from the beach below, and tried to discover whether it was ridiculous or not. He was extremely anxious to do nothing that might be construed into being ridiculous. But his brain, stupefied with whisky, was unable to discover what anything was or what anything was not. His brain was in a humorous mood, a gloomily humorous mood. He discovered himself laughing at a jelly-fish that was floating sideways in the surf beneath, with its filmy fingers sticking from its belly. 'Pull yourself together,' he said, apostrophizing himself. He got up and was going to sit down again, when he realized that the people would notice him getting up and sitting down again foolishly. 'They'll say I'm like a hen with an egg,' he said with a foolish smile. Then he walked on down towards the Pier once more.

Half-way down the road he met John Carmody arguing heatedly with one of the supporters of the Gaelic Revival, while a crowd listened to him.

'You are all crazy with the heat,' Carmody was saying. 'You an' yer goddam soul o' the nation. It's only by the common ownership of the land and the tools of production that ye're goin' to make this lousy country free. Socialism. You bet yer life. Ye don't like it, because you fellahs are a damn sight worse than the English, with yer superstitions and yer Popes and yer politicians. You make me sick. Fight the British Empire? Why, you fellahs couldn't fight a plate o' beans unless the workers went down and done the fightin' for ye.'

'What's he talking about?' mused the curate as he walked past. 'Oh yes, Socialism, of course. Interesting chap, that Carmody. Doesn't believe in hell. I wonder what he would say about the tradition of the ancient saints?'

But he brushed aside the thought of Carmody, an ignorant peasant with bigoted ideas, no soul, no conception of beauty, a man who could not possibly understand the difficulties of an intellectual. He entered the sports field, taking care to walk in the empty parts of the field, so that nobody could smell his breath. Even though it was his last day, he told himself that he must not give scandal. Of course, Paul and Augustine were known to be worldly men. Augustine's loose living was common knowledge in his time, living with a prostitute or something. But then they were not priests at the time of their sins, and even though he were enjoying himself
. . .

'No,' he said aloud, in contradiction of his thoughts, 'I am not enjoying myself'; and Lanigan the tailor, who was standing near by, thinking of his son Denny who was killed in Pinkerton's Detective Force in Butte Montana, and feeling sure that if he were here today he would carry all before him, heard the priest speak, and thought him to be praying. And he himself muttered a 'Paternoster' and three 'Lord Jesus, have mercy on me a sinner.'

The field was almost empty now. Only the weight-throwing was being contested, and that did not attract the people. Everybody knew that John Daly of Kilmillick would win it — Daly, whose brother was the biggest man in the Dublin Metropolitan Police Force, and had won the weight-throwing competition the year before in the sports held at the Viceregal Lodge or somewhere, or so it was said, anyhow, for the Dalys were 'Terrible for boastin'.' The people, having exhausted their enthusiasm on the boat-race, were eating and drinking in order to recuperate themselves in preparation for the night's dancing and amusement.

The curate, walking around the field, spied Lily in a corner talking to an old woman. 'Wonder what's she doing here alone?' he said to himself as he stood watching her at a distance. Presently he saw O'Malley coming out of the dressing-tent and going towards Lily. 'Ha! she's waiting for him. I knew it,' he muttered, and his eyes gleamed. O'Malley turned when he was near her, and stopped to light a cigarette. Then he walked towards the beach, whistling loudly 'Who Fears to Speak of Ninety-Eight.' Lily turned her head sharply and he raised his hat to her. She bowed. The curate walked away to the west, crossing to the beach to the west of O'Malley. He looked back. Lily had left the peasant woman, and walked through a gap in the fence to the beach road. O'Malley moved forward to meet her. The curate followed him, staying in the shelter of the fence around a turning.

The beach was deserted. All the people had moved up along the road towards the town. O'Malley sat down on a rock behind an old boathouse and raised his hat as Lily came up to him. The curate knelt at the western end of the boathouse and prepared to listen. He was mad with the whisky. He didn't trouble to realize whether he was eavesdropping or not. It was his last day. He listened.

'Don't, Hugh, somebody will see us; oh, why did I come?'

He was kissing her, the curate thought, and he panted for breath. His breath came hot up his throat, as if his lungs were on fire.

'What does it matter who sees us, Lily? You are mine, tell me that you are. What is your answer? You promised to give me an answer today after the boat-race; what is it? Tell me, say "Yes," say that you are mine, that you love me, that you will come away with me.'

The curate heard O'Malley pause, and then his voice became low and soft and seductive . . . the cur, like his grandfather . . . pity he hadn't a revolver. He could go around the corner and . . .

'Speak, Lily. We can go to America together, away from everybody; oh, what does your husband matter, you don't love him, it's a crime to go on living with him. I will take care of you. Tell me you love me; Lily, tell me.'

There was a pause. The curate waited intently. There was a mist before his eyes and a savage frenzy surging through his whole frame. His lips were quivering. He was unable to move. He heard a half sob, then a deep sigh, then the sound of kissing. Then came Lily's voice, low and sweet.

'Yes, I love you, Hugh, I love you.'

Then O'Malley's voice.

'My treasure, you are mine.'

Something suddenly snapped within the curate. His rage left him. 'She is his,' he mumbled dully, as his head fell forward. 'She was mine and she is his, she was mine and . . .' He repeated the words as if they were the words of a prayer.

'It's finished,' he said again. His lips moved in a noiseless laugh, his head jerked forward with a hiccup as if somebody were trying to strangle him. His hatred left him. He became weak, too weak to hate, to love, to fear, too weak to feel. Everything dimmed from his memory but the vision of the shore at Rooruck, the oarless boats, and the saints going forth on the sea, with their hands clasped across their breasts in prayer. His head fell on his breast. His lips curled up at the side, scoffing at the world, at heaven and hell, at life, death and ambition. And with that curl of his lip, like the snarl of a beaten cur, he resigned himself to the fate that he himself had planned, penance for his sins, an eternal floating, floating into the arms of death, that or forgiveness, no not forgiveness but death, not death but forgetfulness.

The voices came again, but they seemed distant now and meaningless — voices from a dead past, casual whispers borne on the wind, as one might hear in the street of a crowded city.

'Hugh, I can't leave my husband. I must stay with him, I must. We would not be happy otherwise, not while my husband is alive.'

'Rot, rot!' imperiously. 'What does your husband matter? You are mine, you are mine. Those vile superstitions are good enough for peasants and old women —'

'Oh, Hugh, don't talk like that, you make me afraid. I-I-I have tried to tell myself that, but I must, I must stay until — Oh, I hate to think that I should be waiting for his death, much as he has wronged me.'

The voices died again and he heard sobbing.

'What the hell are they talking about?' he muttered.

'Who are they?' he muttered again, as he took the flask from his pocket.

As he was about to pull the cork hurriedly, he paused. A cunning look came into his eyes. He slanted his head forward, listening, and then looked around him furtively. He pulled the cork, careful not to make a sound. As he put the flask to his mouth he grinned, distending his nostrils and thrusting forward his upper lip. He took a deep draught and put the flask back to his pocket.

'I must be going, Hugh. No, no, I must go. No, I can't leave him, Hugh. Look, somebody is coming. God, it's Polly, Fr O'Reilly's servant. What can be the matter?'

The curate sat still with his head hanging down on his breast. He was falling asleep when he heard a shriek, and he sat up with a start and shuddered. 'I must not stay here,' he mumbled. 'Must go to the shore at Rooruck. What's that? My husband dead. Whose husband? I haven't got a husband,' and he trudged along the beach road westwards.

And Polly, with her teeth chattering with fright, was telling O'Malley that McSherry had fallen dead in the parochial house, right in the hall when they were coming out, and then she hurried away to tell a group of women how he said, 'I'm a priest's bastard, curse you, you devil's breed, you Reilly and your whore of a niece,' and then he dropped there an' then as if the Divil had swallowed him. Lord preserve us from all harm.'

O'Malley looked at Lily, fainted, lying on a cloak at his feet, while a woman bathed her forehead. He shivered as if an apparition had touched him, and then Lily opened her eyes and smiled at him, and he felt happy.

'Where am I going, shore at Rooruck, tradition shtill told,

oarless boats, great future, evangelist, curse the road, shore at Rooruck,' mumbled the curate, stumbling and staggering westwards over the stony road by the sea.

While around the booths and through the streets of Kilmurrage the people sang and danced and quarrelled, oblivious of the dead.

And overhead the sky grew dark, and shadows of a coming wind flitted darkly over the calm sea.

2

It was said in Inverara that the sun never shone on Rooruck. That, of course, was a lie, originating in the impiety of the Rooruck people, who hardly ever went to Mass. And the islanders, and more especially the women, who in Inverara were as credulous as elsewhere, associating the sunlight with the Grace of God and the Fire of the Holy Ghost, were confident that Rooruck was perpetually enveloped in outer darkness.

The truth of the matter was, that when the rest of the island was bathed in sunlight and cheered by the songs of the larks, Rooruck was gloomy and grey and bleak. Grey-black towering cliffs, washed by huge Atlantic breakers, bleak crags, a long stretch of shore, lined by huge boulders, such was Rooruck. While to the west lay nothing, just America. The young men around the forge fire at Coill Namhan debated on cold winter evenings how long it would take a man to walk from Rooruck to America, if men could walk on the sea, but beyond this innocent and impossible calculation, the islanders shunned Rooruck. Even tourists shunned Rooruck, it looked so melancholy and the rocks were so impassable. Even the Land Commissioner, who had been sent specially from Dublin Castle to find out the truth about the townland of Rooruck, with a view to assessing it for rent and to discover the amount of arable land it contained, did not have the courage to go any nearer to Rooruck than Shaughnessy's hotel in Kilmurrage, and sent in his report on the strength of information received from Pat Conneally to the effect that there was only half an acre of land on the whole townland.

And this report was true. In the whole village there were six dogs, three donkeys, and one cow. The cow lived in the half-acre of arable land, the donkeys, after their day's work, tramped into the neighbouring village to have a meal, and the dogs were known all over Inverara as the most flea-bitten curs walking on four legs. The village contained six cabins and thirty-five inhabitants, at that time, including Mrs O'Donnell's twins, who had just been vaccinated. And the whole population, having no land worth mentioning, lived on the sea, metaphorically speaking. They fished in fine weather. They gathered seaweed all weathers and turned it into kelp. When the weather was bad and fish was scarce they lived on limpets and sea-moss. They prayed for storms and shipwrecks so that they might find firewood and treasure washed ashore.

On the very edge of the shore, within two hundred feet of the sea at high spring tide, lived Big John and his wife. Their cabin was propped up in the rear by the huge boulders that had been cast ashore during the Big Storm of 1867. Big John might have had a surname in the past, but he had forgotten it, and nobody else had taken the trouble to discover it. His father had also been called Big John, and his grandfather had been called Big John, and his wife was called 'the wife of Big John of Rooruck.' It was said that he had been in Kilmurrage but three times in his life, once when he got married, once when he had been carried by force there by the parish priest to get confirmed and had established a record in paganism by declaring that there were six gods and he didn't care if there were a dozen, and once when he had gone to the court-house, on a charge of having sequestered to his own use wreckage that was cast ashore and belonged by law to His Britannic Majesty. He and his wife had no children, and in Inverara that was considered to be natural, for the couple were looked upon as not altogether human, being half-human and half-mermaid.

On the evening of the sports day, Big John and his wife were gathering seaweed on the shore at Rooruck, utterly careless of the festival that was taking place in Kilmurrage, a town that was almost as unreal to them as New York, some mysterious place where the enemies of humanity lived, the priests, the doctors, the rent collector and the coastguards, who were always nosing around looking for purloined wreckage. They were drinking their tea in the shelter of a rock at sunset, when Big John looked at the heavens and said to his wife with a gleam of satisfaction:

'Storm.'

His wife looked too, and nodded her head.

Big John then looked towards the east, where the main road from Kilmurrage ended on the edge of the rocky shore. He nudged his wife.

'Priest coming,' he murmured fearfully.

Man and wife looked like two wild savages in the heart of Africa seeing a missionary approach (with a Bible and the agent of a limited liability company), while Fr Hugh McMahon stumbled along the rocky path to the shore. They watched him pause and wave his hands above his head, and then take a flask from his pocket and hold it several times to his mouth, and throw it among the rocks. They looked at one another without speaking, and looked again towards the priest. He was still coming down towards them, stumbling among the rocks. Once he halted on a high rock and looked out to sea, shielding his eyes with his hands. Once he slipped on the wet moss and fell in a pool of water. Again he rose and came on. The couple looked at one another fearfully.

The curate stopped in front of them.

'Is this the shore at Rooruck?' he asked in English.

The couple shook their heads and said nothing, they did not understand, and the curate brushed his eyes with his hands and mumbled, crossing himself, 'Spectres of the dead, tradition is true, spectres of the dead.'

He moved down to the water's edge, where Big John's curragh was drawn up on the beach, with its stern washing in the surf. He seized the prow and began to turn it round to face the sea, wading into the water and stumbling. He brought the prow to face the sea, and then tried to get into the boat, but he fell into the water.

Big John came running down.

'Oh, priest,' he cried in Irish, 'storm coming, look,' pointing to the sky.

But the curate, shaking the water from his clothes, stared at the man and murmured:

'Shore at Rooruck, spectres of the dead.'

Then he laughed, and when the man tried to prevent him from getting into the boat, he cried:

'Begone, you are the spectre of the Devil. Wretch, do you want me to curse you, to blast you,' and holding up the silver cross that hung around his neck, he looked at the man with fury in his eyes.

Big John bowed his head and pushed the boat out to sea, and the curate, sitting in the prow, mumbled, 'Shore at Rooruck, oarless boat' — and in his drunkenness he did not see the two oars lying in the stern.

The tide was ebbing, and a strong swift current was rushing round the headland to the south. The boat was swept along sideways over the calm sea, while the peasant and his wife looked after it awestricken, their means of livelihood being swept away on the current and a storm coming. They looked for several minutes as it swept farther and farther away to the south, and then the woman wrung her hands and cried:

'Oh, John, John, there isn't another boat nearer than Coill Namhan; they are in Kilmurrage at the races.'

The man started suddenly. Then he shrugged his shoulders.

'Come,' he said.

'She was mine, she is his, never, never, while the stars, yes, yes, what is it, my breast shall not lie by thy breast.'

He mumbled, sitting in the prow of his boat, while it slipped away to the south. He shivered with the cold of the evening. His clothes were drenched with the salt sea. His hair lay damp on his forehead. His collar hung loose to the side of his neck. His black clerical waistcoat, with the black ivory buttons, was opened at the breast, and his stock was hanging out. He stared in front of him, shivering, while the wavelets beat against the coracle's sides, pit-pat, flush, thrup. His mind rushed hither and thither, grasping at different ideas and retaining nothing, like a boy chasing butterflies. Everything was so unreal to him. Sometimes he thought himself at the sports, then an evangelist converting Europe to Catholicism, riding on a caparisoned charger, with a sceptre in his hand, at the head of mighty hosts; then he was one of the ancient saints of Inverara, and he murmured, 'Shore at Rooruck, penance for my sins.' Then visions of Lily came; once she was dying in an inebriate's home; at another time she was lying drunk in Brannigan's shebeen with thousands of ghosts around her, weird ghosts with fleshless grinning skulls, while he himself stood over her, driving his claws into her; he had claws like a devil, with flames spurting from the nails, and he jumped up in the boat, and the boat rolled wildly, so that he fell forward against the second seat, cutting his forehead on the hard wood. He struggled back to his seat and put his hand to his forehead. When he looked at his hand it was covered with blood. He felt a nausea and leaned over the side and vomited.

For a minute he lay leaning over the side, vomiting. Then he returned to his seat and washed his mouth with the sea-water. His mind was clearer now. Yes, he was out at sea, in an oarless boat, going to do penance for his sins like the saints of old. He looked behind him at the shore. It was fading away, almost half a mile away now, and he was drifting with the tide to the south. He looked at the water around him. It was dark and covered with shadows. A light breeze was beginning to play on it, coming from the east, circling around in large black patches. The water seemed to shiver as the breeze passed over it. The curate shivered too, with fear, without knowing what he feared. His brain was still stupefied with alcohol. He murmured, 'I am in the hands of the Lord.' He clasped the silver cross that hung around his neck and began to pray, but he forgot how to pray. He searched in his pocket for his breviary and could not find it. Then he began to recite aloud the 'Dies Iræ, Dies Illa,' the chant for the dead. He became excited with the recitation. He hurled out the mournful cadence as if trying to cover the mighty vastness around him with the sound of his voice, singing his own death song. But the wind, mocking his voice, blew more loudly now, coming in fitful gusts, sweeping about his coracle, turning it round in its course, and then leaving it, whirled away to the west in ever widening circles.

The curate stopped half-way through the chant. He forgot the words. He began the 'Ave Maris Stella' (Hail, Star of the Sea), the hymn to the Blessed Virgin, but again he checked himself.

'What the devil am I talking about?' he said.

He sat still, holding his breath, as if he had discovered himself saying something ridiculous in company. He looked about him hurriedly. In the west the sun was setting. Dark clouds were flitting over the sinking yellowish half-circle. The shore was dim now. Nothing was to be seen but the towering cliffs, yellow and grey and green in patches. And overhead the sky was a dark mass of flitting bulging clouds. He became afraid of the darkness about him. He put his hands through his hair and cried: 'God is deserting me, I am condemned, I am condemned.'

Then, as if in answer to his cry, the wind suddenly stopped wailing. The sea became as level as a glass floor, as if oil had been poured over it. A stillness of death reigned for several moments. And then, from the shore, from the base of the tall cliffs, came a dull rumbling, as of drums beating in the centre of a forest. Then the sound died and there was stillness again. He listened, almost expecting to hear the voice of God from the sky pronouncing his verdict. He listened and his heart stood still. His lips fell open. His eyeballs hurt him, like great weights dropped into his head.

A roar like a thousand cannons fired in rapid succession, came crashing across the vault of heaven. The sea, as if galvanized into action by the sound, broke its calm surface. Long deep furrows cut across its level face. Dark ridges, rising and rising, each moment, began to roll towards the shore. The coracle whirled around and began to toss on the ridges, then was hurled into the hollows, then rose again on the ridges, whirling towards the shore. It was the turn of the tide. Dull noises came from the depths, as if mountains were being moved by giants in the centre of the earth. The breakers reverberated at the base of the cliffs. Then another thunder-clap, louder and wilder than the first, and the whole atmosphere was filled with a chaos of sound. The tops of the ridges broke into white foam. Ridges hurled themselves, the one against the other, sending up fountains of foam. The sea became a living volcano. And from the east came the storm wind, whistling now and screeching, riding over the ridges, whipping the foam into cataracts and whirling it towards the cliffs.

The curate shook with terror. His teeth chattered. For an instant of time he thought that it was the voice of God condemning him, and then that instant passed. The veil of drunkenness fell from his eyes. He became sober. For four seconds he sat in his seat, shivering and sober; awakened to his danger, to the danger to his life and the imminence of death. He underwent a transformation. The curate died. The intellectual died. The visionary died. The drunkard died. The lover died. The pious, shrinking, conscientious priest, fearful of himself, torturing himself with doubts and temptations, they all died. There remained but Hugh McMahon the man, the human atom, the weak trembling being, with the savage desire to live, to save himself from the yawning chasm of death that was opened up about him by the storm.

And awakened to his danger and reality, the human atom raised his voice to heaven for assistance. He raised it humbly, like a cringing slave to his master. He cried out from the depths of his soul, 'O Lord, save me or I perish.' He did not think of heaven or hell. He remembered but death and his desire to live. He knew but his desire to see the sun rise, to feel the cool breeze in his nostrils, to eat, to sleep, to laugh, to sing, to live, to live. And like a slave he besieged God with promises. He would scourge himself with thongs. He would wear sackcloth and ashes. he would pray ten hours by day and ten by night. He would spend his life as a missionary. He would go to China.

And joyfully, as if he had found the key to the favour of the Lord, the talisman that would open to him the gates of heavenly assistance, he cried:

'O Lord, Lord, save me and I promise to go to China as a missionary.'

And then, confident that he had made a bargain with God, he sought means to save himself, and he saw the oars in the stern of the coracle. His eyes gleamed with delight. A miracle. God had hastened to his assistance, and before he seized the oars he murmured, 'From my soul I thank thee, O Lord, for Thy divine mercy.'

And then, trembling with excitement, he seized the oars and set them in the rowlocks. He knew how to row, and in the first fury of his desire to live, he succeeded in turning the prow to the shore. But then the difficulty began, to keep the prow facing each breaker that rose, towering above him now, to watch the breakers coming on his flanks, to meet them as they came, to stay his stroke while the coracle was on the summit of a ridge, until he could grip the water with his oars as it rolled into the hollow. His hands were raw after a few minutes. The muscles in his arms and shoulders ached. His back seemed about to break. His breath hardly issued from his exhausted lungs, and still he was making no headway. The coracle was bobbing up and down on the crests of the waves, now down in a hollow between two ridges, now whirled around with its prow to sea, now heeling over to port until the gunwale was almost under water, now heeling to starboard until it hung like a fly to a perpendicular wall of water, and then suddenly being caught underneath by a rushing breaker and hurled clean out of the water several times, while the curate sat grimly in his seat, shutting his eyes with fear, praying. He glanced behind him now and again towards the land, trying to direct his crazy coracle, rowing just to delude himself that he was nearing safety.

Then gradually he realized that he was making no headway, that he was wasting his efforts trying to make the beach. He could not see the beach. The rocks might be in front of him, a worse death than by drowning. He almost gave up hope. He was about to resign himself to his fate and rest on his oars, but as soon as his grip loosened on the oars, he saw a mountainous wave approaching from the right, and with a half-uttered scream of fear, he seized the oars firmly and whirled the coracle around to meet it. The coracle soared like a cork to the summit, and dropped gently into the trough beyond. And proud of his power to master the craft, he calmed again. He gave up the effort to make the shore, and concentrated in keeping afloat.

A cruiser would hardly have lived so long in that gale, but the curragh, as light as a feather, offering no resistance to the waves, hopped around unscathed. At moments it appeared to be engulfed as the towering waves enveloped it, but it appeared again, wallowing like a snake on the crest. The waves lashed against its prow, eager to devour it, but it flew before them, shrinking from their perilous embrace. It stood on end, standing perpendicularly on the sheer slope of water, with its prow pointing downwards and again it came level. It fell sideways, with its bottom upwards and again in answer to a dip of the oars it came level. And the curate rowed and rowed, sitting motionless, using his oars unconsciously. He was not thinking now. He was fighting the waves, while overhead the thunder roared, the lightning flashed, the rain swept fiercely past borne on the winds, and from the cliffs came the noise of a mighty battle, the age-long battle of the sea against the land.

'Jesus, Mary, and Joseph, help me, O all ye holy saints and martyrs, help me.'

He prayed and prayed, with his eyeballs starting from his head, with his lips trembling, with his breath coming in spasms that pained. His strength began to ebb as the hope of succour waned. Fear now possessed him. Death rose before his eyes, gaunt and horrible. The sea seemed to beckon to him. Each wave that arose opened a chasm that seemed to be about to suck him into hell. In a paroxysm of fear he screamed. And then, afraid of the hollow sound of his voice in the din of the storm, he crouched low on his oars and gritted his teeth. With the salt tears starting from his strained eyes, he rowed furiously and cried, 'I will not die, I want to live, I will not die.' But the winds roared in mockery, and the waves came striding towards him, like mountains to overwhelm him, while his hands grasping the oars tugged and tugged, to save himself from annihilation.

He became weaker. The waves became more alluring. The hollows between the ridges began to appear like beds of down, that would waft him into a dreamless sleep. Singing came to his ears, fairy singing of mermaids, that soothed his weary limbs and called him to drop his oars and sink, sink, sink into forgetfulness. His lips ceased crying out to heaven. The tears dried in his eyes. His fears left him and he laughed. His brain dulled into thoughtlessness. And he stared into the black waters. he rose from his seat to hurl himself into the sea, when he sat down suddenly and grasped his oars again and listened.

A cry came to him over the sea from the shore. He listened, and as his curragh mounted another ridge slantwise, with its side to the shore, a flash of lightning lit up the water. He saw another boat coming towards him. His heat thumped with joy. He shouted, but no response came. Again and again, he shouted, but no reply came. He rowed furiously, trying to direct his coracle in the direction he had seen the boat, but after a few strokes he lost his sense of direction. A breaker caught him on the flank and almost filled his coracle with water, but again it emptied itself as it fell headlong down another slope. Then he calmed and waited for another sound. Presently it came again, nearer now. He could distinguish the words in Irish, 'Oh priest, where art thou?' He yelled again. Three times he yelled and then he heard a shout of triumph in response. He kept shouting and still there came answering shouts. He could hear the clash of oars in the rowlocks, and the 'huh, heh' as the men called out to one another, bending on their oars. Another flash of lightning. The other crew saw him. 'Keep on your oars,' they cried. He bent on his oars. He was afraid now of every wave that advanced. He trembled as the waves towered above him, now that help was near. The oars quivered in his hands as he mounted the ridges. His hair stood on end as he fell down into the hollows, and then he shouted with joy again as he saw from the summit of a wave the other boat approaching him.

He could hear them distinctly now coming, calling to one another. He saw the eight oars, glistening white in the darkness, as they were lit by the lightning. And then the boat swept past him on the crest of a wave. It turned on another wave and then it was lost to sight, as he was swept down into a hollow. Afraid that they would lose him, he yelled with fright, and forgetting himself, as he rose again on a ridge, he dropped his oars and stood up in the coracle. The men screamed to him: 'Keep to your seat.' He sat down again, and tried to seize his oars; too late. His coracle was caught in the flank by a wave, it was whirled into the air, it dipped again into the water . . . smash, another wave broke it into atoms . . . he was clinging to the prow . . . he was sinking . . . and then a black monster came down on him . . . it passed over his head, and he felt two hands gripping him . . . and then he was lifted out of the water and fell in a heap in the stern of the rescuing boat.

He lay in the bottom of the boat with his eyes shut. There was water in the bottom of the boat, swirling around his body. He did not trouble to move. He was listening fearfully. Above him in the boat he could hear voices, sharp voices that he didn't understand, but that comforted him. He could hear the rumble of the oars and the voice of the man in the prow — 'Strengthen the right hand, the left, the left now, quick with the right, slow now, wait for the fall, now pull, huh, heh, huh, heh, wait for the next.' He could hear the men's breath, their panting, their groans and the snapping gasps as they lay back on their oars. And he listened fearfully like a child in its mother's arms. When the thunder clapped he shuddered and when the waves towered overhead, and the curragh paused uncertain as if about to founder, he held his breath and gaped in horror. And again when the strokes came in rapid succession and the captain shouted, 'Lay on them now, lay on them, huh, heh,' he felt glad. He prayed and prayed. He thanked God for having saved him. He thought of the promise he had made, to go to China; he thought of the miracle of finding the oars in the boat. He was filled with a passion of self-righteousness. The fear and humility of the hour alone in the boat, in the storm, left him. He became again the priest, the intellectual. But he was a cleansed priest now, a purified priest. He had passed the test. He had come perfect from the crucible. He moved in the bottom of the boat, to get out of the water. He was full of confidence in himself now. God had preserved him for his mission. The temptations had been to test him. He had overcome them. He was free now to devote his life to the service of his Church. His poetry, his nationalism? Nothing mattered but the Church. Then he heard a cheer from the men above him in the boat and an answering cheer from the distance. He heard breakers rolling on a sandy beach. He looked out over the gunwale and saw lamps moving in front, then people rushing hither and thither on the strand. The curragh swept in, paused on the crest of a wave, and then with a rush it swept to the shore, carried up the beach between the people.

They lifted him from the stern and helped him to the beach. He stood among them trembling with joy, like a man arisen from the tomb. They gaped at him awestricken. He offered the crew who had saved him his purse and the silver crucifix that hung around his neck, but they refused, shaking their heads in silence.

They brought him a horse, and one man offered him a coat, murmuring that he was drenched to the skin and the night was cold. But the curate waved him aside.

'I am not drenched,' he cried, 'I am cleansed.'

He mounted the horse and rode into Kilmurrage at a gallop.

'I am cleansed, I am cleansed,' he murmured as the wind blew about him and the rain pattered on his cheeks.

As he rode through Kilmurrage, the town was filled with noise of drunken revelry, and no one noticed him. At the parochial house he dismounted and entered eagerly. He found the door open and people — many people — talking in hushed voices, voices reciting the rosary in the dinning-room over the dead body of McSherry. He paid no heed. He asked the servant to show him into Fr O'Reilly's study. The servant looked at his dishevelled clothes, his bleeding forehead, and his clothes dripping with water, and wondered. She led him to the door of the study and knocked.

'Come in,' came a tired and weary voice.

The curate brushed past the servant and entered. Fr O'Reilly sat at his writing-table with his head between his hands. He stood up suddenly when he saw the curate. His eyes were bloodshot and glaring.

'What the devil — ?' he cried.

The curate stood upright in front of the table, looking steadily into the parish priest's face, with a calm, proud look.

'Fr O'Reilly,' he said, 'I have come to confess, but first I want to tell you that I am going to volunteer as a missionary to China.'

Fr O'Reilly stared.

'What madness is this?' he cried. 'Is this the time, when death is in the house — when — when — what do you mean?'

The curate never moved. He kept looking into the parish priest's eyes.

'I have promised,' he said simply.

'To whom have you promised?'

'To God.'